Red Love

Lijian Zhao

authorHOUSE®

AuthorHouse™
1663 Liberty Drive
Bloomington, IN 47403
www.authorhouse.com
Phone: 1 (800) 839-8640

Published by AuthorHouse 06/20/2018

ISBN: 978-1-5462-4559-9 (sc)
ISBN: 978-1-5462-4557-5 (hc)
ISBN: 978-1-5462-4558-2 (e)

Library of Congress Control Number: 2018906631

Print information available on the last page.

To my father

Acknowledgements

In the decade of writing, editing and searching for a publisher, my husband Mark Kantor has rendered me boundless help. Without Mark, Red Love would not have been born. Thank you, my love! Thanks also to my younger brother Xiaoshi and my sisters Xiaoyan and Jianfei who provided photos for me to rekindle the old memories.

There is absolutely no such thing in the world as love or hatred without reason or cause.—Mao Tsetung

Part One

Chapter 1

Today the sky will be blue. She read the weather report through her shut eyelids. The screen of her closed eyes was red, not black: sunbeams. It should be a transparent autumn day.

"Good boy, you got up as early as the adults."

Jianfei pulled the quilt up to cover her ears.

"Dad is going to the athletic field. Are you coming?"

"I will wake up Big Sister first so that we can go together."

Annoying imp! Go away! She turned her back to the door.

"Could you wait outside?" her back said, "Sister needs time to get dressed."

"All right," her seven-year old brother Xiaoshi, Little Rock, waddled out.

Procrastinating. *Bed is so comfortable. It requires strong will to get out of it.* She debated with herself. Procrastinating, one minute, ten seconds, she began to count: eleven, twelve…Suddenly the alarm clock screamed, shooting her out of bed. Six thirty. *Li Shan and Huifang must be there already.*

Once outside, she was deeply touched by the brilliance the world offered her. Almost with gratitude, she inhaled the essence of fall; her eyes drank the grandeur of green. Green, green everywhere, young, handsome, and full of virility; it was a picture of youth and glory, these cadets. In her eyes they were all Alex, Ivan, Dmitri and Gregory, and she herself was Natasha. A Soviet ideal.

As China's first, and the only, institute to educate and train its commanding staff, the Nanjing Military Academy occupied the address of its opponent, the Department of National Defense of the Kuomintang. Since Nanjing was the old capital city, the location suited the Academy

1

in size. Nestled at the foot of the picturesque Purple-Gold Mountain, the Academy was kept away from the hustle and bustle of the city life and stood secluded behind thick walls and curtains of trees. To the south, a bus line ran in front of the main gate, though not very frequent, sufficient enough to carry the studious cadets downtown for a change of scenery on weekends; a tributary of the Yangtze meandered to the east, severing the campus from the market with its boorish haggling and daily shopping on the opposite bank; to the north and west, a stretch of forest merged with a great expanse of farmland.

There were four campuses. Compound One, the North compound, was the headquarters, the buildings of the Administration and the President's office. In the old days, this was also the site of the enemy's brain. It was here that the strategists and tacticians, prestigious military celebrities, passed the prime of their lives: Marshall Liu, who had lost one arm and one eye in the battlefield, one of the founders of the Academy; the three-star General Yang, a radical hot pepper addict from Hunan, who later was promoted to Secretary of National Defense; and numerous other three-star and two-star Generals. Not only were they the trailblazers, but they had opened a new phase of military training, teaching the fledgling republic how to build and strengthen its commanding officers, creating the foundation of its national defense. Compound Two, the South Compound, was the residential area for all the officers and faculty members. Ironic that this compound was formerly the cavalry regiment. Where the Nationalists raised horses, the Communists were now raising their families. Jianfei grew up here in Building Seven. Compound Three, the West Compound, had a strange name in the old days, "Little Barracks". It was now the teaching area. Every morning people stopped on the streets to watch the cadets in their smart green uniforms marching in synchronized square formation to the classrooms, slogans and songs maintaining their harmony all the way along. Compound Four, the East Compound, the old "Artillery Regiment", was now allocated to the Department of Provisions and Warehouse.

When Jianfei got to the field, the morning drills were at their peak. Young cadets filled the air with rousing patriotic songs, punctuating their precise march, arms swaying to the height of their second button, legs raised in a line as straight as the one on the blackboard the math teacher drew with a ruler.

"One, two, three, four," shouting, they brought unison to their gait.

Incessant slogans accompanied their marching, striking the ears like firecrackers. Green, green, green everywhere —the sports ground was a green sea. The department heads passed greetings in front of each perfectly formed squadron. Discipline was addressed and a weekly song sung: *The Red Flag Fluttering on Jinggang Mountain* or *The Anthem of the New Fourth Army*. Sometimes a Soviet song was taught and the cadets displayed higher spirits, louder voices and greater passion: "The sun sets behind the mountain…Soviet soldiers are returning from the battlefield…"

The philosophy department was in the east corner of the field. Jianfei spotted her dad who was inspecting his green square marching across the field like a piece of moving turf. Since last Sunday's National Day drill rehearsal, the day by day competition among the departments intensified, drawing large audiences. To Jianfei, it was more interesting than a movie, not only because of the beauty and heroism embodied in masculinity, the marvelous clean-cut lines of human torsos and limbs, but also because of the great spectrum of emotion registering on the faces of the department heads from uneasiness, concern, foreboding, worry, complacence and smugness that passed revealing the secret code hidden beneath the pageantry of the drill competition. Whoever won would go to Beijing and demonstrate to the great leader Chairman Mao himself, a display of our powerful national defense! Who would not want such an honor? As the holiday drew closer, the drill rehearsals replaced the daily exercises. In the History Department, the cadets stood on one leg in mid-stride, the other leg suspended parallel to the earth.

"Together, together!" the trainer tilted his head, measuring the line with a pair of slanting eyes, "You, one inch shorter! Keep it in one line!"

In another squadron, the performers' arms thrust backwards, forking a forty-five-degree angle at the armpit, the other arm hoisted to their chests.

"Number six, right arm, wider! Number seven, left arm, higher!" the instructor roared, "Discipline your eyes, straight ahead, no rolling around!"

Sweat beaded down, their uniforms pasted to their backs. And then there was the band that contained faces puffed up with earnest self-importance. The drummers produced an emphatic rhythm for the marchers to keep abreast and accentuate the straight line of their strides. In the Department of Chemical Warfare, a voice led, "Raise our health; strengthen our defense!" The Song of the People's Liberation Army soared in the air joining with the early autumn heat to mobilize every young heart within earshot including that of the juvenile whose eyes had never left the green, moving squares.

Jianfei concluded that man as an individual was boring but as a collective, fascinating. She fell in love with men on the whole, but decided that to fall for any single man was folly. A disdainful glance was cast from the corner of her eyes to the far end of the field where an undisciplined group of grey, brown and blue boys assembled. *Look at those good-for-nothing loafers!* A natural sense of superiority arose in this good-for-everything girl.

The sky, as if vacuumed, was free from even a speck of cloud. The buildings, the trees and the uniforms were gilded in the sun. The air was charged with the ebullience of youth. This was the color of a September morning: blue, gold and green, blended in unison, woven into one piece called the Military Academy. Everything was in unison.

Chapter 2

To its east and west, the sports ground was flanked by two lines of residential buildings. To its north was the Officers' Club which was a haven for chess players in the evening and a beehive of ballroom dancers on the weekends. To the south was the children's playground where slides, jungle gyms and seesaws were commanded by toddlers. Brave ones tried the swings. Timid ones popped their curious heads from the cave of the miniature mountain, a large block of West Lake stone. Boys of Xiaoshi's age ran amuck, leading their maids on wild-goose chases. In their consternation, these maids often stubbed their toes on the holly bushes, worried to death that their career might stop short if their charges tripped over the curbs or got scratched, even injured, in God knew what way and where. They found themselves in an evil cycle; the more anxiously and desperately they tried to catch the kids, the more joyful the kids became. A permanent smirk lit the toddlers' eyes and their faces, red and steaming, gleamed with their mastery of mischief. Perspiration oozed out of the maids' foreheads, evidence of their devotion to their masters.

Here and there, in the blue air, as yet unpolluted by the daily routine, was a diversity of names, shouted with the precision of a drilling cadence.

"Little Ocean, come back and eat your breakfast."

"Building the Country, your dad will give you a spanking if you keep playing cat-and-mouse with me!"

Little Ocean adroitly skipped from one cave to another; while Building the Country stepped out from his hiding place, surrendering to the maid who grabbed his swiveling arms and dragged them home.

"No, no, I don't want to go to school, I want to play!!" like a piglet towards a butcher's knife.

These little ones were a real nuisance. While their more mature siblings primly engaged in fitness exercises to cover their ineffable social interest, the little ones tailed them, spied on them and quickly tattled on them to their parents. And while their teenage siblings were scolded for improper behavior, an unnecessary word or glance exchanged with the opposite sex, the brats wagged their tails like running dogs but were quickly deserted by their older siblings.

Jianfei looked around. Her tail was nowhere to be seen. She sighed with relief. Shaking off her tail had become a constant challenge, first daily, now hourly.

When teenage boys gathered in twos and threes in front of the Officer's Club, aloofly observing morning drills from a distance, or when teenage girls, scared away by the boisterous masculine activities, sheltered themselves in a remote corner, they all had two pairs of eyes: one skimming over the lively drills and cadets; the other, alert behind the first pair, studying the opposite party. Like predators crouching for their prey, with camouflaged patience and curbed expectation, they loitered, moving slowly.

A scarlet dot decorated the green field, like a rose standing out against its leaves, Huifang's jacket. Jianfei waved and headed towards this sole, female presence. Sure enough, the two friends of hers were already waiting. Of the same age, twelve years old, attending the same girls' school and in the same grade, with a father of the same profession, these three girls found a natural bond among themselves. Whether they chose to live a life of three as one and act as a league so as to draw more attention in public or pass the masses unnoticed as individuals was quite vague in their mind. All they knew was that this bond, like a cocoon, had wrapped their teenage timidity and audacity seamlessly and made their lives cozy and safe.

"Hi, girls. The early bird catches the worm. How many worms have you caught?" Squinting in the direction of the Officer's Club, Jianfei patted Huifang on the shoulder.

"You're asking the right person. Huifang is a worm expert," slowly, Lishan, her name Mandarin for Beautiful Mountain, echoed, a wisp of a smile hanging over one raised corner of her closed lips, squeezing out a couple of dimples, her lips protruding towards the Officers' Club.

"Hey, it's unfair I should come all the way from Beiji to be made fun of by you," Huifang pouted.

Beiji, the North Pole, was the short name for Beiji Xincun, the North Pole New Village, a compound which otherwise would be ranked as Campus Five along with the other four if not for its inferior image in the eyes of hundreds of cadets. Yet it held a unique position and enjoyed special favor from the Beijing leaders because the residents here were the nation's old foes whose hands were smeared with Communists' blood. They were the former KMT officers, now part of the faculty of the Academy.

Before the Chiang Kaishek administration sluiced down to Taiwan like waves dissipating as they pounded the immovable rocks of shore the Nationalist Party had undergone another crisis from within. Secret liaisons had been established between some of its high ranking commanders and the underground Communist forces, among them, the Navy General Lin, the descendant of the celebrated Lin Zexu whose name was associated with the infamous First Opium War that opened China's modern history. These officials, after years of observation, deep thinking and calculated planning, had turned their backs on their comrades in arms and walked towards the opposite side as the cannons sounded closer and closer. They had played a decisive role in the Red Army's intelligence and helped the Communists in their effective campaigns and final seizures of the major cities. They were rewarded for their complicity, and the reward, dramatically, was to let them keep their original ranks, but in the People's Liberation Army. To show its generosity and magnanimity, the Beijing regime later even appointed the above-mentioned Navy General Lin, to be President of its Naval Academy. Without shedding a single drop of blood, these renowned historical figures had completed the metamorphosis from bloodthirsty monsters, in their enemy's eyes, to Buddha's; from commanders to professors. Some weren't so lucky. Dashing through the rain of bullets and braving the forests of bayonets, in the fire and smoke, refusing to bow their heads, they were captured in the battlefields. Huifang's father was one of them, as was Colonel Wang, now his neighbor.

When Mao Tsetung came to power, announcing in his heavy Hunanese dialect on the rostrum of Tian An Men, the Gate of Heavenly Peace, "China has stood up!", he was well aware that his army, though tempered in the Long March, the Civil War and the eight years of the Anti-Japanese

War, was still a fledgling army, whereas his ill-fated enemy, though long passed their Waterloo in the three major battlefields of Pingjing, Liaoshen and Huaihai and reduced to a tiny island home, had been much better equipped with formally trained military talents, some of whom were western educated. The People's Liberation Army was still in its infancy. His Military Academy needed strategists and tactical operators. Now a large body of this enemy force had fallen into his hands. It would have been easy enough to dump these defeated warriors into the jails; easy enough, but not easy for Mao, whose mind teemed with the intrigues and stratagems of five thousand years of Chinese emperors, generals and eunuchs. To use them to benefit us, to employ the KMT resources to arm the PLA staff, to see ourselves from the eyes of our enemies, especially from a defeated army, was Mao's keen interest. Mao sorted the trash and decided to put some in the recycling bin. Eagles with clipped wings, these officers could hardly fly. Their insurgence was an impossibility. When the time was ripe for recapturing Taiwan, our intelligence would work even better this time. Mao proved to the world his gamesmanship. Enclosed and separated from the other four compounds, the North Pole New Village was nearest to the Administration campus, under immediate surveillance.

"It's great you can join us at an early hour every morning," Jianfei proffered a hostess' hospitality. "How long did it take you by bike?"

Huifang was the first among the two hundred seventh graders and one of the only five out of six hundred students in the junior high who rode her bike to school, drawing avid eyes from all directions wherever her red Flying Pigeon carried her. Now her enviable Pigeon stood perched in the corner, leaning against the wall.

"Not long, ten minutes at most, but I could not wallow in bed. See, I have already had my breakfast but you just got up." Huifang was chewing a candy.

"Want one?" she produced from her pocket a handful of nougats. Jianfei and Lishan each took one.

"You are different from us," calmly peeling the rice paper and sticking it to her tongue as a prelude to a serious speech, Lishan said in her hoarse, nasal alto, "At such an hour? For breakfast?"

Huifang giggled, shrugging and nodding, in denial and admission. Her cheeks were like marble shaded with red blossoms, another outstanding feature among hundreds of faces at school. Lishan called her "Natasha" as they stepped out of the Soviet movie. Her personality was like Natasha's, a merry-go-round, carefree, singing "Lalala-lalala" all the time. Today she was wearing a pair of black leather shoes, which made Lishan's jaw drop the third time in five minutes.

"My gosh! The only one riding a bicycle, the only one wearing a skirt in September, now what? The leather shoes?" Lishan nailed her eyes on Huifang's quaint toes.

"Do you have the slightest instinct of self-protection? Aren't you afraid of the dean?" Jianfei asked.

"Hide your beauty, be a forsythia and not a rose," dad's words came back visiting Jianfei's mind. She realized how correct dad was ever since she entered middle school.

"Why?" Huifang's eyes like a pair of saucers. "It is a gift from my father to celebrate my middle school. Don't you like them?"

Lishan stretched her arms, turning her palms upward, drawing her lips downward while Huifang expressing bewilderment that her shoes could prompt such aesthetic and ethical valuations.

Lishan's father was a professor of the history of the Soviet Communist Party. They lived in Building 11. Jianfei constantly caught him talking to dad in the late afternoon on their way back from the Little Barracks. A pair of glasses, a bit bookish and a torrential speaker, he somehow reminded Jianfei of Trotsky, on whom he was an expert. In comparison, Lishan and Huifang formed a black-and-white contrast. As striking as Huifang's September skirt, Lishan's uniform pants stood like a pair of green balloons floating at her sides, serving as Lishan's trademark and were eye-catching in their own peculiar way. She carried this mark at school, but even more so away from school where officers and juvenile boys converged in life's daily stream, widening their eyes, questioning her queer attire. She was tall, her dad short. The army trousers were a good fit without any alteration. A blue jacket and black shoes contributed more drabness to the sketch of the most unadorned girl; a pair of white socks completed the portrait. Just a week ago, she had cut off her last link to girlhood. A pair of scissors relentlessly glinted over her cascading hair that was braided for the sheer purpose of female elegance. With a few resolute clicks of the scissors the two long braids, and their sheen of reflecting blackness, dropped, bidding good-bye to feminine softness and sweetness.

"Those three-year-old, long pigtails are too time-consuming in the morning." She appealed to her mom's sympathy and won her consent, who insisted that the long braids were a necessary emblem of propriety for a girl with a decent upbringing. Ever since, she had taken pride in her mannish new bobbed hair.

Lishan was the only girl in her family. It was this tomboy appearance that came to her most naturally and set her mind at peace. No matter how much of her physical development was flattened and preserved under her fading and baggy clothing, what she could not hide was her almond-shaped eyes, dark and unfathomable, like the "autumn water", a classical term to describe an ancient beauty, and her red mouth, habitually curving upward to emit an almost imperceptible smile. Her slightly nasal voice was a perfect companion to her sensual lips, the two together, created an attraction which was not easy to discern. At a time when girlish beauty meant bright colors and a high voice, she had her own taste, the taste of an artist, a painter, since her childhood, subtle and not readily comprehended nor accepted by her peers.

"What book are you carrying this time?" seeing Lishan's bulging pocket, Jianfei asked.

Lishan pulled the book out of the green balloon:

"*How the Steel Was Tempered*. This Soviet novel is really popular now. May I borrow it?" Jianfei leafed through and was fascinated by the illustrations.

"No problem. I took it from dad's bookshelf."

Lishan and her dad shared almost everything and this father-daughter Communism greatly broadened her vision and made her the most knowledgeable in school.

Chapter 3

"Where is that little tail of yours?" Huifang looked around.

"There he is, with a bunch of boys… Over there, by the club!" Lishan's fingers leading their eyes to Xiaoshi, who was jumping rope near the uneven bars.

"Let's go over!" eyes sparkling, Huifang was itchy for a departure.

"No way! With all the boys around?!" Lishan wouldn't budge an inch.

As usual, Jianfei found herself caught in the middle; it was always her decision that balanced the two and settled the situation.

"I have to go home with my tail attached anyway; otherwise dad will see me incomplete."

Huifang's mind was easy to read, her keen probing and secret coveting of boys were shallow to detect. Yet Lishan was an enigma. Not only her indifference towards her adolescent contemporaries across the sports field, but her determination to be contrary wherever she appeared and her refusal to compromise all were beyond Jianfei's comprehension. Though seldom did she take Huifang's side, this time however, Jianfei readily agreed to cross the field to fetch the little nuisance. For the beautiful Huifang, the spot on the opposite side, of an opposite nature, was magnetic. The three female figures were thus seen making their way to the club, one leading, the other two following, one reluctantly, one eagerly.

The boys were fully engaged in fitness exercises and paid no mind to the approaching party. No greetings were exchanged between the two teams, but Huifang's narrowing eyes and widening lips suggested a hello.

"Xiaoshi, let's jump together." Awkwardly, Lishan tried to rescue herself by feigning a friendship with a seven-year old.

"Yes, let's play together." Jianfei, too, began to shield herself behind her brother, posing as the caring sister.

Startled by his sister's unusual favor and the somewhat condescending patronage from her normally cold friend, Little Rock jumped vehemently, smiling from ear to ear.

Huifang was grateful that the two friends of hers had quickly adjusted themselves to the presence of the alien clan and created an atmosphere natural enough to brave an approach; she was also amused by how they made the best use of the otherwise annoying Xiaoshi. Now two of the girls threshed the rope, swirling it in the air; Little Rock bounced in the middle, while the fourth one waited aside to cut in.

"One, two, three…fifty one…one hundred…" The counting created by Xiaoshi and Huifang was deliberately loud intending to catch the boys' ears. The male teenagers poised in the distance; their limbs rested on the bars and their eyes cast careless glances at the little jumper and his three pretty girl companions.

Little Rock made it to one hundred and four, elated in his success.

"One of the big brothers over there can do a triple jump. He showed me the trick. I want to learn." His aspiration was bolstered by his record jumping accomplishment.

Snatching the rope, he darted for the big brother and then waved at his sister. Huifang, dragging Jianfei, proceeded to join them while Lishan shuffled over, hesitation written on her face.

The big brother stepped calmly from the lawn to the pavement, ready to show off his prowess. All heads on the uneven bars, the parallel bars and the pommel horse swerved towards the young player, eyes riveted on his legs. A pair of glasses, navy blue sweater, slender build, that was the performer. The rope was doubled and redoubled to the shortest possible length in his hands and taut against his calves. Like an arrow on a stretched bowstring, he bent over, ready for a flight. A flash of lightning! The rope whipped down and shot up time and again, whistling in the air, his feet sprang up and bounced back, allowing the electricity to run through three times before an abrupt circuit break. All this happened in a wink! An outburst ensued. Boys bravoed; their faces revealing great pride; their eyes narrowed, posing a challenge to the silent party who seemed to have enjoyed a free show without any intention to pay applause. Among the opposite panel, Xiaoshi was the sole contributor to the cheers.

In a second, Xiaoshi stepped forward and followed suit. The rope flew in the air and then whipped down striking his foot like a firework fizzling in the rain. Not reconciled to one fruitless attempt, he coiled the rope and doubled his tiny body again. The whip cracked on the ground once only and dropped like a dead snake lying listless at his ankles. Another aborted trial.

"Sister, you show me how to do it!" Dejected, he nudged Jianfei.

Once a tail, always a tail. Jianfei glowered menacingly and shut her little brother up in the nick of time.

Vigilantly, the girls looked at each other. The threat of the boys was imminent, a phenomenon foreign to their daily school life, immersed in an ocean of girls.

"Hi, my name is Yang Bing, Yang as in poplar, Bing in ice." Extending his hand, the blue sweater was quite diplomatic.

An embarrassing moment, a fleeting yet everlasting moment.

Jianfei held her fortress, her arms folded and face expressionless. On Yang Bing's face, the smile froze and then evaporated ephemeral as a rainy-day sunbeam, his hand hanging in the air not knowing which direction to go. Abashment and courtesy caught him in the middle. To break the ice, the three girls pronounced their names one by one, as if reporting to their homeroom teacher the first day at school. Jianfei delivered absent-minded thanks and then turned to Xiaoshi. With clenched teeth, she goaded him at his back, "Go home!"

Her little brother, overpowered by the unusual heaviness in her tone, took to his heels after making a timid request, "Big brother, may I see you tomorrow morning, the same time and same place?"

Jianfei and Little Rock followed the curving track and entered the west door, where their family resided in Unit 101. From the corner of her eyes, she caught a smudge of blue, which disappeared behind the east door of the same building, Unit 301. How come I never noticed the four-eyed blue sweater? Oblivious to the fact that this was the first year she lived at home after six years of the primary boarding school, the discovery somehow made her euphoric.

Chapter 4

In Jianfei's bedroom, Huifang hastily scribbled her homework, while Jianfei hastily swallowed her breakfast. Then the three girls took off and chattered their way to school, thinking the best of the day was passing away.

"The biology teacher has a gold crown hidden behind his upper lip," Huifang giggled again.

Lishan seemed to be choking with indignation, "The most despicable creature on earth! Imagine! He wants to unravel the secrets of the female body in front of us?! Lord! Turning these pages makes me blush! Those terrifying illustrations of sexual organs!"

Lishan covered her eyes.

Jianfei concentrated on the bun she snatched from the breakfast table. Suddenly she blurted out, "Wait! Are we having a math quiz today?" Her steps halted.

Lishan stood petrified, her face ashen, her expression suggested great pain.

"I hate your homeroom teacher, that Canine Teeth!" Lishan spat out at Huifang who remained lighthearted despite the curse. Lishan and Jianfei were in the same homeroom therefore the same math class, but today Huifang didn't have to go through the same nerve-racking ordeal.

Jianfei and Lishan entered Classroom A and Huifang B. Theirs was, formerly, a Catholic school built by British missionaries during the thirties. Two teaching buildings stood face to face with a lawn between, and a hedgerow of dwarf hollies skirting its edge. The three-story building to the south was the high school, each floor given to a grade higher than the one below. A wooden veranda with banisters ran along the façade on each floor allowing the students to look out on the lawn and displaying their daily activities to the eyes of their younger sisters in the opposite building. The northern building holding the middle school was similar in size and style.

The fourteen hundred students in these two beehives went in and out, uncovering the mysteries of literature and history, taxing their memories in English and the classics, building their skills with triangles, circles and squares, hearing for the first time the great names of Newton and Li Bai and sharpening their political instincts. Each classroom held fifty to sixty students, spacious and sunny, echoing ringing voices, some childish, some youthful. Faculty rooms were in two small, two-storied red brick buildings, square and modest, behind the high school, surprisingly aged, reeking of British decadence. A red brick wall with the same color and worn appearance surrounded three sides of the school campus enclosing to the east a wide open sports ground. Preserved to the west of the lawn was the school's old gray church. This remarkable relic had kept its steeple, pulpit, apse, and large vaulted ceilings intact, despite the ravages of Japanese invasion and Civil War. The pews were long gone but the large space inside was ideal for a number of functions. It was now utilized as the students' dining hall as well as the auditorium where poem recitations, singing competitions, speech contests and dramas were staged and political assemblies and all sorts of celebrations held.

Ms. Guan's full name was Guan Ziyi, Self-Leisure Guan. A short lady in her mid-thirties, she was Jianfei and Lishan's homeroom teacher, teaching Chinese Literature. Inserted into an oval face was a pair of almond-shaped eyes sparkling with wisdom. The short nose somewhat tilted up, speaking for her pompousness and carefree temperament, a perfect match to her thick, pursed lips which seemed to always say "no." Her permed hair was cut even to the earlobes, neat and sharp, blossoming in a modern fashion. A pair of semi-high-heeled brown leather shoes, spotlessly polished, peeped out from under a pair of woolen trousers with two knife-cut pleats. On top was a Chinese navy blue jacket, on the right side, white buttons twined into tiny frogs lined and guarded the border. A long silk scarf of pale green embroidered with black velvet flowers embraced her face, and then trailed behind into a piece of cloud wafting in the breeze. Whenever she strolled in the hallway, she stirred up a gentle ripple. Girls' eyes tailed her in admiration, each picturing herself trimmed as elegantly as Ms. Guan.

Lishan bragged about her teacher, but vilified Huifang's homeroom teacher whose protruding front teeth had become her trademark and obstructed her speech. "Huifang" was pronounced "Feifang" through those jutting yellow slanted little squares. The meaning of her name was thus twisted from "Amiable and Fragrant" to "Lung Fragrant". Laughter exploded and the amiable Huifang was slightly ruffled.

"Your 'Canine Teeth,'" Lishan burst out laughing and doubled over, gloating for her creativity in coming up with such a nickname, "deserves to teach only boring math."

Canine Teeth, the ugly metaphor, had since become a substitute title for their math teacher. Huifang, though scarcely appreciative of the mockery of her homeroom teacher, like her friends, remained a faithful disciple, a keen observer, and a truthful imitator of Ms. Guan.

Lishan's worship of Ms. Guan was quite personal. The literature teacher was also an avid artist and a tireless patron of the arts, whose spare time was mainly devoted to promoting art. Lishan went to her dormitory almost every Sunday to consult her on her own works. Evidence of such a teacher-student friendship was the painting placed under the glass cover of her desk which displayed the artistic talent of her favored student. Out of the dozens of paintings and sketches that Lishan had tried her hand on since her days in primary school, Ms. Guan singled out this one. A wilderness of green and yellow, a sweep of blue and white and a stripe of brown presented a dazzling rape field under the azure vault threaded through with a narrow path imbedded with footprints. A grayish smudge beyond suggested a village. The blooming of the spring, the revival of nature, the lives refreshed in the first thunder peal, the renewal of the world were all explained in the title "The First Rain". No people, just footprints. A painting out of a twelve-year-old brain, so straightforward yet so oblique, deserved focused attention. Ms. Guan wanted the school to know about Lishan.

"That touches the theme, the footprints," Ms. Guan was heard commenting.

"Theme" was the theme of a literature teacher.

She expounded to her colleagues, "the footprints imputed a busy society backed by the smoky village in the distance."

Her coworkers scrutinized, nodding faintly, wondering why a teacher of literature should go beyond her profession to delve into a field not her proficiency.

"And the employment of sharply contrasting colors; the strokes, some casual, free flying; some constrained and disciplined…"

Her coworkers smiled and glided out of sight. Nevertheless, she sat down with the artist Lishan and together they dissected the work in minute detail: how to make it mature and deliver the best of it. The literature teacher submitted the painting along with their critique to the editor of *Literature of Youth* who, without delay had chosen to include the image in an upcoming issue. The issue had now been published a month ago. Lishan, now a minor celebrity, had her first taste of success.

Chapter 5

Dusk. The girls wrapped up their homework and left Jianfei's house. Working together would ensure they get the same grades as Jianfei. Six o'clock. The bugle blasted from the loudspeakers. It was time for dads to return home. The two girls made their way home, one on foot, one on bike. In the west, where the heavens met the earth, rows of poplars appeared silhouetted against the burning sky. Birds fanned their enormous wings, like a Chinese paper-cut pasted on a large orange sheet. As if shied by the sudden blinding grandeur, they broke into chorus, scattering home amidst the massive foliage. Jianfei walked her friends out. The printing on the west sky delivered a perfect match to a picturesque poem dad had taught her:

> The fading sun
> The empty mountain
> An exhausted crow returns
> Without a sound.
> Hurriedly rushing home
> It is startled.
> In the ancient temple,
> Are the monks having dinner yet?
> From the wooded hollow,
> From time to time,
> A bell is tolling:
> Go home, go home.

In the smoky twilight, maids too scurried to the dining hall, fearing they might be unable to catch the best dishes. One by one, windows were lit. Countless stars blinked at the stars in the sky, reflecting a variety of family stories. Each frame displayed joyful scenes, harmonious units, incoherent movements, tacit or garrulous mouths, hugging arms, pattering feet, scolding, laughing and bickering.

What was framed in Jianfei's window were four dishes arrayed on a round table sitting squarely, waiting for the head of the family to pick up his chopsticks, look at each of his family members and announce "start". A meat dish, a tofu dish, a vegetable dish and a soup were designed to bring balance to the table, not only in taste, but more importantly, in nutrition.

Mom was always the last to join, busy running a department in the municipal government. In Jianfei's eyes, her mother was alien to this compound. She was too beautiful to be a politician, compared to the other officers' wives. Those women, because of their husbands, occupied more or less prominent positions in the government, depending on their education, experience, caliber and the length of their tenure with the army. Mom, an orphan at the age of 14, grew up destitute. Her luck was built on her friendship with a wealthy classmate who helped her with her board and lodging and half of her tuition—the other half was waived due to her high grades. Having matriculated to a Catholic school run by the British, she became a teacher. War broke out and the Japanese approached Shanghai, a hundred miles from where she was teaching. Flames licked and parched the earth; fresh blood flowed in the field; bayoneted bodies lay on the roadsides; classrooms rumbled and the groans filled the ears. Her rich friend whispered to her about the existence of a party, the Chinese Communist Party, and its charismatic leader, Mao Tsetung, who was planning a strenuous war against the Japanese to pull the nation out of the deep water. She started reading some of the Communist literature and that was all it took. Throwing aside the writing brush and picking up the gun, she joined this Party and its force the New Fourth Army.

The war weathered her but did not wear out her looks. Her brisk pace matched feet ten years younger. The invisible smiles that flipped over her face and lingered between her upward lips, the noiseless way of opening the door and the footsteps that were reminiscent of a cat were more attractive than the thumping steps, determined looks and executive phrases paraded by other female politicians. In summer, a white silk shirt tailored artistically for her body, a black silk skirt and a pair of white leather sandals drew a demarcation line between her and a group of stupidly garish, flowery dresses. Her enticing breasts contrasted with their pavement-flat chests. A pianist, a painter, a calligrapher, she took full advantage of the Catholic education and cultivated herself in many ways that other housewives could only covet.

Though evening was her favorite time, Jianfei hated dinner. It was at the dinner table that homework was checked, the day's performance reported, and each incident scrutinized; each subject reviewed, comments made, mistakes called out, and the scolding began, a routine investigation and interrogation. Dinner turned cold while hot tears dropped and seasoned the rice.

"How was your day, kids?" Dad's eyes were a pair of crescent moons.

"Great! I got two A's, one on a math quiz, and one in Chinese character dictation."

Taking advantage of his good scores, Little Rock threw a four-bite portion of "lion's head" into his bowl, and two helpings of tofu in addition.

"Also something real special happened today. I am going to learn the triple jump from the big brother in Unit 301."

"Who is this big brother?" mom turned to dad.

"Commissar Yang's son, one year senior to Jianfei." Dad's chopsticks nodded and pecked in the dishes, prodding out a good piece to reward the girl for an expected high mark, "A genius, a tiptop student. At a parents meeting, his physics teacher, recalling his twenty years' career, assessed young Yang as number one. I just consulted Commissar Yang to see what formula he feeds this prodigy."

"Well, genes and upbringing, of course. With that kind of parent, the children are born geniuses. How many of us could afford the Central University, going to bed with empty stomachs and walking in the snow with shoes so worn our toes would stick out?"

Jianfei pricked up her ears. Her judgment of mom's remark wavered between sincere admiration and acrid jealousy. While the family conversation continued to drone in her ears, the term "Big Brother" rang in her heart like a bell. *Why does the name stand out?* She asked herself, but no answer was provided.

"How was your quarterly examination, Jianfei?" the interrogation carried on between green leaves, light pink balls, and white tofu. Dad's chopsticks ceaselessly tried to ensure that every good tasting morsel from dinner landed in the children's bowls before someone else took possession in her mouth. Fortunately, mom was still oblivious at this stage that such a drama was unfolding.

"Algebra, 100, Chinese Literature, 96. Geography and biology will be announced tomorrow."

When her grades met dad's expectation, Jianfei liked to put on a sullen face. She enjoyed the retaliation because in a case like this, it was dad who was in debt, and not she. And sure enough, a pink piece of pork flew over.

"Good! For Chinese literature, 96 is considerably high," dad smiled, a trait of smugness in his tone. "Like father, like daughter," he said in his head.

Jianfei read dad's mind. He was reviewing his old days at Hunan Normal School, well known for its alumni, Mao Tsetung, who was eight years his senior. Professor Tian Han, the celebrated dramatist, one day examined his essay and was so carried away that his brush immediately swayed a "110", topping the peak. "Genius," he said.

"Is yours the top?" dad asked.

"No. There is a 97."

"That is quite surprising, you know, being my daughter." Dad's jaw slowed down his chewing. "From now on, you should always bear in mind if Commissar Yang's son can be number one, so can Professor Zhao's daughter."

Furious and eager to exit, Jianfei snatched the soup bowl and poured half into her own, letting one spoonful splash unctuously and erode the red paint of the tabletop. Big Brother was now an inflicted challenge for her.

"Are you listening to me?" Dad put down his chopsticks.

"Brr..r..r..." burying her face in the bowl, Jianfei gave happy consent through the loud gurgling into her soup.

"By the way, you'd better keep an eye on your little brother when he learns the triple jump. He could easily hurt himself."

Jianfei was on the verge of "I am not my brother's keeper," but on second thought, returned to her soup and buried her face there until dad spared her a reply.

"One more thing, I must remind you of your table manners." Dad picked up his chopsticks and resumed his rummaging among the colorful pieces.

Jianfei was about to give her face a third dip when a rapping was heard on the door.

Jianfei extracted her face from the swimming bowl and sat up straight, waiting for the unexpected caller.

Chapter 6

"I'll get it." Xiaoshi hopped off his chair and darted for the door.

"Look who's here!" Xiaoshi's voice harbingered a guest, his thin arms entangled with a pair of thick arms. In he dragged his Big Brother.

Good Gracious! Jianfei secretively dabbed her cheeks, hoping no specks would shine there. Shamefully, she stole a glance at the dinner table. Green, white and yellow, the stout red table was studded with bits of fat and congealed drippings. The spilt soup expanded and bubbled up the paint like a baby's soiled bedding. Coarse and plain-looking bowls exposed uninviting remnants like a stomach turned inside out. In her mind, she pictured a tall, white table covered with embroidered white cloth, fine porcelain plates bordered with orchids, peonies encircling their rims, ushering in stir fries, stews and cold dishes. Slices, shreds and juliennes were displayed in a marching array of culinary supremacy, each piece perfectly shaped—an enticing menu, color, taste and flavor all coordinated to whet the appetite just as had been seen at dad's higher-ranking friends' houses. She wondered whether this Big Brother belonged to one of those tables.

"I am sorry to interrupt your dinner," Yang Bing was also blushing, "but my father sends you two movie tickets; *The Gadfly*, a Soviet movie adapted from an English novel."

"Oh, the one about the 19th century Italian revolution, right?" Dad took over the tickets.

"Saturday evening, seven o'clock. Dad said you might already have your tickets. I brought these extra ones, hoping Xiaoshi's seat could be next to ours."

Big Brother draped his arms around Xiaoshi's shoulders from behind. However his invitation sounded in Jianfei's ears cautiously but casually directed towards her.

Emboldened by the sudden favor, Xiaoshi turned his face to Big Brother, "May I spend my evening with you?"

"That'll be great!"

Xiaoshi was about to slide off, but detected a cloud on dad's forehead. He checked his steps in time, "I will wash my bowl and leave the homework on the desk for dad to check. Dad, may I go now?"

"Make sure you leave Big Brother alone with his homework. You only have one hour."

When Xiaoshi came back and tiptoed into her room, Jianfei was absorbed in thought. *How the Steel Was Tempered*, which Lishan had browsed the last few pages of during recess and passed over to her, was laid open on the end table. Xiaoshi kicked off his shoes, climbed onto her bed and stared straight ahead through the window. Jianfei kicked off her shoes, climbed onto her bed and followed her brother, staring straight ahead. The discovery in the window opposite her bedroom nearly knocked her out of bed.

Building seven had three entrances, the east, the middle and the west. On the two ends, Unit 101 and Unit 301 stood face to face in the shape of the letter E without the middle bar, with a distance of around thirty meters in between. Her bedroom and his were the two identical E bars; each had the bed positioned just under its window.

Yang Bing was doing sit-ups on his bed!

My God! I am sleeping face to face with a boy of my own age.

Jianfei rolled off the bed, stumbled to the door and snapped off the light. *He can read my life just as I can his!* In a minute, the maid hung up a curtain for her. Now she could snuggle behind the curtain and watch the show.

The curtain made Xiaoshi a bit crestfallen, but the evening at Big Brother's, still vivid, enlivened his mind.

"So much amazing stuff! Big Brother collects everything! Coins, stamps, lead figurines, miniature ancient weapons, marbles, paper cuttings, wood carvings…you name it, he has it. Pebbles, beautiful, beautiful pebbles! Red, green, yellow, blue, transparent, opaque, with intriguing lines, in fantastic shapes that trigger the imagination. A rabbit, a pig, a fish. There was a stone just like a crouching dog with a tail coiling around the bottom. Round, triangular, elongated, slippery and smooth! His room is a museum and a library. You should see his stamps, ten times more beautiful than ours! Olympic Games, Russian paintings, Ancient China, each stamp is a picture, telling a story, showing me the world. And they are countless. Countless!"

As the manager of Xiaoshi's stamp and other collections, Jianfei felt inferior, but she immediately came up with an idea to partake of Big Brother's possessions. "Bring your stamp album and trade with him. I will be your adviser."

"Shall we?" Little Rock jumped in the air. "Big Brother has twelve stamp albums, all bought from Beijing!"

Another pale comparison, Jianfei was determined to catch up. "Let's ask dad for more albums."

Little Rock babbled on, counting other's treasure as his own.

"He even owns a bookshelf, like the one in dad's study. Literature, math, chemistry, physics, picture books, magazines…countless, countless! No wonder Big Brother knows everything. He told me a story called 'Straw boats borrowing arrows'. Zhu Geliang, do you know Zhu Geliang? He is the wisest man in *The Three Kingdoms*."

Given a chance to show the bit of superiority, Xiaoshi gloated.

"Anyway, Zhu Geliang outwitted Zhou Yu by luring his army to shoot the thatched boats, while he sat inside, safe and sound, drinking. Hundreds of arrows became buried in the straw and were collected to be used for his counterattack."

"Take a break," Jianfei interrupted.

"Oh, he has the same book you are reading now, *How to Temper the Steel*."

"No. *How the Steel Was Tempered*."

"Yes, *How to Temper the Steel*," brother yawned.

"Now, go to sleep," yawned the sister.

Reading a book adults read was not easy at her age. Unfamiliar words covered the pages; phrases she could only half-digest tripped her up; long sentences like noodles in the porridge slowed down the fluency.

The Whites, the Reds, Bolshevik, Menshevik, proletariat, bourgeoisie… however, what kept her eyes glued to the book were the twists and turns of the relationship between Pavel and Tonia. The two protagonists met from different backgrounds like the North and South Poles, one in abject poverty, one from a well-to-do family. They fell in love. As the teenage lovers entered their youth, their lives diverged. One became a Red Army soldier, constantly shuttled between the endlessly stretching railroads and the smoky, swirling battlefields, in a permanent bedraggled or bleeding state. The other, in her fur coat, apathetically observed from the brightly-lit car as it slowly glided past the railway builder. Now Pavel, an attentive angler, became annoyed when a well-dressed pretty stranger of his age sneaked up on him from behind and ruffled the water with her untimely greeting. A fish nipped his line and swam away, leaving behind only a jiggle. A love germinated here.

Jianfei's mind roamed to the other end of the building. *Is he reading the same book?* In a wink, she saw Yang Bing holding the fishing rod, kneeling down on the meadow, she herself wearing a summer hat, teasing him from behind the willow tree. The vision vanished instantly. *Shame on you.*

Turning off the light, she furled her curtain leaving a small slit to peep through. A shadow play began. In the far room, dimly lit by the desk lamp, a father and son walked onto the stage, big glasses and small glasses. She glued her eyes on the opposite window. The next two pantomime characters entering the theatre wore two pairs of female glasses, one tall, one short, hands up, hands down, sitting down, standing up. The show told a family's wrap-up story of the day. In a society where glasses symbolized knowledge and classiness, Jianfei analyzed the drama and assumed the four glasses were super-intellectuals.

The hodgepodge of the eventful day refused to subside and her brain raced on. The sports field resurfaced in the darkness with a reanimated vividness. Rope skipping, whipping, three electric shots… her mind's eye now saw the movie tickets, the blue sweater, Pavel the teenage fisherman and Tonia, the lit window and its silent movie.

Tomorrow morning! She couldn't wait to see that lightning rope again. With a thrilling expectancy, she counted sheep. The day's happenings gradually blurred into a colorful tapestry hanging over her head that glided into black water and moored there.

Chapter 7

In an era when movie theatres were infested with *Red Storm* and *Red Children* and the street urchins flung bamboo poles on their shoulders and chorused, "We are the Communist Children Corps," the Academy was privileged to view quite a different caliber of pictures. *Oliver Twist*, *The Pickwick Papers*, *Hamlet* and the Soviet version of *Twelfth Night* enjoyed popularity on campus. The three girls were their devoted audience. Not only did these movies flavor their life and enhance their tastes but also equipped them with the most avant-garde fashion tips. They hummed "The Song of the Willow" of the crazy Ophelia when her sweeping hair drifted aimlessly in the silky water. All these pictures were restricted within the boundaries of the Academy where Soviet life was in fashion and fervently promoted by the officers' wives.

The movies took the lead in the officers' spare time and were the core of their privileged life behind the walled compounds. Officers were given free tickets, their families included. The ex-KMT officers in Beiji chose not to mingle with the Communist compounds; therefore tickets were spared and circulated the second time among the Communist high ranks. A child quickly lost social status if he was not spotted with sufficient frequency among the audience. Little kids from the North Pole were constantly patronized with tickets from their friends. Huifang considered herself lucky enough at her age, as a "walled one" by her classmates, though a Nationalist child, to be blessed with Jianfei's generosity that always ensured her a ticket. The coming weekend was drawing near and the excitement over the approaching screening of *The Gadfly* was shared between her and her friends. The movie was always a great social event and the girls elevated this in their heart. Huifang, Jianfei and Lishan counted the minutes.

Saturday finally arrived.

Lishan was forced to straighten her arms along her ears and let mom pull the brand-new sweater over her head. When she showed up at Jianfei's, her whole body moved robotically. Her legs appeared stiff as if frozen. She detested being dressed up like a doll. Embarrassed, clumsy, unsure how to dispose her limbs, Lishan stood at the door waiting to be directed. Jianfei was amused. Lishan's attack-dog tongue directed, by habit, at anyone who indulged in a bit of color or a touch of new fashion was kept in check at the moment. Day in day out, Lishan took great pride in her plain clothes because her no-fashion fashion, no-color color had struck the whole school and was widely known as "Lishan-style." Now her purple sweater prepared the way for an unusually quiet reception of Jianfei's brand-new green sweater which on any other day would have been subjected to Lishan's caustic remarks.

"My mother said I would look like a grandma standing beside you two in the cinema," Lishan's words trickled out in a murmur. A shamed face and a faint smile followed to suggest a possible apology for her routine sharp criticism, sometimes straightforward, sometimes oblique, of her companion's attire. Beyond her sarcasm and acid tongue, a dread of bright colors and the public attention that accompanied them was the real source of her catty comments towards the more sartorially inclined.

Surprised by the newly purple Lishan, Jianfei and Huifang traded a meaningful glance. Huifang was in a pale yellow cashmere sweater; the fine texture and soft color added sweet tenderness to her whole being; her budding breasts were cupped underneath. Unlike Jianfei, Huifang never gave a second thought as to what to wear to school, despite the intimidating atmosphere exhaled from Lishan's acrid comments.

Jianfei's green sweater was a gift from her parents after she was elected by the fifty-two Young Pioneers in her class as their leader. A white arm emblem with two red stripes, the leader's identification, satisfied her parents' vanity.

Now the green, the purple and the yellow strolled to the movie theatre like three pieces of dazzling clouds in a Chinese fairy tale, pleasing mothers' eyes, and alerting the males across the campus.

The auditorium, where the movies were shown, stood in the center of Compound One. A red star crowned its spire, shining in the clear blue sky. Majestic pines deferentially guarded its flanks; their lower, stretching branches skirted around their trunks, graceful but stately. Embraced from all sides by autumn's red, yellow, orange, gold and russet, the auditorium's marble columns stood in a glistening white contrast. Granite steps led to the main entrance and spacious foyer beyond. Magnificent, solemn and classy, the auditorium, nevertheless, was a legacy from the Kuomintang. Deep from the bushes, modest and unnoticeable, the tiny laurel flowers breathed out an enticing scent, thickening the air.

The green, purple and yellow clouds sauntered into the rock garden adjacent to the auditorium. Leisurely taking in the traditional Chinese atmosphere of the garden with its rustic wooden bridge, large moon gate and vermilion flying eaves descending from atop the raised pavilion, the girls took delight in the contrast with the pinnacled Western auditorium in its backdrop. Meandering through the lawn was a pebble path along which the dwarf maples and the miniature mountains were laid out in a symmetric display. West Lake Rocks stood upright, with their large natural holes running from top to bottom like numerous windows. Bamboo thickets, a wooden bridge and a jingling brook assembled a landscape in harmonious ancient beauty.

"What do you think of Pavel?" out of the blue, Jianfei introduced the foreigner into their presence.

"He serves as my role model," Lishan came up with a lucid swift answer as if Pavel was in her pocket with a ready answer. "You know, I've realized I am drawn to a certain type of male protagonist. Their minds are set straight and never give up. They are their own masters and never drift with the tide. Pavel is one, and Arthur, in *The Gadfly, another.* You will see in tonight's movie. This kind of man shares the same quality: the willingness to endure pain, the stomach for bitterness, the limbs and bones built for hardships, and a shining charisma, of course. Do you know who possesses these qualities?"

"Who?"

"The boy we saw this morning. My brother told me he runs every morning for an hour. He's done so for the past two years. Starting at five thirty sharp, in rain and snow. He is your type."

Jianfei felt a pumping in her heart and a faint blush.

"Me?" and her mind went astray, asking why her friend, a girl seemingly nonchalant and stoic about boys knew the life pattern of a boy who lived under her own nose while she herself was in total darkness.

"He is envied by my wild brothers." Lishan's voice became nasal again.

"How do you like my ponytail? I am going to wear a big red bow." Huifang pulled her hair back and cocked her head. Her facial muscles pinched out an amorous smile.

"Why don't you give yourself a Western name? Natasha something... Natasha the Beauty." Lishan's waspish tongue returned. Her lips tilted unevenly, squeezing out an acid smile.

They followed the winding path paved with black and white pebbles. Red stones were inserted in the center of tessellated flowers. Under the bridge, a weeping willow cast a generous canopy, overlooking a small pond. An autumn breeze flipped by, wrinkling the surface on which the sun danced in its silvery, sparkling costume. The water furled and unfurled like a giant fish with thousands of shining scales on its heaving back. The brook frolicked, kissing and glazing the pebbles.

At a distance, painted on the blue canvas of the sky, was the Gold Purple Mountain, hazy, almost smudged, in the waning sun. The Academy nestled, as if in the arms of a grandfather whose face wrinkled with motley autumn foliage. The sun reclined, projected on its green screen and tinged it with gold. From its belly, an unknown bird echoed a sad song, touching the strings of the girls' hearts.

Lying down on the lawn, Lishan took a deep breath. "I wish I could remain like this forever. Tomorrow I will bring my painting kit and spend the whole afternoon here."

"Are we going or not?" Huifang raised her head and glanced at the time that was ticking on the auditorium clock, "Only twenty minutes left."

Lishan rose to her feet in no haste. The green, purple and yellow clouds drifted back.

In front of the auditorium, people streamed in from all directions. Jianfei's eyes were busy searching among children who arrived in different modes: hopscotching, whipping tops, trundling hoops. The spinning tops painted in green, pink, yellow, white and blue radiated circles in blurring brilliant spectrums as they were whipped along. The hoops rolled smoothly when the asphalt roads came to greet them, but stumbled, skidded, skipped if they swerved to the sidewalk where adults' feet were annoying obstacles or simply slumped when they struck the grass. Her brother was nowhere to be seen among the players of trundling hoops and spinning tops, nor the hopscotch crowd. Her eyes searched around. *Who are you looking for? Your brother?* She was not sure.

When the three girls in dazzling colors emerged from the hullabaloo, they found themselves tailed by admiring eyes. In the lobby, social life was in full swing. Different ranks gathered in different manners. The seniors with their wives at their heels headed directly to the small tables in the corner and engaged in quiet conversations. Their demeanors were much more composed in contrast with the dashing, young ones, usually seen with one stripe on their epaulets who now grouped in threes or fours at the windows, smiling broadly. Their eyes roamed around, hunting for pleasing colors and outstanding figures. Ostentatious and frivolous they might seem in the eyes of their seniors, for women, their gallantry was the usual magnet.

It was this chivalry that enlivened the lobby and drew Huifang's eyes. Tightening her lips, she successfully printed out a pair of dimples beside each mouth corner. Her eyes constantly rolled sideways, two or three glances a minute.

Pointing her chin at Huifang, Lishan nudged Jianfei, and in a low voice, "What a social butterfly!"

Jianfei nodded absent-mindedly. Neither Huifang's flirting efforts nor the air of chivalry interested her.

A chandelier hung from the center illuminating the lobby. An oil painting of Mao Tsetung meeting the Academy's top leaders brightened the east wall. Red velvet with dazzling gold tassels highlighted the window frames. Brilliant and sparkling, yet still, somehow, in Jianfei's eyes, the hall looked dim, hollow and colorless. She was waiting for something, someone to fill it with solid content, to repaint it and set it aglow. *What is it?* She probed her heart. Finally what she had been waiting for came to reveal itself and this disclosure shook her. She argued with herself, rejecting the exposure.

"Yes, I am waiting for my brother," she heard a self-defense in her head.

"No, you are waiting for someone else," a second Jianfei retorted, sneering.

"Who?" her own voice again, meekly.

"The blue sweater," the other Jianfei thundered in her ears. She now saw herself in the mirror of the other self, quivering and blushing, her heart accelerating and feet nailed to the floor.

The bell rang. Six fifty. Crowds thinned. Xiaoshi was nowhere to be seen. Jianfei knew whom he was with. Her parents had already entered without him.

"Shall we go in?" urged Huifang.

"I have to wait for my younger brother," Jianfei faltered. Lying was not easy.

The bell blasted a second time. Two minutes left. Now they were the only ones left in the foyer. A bit fidgety, Jianfei tiptoed for a look like a sailor searching for shore.

Huifang laughed, "What can you see behind the closed door?"

The door clicked open. Six eyes shot simultaneously to the entrance. Jianfei could hear her heart thumping. A sudden wish seized her that she should have left the lobby earlier, but now it was too late. Five people strung in, Xiaoshi's voice rang in the air.

"Look! My sister is still waiting for me! I told you she would!"

He ran straight to his sister, dragging with him his Big Brother. His face radiated. So did Yang Bing's. His eyes fixed on her arm emblem. Jianfei smiled a casual greeting to Yang Bing's parents and his sister, her eyes eluding him.

"Jianfei, you are a young pioneer leader, eh?" Yang Bing's mother, the Assistant Director of the Department of Education in the Municipal Government, was a keen observer. Jianfei nodded indifferently.

The three girls groped for their seats which were two rows behind the Yangs.

As the projector reeled on, the screen unfolded the story: With their torches held high among Italian revolutionists, the Englishman Arthur and Gemma swear to be loyal to the revolution: Arthur confides his secret to father Montanelli, later elected to Cardinal, who unbeknownst to him was his natural father...betrayed by his father, Arthur is jailed...his cellmate

Giovanni Bolla, the leader of the group, spits out "traitor" into Arthur's face…Arthur is released …Gemma welcomes him with a bouquet… Arthur's confession is revealed and Gemma slaps the traitor's face… Arthur disappears, leaving behind a note: "Find my body in the river"… Gemma marries Bolla…"Gadfly" visits Gemma's parlor …something about "Gadfly" reminds Gemma of her deceased lover Arthur…Gemma asks Gadfly about Arthur, Gadfly denies his identity…Gadfly is arrested… Gadfly goes to the execution ground…gunfire…a letter delivered to Gemma, a poem, which they shared many years ago, "Wherever I go, I am always a happy gadfly.".…tears roll down like beads falling from a broken string; Gemma has lost her dear Arthur the second time.

From time to time, Jianfei allowed her eyes to roll away from the screen to Yang Bing, secretly hoping to peer into his unguarded heart, to understand what made his hands and head move whenever the screen showed the twists of the lovers' relationship. *What does he think of a love that takes such a treacherous road only to reach its tragic terminus? Does he scorn these lovers torturing themselves or would he dare to do the same? Would he wholeheartedly pursue a love which was doomed and only able to express itself in pain?*

The lights came on. The three girls dabbed tears. Jianfei stole a glance at the Yangs. They, too, were saturated with sorrow and no one spoke. Even the seven year old seemed lost in thought.

Jianfei's mind was ablaze. Unsolved questions gripped her, filling her head like fireworks against a black sky. As the three girls parted, Jianfei spotted her parents a few steps ahead among the dissipating audiences. She followed.

"Revolution plus love, this is the formula of Soviet literature," dad's voice.

Curiosity drew her closer.

"Like their major ingredients, bread and salt, revolution is the bread without which the book is not a book; and love is the salt, to make the story tasty."

Refreshing and brisk like the fall night, Jianfei thought, eavesdropping at her dad's heels.

"What do we have? Plain rice only, that's what our literature has had after 1949, tasteless." Dad's usual suavity failed to conceal a surprising bitterness.

Hearing steps, dad steered around and found himself face to face with his daughter.

"Jianfei, I know you like foreign movies. There is nothing wrong with that. But western movies contain some unhealthy elements that might not suit your mind frame, even in the Soviet movies. You must not let these scenes hamper your growth."

"Like what?" a bit belligerent.

"Like…er…like the relationship between Arthur and Gemma. You are too young to understand such things."

So, love is unhealthy? Jianfei replied not without poignancy and almost in rebellion, "Such things? I am grown up just like you and mom."

"Well, yes, but… However, Arthur's character, especially his strength in the face of adversity should always be your model, including his sacrifice of personal feelings for the cause of revolution."

It was not until six years later was dad's true meaning divulged to her.

"And that explains why Gadfly denies his Arthur identity." Dad seemed to hold all the keys to the mysterious details that baffled Jianfei but her interest in prying into them stopped there.

Chapter 8

In the year 1957, thousands upon thousands of intellectuals, including teachers, professors, doctors, journalists and writers who, candidly and ardently offered their criticism for the Party as Mao encouraged, were branded as "rightists", a label indelible for the remainder of their lives. They were sent to the remote countryside or the mountainous regions or some unknown camps to "remold themselves" through physical labor where some simply vanished. Mao's campaign "Let a Hundred Flowers Blossom and a Hundred Schools of Thought Contend", known as "the double hundreds", landed thinkers in jail and froze the flowers. For the intellectuals, their first crime was being gullible and outspoken. Here, once again, Chairman Mao proved to be a masterful game player. First he lured the people into outspoken criticism and then launched a ferocious counterattack, branding them the enemy.

No school, factory nor work unit was spared when the storm swept every city and village across the nation. Teachers burrowed in their offices, their hands gliding along their teaching notes which on this day turned into something confidential and irrelevant to their teaching. These writings were to be submitted to the General Party Committee for minute scanning of each teacher's performance in the light of Socialism and revolution. The commandment was to "reveal your heart to the Party." Failure to comply would mean the end of a teaching career. Confession was welcomed and snitching one another out was most encouraged. Socialist education could only be carried on by a Socialist staff. Their minds needed to be purified. From time to time, a window was pushed open and a head popped out measuring the temperature on the red walls like a groundhog testing the sun.

On the four walls surrounding the central campus courtyard were pasted long scrolls of white paper cascading three meters down, emblazoned with big characters written in black Chinese ink, boldly gutting the entire faculty and scrutinizing their intestines. Now the teachers, like mice, scurried out with heads slumped between their two hunched shoulders. Peeping and sniffing, eyes shifting, they paced a dead man's walk to view the poster site where they feigned piety by fixing their sights on each big character and suckling the humiliation. Their heads were buckets holding filthy, black water in which their names were wallowing: "bourgeois," "capitalist remnants," "rotten" and "rotten to the core." Adroitly moving their fingers over their notepads with a velocity compatible only to that of young hands taking notes in their classroom, the teachers had reversed their roles. They had become the students of their students and the subject of study. The commonplace, warm, respectful, smiling morning greetings had turned curt, indifferent, detached or simply went tacit. Gleeful eyes were scarce and merry faces undetectable.

You ought to taste what we have gone through in your classes!

The posters were blatantly protesting.

You think standing mute at your questions is fun? How can you justify our suffering through your frowns and scolding mouths? You think public criticism will glorify us? And the red D's on our examination papers add make-up on our faces?

The black and white of the posters, striking against the formerly unnoticed red bricks and green trees, triggered Lishan's memory of a Tang poem and she recited a line in modulated tones:

"Tens of thousands of pear trees blossoming overnight."

To the mind of the Tang poet, the sudden winter storm which covered the bare trees was transformative, bringing pear blossoms in its snowy embrace. So too in Lishan's view was the whiteness of the school courtyard she looked upon. The stable political world she thought she knew was now overcast in a white shroud.

"Shut up! This is no joke," Jianfei, flabbergasted at the overnight snowfalls, glued her eyes on Lishan, whose nostrils dilated with grunts which then fizzled out and ended up with an "ouch!"

Jianfei whispered into her ear, "Watch out!" and looked around vigilantly.

The auditorium, which also served as a dining room for the boarding students and as a lunchroom for those who lived far away, was another battlefield. Hanging outside the steeple of this converted old church, large white scrolls of paper scrawled with black slogans—"Down with the Bureaucrats!" "Power to the People!"—cascaded down, like banners suspended from above. Its spire spared, the church's nave was not. Inside, it looked like an animal gutted out and stuffed with new black and white intestines. The dining tables were shuffled to the center like back-to-back mustered prisoners. Stools were stacked seat to seat or legs to seat as if waiting for some acrobats to perch their precariously balanced torsos on the ends. Along the walls where black characters were scribbled or squarely presented on white paper, four sets of tables and benches stood underneath, separated from their rank, ready to sacrifice their gleaming surfaces. They were smeared under sordid feet whose ardent owners were eager to paste more posters high to furbish the battle with newly produced bullets. In any case no one was going to mind; the diners at this juncture were likely to consider hygiene as yet another bourgeois nicety and not likely to pamper themselves with it. The trod-upon victims really meant nothing. The former pulpit and apse were smothered in posters as well, and the windows had been blindfolded. The only available light enabling the diners to avoid shoving their food into their noses was provided by the door now wide open gulping in hostility and frenzy from the dozens of white tides that bellowed out from their classrooms.

The three girls threaded through the white forest, marveling at its might and wondering when their turn would come. The loudspeaker ordered all to resume their seats in their homerooms.

The classroom boiled. Every face was set aglow. The hurricane swept over, with the imminent involvement of the freshmen and this charged every nerve in Class A.

"I bet we are not going to have classes today."

Minming, Fast and Bright, was the daughter of the dean. She was now finishing the last piece of breakfast that was tossed high in the air and intercepted by her swift moving head with its wide open beak like a fledgling in the nest.

"I overheard mom talking to dad. Most likely we will have big-character poster sessions instead."

The freckles gleamed on her face in the morning sun as it moved to its gradual brilliance.

Minming's prediction about the big-character posters triggered Jianfei's memory and brought her back to the lunch she was honorably invited to at her friend's house to celebrate her primary school graduation. Her friend's father was a revered three-star general. His name was mentioned daily in the nation's media.

At their elongated mahogany table, the General sank into the master's armchair, commanding his tablemates on the other end. The dining room was the centerpiece of his sprawling bungalow complex, formerly occupied by western dignitaries, and huge by any standards. Jianfei's amazement at the size of her friend's dining room turned to speechlessness when she was shown around the complex. Flanking the dining room to the west was the ample conference room which had recently grown familiar with the nation's most distinguished political figures. A colossal elongated table similar to the dining room table was covered with a light blue cloth, its border lined with white, orchid-embedded tea cups. To the east was a miniature copy of the western conference room, secluded and reserved for Beijing correspondence only. This room was distinguished by a small round table on which a direct long-distance army line to Beijing was found. Since political unrest had increased in the spring, the ringing no longer alarmed the compound occupants. To the north, overlooking the bungalow, was a two-storied Tudor house, before 1949, the embassy of some western country. Here the General's family could enjoy the sun on its balcony with a bird's-eye view of the south garden where jasmine and laurel infused human lungs in fall, and the pine trees soared four seasons long. In the center of the garden, a small lotus pond opened to shoals of fish, red, gold, yellow and white, swaying their fins, frolicking with the West Lake Rock that emerged from the water with its numerous holes, like the monster Argus sleeping with its hundred eyes open. Well-manicured lawn was seen stretching between the bungalow and the Tudor house. Layers of trees removed the compound from the plebian city noise with their absorptive sound insulation.

The General insisted that her daughter's friend stay for lunch because Jianfei's father happened to be another Hunanese, born not far from where he himself started his career.

"Hunan people are pepper eaters and therefore hot-tempered. We are diehards and the most ferocious in the battlefields…" the General was a chatterbox. "By the way, do you like turtle eggs?"

Between his resonant self-introduction and energetic chomping, the General skillfully maneuvered a delicate ball from its slimy pond and ushered the slippery egg to a safe landing on the white tip of Jianfei's rice bowl. Wary and curious, Jianfei tapped it with her chopsticks. The marble escaped the bowl but was recaptured by the General's spoon and embedded in the white mound a second time. Jianfei's chopsticks hesitated but her tongue was willing to give it a tentative lick, seeing her friend gulped down another marble without wincing. *Turtle egg?* She examined it. *Isn't that how people cuss, calling each other names? You turtle egg! Wang Ba Dan!*

Her chopsticks were about to make a daring move when a thunderclap shook her hand. The barely stabilized egg in her grip gave a quiver and retreated to her bowl again.

"Report!"

Her eyes traced the sound to a guard at the door, saluting squarely.

"Come in." The General narrowed his eyes. His entertainment was uninterrupted.

"Report!" The guard now was at his General's elbow. "The college students are here again. The compound walls are packed full."

"What do the posters say?" the unmolested jaw questioned through vigorous moves.

"Report! They say, 'This compound…should…should open to the public as…a model bourgeois kingdom.' They say, 'the General should…move his two legs…like ordinary citizens…and the car should be confiscated and…return to the government…no privilege, no high salary…etc.'"

"How many of them?"

"Report! Approximately two to three hundred. They are still gathering in the street, shouting, 'freedom of speech, freedom of press, freedom of assembly …down with bureaucracy, down with the warlords…'"

The disciples of Nagy, the Hungarian ring leader of the counterrevolutionaries, the General thought. *Where there are intellectuals, there will be another Hungarian Incident.*

"Eat it. It's a delicacy," adding one more egg into Jianfei's bowl.

"Report! The comrades of the Guard Platoon are requesting to take down these vicious, anti-Party, anti-PLA posters. May we have your order, sir?"

"No," abrupt and resolute. "No one is allowed to touch the posters." *Not until Beijing, Chairman Mao himself, issues the order*, he said to himself.

The general's chopsticks leisurely strolled over the white porcelain. The "double hundreds" movement was not offered for free.

"Yes, sir." The guard clicked his heels and veered to the door.

"Wait," the General knocked his chopsticks in the empty air, sinking into deep thought, "Call the PLA Daily and have a journalist sent immediately. These posters need to be documented. Make sure the students' signatures are all visible in the photos."

The lunch went on with sufficient flavor and abundant laughter. Jianfei allowed the mashed turtle eggs to stick to her palate longer than needed in order to analyze its texture and memorize its complex taste stratum as a rare delicacy. What she did not know was that the round, smooth marble which she had some reservation in eating was at the time only affordable by those who could sit at an elongated mahogany table in a private bungalow surrounded by an ex-foreign embassy, a miniature mountain, a goldfish pond and rustling pine trees.

The noises died down. Silence reigned over the classroom. Jianfei switched her focus to the front. Almost immediately everyone noticed that Ms. Guan was not her usual self today. Her head, on which every single hair used to be disciplined and stick to its proper position, was now entangled in a seaweed ball. Her eyelids, drooping, red and swollen, told the tale of a sleepless night. The absence of the silk scarf and the replacement of the leather shoes by a pair of flat-heeled cloth shoes shortened Ms. Guan's stature. From her moderated pace and softened eyes, the self-assured, world-ignoring lady seemed not sure about herself and the world seemed all she wanted to know about now. Throughout the classroom students exchanged glances with one another. Keeping her eyes on Ms. Guan,

Jianfei nudged her desk mate Lishan, who responded with her own elbow movement.

"As you… all know…" Ms. Guan cleared her throat and tried to regain yesterday's clarity but the voice produced was like a faltering microphone. Girls straightened their backs. Their curiosity about the seaweed ball and the cloth shoes soon evolved into an itchiness to throw themselves into the storm itself that snatched away their teacher's modern equipment as Ms. Guan's mouth opened their eyes to a bigger picture.

"Chairman Mao and the Central…Committee of the… Communist Party, have launched the… campaign of 'letting a hundred… flowers blossom and a hundred… schools of…thought contend'."

From then on, the microphone seemed to have restored its circuit and her speech regained fluency.

"Criticisms are most welcome. Suggestions and proposals, any ideas about the school, the government, the neighborhood community, the army, a store, a factory, a doctor at a hospital… anything and anyone, are free to be voiced. Middle schools are catching up with all walks of life. Yesterday, the whole school, except the freshmen, had a rally. The principal called for a thorough review of our work. Everyone has the right to contribute her opinions on the faculty and their performance because what you are doing is dumping the bourgeois elements into the garbage and building up a new, healthier body for our society. We, the faculty, educated under an old system, walked into the sun with the dark shadow of our history. Please help to perfect our team so that we can adapt ourselves better to the New China. As the youngest of the school, you, too, have the obligation to point out our mistakes like your older sisters are doing now."

To wrap up, Ms. Guan issued an order, "Now everyone, go out and read the big character posters, then come back to write your own."

Chapter 9

Like sparrows scattering at gunshot, girls darted. From the third-floor balcony opposite their building, three five-meter long slogans streamed down. Red ink like fresh blood read:

Communist Party, Step Down!
Return the Power to the People!
Two Parties!

Jianfei felt as if she had been hit in the face and punched in the heart. Of course, just a few months earlier, Hungary had been her family's hot topic. The Communist Party members and government leaders were butchered; their bodies littered the streets. Instantly, her parents hanging from the lampposts flashed in her mind. *Is this it?*

Gathering outdoors, the older sisters resupplied the battlefield with new bullets; flying out from their hands were new posters, fresh ink exposed to be dried in the caressing morning breeze and enhanced by the sun. A familiar term, PLA, dear and close, bounced into Jianfei's eyes. The red title in which the two enemy forces were put in juxtaposition scorched her and set fire in her heart.

The PLA and the KMT Officers are Birds of a Feather

A red light. Jianfei came to an abrupt stop. *Something has to be done.* She heard the wailing of a train, a siren, an ambulance blaring. The Hungarian movie flashed again. Her mind searched every nerve and pore asking for immediate answers while her eyes hastily ran down the lines:

…its luxury…

…its overbearing manner…

…the same privilege…the house…the car…

…the same flippancy with women…

………

Warlords are warlords no matter what brand.

At the bottom, a signature was scratched like crow's feet: Zhao Shihe, World Harmony Zhao. Moving slowly up, Jianfei's eyes traced the name to a pair of stumpy hands that took the paper in their firm grip, and a flat face poked with a pair of triangular eyes whose whites were not sufficiently white to be called white, and whose pupils were more grayish than dark. Its bushy eyebrow threw the whole bleak appearance into disarray. A pair of drawn lips seemed to be always grunting. The face was studded with a nose without a bridge which nevertheless supported an exuberant growth of hair. Two tufts stuck out from behind the ears, vibrating in response to each of her body movements.

What a moron! Eighteen years old, wearing a child's hair style. Jianfei felt truly repulsed, even without the poster. *What a hideous sight!*

Jianfei's classmates seemed to have been run over by traffic. The audacity of the seniors hit them, dizzying and disorienting them. The itch to join the battle half-vaporized. They needed a leader. They gathered around Jianfei as children at their mom's tail about to cross the street.

The Power Must Be Shared!
Why One Party?

As they poured into the dining room/auditorium, exclamation and question marks jumped off the paper and screamed in their ears. Their minds seemed to be churning and whirling in the white snowstorm. They didn't know what to think, yet they remembered they had clear minds a moment ago when sitting and listening to Ms. Guan. Do minds grow up with different answers to "how much is one plus one"? Their eyes scavenged the walls for an answer where the white and black ocean seemed to hold a "yes" to that question. The seniors' posters encouraged a change in social formation, advocating a greater diversification of the elements of

Chinese society to allow for a more peaceful environment. The standards to which they held their government accountable went far beyond the juniors' imagination. Some of the more daring posters even called for a multi-party political system.

"Jianfei, what should we write?" a classmate turned back, utterly at a loss.

"Are we allowed to debate? The seniors are full of erroneous ideas." Minming seemed to have acquired a level mind in this bazaar of ideas.

"What they say runs counter to what we are taught in class and to what the newspapers tell us," another girl echoed.

"Lishan, she is spreading bullshit about our fathers. Read this one," Jianfei pointed her chin to the bushy eyebrows and turned to Lishan. But her friend was nowhere to be seen; she had moved on.

Eager to find an ally in the debate against the ugliest features on earth, Jianfei elbowed through the throng of her schoolmates, braving the white and black storm. She had confidence that Lishan could offer thick armor in defending their fathers. Her waspish tongue, seamless logic and profound analysis seemed to have been built specifically in preparation for this day.

In one corner heads craned towards a particular poster. Most of these heads belonged to the freshmen. Jianfei's eyes swam over this section to discover balloon pants and bobbed hair, Lishan's trademarks. The monitor of her class Xiaonan was talking to Lishan who absentmindedly delivered an answer to the monitor while she gazed at the poster, her face covered with lingering clouds. The pained expression on Lishan's face told Jianfei Lishan was not herself. As she pondered her friend's frame of mind, the rest of class A along with many other freshmen mustered under this poster. Heads rocked in the front rows from which sighs of sorrow, pity, marvel, bewilderment, merriment and relief could be heard. Jianfei held her breath while watching the freshmen from the other classes milling around, nodding in acquiescence and uttering cynical remarks. Some faces were satisfied, some reserved, but the majority showed celebratory expressions. They bent over laughing at the caricature but immediately muffled their mouths when their eyes rolled aside and caught sight of members of Class A. One or two giggles leaked out. A short girl cocked her head, swayed her arms, tipped her heels and waltzed in front of all the readers. The imitation of the figure on the poster triggered a chorus of sincere appreciation. Cheers burst out.

Jianfei's eyes climbed up to the three-meter long poster which explained why it was the freshmen's particular interest and also the source of Lishan's special pain. Ms. Guan was sitting in a cloud with which her trailing scarf merged; blossoms of permed hair enlarged her head making it twice the size of her body; her shoes were a pair of black sickles, dazzling and hooking up to her sharp nose which was presented as an upward banana; a cigarette was her sixth finger, drooping, hanging with the other five from her scornful lips; her eyes were shaped as two worms in whose bellies gun barrels were stored. The title was *What Ms. Guan Is Made of.*

"Let us dissect Ms. Guan. Looking into her soul, a bourgeois kingdom is what we see. Her eyes never bother to glimpse the workers' offspring. Those who were born in the purple enjoy her special favor and share her tastes… Aesthetics, as everything in a class society, is branded bourgeois or proletarian… art for art's sake… no art could ever be detached from its producer... Ms. Guan exerts her utmost to launch a tug-of-war against our Party…swaying a generation…leading them astray…sinking them in the quagmire…corrupting their young hearts…it's high time we stopped this malicious intent of Ms. Guan!....."

There were buzzards in Jianfei's head, hard to chase away: *Is Ms. Guan that vicious? What does this mean to Lishan?* This poster and all the posters were unsettling. *Why should father be compared to a warlord? Who is this Zhao Shihe?* Arrows shot from all directions. Her palms felt soaked. Her ear drums throbbed. Finally the swirl subsided, leaving only one question afloat in the air: *Where to start? Who to defend first? Her dad and his PLA or Lishan and her Ms. Guan?* This quandary produced a startling reaction in Jianfei. An anger that had been hidden for a long period, that up to this moment had been smoothed by their daily playfulness and painted over with thick layers of friendship, emerged. *Maybe this is Lishan's own fault. What has fed Lishan's constant biting remarks towards her peers? What has produced in her either this detachment or this condescension whenever she approaches?* Lishan's slantingly drawn lips, her acid smiles and frowning countenance flashed in her mind, fueling this anger. *Lishan was like a drop of oil on the water of her class. No one liked her and she could merge with no segment except one. Lishan's world view clearly proclaimed, "No one is worth speaking with but everyone deserves a good lashing by my tongue."* If *her reading brings along sophistication, profundity as well as cynicism, Lishan deserves no more books,* Jianfei said in her heart.

The possible precariousness of Lishan's social standing became clear. Jianfei sensed that the hubbub surrounding her might encourage scapegoating. It would be a tremendously formidable task for Jianfei to protect her friend. As if to verify her prediction, Xiaonan left Lishan and joined her classmates.

"What did she say?" Jianfei asked with caution.

"I don't know and I don't care," was the answer.

Jianfei now faced the mission not only to parry the bullets from other classes in the front before they wounded Lishan but also to shield her from the arrows aimed at her back by her own classmates. Lishan was directly involved and obliquely targeted on the poster. Grabbing Lishan by the arm, Jianfei yanked her away.

Lishan broke loose and attacked Jianfei with her ferocious eyes, "What did Ms. Guan do wrong? You tell me!!"

The bell blasted. The sparrows flew back. Chinese Literature had given way to poster writing, to everyone's satisfaction, especially Minming's who now gloatingly led a group of fifteen towards Jianfei and encircled her desk.

"Let's write together. Let's show our strength!"

Everyone had bottled zeal that needed to find expression. They knew Jianfei could make the team work.

"The 'Birds of a Feather' poster is a vicious slander of our army and presents an imminent danger to the security of the nation. We should start here."

Any thought of giving priority to a defense of Ms. Guan or Lishan was gone. Xiaonan, arms akimbo and scowling, picked up a pen and handed it over to Jianfei.

"Here! You're the scholar!"

Jianfei took over the pen and moved it over her notepad.

Warlords or the Great Wall of the Nation?

The title struck her there and then. Yes, her father and thousands upon thousands of dad's colleagues stood like the Great Wall defending the nation.

"Every mouth must participate. This means we'll have fifteen bullets. Go ahead. Pick up your own and arm yourself."

"The PLA serves the people," a voice from a corner took away the easiest line.

"Yes, No People's Liberation Army, no New China," a butterfly bow took the second easiest one.

"I need facts, facts." Jianfei stopped writing. "Empty words are soft tissue. I need the bones."

"They helped to build the new highway in Tibet. Remember? 'The Twin Peaks are a thousand miles high'…" a ringing voice began to sing a popular song eulogizing the highway builders in Tibet. A few accompanied.

"They come every Sunday to do house chores for Granny Wang, whose family was buried alive by the Japanese devils," a steadier voice offered from the back. It was the calligrapher Wu Feng, whose duty it was to enhance Jianfei's essay by transporting her draft to the poster in beautiful handwriting.

"Right, right," everyone chimed. Granny Wang lived next door. The girls sometimes dropped by to check on her.

"They help children to find their way home," Minming said. Everyone knew the story of her little brother and his PLA friend. Heads nodded.

"They were the first to arrive when the paper factory was on fire," a mosquito droned. Heads nodded.

"They built the dike on the overflowing Yangtze River every summer," a soprano.

"And the radio said they never leave the site, without food, without sleep, watching the rising line of the rampant water," some supplementary remarks.

"They rescued a drowning boy. Yesterday's newspaper had the details."

"They…"

"They…"

The girls effused. Ideas flew out of Jianfei's pen. The facts and the logic worked hand in hand, making the argument airtight. Jianfei couldn't wait to see Zhao Shihe's reaction and expected a seesaw battle between the classes. While engrossed in her arms production, Jianfei did not let the fact that her desk mate had never uttered a word detract her writing. Jianfei's naïve reliance on Lishan's solid protection of their fathers was a pipe dream.

Sketch drawn, Wu Feng was ready to paint. Someone needed to get the brush and ink which was stored in bottles atop the chained prisoners— tables back-to-back shuffled to the center of the dining hall. Everyone volunteered to go. Any scrap of time to get a second glimpse of the battle field was a golden opportunity. Minming dashed out without being chosen despite a dozen other raised arms. She returned in ten minutes from her one minute trip.

"More posters there. Exciting!…and more about Ms. Guan." Whispering, Minming stole a glance at their homeroom teacher who now stood woodenly at the open window facing the green lawn and the white snow thickened with each gigantic flake drifting out of the opposite building.

Grabbing the writing brush, Wu Feng began to brandish over the paper for the prominent title. The majestic vertical strokes stood boldly erect like soldiers each standing on thickened soles. Her horizontal bars were evened from left to right with studs on each ends like shoulder poles. The left-right sway flew and thinned to elegant and graceful tips. Girls' eyes glided over the white sheet now gradually filled with black word by word.

"Black is black, white white, they are not to be confounded!"

The line went through everybody's mind in a loud voice. Confidence filled their hearts that theirs was a heavy bomb. Jianfei was rhetorically gifted. Her deductive reasoning and diction had been repeatedly demonstrated as an example of effective writing for the whole class to follow. Wu Feng's hand, trained by her professional father, would impart a striking visual effect and convince the whole school that Class A was a rock solid unit. This visual tour de force was now being completed as Wu Feng put a period to the last character, dipped the brush in water and capped the cleaned brush. Girls grabbed the brush, reopened it, dipped it in ink and proudly added their names. Led by Jianfei's free-styled signature were Xiaonan, Minming, Wu Feng…Jianfei scanned the list. *Where is Lishan?* She stepped back and took a second look at the names. *No, there is no Lishan.* Now Jianfei's writing was reinforced by Wu Feng's calligraphy, speaking for a collective mind and a unanimous voice, hard for the senior Zhao to refute. It was laid open on the desk, waiting to be posted.

The bell rang for math, which no one was in the mood for. Canine Teeth walked in. The change in her attire and carriage stirred up a ripple in the classroom. Eyes were riveted on her brand new jacket which seemed to have not only suffused her in color but also to have washed away the rust on her façade. Canine's contrast with her old self and with the new Ms. Guan was apparent. The spry gait also proved redemptive of her stagnant mind. Her hair seemed to have undergone an exchange with Ms. Guan's. Where had been a disheveled nest was now a well-arrayed, finely crafted exhibition.

"Wow...woo...oooh!" Marvels and admiration ensued. Canine modestly nodded, her full-moon face lit with genuine appreciation. The tailor makes the man. Jianfei nailed her eyes on the brand new Canine and tried to read her mind. Suddenly she was struck by the fact that among the hundreds of big character posters, none had touched the name of the math teacher. It began to dawn on her how correct the ancestors were when they concluded "women lacking talents must be virtuous." Talents down, dummy up, Chinese logic.

"I have four equations," Canine opened her notes and procured her treasures on the blackboard. "I want four of you to come up and each to solve one," her back said. "Any folunteers?" A leak from her teeth.

Nailing her eyes on Canine's teeth and her equations, Jianfei raised one hand and the other slid her book down to the other end of the desk towards Lishan. A note lying face up wedged between two of the pages, showing her hurried scratchings, "Where is your tongue?"

"Any folunteers?" Canine pointed. One, two. "We need two more." Jianfei's forearm remained upward. "Jianfei, you do the last one."

As she returned to her seat, so did her book. Between the open pages a slip of paper newly inserted, "My tongue is locked up. Don't even try to pry it out."

Recess. Girls hung the dried posters on their arms, five pages altogether, and paraded to the auditorium. Their eyes scanned the ocean, looking for the sail marked "Zhao Shihe" so their posters could be exposed side by side and the whole school could draw a parallel between the contending proclamations to reach their own verdict. However all the sails seemed to bear the same brand now. The posters were either by Zhao Shihe or addressing her. The walls, in two hours, between Canine's "folunteer" and Lishan's locked tongue, seemed to have undergone a facelift and were branded with more posters from Zhao Shihe.

"Ten Questions for the Communist Party," began one sequence.

Whose Fault?
Lord-It-Over: a New Image of the People's Government.
To Educate or be Educated—for our Principal and Dean.
Master or Slave?—Workers at Work.
Get Off your High Horse—to Chairman Mao.
……

What Jianfei and her team considered an ideal shooting range had been claimed by other hunters. Exclamation marks became an avalanche in response to Zhao's question marks. These posters, in equal severity and harshness and with more torrential eloquence, encircled Zhao's, creating a verbal siege from which there was no escape. Dynamite was in the air. Any bit of verbal confrontation could trigger an explosion. The seniors' indignation was apparent in their stanchless white flood that soon would submerge Zhao's signature and muffle her voice. No one could hang back with folded arms when the Party, the Army and their Leader were under such malicious attacks from such an ugly creature. And the bombardment continued.

The girls of Class A were a bit crestfallen when they saw the terrain couldn't be utilized as they wished but their slight dejection was soon replaced with glowing pride. To be the first among three hundred some freshmen to stand up and write with the same momentum as the seniors was exhilarating. They glowed pasting their first big-character poster. Just two months ago, they were no better than those who hung around with toddlers and bickered fervently with their seven-year-old siblings. Now in a few hours, they found themselves entering adulthood. A year later they realized what they were doing in the early fall of 1957 was history making.

With their enemy barraged from upper and lower streams and in a shambles, Class A departed the auditorium victorious. Under the arch of triumph, face to face, they ran into a cluster of Class B. Their monitor was at its head, flanked left and right by two activists. Just behind them, holding a pasting broom and a bottle of ink was the ever-smiling face of

Huifang. A poster fluttered. Jianfei's eyes skidded over and a line flew into view, revealing the animosity from Class B, "Literature: Proletarian or Bourgeois? A question for Ms. Guan."

The two groups stiffened their necks and glowered at each other like ruffled roosters.

"Parroting others! What genius!" Minming launched a counterattack.

"How is your teacher, by the way?" a lazy greeting behind Jianfei. It was Wu Feng.

"Right!" a white bow said quick-wittedly. "Ask her to step out!"

"Correct! No need to hide behind her students!" touching to the quick.

"Good teacher's pets!" spitefully.

Huifang took shelter behind her leaders, her eyes evaded contact. The paste smeared her left palm, and the ink the right due to too tight a grip. The trembling Huifang entered the auditorium furtively, dwarfed by the majestic vault that witnessed a grave struggle between foes.

Eyeing Huifang as she was shielding and tailing others, Jianfei registered a name: "Tide Drifter". In an instant, issues more crucial than attacking each other's teacher loomed.

Chapter 10

Three sullen faces sat around the table, waiting for each other's tongue to pry open the other mouths and begin the battle, each mind tinged with acrimony. The ongoing ceasefire delayed their homework.

Lishan began to sharpen her pencil with a razor left from her dad's shaving. Blunt as it was, it cut Lishan's forefinger. She sucked out the blood and spat it out vehemently, "Even my own pencil bites me."

She flung it on the floor. Now the tip was broken.

"Damned math!"

She stomped her foot. The pencil snapped briskly and split into two.

A symphony was being played in the kitchen. Spatula clinking and clanking, spoons dinging and ringing, chopsticks whipping and hitting, with here and there a gurgle of bubbles and an explosion of sizzling onions, ginger roots and other unknown victims—a fish or a pig, slaughtered in the field and further killed in the wok until their skins turned golden crispy. The aromas of renowned culinary traditions tantalized their nostrils. In the delectable air, Jianfei detected a touch of cheerfulness, or at least a chicken, and she knew she couldn't afford a longer session of silence.

She brought her tongue to work, "Huifang, I would be most grateful if you could offer an explanation of your attack against your admired Ms. Guan."

Huifang's mind was not with her friends but preoccupied with a warning her dad supplied a week ago, a warning which meant very little to her until the reality of the current political climate struck her sharply. In her mind, she saw her parents, hunchbacked, trudging among white posters, a snow-clad peak, where they could find no way out for their daughter and were in constant fear that something might go terribly wrong at school.

"Huifang…Huifang! I am asking you a question," Jianfei's voice echoed from the white peaks which offered the only path for Huifang to follow down from the rugged mountain path to Jianfei's table.

"Ms. Guan?" her mind landed with a lurch. "Oh, Ms. Guan." She chewed her name, still a bit disoriented. "I don't know. Full Teeth walked in and goaded everyone to write." She offered a moderated version of Lishan's "Canine Teeth". "And then the next thing we knew, the poster was hanging from our monitor's hand. We all signed. That's all."

The eternally beaming eyes were on the verge of tears. That mortal poster would doubtlessly hurt her friends' feeling, but her signature was irretrievable now.

"Traitor!" Lishan spat out, through grinding teeth and fiery eyes.

"Stop! Lishan! Don't litter your venom everywhere." Lishan's horrific accusation softened Jianfei's resentment towards Huifang. "Give her a chance to clarify herself. But, Huifang, you like Ms. Guan and imitate her. Is there any other reason?"

"I don't know," Huifang began to crumple.

"You don't know?" Lishan lifted the left edge of her mouth, "You surely knew what you were doing when you kissed the Canine's ass!"

"Shut up!" Jianfei's voice vibrated.

Huifang's carefree and happy-go-lucky nature reinforced by her tacit demeanor had emboldened Lishan who intensified her acrid barrage. On Huifang's face, the dark clouds finally produced rain that streamed out of her almond-shaped eyes. She began to whimper like a child.

"Well, you know…my father…my family…we are different…" Words chopped up like in the winter winds, "My father…warned me against… any impromptu reaction…any tomfoolery…He advised me to…go with the majority…'Stay away from the center…but be one of them'…We are different, you know…I am black, dad said, you two are red…"

Jianfei was tongue-tied. For the first time, Jianfei realized that their innocence had come to an end and their friendship could no longer hold an unblemished façade. Their laughter would begin to contain some jarring sounds along with Lishan's acid tongue, which up to now was taken heedlessly by Huifang and rendered no harm. This painful realization arrested her and she sat there motionless.

Lishan rose to her feet and departed without a farewell, leaving her books behind.

Shortly following the girls' departure, dishes were laid on the table in splendor, but there was no sign of the parents. Checking the clock every few minutes, Jianfei, buried her head in homework, forced, for the first time, to do it alone. Next to her room, Xiaoshi went on with his solicitation. In trading stamps, Xiaoshi obviously benefited from the inexplicable generosity of his Big Brother. Jianfei's objective to enhance her little brother's collection to the level of competitive abundance was now attainable.

"How about one Chairman Mao to one of your Olympics?" Xiaoshi extracted a miniature of the great leader from his album. The portrait lacked one eye and the nose was a blotch of blue ink to which the mouth smiled to join. He grabbed the great leader in his slightly soiled palm.

"Wait," Big Brother produced a quaint penknife from his pocket and clipped the small square. "In handling stamps, you should always avoid fingers. Stamps are valued by their rarity. Their issued year can be found on the bottom. Look."

Big Brother pulled out another device. It was a magnifier this time. Xiaoshi grasped the handle and moved it to the left and right. Under the glass, below the disproportioned beloved face, no year could be traced. The stamp in the small round boundary of glass showed emptiness along the bottom margin.

"This one has no printing date," crestfallen, Xiaoshi mumbled.

"That proves the value." This time, the magician opened his book bag and flipped out a magazine *Stamp Collection*. "Your Chairman Mao was issued in the liberated area even before new China was founded. Nothing could be more precious than yours. My Olympics are only a few months old."

Xiaoshi's eyes flew between a profile murky with crude technique and a missing date that inaugurated China's stamp prosperity and the sixteen Olympic swimming, skiing, skating, and boating, mini-paintings in cheerful blue, green, red, yellow, unable to determine where to land.

"Why don't you keep your Chairman Mao and I will give you the whole set of the Olympics?"

Big Brother's voice seemed to be also magnified by the magnifier in his hand, ensuring every syllable reach the next door. In her smugness, Jianfei congratulated herself on the scheme to open the stamp trade. As for the trade inequality, among the three, the only one in the dark was the little beneficiary whose hands danced in the air holding the colorful squares.

With an ejaculation of rapture, Xiaoshi pushed the half open door wide open, waving Big Brother's album in the air, "I got them all! The sixteen Olympics!" Jianfei's glowing eyes glided in Big Brothers' direction. "Don't let the paltry glitter fool you." Not knowing the meaning of it.

Big Brother echoed to the little one, "Paltry glitter finds no place at the Zhao's." A pink cloud flew over Jianfei's cheek.

Dad and mom returned home quite late. Meetings, always meetings, and always more and more important. Xiaoshi left Big Brother in his room with a whole bunch of his sister's books and walked into the adjacent dining room.

Today's vegetable dish was tofu. Tofu sheets were sliced, thin as rubber bands, and mixed with yellow ginger roots as thin as spring grass. They were submerged in the golden chicken soup. A fine porcelain bowl embraced the yellow, green and white like a picturesque miniature of a lotus pond, tasteful and visually appealing.

"Wow!" Xiaoshi was drooling.

Mom nodded. Finally, after hiring and firing, testing and tasting, the perfect maid had been selected. She had proved herself a real Yangzhou hand, a city famous for its cuisine, a city which had cultivated the most sophisticated chefs. A chicken, yellow and glossy, as if painted, was dished out. Its half-closed eyes were peering at the surrounding predators submissively; its mouth was also half open, as if gasping for its last breath, ready for a French kiss with humans. Elegant slices of green onion stroked its beak like a moustache. A small white cup with soy sauce and pepper sat devotedly at its side.

"Beautiful! What a change! I like the new maid, Auntie Gao." Jianfei clapped her hands, hoping to deliver the dinner image to the one reading in the next room to redeem the sordid picture he had encountered before.

"What is the occasion?" dad put on a sour face. "Who gave the menu?"

"I," mom answered with composure.

To receive a confession from the mouth of the offender of whose guilt he was already assured was dad's consistent strategy at the dinner table, only this time, the offender was his wife.

"Why so extravagant?"

"Extravagant?" mom put down her chopsticks, with a suave smile. "We fought the war, shed blood, crushed our bones, waddled in mud and braved the rain of bullets. Every inch of this land was saturated with our blood and the blood of our fallen comrades. Does the bullet in your chest still hurt you on rainy days?"

A pause ensued. With her mouth agape, Jianfei stared at dad, feeling an acute pain in her chest. For the first time, she heard about the bullet. Mom was very dramatic; she left ample time for her husband to contemplate before she drew a conclusion.

"We paid for it, for this bird, with our lives. We have the right to enjoy life now. Who has if not us?"

"No! We don't!" dad controlled the volume but his voice was heavy. "Sorry, comrade, but we don't have the right to enjoy this bird until every household in this country has chicken on their dinner table."

Dad picked up his chopsticks. The volcano continued to smolder.

"No one acts like you, not even your presidents! Look at their houses, their cars!" Mom sneered, "Fool!"

It was this "fool" that escalated the war. Dad put down his chopsticks with such force even the chicken shook its head.

"Don't forget where we come from! Comrade. Don't forget what we fought and are working for! Don't forget that our mission is far from being fulfilled!"

Though the dinner table was always a battlefield, tonight's skirmish would be etched deeply in Jianfei's mind, known hereafter among the siblings as the "Chicken War".

"Remember, in this house, no one is going to live a life above average!" word by word, resounding in the air.

The next month, *PLA Literature* carried a poem "Remember, Comrade!" with dad's pseudonym beneath.

A sumptuous dinner is going to be ruined! Save the chicken! Jianfei shot an urgent look at her little brother. Their chopsticks flew over like a pair of airplanes and dived to bombard the peaceful bird. The sister snatched its heart; the brother tore off a drumstick.

"Some seniors want the Communist Party to give up power," adroitly placing a piece of white meat into each of the parents' bowls, Jianfei picked up a topic she was sure would avert the crisis.

And sure enough, in an instant, the dispute digressed; the adults were appeased and began to prick up their ears at the school situation. Nowadays school was everyone's focus. Jianfei gave a vivid description of Zhao Shihe accompanied with dramatic gestures, while her mute chopsticks pecked surreptitiously at the defenseless chicken, a motionless swimmer in its golden pond. Harboring an intent to broadcast her dialogue to next door within Yang Bing's earshot and bring him into the family conversation, Jianfei pitched her voice higher than necessary and exaggerated her narration. Her goal was soon attained, beginning with mom's compliment, "Well done, girl! A leader should show her leadership, first and foremost, in a political setting. The diction in your poster sounds quite appropriate."

Dad's appraisal was reserved, "Well, you could choose a different topic. Your debate is too personal. It is very easy to let your emotion lead your words and frame your minds."

It was her little brother who dragged Big Brother into the family picture, "Big Brother! By the way, Big Brother is reading in my room. Big Brother, did you also write big character posters?"

Dad hurried to push the door open, "Sorry for ignoring you."

Yang Bing stepped into the family circle. *At least the dinner table is first class this time*, Jianfei said to herself.

"Did you write big character posters?" dad parroted his son.

"Yes. I suggested that the school library be open from seven to nine in the morning and four to nine in the evening. Who will sit in the library from nine to four when everyone is in class?"

Dad listened attentively and then asked, "How have the seniors performed at your school?" Dad turned to Jianfei, "Listen. I believe the class struggle in a mixed school is more complex than a girls' school."

"Quite alarming," but Yang Bing's demeanor showed placidity, "'Down with the Communist Party' is today's fashion. You know, our school neighbor is the prestigious N. University, whose rebellious youths blow their so-called fresh air into our classrooms day in day out with their loudspeaker facing our windows as if intentional."

"What are their actual words?"

"The Communist Party must share its power with other democratic parties. Today twelve senior boy students in my school posted a ten-page declaration on the front gate, attracting downtown pedestrians. They called themselves 'The Chinese Democratic Youth Party'. They demanded the school be run by the students' Autonomous Committee. I have never read an article so well structured and language so lucid. The terms were so sophisticated, the arguments so logical and the thoughts so profound. It doesn't echo young voices at all and everyone believed it to be the work of an older hand. They even designed their Party flag, white and blue, quite similar to that of the Nationalist Party."

A cloud darkened dad's face.

Mom seemed more concerned for the youngsters, "Do these boys know that they are jeopardizing their lives? The writing definitely indicates an adult pulling the strings behind them. What they are doing is organizing an opposition party, a counterrevolutionary clique. This could easily bring them life imprisonment or even a death penalty."

"I don't think they are aware of this. This afternoon at closing time, some people came onto campus and took pictures. The scuttlebutt is that the police in civilian's clothes are keeping an eye on them."

Jianfei's jaw dropped. I thought the seniors in our school are rampant but they are nothing compared to these daring boys. She never imagined things could go so far. At this point, she abandoned her girlish bashfulness and raised her eyes, "Have you considered fighting back?"

"No. Dad asked me to keep a low profile." Yang Bing also cast away the barrier.

"What did your dad say?" Jianfei's father cut in.

"Dad asked me to stay away from sensitive issues regarding the Communist Party and the government but focus on the school system. He said, 'Patience will pave the way to revenge.' I don't see how his words predict the future."

"Before the hurricane, there is tranquility, on our part." Dad quoted a Chinese proverb, and then lost in his thoughts, "Your dad is right. I am sure Chairman Mao has his strategy."

Mom let her slender fingers cling to a chicken wing. Her jaw moved left and right as if playing a mouth organ. No further comment was issued from her busy mouth.

Chapter 11

The lamp on the nightstand cast a circle, capturing a prostrate Lishan. Her hands and legs widely spread, forming a Chinese character "big". Digging her face into her pillow trying to suffocate herself had created a self-abusive diligence that served as a punishment for what she had done during the day. *But what did I do to turn the world against me?* She remained in this self-torturing posture until she felt her vengeance fulfilled. Turning her face to the ceiling, she began to outline the tiger again. The tiger, in actuality, a water stain on the ceiling, was an accidental masterpiece by some unknown maintenance hands from no one knew when. It crouched above her head, commanding a bird's-eye view of Lishan's life. It even had a distinctive tail that was docilely hanging from its plump bottom. A bit of rust planted one slanting eye, as if mocking the bed down below. Later Lishan added another oblique eye, making the tiger cross-eyed.

"You are satisfied now, aren't you?" said Lishan to the tiger.

In her head she argued with the tiger every day, her disdain for the world found a convenient vent. *If the world consists of tigers and lambs, and if I am surrounded by tigers, at least I have one tiger in my cage.*

"OK, you won again," she stared at its rusted eye.

How does beauty offend this world? Isn't Ms. Guan a victim of jealousy, whose elegance and talent, charisma and popularity are precisely what the ugly Canine Teeth lacks and aspires to? My painting irritates them because they know nothing about art. But my paintings will multiply, she told the tiger, "Just keep your eyes peeled."

"Lishan, dinner!" outside her door, her second brother was beating a plate with his chopsticks, making a jingling dinner call as in her boarding school.

Lishan covered her face with her quilt. It would give her a temperature of one hundred two degrees. Brothers, she had a string of them. They were an army, enough to isolate her, to exclude her from any domestic fun and deny her participation in any family decisions. When they walked, they strutted like a flock of geese; traffic stopped. When they ran, they swirled like a hurricane; people got out of their way. They droned like a swarm of bees; they bickered like roosters pecking each other's crowns. She was accustomed to being the minority, being a recognized loner, a controversial figure and no one's favorite child. And her poor grades would keep her at this position permanently. In this household, where female inferiority was eternally established, she wallowed in self-pity and shut the door in self-preservation. For her, Jianfei's companionship was a haven on a turbulent sea, a cave in a stormy forest. In her reclusiveness at home and school, her rancor dissolved at the thought of Jianfei; her eyes softened at her sight; her face kindled and her heart blossomed. The scathing poster against Ms. Guan had destroyed any flickering hope for the outside world. Her pain was further intensified by her refusal to sign Jianfei's poster. Hurting Jianfei was the last thing she wanted to do. Now she was waiting for Jianfei's appearance. *Leaving something behind was a hook for Jianfei to return. An unanswered question would draw her to me.*

A tap on the door.

"Lishan, dinner is getting cold," mom said.

"I am not hungry."

"Then we will start without you."

Mom tiptoed off.

Jianfei, Jianfei, she moaned in her heart. Breathing through an open mouth inside the quilt, she quickly heated her temperature to one hundred degrees; she was yearning for Jianfei's hand on her temple.

A second tap.

"I said I am not hungry."

"Lishan, Jianfei is here," dad's voice was never so sweet which irritated his daughter.

Her heart leapt to the door but her body refused to move. She knew the tricks. Only a near-emergency could catch her parents' genuine concern whenever she could no longer put up with the male partisanship in the house. Removing her face from the heated bedding, she lay still.

"Lishan, are you okay?"

With eyes closed, Lishan tasted Jianfei's soft finger as she touched her temples, sucking in her scent. Enjoying her presence alone without Jianfei's knowledge was real luxury for Lishan. She wished the world would stop there.

"You have fever," this was exactly what Lishan wanted to hear. Eyes closed and with limbs limp on the edge, she continued to sham illness.

"I am sorry I was rough with you."

Seeing no response, Jianfei said, "I don't mean to bother you. Have a sound sleep and the fever will be gone in the morning."

Jianfei rose to her feet.

"Listen," grabbing Jianfei's hand, Lishan sat up, "I would have signed my name if not for that absurd poster. I still don't see anything wrong with Ms.Guan's supporting my painting. Tell me why Ms.Guan was targeted and I will follow the logic. I will redeem myself."

"Lishan, I know you are greatly wronged, but the situation is much graver than any of us could have imagined. Remember the boy who showed off on the playground? The one who tried to use his triple jump to hook up with us?"

Lishan, though still holding the vivid triple jump in her vision, could recall no "hook-up" plot. "Who tried to hook up with us?"

"Never mind. Anyway, the boy's name is Yang Bing. He just told my dad about a reactionary clique among the boy seniors. They are organizing their own party with an attempt to overthrow our Party. They have their own constitution and flag, everything."

"My lord! These boys are more audacious and outspoken than Zhao Shihe!"

Lishan's disease vaporized. She jumped out of bed.

"Exactly! In the face of the anti-Party activities, our personal pains are trivial. Without the Party, there will be no you and I, not to mention your art."

Lishan locked Jianfei in her arms and sobbed into her hair like a child. Jianfei was astonished to see that this tough friend of hers, to whom any female sign including tears was alien, also had her moments of weakness. Resentment, grief, humiliation, rage and chagrin, all the emotions that summarized Lishan's long day now melted to rain. She let her chin rest on Jianfei's shoulder as long as possible.

In a moment, Lishan dried her tears and was herself again. She began to pace in the room, slowly droning a Russian song:

The prairie is misty and vast,
The road stretching far;
......

The mysterious and unfathomable Lishan! She reached her desk, pulled out a hard cover notebook and presented it to Jianfei, "I will let my diary do the talking. Read but don't open your mouth."

Jianfei started from the last page, fresh with ink:

My love for our country and Party is unswerving; my love for my dad and our army is unshakable. But if listening to the Party means giving up my art, I won't listen no matter what the cost. There should be no boundaries for the human mind and talent. In pursuing my goal, I am unflinching.

Jianfei turned the pages backward, starting from the beginning. To her astonishment, Lishan had kept the writing continuous since the fourth grade when the two girls first struck up a friendship. The pages were filled with her own name which at first glance honored Jianfei but as the pages turned thicker, clouded her face with malaise. A feeling of eating ten pieces of candy in succession filled her stomach. On the newest pages, Ms. Guan's name was studded everywhere like a busy bulletin board with pins.

Lishan regained her composure; her lips began to tilt again. Something in Lishan's diary brushed Jianfei's heart. She scrutinized Lishan's face: an enigma.

Chapter 12

Girls were girls. They quickly forgot their disagreements over the big character posters. When they rallied on the sports field in the sun and their eyes zoomed in on the Officers' Club with the boys clustering around it; when they chatted on their way to school about Sir Arthur Conan Doyle whose murder scenes chilled their spines even in the bright sunlight and on the busy street; when they teased the biology teacher's bald head adorned with a few well-disciplined gray hairs, calling it "light bulb"; when the two made oblique jokes about the more and more frequent visits to Jianfei's house by the triple-jumping blue sweater; when they tried to piece together a song from the latest movie they watched together two months before it was shown to the public, in all these moments of friendship pulled from their young lives they came to realize that holding a grudge was not worth it. Neither Huifang's poster vilifying Ms. Guan nor Lishan's standoffish gesture towards Jianfei's poster could stand long in their insatiable pleasure-seeking together.

The big character posters fizzled out as winter drew near. The winds whipped up, chasing bundled pedestrians, shaving their faces with invisible razors. Children's cheeks became rosy with chicken scratches. The dark earth hardened, patched with white puddles, skimmed with overnight ice. Jianfei coiled in her quilt like a serpent exuviating. She had already counted to four hundred but still grappled with herself over when to wriggle her body out of the comforting tunnel. Her eyes rested on the windows where crystal flowers like glass paper were pasted, scintillating in the pale morning light. Taking a deep breath and then slowly exhaling, her gaze chased the steam whitening in the air. She knew that once out of the tunnel, her toes would come to a dull numbness and then her classroom hours would have to concentrate on how to thaw them: jumping on the floor, stirring up a gale of dust or chasing each other in the hallway, annoying the faculty.

The three girls had cancelled their morning sessions because, first of all, the weather had entered a zone unbearable for the outside meetings, and secondly, the final exam was at hand. They needed some serious individual memorization work such as the author of *From the Hundred-Herb Garden to the Three-Scent Library* - Lu Xun. "...Laughing at somebody's missing tooth, alluding to a wide-open doghouse..." Her mind wandered about in Lu Xun's garden and humored at a random, unessential but sort of enigmatic line when a boy's voice intruded, "Xiaoshi, you must wear thicker gloves tomorrow."

My lord, HE is here! Jianfei slipped from the fringe of the quilt and shrank her body into the deeper inland.

"Big Brother, may I join you in your jogging?"

"No," a muffled answer seeped through the thick cotton. The two boys were in the hallway now.

"Why not?"

"Because I get up at five thirty and run about an hour. It is beyond your endurance."

Good heavens! Five thirty? In the dark? Before the sun wakes up and exchanges the post with the moon and sends the pale stars to their slumber? Shamefaced, Jianfei stole a glance at her alarm clock, seven fifteen.

Jianfei considered herself strong-willed. However her body refused to follow the headquarters today. Get-up orders repeatedly issued but repeatedly tapered off in the quilt too warm and cozy to be abandoned. Her throat felt strange. She tested it again by coughing up a slimy piece. Her glands asserted themselves, her voice hoarse and heavy. *No, no,* she screamed in her head. *Not again!* Getting sick two weeks in a row was no fun at this juncture. She simply could not afford it. All the classes were heating up for the final exams and all the teachers brazenly dropped hints on what would be shown on the final paper. Scopes of knowledge were largely narrowed as if the absence of the whole semester would not matter so long as you attended the reviewing sessions. Driven by her imminent finals, she slowly pulled the sweater on despite the resistance from every part of her body. She thought, in agreement with the great writer Lu Xun, how a harmless trivial illness should really be enjoyed if the little tingling sore in one's head and the faint ache in one's throat could be arranged at the beginning of the semester when the mild and soft weather virtually gave no reason for being sick and the class was also mild and soft. Then all the little physical discomforts could be paid off with the extravagance of bedside care and the ambitious achievement of diverting the parents' favor from the younger one. And if she could succeed in bringing her temperature past one hundred and two, dad might even spoon feed her.

The advantage of possessing an insignificant pain was also demonstrated by her classmates who in her first sickness took turns to show their concern with their after school visits. She relived their day. They enlivened her hour with stories of the biology teacher's light bulb getting brighter or Canine's v-f pronunciation becoming more strident. Her bedside saw Class A in rapport. The visitors came in different batches. Wang Gui, Wealthy Wang, the leader of the Communist Youth League, whose name conveyed her poor parents' sole ambition, was the first to come, three of her comrades at her tail. Their profuse "take care's" and abundant "we miss you's" deepened Jianfei's guilt. Jianfei had cultivated a distance and reserve towards Wang Gui and her disciples since the very beginning of school.

In her categorization, Jianfei's classmates were split into three: The class strata started from the patriarch Wang Gui. This group was a group who showed no interest either in knowledge and skill or in learning and practicing. They stood up blushing at any questions on any subject. Their tears gradually dried up at the red on their paper that signified discipline was not a substitute for intelligence. They won constant verbal compliments for their straightened backs, mute mouths, and dull stares at the teachers and the boards. Irresponsive in class as they were, they were swift contenders in school's political arena. Above all, they were the eyes and ears of the authorities. Their ultimate goal, single-mindedly, was to become a glorious member of the Communist Party in the foreseen future when they reached their maturity.

The second and largest strata of the class were Jianfei's followers. They were the ones who monopolized all the subjects, the ones who shared mastery in music, painting, drama, international affairs, rhetoric and debate. They were the problem solvers as well as the challengers of the teachers in the classroom. They swept away all the highest records and picked up all the championships in the fields and on the forums.

Quick-witted, mischievous, carefree, easy-going, and always on the run, they were jokesters who enjoyed producing laughter and great storytellers who made merriment. Easy to take offense and easy to forget, they never missed any collective amusements. Lighthearted and simple-minded, they never guarded against anyone and they allowed their tongues free rein to bring them trouble. They were a medley of singers, poets, dancers, theatrical figures, clowns and dreamers.

The third group was comprised of a few stragglers. They were loners staying away and looking on. With no intention, whatsoever, to communicate or participate, they rejected any help and were gradually rejected. They let their grades stay low because their sole expectation for schooling was to make meager money at the earliest possible age to help their parents who were either disabled or came from blemished backgrounds and therefore lived on the verge of destitution.

Chapter 13

The battle between a warm bed whose attractiveness was bolstered by a sore throat and a freezing classroom whose repellence was equally reinforced by the looming finals later turned to be insignificant and Jianfei's self-disciplined choice of the cold classroom proved to be an historical mistake. A question whirled in her head in later years: what if I chose not to go to school that day? The answer dealt a telling blow to Jianfei. The answer was: it was just a matter of time. The outcome would have been the same.

When she walked into class A that morning she was not greeted with good morning smiles. No friends' hands were found on her shoulders as she went to her desk. No invitation to a volleyball game against Class C that afternoon was to be heard. Cold, stoic or dubious eyes met her as she came in. Puzzled, she remained calm until her eyes finally met the sources of all these changes and rested there. On the blackboard in the back of the classroom laying open to everyone, was the Class Correspondence, a monthly periodical published by the Communist Youth League branch. Jianfei's name bounced to Jianfei.

Some Suggestions for Jianfei

Red title, white text flowing down the black background, trapping her emotions. With shock and confusion, Jianfei's eyes moved along the lines:

> …Your pale green sweater is eye-catching. We suggest you wear it under a black or blue jacket to cover the sharp contrast with us, to bridge the gap between the privileged few and the plebian majority. Look around you. People in rags are everywhere.

Jianfei's regular attire was reviewed day by day in her mind. *OK, I did wear the sweater to school once but that was for the duet at the National Day celebration.* A moment of self-defense and then she pled guilty.

> …Your grades top the class. We suggest you stay three hours after school to help those who lag behind. What draws you back home in such haste? That petty bourgeois nest of yours under the wings of your aristocratic parents behind closed walls?

I could spare anything but my time. Why should I give up my privacy for someone's laxity and incompetence? To this charge, Jianfei pleaded not guilty.

> The two suitcases of yours must contain more dazzling clothes. We suggest you go through them and pick out only the plain ones because splendid clothes will serve only to startle ordinary eyes and provoke wretched souls.

Her brain went inert. Her eyes rolled back and her lingering gaze rested on the two suitcases. *What are they talking about? Is this a metaphor? My two suitcases? A figurative usage?*

There was no signature. A collective noun "The Communist Youth League" stood out stark at the bottom of the board, shielding the individual responsibilities.

Wang Gui's desk saw unprecedented prosperity today. The usual hustle and bustle had shifted over there from Jianfei's seat. A small circle of students was putting their finishing touches on their monumental masterpiece, making sure there were no slips of the pen. There was a smirk hanging on their faces, celebrating their patent beyond mere academic achievement.

"Vicious liars!" Lishan clenched her teeth. Midway in her reading she turned to Wang Gui's desk, "Those good-for-nothings in class should at least shut up!" And she shut them up.

The two suitcases buzzed in Jianfei's head. They bumped from wall to wall, slipping from the dining room, storming into the study, droning into her bedroom. Her brain cells unfolded, launching a room-to-room search.

Her eyes rummaged under the table, scraped the shoes out from under the bed, knocked over the books, tumbled over the ink bottle. *Suitcases, where are you? Stand out!* A desk, a bed, a chair, a lamp constructed her room. *Is there an alcove, a cubbyhole, a tunnel, a cave, a burrow that could possibly hold the culprits?* Scouring, ransacking, scraping, overthrowing, the house was turned upside down, the guts inside out. *Where are the suitcases?*

In the thick of her suitcase digging, Jianfei saw Lishan jab her chin into the air. Her eyes followed her chin and met a new face.

"Stand up!" Jianfei called the class in a flurried manner. She almost missed her routine duty.

Ms. Guan had long been suspended. The substitute teacher from a normal college who had filled in in the interim, with a mediocre performance, too, had disintegrated.

"You already know me," the face in front said, "Lin Huiqing. Hui as in wisdom, Qing purity, Lin forest." She stroked elegantly her name on the board, "From now on, I will be your permanent teacher, Chinese Literature and homeroom."

The new teacher was frugal in words and spoke them quickly. Her jaw clattered at the pace of a machine gun. "I'm the branch Party secretary, in charge of the freshmen."

Jianfei cast a warning to her desk mate. They surely knew her, a graduate from a prestigious university, plain looking, clean-cut, so far with a low profile. She was no fun.

Still chasing the two suitcases that buzzed in her head, flying from room to room, Jianfei took a break and let her eyes cast a casual glance at the face. Her eyes froze there. She vaguely remembered a week ago it was this face that walked shoulder to shoulder with the class Youth League secretary, talking head to head. It suddenly dawned on Jianfei that this blackboard journal was a welcome gift from the League branch to the Party branch. And what a gift! The sacrifice of the Young Pioneer leader! Jianfei recognized her own blood on the altar. The two blackboards in the front and the back of the classroom stood face to face.

"Some of your names have already registered in my mind," a significant pause ensued, and then Ms. Lin picked up her train with a semi-smile. "I wish those registrations are all under good deeds."

A hung dog, Jianfei knew that the imposing figure in front was now commanding a view of the journal and its related face. She was sure that each performance evaluation would be in her firm grip, flow out from under her pen, and be safely passed on to parents and archived. And then in six years these evaluations would constitute the bulk of their college application, and if lucky, usher them into their future schools.

The teacher swerved to the final exam preparation, "Li Bai's poems need to be memorized. All of them."

Lishan made a wry face but the face was arrested by Ms. Lin's sharp gaze.

Closet! All of a sudden, Jianfei made a discovery. Yes, there was a closet right next to her room but dad used it to store his miscellaneous papers.

"Turn to page 144. Lu Xun's conclusion of *A Mad Man's Diary*, 'children without cannibal records may still exist? Save the children.' What is the suggestion here?"

She paced the aisles. Now her back faced Jianfei.

A tiny ball escaped someone's hand and in a lightning speed, shot across the aisles and landed on Jianfei's lap. Her eyes rolled around and then glided cautiously to the unrolled slip of paper, "Why let the retards bother you?"

With utmost gratitude, Jianfei's eyes skimmed over the classroom, a black ocean, unruffled, buried in Lu Xun. Could it be Minming? Minming's elbow was sliding over her notebook. Wufeng? She was sharpening her pencil. Xiaonan? Her fingers were underlining the last two lines of Lu Xun. *Thank you whoever you are, friend in need!* She said to herself.

Yes, there is a storage room. Books, papers, documents, dad's lectures, certificates and awards, manuscripts of poems, dad's publications…to which Jianfei never paid a formal visit. "That is my stuff, please don't touch it," dad warned the inquisitive Jianfei once.

Are there any suitcases in the closet? Jianfei was lost. The league members apparently knew more about the house than the house owner. Jianfei was aching to get home.

Chapter 14

Sure enough, crouching like a pair of family dogs, hidden among the yellowing relics were two rickety wooden boxes. Papers bound with ropes brittle with age, newspapers without news, flyers showing Japanese bayoneting Chinese...cradled each other and nestled against the two boxes whose existence had launched a war against their young master and baffled her throughout Chinese, math, geography, music and biology classes.

"Oh heavens!" Lishan's lips warped. "How did these worms wriggle in? Their eyes drilled through the wall? Even we everyday visitors are in the dark. Those spies!"

"Correct! To spy on someone, one visit is all you need," Huifang echoed, turning to Jianfei whose face displayed her incredulity.

The closet door was kept shut in the house because no one bothered with the history. But in Jianfei's ears, a click echoed from her recollection of a week ago when she was in bed feeling guilty about her distrust versus the Youth League sister's genuine friendship, apologizing for not being able to walk them to the gate. The click was distinctive because it was produced right outside her bedroom door. Accompanying the click was the exclamation of: "So many doors!" "So many rooms!" and the clicking of the tongues as children did while sucking sweets.

"Hypocrites! Smiling tigers!" Lishan's lips foamed after hearing Jianfei's story. "A typical 'knife hidden in a smile'."

Huifang sighed and shook her head. Words failed her. Finally she found her tongue and drew a conclusion, "You know, some people are simply too poor to picture beautiful clothes and decent suitcases."

"Right," Lishan nodded in concordance, sullen-faced, "poverty and jealousy go hand in hand."

Jianfei cuddled in her quilt. Tiny hammers continued to pound on the sides of her head. Her glands grew like a pair of puffballs after the rain, her body shivering like a leaf in the autumn wind. A pair of shoes stepped into the lamp's circle. A tray entered her visual field presenting steamed egg and white porridge dotted with jade green vegetables and pink dices of pork. But this time the special favor from dad cost her too much. Tears broke loose.

"No, no, no," dad shook his head, feverishly rejecting his daughter's reaction to his tenderness while carefully maneuvering himself towards Jianfei's bedside holding the patient's privileged tray aloft between his hands.

"'Jianfei' means you don't cry. 'Jian', sword; 'Fei', evil. 'Cutting off evil,' that's you. That's what dad expects from his girl."

"What the hell is in those two boxes in the storage room?!" A sudden burst of anger rose against her dad, whose two shabby boxes had been promoted to suitcases and had become a canker in her life, aggravating her illness. A patent wound was born on her face.

"Nothing. The remains of the war, that's what they are. A carpenter's quick handiwork. We were stationed in a village and a carpenter built them for me when he spotted my backpack bulging with important documents."

"We must get rid of them."

Now the two boxes were her eyesore. They seared her from inside.

"Get rid of what?" dad beamed. "They are the exhibits for the Military Museum! Among them are Marshall Chen Yi's personal letters and the orders for the last campaign!"

"But they have been transformed to golden cases containing glamorous dresses!"

Dad held his tongue, but employed it in blowing the steaming porridge, and then beamingly, "Feeling like eating a bit? Looks really good."

The daughter stuck her mouth out to meet the spoon, feeling ashamed of her infantile behavior.

Dad scooped more and blew again.

"It is just a matter of names. What we call boxes they call suitcases. No need to be so sensitive."

Jianfei's face began to darken as dad continued, "Feeling wronged, brooding over it and building a longstanding resentment will only degenerate the relationship. Forgive and forget. These are the balms to heal the gash."

The yellow jelly of the steamed egg quivered in the spoon on which dad blew and cautiously fed the mouth that now showed a bit of reluctance to open.

Dad continued, "Magnanimity adds grace to your beauty. Look at a valley. Deep, hollow, and open. In its vast chest lie lush lives, verdant and exuberant. Vegetation and forest find the best habitat in it because a valley absorbs more rain and snow and provides the best for their lives. Embracing and tolerant, your chest should be like a valley and only then will you be strong enough to meet the world. What do we call this? Xu Huai Ruo Gu. Xu: modest, humble; Huai: heart, bosom; Ruo: to resemble; Gu: the valley. Remember Xu Huai Ruo Gu, a modest bosom is like an open valley."

Another spoonful of yellow jelly approached her mouth.

"For example, has it occurred to you that it is your obligation, as one of the leaders of the class, to lend a hand to those who have lagged behind?"

As usual, when dad's didactics were aided with idioms and proverbs, made vivid by similes and metaphors, backed with quotations and allusions, she found it hard to talk back. Nevertheless, she turned her face to the wall, glad that she was full just on time.

"Here, take some penicillin. Dad is going to peel an orange for you."

Drowsy, drowsy. Her sleep brought forth a procession of pantomimes going through an unlit tunnel. The Party Secretary and the Youth League sisters danced around two suitcases, a clown bouncing to and fro, silk gowns gleaming in the dark, red, gold and blue.

Between her fragmented dreams, dad's voice wafted in, turning the silent movie into a talkie, "...this is what Lishan told me...spying on people, sowing discord, spreading rumors, vilifying innocents, poking their noses...this is their profession..."

Jianfei's anger simmered.

"Did you just say their new homeroom teacher is a Party branch secretary? This might be good for Jianfei," mom hissed.

"That explains the whole situation. Jianfei might simply be used as someone's stepping stone to sneak into our Party. I am concerned our new blood may be contaminated!"

"Are you serious? At the age of fifteen or fourteen even?"

"Has age ever deterred fanaticism? Do you know how old Hitler's Third Reich soldiers were?"

"What if Jianfei has to stay at home and they come for a visit again?"

"No. That won't happen. I am going to give the guards an unwelcome list now."

"Wait! This afternoon the Municipal Committee called a special meeting addressing issues regarding the current movement. Here is the document."

The paper rustled. Dad sounded lighter-hearted. "Good. Some issues are clarified. Of course, on no account, should big character posters be utilized to target ordinary masses and children at such a young age. The vicious blackboard journal against Jianfei is nothing but a big character poster. It is a distortion of the Anti-Rightist Campaign."

Particles of dad's words deposited like dust, whirling and mixing with faceless shadows that crisscrossed the dark space like a chess board. The first emperor of the Qin dynasty was solving an equation for Canine Teeth; Lu Xun was reciting Li Bai's "Thoughts in A Still Night"; and Li Bai was waving an orange. An orange. Dad is going to peel it for me. Her eyes opened. The lamp shade cut an orange circle out of the dark square; eight enormous oranges were arrayed for temptation, exuding a sweet scent ready to quench her parched lips. She stretched out her arm.

"I'll get it for you."

From the shade rose a voice whose rasp and acrid tone had long been accepted by Jianfei's ears. Lishan stepped into the circled region.

"These oranges are from Huangyan County, well-known for their oranges. My cousin mailed us ten pounds."

Jianfei was so used to Lishan's bitterness that her sweetness sounded off-key in her ears. Lishan ignored the chair and occupied a bedside seat. Inch by inch, in her furtive invasion, she edged towards her pillow.

"Let me peel it for you." Lishan said, grabbing an orange.

"I'll do it myself."

"No. I told your dad I'd take care of you." the gift giver insisted with authority.

The orange was peeled meticulously; even the light yellow membrane was carefully removed. Jianfei could hardly picture Lishan as a loving, deft caretaker. An extreme uneasiness snuck into her heart. The delicate section dropped into Jianfei's mouth. Repulsed as she was, Jianfei was too tired to bargain. She let Lishan feed her like a helpless baby but was disgusted at heart. Lishan continued her role as ward nurse. In a wink, a second slice was peeled smooth and clean, hanging onto Jianfei's lips. Jianfei couldn't hide her loathing this time.

"How long have you been waiting in my room?"

"Don't worry! I have completed my review plan." Lishan had brought with her a ready reply.

"That is not the point," but Jianfei held her tongue.

However whatever the point was was a blurry cloud. You turn my stomach? I prefer your aloofness and your sting? She couldn't bring these thoughts to words. An abrupt, complete rejection was not what she was seeking but some distance, an adjusted distance, to keep the friendship warm but not burning was what she was expecting. This hand-feeding gesture on Lishan's part seemed natural and heartfelt but Jianfei regarded it with antipathy. She flinched lightly and the transparent orange petal dropped on her pillow. Lishan withdrew her fingers but held her position close to her friend's face. Her placid eyes met Jianfei's peevish ones.

"I couldn't sit at home with the thought of you being slandered. Whoever offends you offends me. Your adversity is mine. I feel we are one. Do you think I could sit quietly reviewing for the stupid finals? I cannot picture myself with folded arms standing by while you combat single-handedly against those conspirators! The green sweater! Wasn't that the music teacher's order that everyone must put on her best for our National Day? The accusation is groundless and atrocious! If this is what the Communist Youth League is committed to, I will never become one of them!"

With these words, Lishan bent over and printed her lips on Jianfei's forehead. "Sleep well!" in a sugary voice. Then she rose to her feet, closed the door and disappeared.

Lishan's intrusiveness and imposed tenderness exasperated Jianfei. Her forehead burning with shame, she felt defenseless and belittled. Along with her indignation, there arose in her heart an uncertainty regarding their friendship. Jianfei rubbed her forehead feverishly to make sure that the female kiss which she considered a mark of contamination and blight was obliterated.

The tunnel returned. This time it was a single runner overtaking her view. She saw a window that was lit as the startled alarm clock pointed to 5:30. A boy rose from within the window frame. This window was one of the few that were seen bright before reveille and after taps. The sun was too late getting up in the east when the boy's footsteps began to echo on the track and the moon was too early sinking in the west as it shone on a young body bending over for the final preparation. This was Pavel, the diehard Bolshevik whose whirling saber glistened in the sun; this was Arthur, the English revolutionary whose life was dedicated to the emancipation of another nation. Both had conquered their disability through unbridled zeal and enduring an unthinkable ordeal. This was Yang Bing. Now the three were running shoulder to shoulder into her intermittent sleep. Thumping, thumping, their feet thumped into her ears.

A silhouetted runner opened his mouth, "Your sister is still asleep. Hush!"

The voice alerted Jianfei who jerked up, staring at the door where two shadows stood revealed by the lamplight, one big, one small.

The small one yanked the big one, "Look, she is up!"

With these words, Xiaoshi walked headlong to the group of oranges, leading Big Brother by his fingertips.

"Oh, great! Big Brother has also brought some gifts. Look!"

He tried to lift Big Brother's hands in the air but the hands stiffened along his two wooden legs, too fuddled to bring them out in front of his chest. Xiaoshi came to his rescue just as the other two expected. In the past several months this little one had served as a go-between to join the two parties, too awkward to face each other, too ashamed to open mouths, as he did now.

"One is canned lychees," Xiaoshi exposed Yang Bing into the full circle of the lamp. His little fingers adroitly unraveled a net bag that had hung humbly along the seams of Big Brother's trousers.

Jianfei kept her eyes on the oranges and Yang Bing kept his on the lychee can as the second can of fruit, this time yumberry, was also captured and exhibited on the table. His feet alternated in holding the floor as the two cans were saying in loud voices "I do care about you," the words unspoken yet able to redden the four cheeks of the two mute teenagers at once. Despite all the rehearsals inside each of their heads as to what to say, how to wear their facial expressions, to what extent their smiles should spread, how wide to open their mouths, how many teeth to reveal…when the time for the real show arrived, they both fell apart. Neither had been prepared how to deal with stage fright.

As the two mouths grappled for words, Xiaoshi prompted, "Which one should we open? For you, I mean."

Jianfei frowned at her brother's manner as if he were she. The little one gave up but turned to the shining, tantalizing fruit whose color brightened the lamp and scented the room, "What lovely oranges! Take one, Big Brother!"

"Yes, please."

For the first time, she let her eyes rise up and rest on his face. She was glad she had something to offer in return and found a topic to subdue the tension.

"From Huangyan."

By now the other party seemed to have found a key himself and the door was opened.

"I heard about the happenings at your school."

He was himself again.

"If I were you, I would simply turn my mind aside from these distractions and concentrate on my finals because my failure would signify their victory."

Jianfei nodded with gratitude. Big Brother is indeed a Big Brother! She looked up and the four eyes met for the first time. They spoke a common language.

"Good night then," Yang Bing said in a tender voice.

Xiaoshi snatched two oranges, thrusting one in Big Brother's hand. He cast a despondent farewell glance at the two canned fruits and followed the big one in retreat.

"Fool, fool! What a fool!" Jianfei cursed inside, "Why couldn't you drag the meeting longer than five minutes and enliven the conversation? Why didn't you offer him a seat? You could have fabricated some news, invented a question, and consulted him on algebra…"

The drama and rehearsals started again and she was already itchy for the next bout of stage fright.

At the opposite side of the building, framed in the lit square was a face vexed by the similar questions: what made you so tongue-tied? Did the net bag make you look dorky? Maybe the fresh fruit will add more weight to the gift? He, too, started rehearsing for the next performance.

As the evening was replayed over and over again, it occurred to Jianfei that Lishan's kiss could only make sense if delivered by a boy. Yang Bing should occupy a bedside seat; Yang Bing should be the one who spoon feeds her lips. With the taste of Yang Bing's feeding spoon and a touch of his lips on her forehead, Jianfei was lulled into night.

Chapter 15

The academic reports were on their way out to the parents; the long-sought winter vacation was made official. Dog-eared books were shut in their drawers like criminals sentenced for one month imprisonment. Movie tickets were booked, Spring Festival parties scheduled. Correspondence lists were distributed from hand to hand. The last two school days were nothing but assemblies of all sizes. Semester performances were surveyed, punishments and awards were announced. Homework was the last to be issued and finally, the cleaning up.

Despite the blackboard incident and the flu, Jianfei's grades remained the top. Yang Bing's prediction proved true. As she ascended the platform, as one of the two in Class A, to receive her first award certificate in her middle school, her classmates clapped with exhilarating enthusiasm. The Youth League applauded along except for Wang Gui whose palm seemed to have a thorn in it and hence averted her eyes from the award recipient on stage. Jianfei's prominent image was sculpted by her doubled efforts thanks to Wang Gui and her well-manipulated journal. Nevertheless her popularity did not make her head light as a feather but deepened the imprint of dad's words: Xu Huai Ruo Gu. Big Brother had played an indispensable role in her successful finals.

"The first and foremost thing to maximize our vacation enjoyment," Jianfei gathered Huifang and Lishan, "is to get all the homework out of the way. Then the whole month will be pure fun, unalloyed bliss!"

They devoted the first afternoon and evening to eliminating math, biology and geography. The next day, with their eyes shuttling between the clock and their papers, they battled against the four compositions and done with them in less than four hours, a record speed: four two-page essays were glibly concocted.

Now the girls indulged in a long sleep, compensation for what they had missed during the school days. However, it was not long before they realized that aimless self-indulgence could also mean boredom. A life of fun was a life in a team.

The third day they gathered in light snow and made their way to the Academy library. The library was a two-storied brick building in juxtaposition with the auditorium to its west. Like a twin sister, the library's facade was also glorified with marble pillars and granite steps leading to its sprawling lobby. And it, too, was the legacy of the KMT. Opposite the library stood the stately indoor swimming pool built in the late forties by the Americans. In summer, a manicured lush lawn lay between the library and the swimming pool like a green carpet laced with exquisitely cultivated clusters of wisteria, snapdragons, roses and dahlias. The well-trimmed hedges stood around with neatly shaved heads. Now the lawn was snow-shrouded. The surrounding trees were sheathed in white like spreading fingers in silver gloves. Pine trees laden low like obsequious servants cringed in the severe elements.

As the girls submitted their exposed faces and necks to the sullen-faced sky, petals of white whirled, spun and alighted on their dark hair. Their rosy cheeks emitted a contrasting beauty. They hurried up the library steps and shook the flakes off. Their feet thumped at the entrance as they stepped onto the tiled floor. They took their time browsing the shelves and examining the numerous titles. Finally they made a selection. Using their fathers' library cards, they each borrowed a classic novel: Pu Songlin's *Strange Stories from a Chinese Studio* and Wu Chengen's *Pilgrimage to the West* and Ba Jin's *Family*.

As they came out of the library, they took a detour through the rock garden next to the auditorium. Like grizzly-haired old men, gray rocks braved the gradually thickening flakes, their heads slowly coated in a feathery whiteness. With longer patience, these brave old men waited together with the wisteria's sinewy arms and the naked dwarf maples, for the resurrection of the dead earth. A small brook ran through the rock garden. Ice gathered along both sides of the brook creating jagged transparent edges but leaving a small gap in the center. Under the ice hollow, the jingling water, babbling even more merrily in the brisk air, continued its flow joining a pond which also was skimmed with ice freshly frozen during the night. The sun finally pierced the gray iron curtain with its solid shafts. The snow-bound pond became tinged with red and gold. From time to time, a clump of snow peeled off from a twig and melted into the earth. Willow branches had transformed into icicles, glittering in the late arriving sun. Stillness embraced the garden, occasionally broken by the cracking of the ice, the falling of a branch and the snow pulverized in a gust of wind. It was a stillness impregnated with life, a silence breeding sound.

Lishan spread her arms and inhaled the wintry air, "How fresh! Like a newborn baby!"

Huifang, her eyes roaming far, pinched her lips and smiled furtively.

"A penny for your thoughts," Jianfei said.

"Sorry, my mind has nothing to do with the purity of snow, actually quite the opposite." A mystery circled her beautiful eyes, "Do you know what 'xingjiao' is? I met some university girls hanging around in our compound and I overheard them talking about 'xingjiao'. Do you know what it is?"

"No clue." The knowledgeable Lishan shrugged her shoulders; Jianfei shook her head.

Huifang looked around vigilantly as if fearing the snow might tell tale. "Xing, sexual; Jiao, intercourse."

"Meaning?" Jianfei asked.

"Stupid! Just put the two characters together: Sexual—Intercourse. Sexual Intercourse!" Giggling, Huifang felt she had something to show off now.

"What the hell is this stuff and nonsense?" Lishan perked up her lips.

"What is sexual intercourse?" Jianfei's face, too, was foggy.

"Shhh!" Huifang lowered her voice, "that is… a man puts his thing into your body."

"Yuck!" clicks of tongues from the other two.

"How?"

"I don't know."

Another smile snuck out from Huifang's mouth.

Lishan, dumbfounded at Huifang's possession of such vulgar knowledge, seemed to be profoundly disturbed. She jumped away from Huifang as if from a heap of stinking meat, examining her from head to toe. Jianfei rose to her feet and stepped back, flabbergasted.

"Yuck!"

Lishan flapped her two arms vehemently in the air as if swatting a fly. "It gives me gooseflesh all over."

"Me, too." Jianfei dabbed her clothes subconsciously. "What dirty thoughts! Good gracious!" She felt truly filthy.

Picking up a dead branch, Lishan began to scratch on the snowy surface of the icy pond: a pine tree, many layers, like a gigantic umbrella; the auditorium tipped with a star like an English letter 'i'. Then the stick swerved to sketch a female profile: permed hair, high heels, trailing scarf.

"What brought Ms. Guan back to your mind?" Jianfei asked prudently, knowing how sensitive the topic could be to Lishan.

"She has never left my mind."

Yes, Ms. Guan was still fresh and vivid in some young minds. But who could link this image with handcuffs and the police? Yet it occurred just two weeks ago, in front of all.

At the semester assembly, the dean commanded the school from the platform and made an astonishing announcement: four senior students were labeled as "rightists," including Zhao Shihe, whose penalty was immediate expulsion. Next, Ms. Guan was called to the front, facing an ocean of her students.

A policeman came forward, and in a resonant voice listed her crimes.

"During her university days in the forties, Guan Ziyi, was an active member of the Three Youth League attached to the Nationalist Party. Her initiatives at that time led to the arrests of a dozen Communists and their sympathizers, supporting the KMT's suppression and persecution."

The accusation went on and on, "Her hands drip with the blood of revolutionary martyrs. However, this pair of bloodstained hands is holding our text books now and she is preaching to our youth on Communism and patriotism! How can we let a murderer be a teacher? She is a time bomb…"

As the police enumerated the charges, Jianfei stole a glance at Lishan. Her eyes focused on some spots on the ground, her brow tightly knit. In a minute, the counterrevolutionary Ms. Guan was taken away, hands in cuffs. How, in a wink, could this art lover and promoter be transformed into a monster? A voluminous lecturer on Li Bai, Lu Xun and Maupassant, now a bloodthirsty killer? How did a life stumble off a sunny plain into a dark abyss and a promising career become a nightmare? Incomprehensible lumps blocked Lishan's thinking.

Her mind sneaked back to her classroom where Ms. Guan patrolled, fifty pairs of eyes riveted, "Today, we are going to learn 'The Last Lesson' by Alphonse Daudet, a nineteenth century French novelist."

With expressive modulation in her tones, the Chinese teacher began to imitate the French teacher's farewell class to his beloved mother tongue during the Prussian occupation. "Adieu!" She wound up her reading, her eyes laced with red. That was her last lesson. The next day, a substitute teacher showed up. It was in November.

"Adieu!" Skimming a last glance, Ms. Guan was saying goodbye to her class as she was dragged away among the forest of raised arms and in the thick of thunderous slogans,

"Down with the counterrevolutionary Guan Ziyi!" Hundreds of necks craned, fighting for a closer glimpse of this she-monster.

Ms. Guan's eyes searched the crowd for her favorite student, who failed to bring herself up to send a farewell glance to her art instructor.

Lishan gazed at the silvery Ms. Guan now scintillating on the sunny snowy surface and almost inaudibly, "She is gone, gone forever."

As if responding, a gust of wind swept over Ms. Guan, the sun vaporized her, Lishan's eyes brimming.

Chapter 16

Amidst white flakes and soprano winds, Spring Festival danced in. Music blasted over the loudspeakers with the incessant explosions of gongs, cymbals and drums. Firecrackers popped sporadically like merry insects chirping here and there on summer nights. Little children tailed their older siblings, faces radiant in the variety of New Year's engagements. Strings of firecrackers dangling from their puffy hands chapped in the bitter cold embellished their annually renewed wardrobe and became the centerpiece of their playful lives. Housewives and maids lined up at the market in long queues, waiting for preserved eggs, ham, yellow-flower fish, pig's feet, lamb and chicken to fill up their baskets. Startled hens chuckled more loudly this time of year, preparing to run for their lives. Their cumbersome wings offered little help for a successful escape flight when the maid was in pursuit, bounding left and right with a sharpened knife in hand and a cutting board laid aside. The woman finally took hold of the wings, crossed them while the chicken was still kicking and screaming. Relentlessly, she slit the throat and held the head back to let its warm blood drain into a bowl of salted water. A pot sizzled; water was boiled for feather plucking. Dipping and soaking, the maids' hands were happily reddened and her fingertips wrinkled. Deep-fried fish, soy sauce pork and boiled chicken permeated and thickened the air; each distinguished from the other by its uniquely savory flavor. Salted ducks and smoked pig heads hung side by side on balconies to air dry meeting the eyes of passers-by with tragic faces. Newly ground glutinous flour was spread on huge bamboo sifters, ready to be combined with freshly processed black sesame, red bean paste, and peanut butter producing the season's glorious sweet dumplings. The Cooperative of the Academy had recently offered some special services: popping dried sticky-rice-cake chips, grinding rice, and wrapping dumplings.

Auntie Gao had glued her hands on the cutting board and the stove for two days. Now her two projects were laid out shining in yellow and white. The yellow was egg dumplings whose creation required calculated portion of fat and lean, fine chopping, even mincing and finally the painstaking churning and turning of the beaten egg to make the delicately thin sheets. The white mound was "eight treasure glutinous rice", whose assembly cast a magical spell on Jianfei. She was entranced by the red, pink, and green jewels of dried fruits diced and laid in the artist's sticky canvas. Then came the "lion's head," the third item in Aunt Gao's menu. She laid the white and pink on the cutting board, giving instruction to the curious kitchen visitor:

"Remember, the key is tenderness; the meat ball relies on its tenderness to succeed…"

"Auntie, I need another fifty cents. Big Brother told me there are some fireworks for sale in the Cooperative! We are going now." Xiaoshi panted at the door, beaming brightly, his fingers blackened by the soot of the firecrackers. With the mention of Big Brother, Jianfei prepared a retreat from the kitchen.

Auntie Gao dug out a crumpled bill from her folded handkerchief:

"All our New Year's delicacies have been traded for your firecrackers! You consume firecrackers like they are sticky-rice-cake crackers!" the maid scolded, her hand about to swat his little rear.

Xiaoshi ducked under her arm and slipped away from the spanking like a fish. Being Big Brother's follower, Xiaoshi had become his sister's best friend. A hint from Jianfei, and the message would be parroted to Yang Bing and vice versa.

Snatching her gloves, Jianfei chased him out of the kitchen, knowing that his Big Brother must be waiting outside.

"Brother, wear my gloves!"

"I have my brand new ones, don't you remember? Here."

He pulled the string on his neck at the ends of which hung the gloves.

Of course, the gloves were only an excuse to take a look at the one whose more and more frequent appearance in her mind had become a constant longing. The explanation for all the impetuous acts on the part of Big Brother and his sister remained vague in the mind of Xiaoshi, the envoy, running errands, shuttling between the two. This time the New Year message cost his parents fifty cents.

"Xiaoshi."

Seeing Jianfei, Yang Bing raised his voice, "We'll set the fireworks together tomorrow evening, right after the New Year's Eve dinner, OK?"

His eyes glued on Jianfei expectantly.

"Of course, didn't we just talk about this a second ago?" The little, naïve one asked.

Having passed the message, Yang Bing was looking forward to celebrating the Eve of Chinese New Year with Jianfei.

Bong-Ba! Firecrackers popped on every doorstep as the year's most important meal unfolded within. What Auntie Gao had in store for her employers was a real art show. The colors of her template, green, red, pink, yellow, purple, spent the afternoon somersaulting in pots and pans, acrobatically moving from board to pot to plate, delicately arrayed in flowers, petals, orange slices, marbles, fans, leaves and grass blades, preparing to be conveyed onto the table as the opening cold course. The porcelain plates were as fine as those that had impressed Jianfei at other's dinner tables. Chopsticks, dipping and rising, boarded the merry-go-round of delicacies. Quickly, the eight cold dishes were wolfed down. In rapid succession, the stir fries marched to the table in the same parade of elegance. Few words were exchanged in the first two minutes. Insatiable, everyone was appreciative that dad had lifted his prohibition on chicken, providing the banquet with its gustatory pinnacle.

Jianfei's thoughts strayed. The image of a shabby, bare table scattered with rice grains and painted with soup drippings was still vivid in her memory. The embarrassment of having exposed their sloppy family dinner to the eyes of Yang Bing still burnt her cheeks. Now she craved Yang Bing's presence before the sumptuous, exquisite pieces were mangled by the ruthless chopsticks. To her disappointment, he showed up late and missed all the colorful courses. All the distinctiveness of the edible realist paintings had blurred into a mass of impressionism. Luckily the timely arrival of dessert largely compensated for what he had missed. The "Eight Treasure Rice" did catch Yang Bing's eye. The dessert soup, a sweet medley of light yellow "wood ear" fungus, white lily cloves and lotus seeds, complemented by yellow chestnuts and red tomatoes culminated the feast.

"Please join us," mom grabbed a chair and delivered into Yang Bing's hand a small, quaint plate whose subtle light blue filled Jianfei with contentment.

Yang Bing shook his head. "I am full." He patted his stomach but took the seat wedged between the hostess and her daughter, pasting two rose petals onto the young, timid face. Ignoring his refusal, Auntie Gao quickly filled his plate with a spoonful of "Eight Treasure Rice." Jianfei was glad that he could witness this atonement dinner. Fed by her inferiority, she imagined the foods on Yang Bing's dinner table were somehow never touched and the paintings were permanently fresh.

Yang Bing was wearing a navy blue woolen jacket, a narrow opening on the zipped top revealed a white turtle neck covered by a second layer of a black sweater. His thick brown overcoat was hanging behind the door. Jianfei was attracted to the white and black combination and craved a touch. He is handsome and has taste. For the first time, she noticed this.

"Happy Spring Festival!" Yang Bing turned to everyone, one balled hand clasped in the other and extended in front, delivering a traditional Happy New Year gesture.

"Happy Spring Festival!" returned Jianfei.

She was glad that the festival had created for them both a chance to exchange a public greeting and give each other a square look in the face without inflicting the uneasiness of harboring a guilty secret.

Dinner was over. Xiaoshi dragged his sister by the hand, "Please join us to light the firecrackers."

"I have to wait for Lishan and Huifang,"

Knowing that the streets outside would be filled with juvenile boys whiling away the hours before the New Year's firecracker orchestra, Jianfei tried to avoid a public appearance in the companionship of a boy of her own age.

"Come on, you can wait outside," Yang Bing beseeched. "You don't have to be near me," almost inaudibly, as if reading Jianfei's mind.

This is no different than making a public announcement that something is going on between us. This enlightenment made Jianfei's heart beat fast and her whole body twinge.

Behind his glasses, Yang Bing took a careful look at the New Year Jianfei. Black flowers sharply cut out from their orange background, Jianfei's new padded jacket was precisely measured, cut to match her well-curved young body. A line of elaborately coiled butterfly buttons flew from under her chin down to her waist where her braided hair danced with two orange bows at the ends. Slender and tall, her body pulsed with youth and vitality. A baby blue scarf cupped her pointed chin that sharpened her oval face. A pair of willow brows, naturally painted dark and thin, lifted her long, meditative eyes. Her straight nose bridge matched her firm and clear-cut lips. Suavity and strength were alloyed seamlessly; this was a girl of his type. *A subtle beauty,* Yang Bing reflected.

Jianfei regained her composure when Lishan and Huifang joined her for the celebration. Immersed in a group of girls, she felt she could take liberty to cast glimpses at Yang Bing. However despite such attempts at modesty, the three of them were already conspicuous figures in the compound. The striking beauty of Huifang, the queer attire of Lishan, and the leader's emblem on Jianfei's arm were each eye catching.

The three girls kept a distance from the firecrackers, their eyes focused on the fuses that blinked here and there in the dark, their fingers plugged in their ears and their bodies arced backward in apprehension of the explosive moment.

Hanging from Xiaoshi's hand was a braided whip of two-hundred small firecrackers. When ignited, the red string cracked like popcorn. In a wink, it fizzled out. The girls seemed uninterested and Xiaoshi was crestfallen.

"Cheer up," Yang Bing came to rescue the holiday mood, "watch mine."

Armed with firecrackers of various size and color, and with some fireworks, Big Brother quickly became the king of the New Year's Eve. Driven by curiosity, the girls edged over.

"Heaven and Earth Resounding" was the name of the gigantic one, the size of a cigar. It shouted a majestic "Bong" when hitting the ground and "Ba" when bouncing up in the air, in two consecutive explosions, then vanished behind the shadowy, soaring pine trees.

"Wow!" the girls moved their palms from their ears and clapped.

Xiaoshi was beside himself. Any of Big Brother's successes belonged to him.

"Xiaoshi, you try." Yang Bing handed over a tinfoil stick to Xiaoshi whose hands wavered in holding it. Yang Bing took back the stick and lit the bottom. Silvery stars erupted and then dripped to the ground. Tightening his grip, Big Brother swayed his arm in the air, drawing enormous circles dancing and sparkling in the dark. Spectators were mesmerized. Then came the "Mickey Mouse." When lit, a small disc began to spin and accelerated like a scurrying, fiery mouse, in its frightened whistling shriek.

"Amazing!" the audiences clicked their tongues. Xiaoshi gloated, "Let's show them the fireworks, Big Brother."

This time Xiaoshi volunteered to light the fireworks. Too scared, his hands jerked back before the lit paper stick touched the fuse.

"Try again," Yang Bing encouraged.

Holding the fireworks in his right hand, Big Brother's left hand drew the little boy close. Xiaoshi stretched out his hand again, but again wrenched it back as his scared little body recoiled.

Furious at her brother's cowardly performance in public, Jianfei snatched the paper stick and drew herself near to Yang Bing. The corner of her cotton-padded clothes slightly brushed against Yang Bing's woolen coat. Her heart was immersed in a dull sweetness, a feeling new and fresh to her. The red dot in her hand kissed the black fuse in his. A flower rocketed up and blossomed in the diamond-studded night sky, shedding hundreds of petals, green, red, pink, purple and yellow, resembling her heart, colorful and blossoming, embracing the New Year.

Chapter 17

On the lunar calendar, the 15th of the first month of the year was the Lantern Festival. Tenderness snuck into winter's severity. The hot-tempered north wind tapered its howling to a whisper. All of a sudden, between the lethargic sunlight and the tamed winds, thousands upon thousands of naked trees became green-tipped. In a week, these tiny fists would gain a grip and then their fingers would stretch out. Cumbersome winter jackets were cast aside, agility and briskness changed the motif of life.

The Confucian Temple on the Qinhuai River, a market place known for its large variety of foods, striking traditional architecture and arts and crafts, was exceptionally boisterous during this season, although its year-round popularity seldom slackened. An annual lantern exhibition would be held along the river throughout the night and this made the place the city's pivotal attraction for all walks of life.

The three girls had planned their trip to the lantern show long ago. They left home at dusk. To cast off her tail, Jianfei lied to Xiaoshi saying she was going to Huifang's to finish their winter homework.

Flying eaves tilted up on all buildings, their clear-cut silhouettes pasted onto teal blue backgrounds. Along these ridges, pygmy lions, dragons, tigers, dogs and frogs crouched on their haunches, overlooking the streets streaming with shoppers and sightseers. Shops in spacious bungalows stood in a line. Their verandas wound along the river, allowing the strollers to feed their eyes with the indoor glitter and the outdoor reflections simultaneously. Grated windows were pasted with opaque rice paper, soft lights seeping through. In the summer, blazing sunbeams were blocked out and the heat was largely reduced. Red wooden doors were wide open demonstrating traditional goods from palm leaf fans to chamber pots alongside of those catering to a more modern life such as electric fans and radios.

In one store, the girls found bottles with elaborate detailed pictures painted on their insides, a traditional Chinese handicraft. "Twelve Jinling Beauties" depicted the ideal women of the ancient Chinese: genteel, amiable and submissive. Jianfei's eyes fell on a bottle with a miniature of "The River Fair on a Clear and Bright Day", a famous Qing Dynasty painting. The bridge spanning the river, the sprawling boulevard, the prominent merchants and obscure fishermen, the peddlers and food stands, the goaded donkeys and their straddling, imposing masters, the stately horses and humble sheep, men in gowns and pants, boats cleaving the water, houses with balconies commanding a bustling view of the banks… in a bottle half the size of her palm, a panoramic view opened her eyes to the ancient prosperity.

Jianfei thought of her little brother. *For my lie, he deserves a New Year's gift.* She paid three yuan and asked the clerk to wrap the bottle with silk and put it into an exquisite embroidered box. With the silk and embroidery, Jianfei felt fully redeemed.

They discovered more wonders as they stepped in and out of the stores one of which was the drawings on a grain of rice. The grain was fastened to a metal device with a magnifying glass placed on top, under which the painter's ultra-thin brush was moving. A garden with a green bamboo grove, a red azalea bush, black rocks and a rippling fish pond was built stroke by stroke along with the artist's moving hand. Gold and red fish were given life and swam vigorously in the pond. It was a live Chinese garden under the magnifier but an ordinary rice grain smeared with some colorful dots without the magnifier. The girls moved the magnifier in and out to verify the marvel. They meandered through the narrow alleys hoarded with treasure. The flower and bird stores offered an early taste of spring. "One Hundred Dumplings" exuded enticing aromas. "Rain Flower Stone" beckoned with an exhibition of red, green, yellow, blue and purple stones with intricate patterns and miraculous shapes sitting in white bowls filled with clear water. Each stone presented an amazing picture and told a story. "Three Pine Trees in the Snow", "Sunset behind the Twin Peaks", "The Face of the Monkey King", each had a name.

Crowds swarmed the Qinhuai River Square. The girls crossed over. Thousands of lanterns were hung along the river, making the water a shining belt and bringing daylight to the square. The River Qinhuai, the pride of ancient Nanjing, had inspired generations of poets.

Mist enveloping cold water and the moon embracing the sand,
At night I moored on Qinhuai by a wine stand.

Lishan's memory was kindled and the two lines from Dumu came to the tip of her tongue.

"The river carries the poem on." Jianfei said.

"No. The poem keeps the river flowing." Lishan looked at Jianfei, smiling.

"OK, OK. Stop your chicken-and-egg discussion." Huifang said, sulky-faced.

"Good point! Art and life, which creates which?" Lishan was in a deep thought.

"Chairman Mao says that literature and art germinate from reality. Didn't we learn that in Chinese class?" asked Jianfei.

"I believe artists design a better world for us to follow," Lishan retorted.

"Stop, you great philosophers," Huifang dragged Jianfei by the arm, "Let's go see the frog lanterns!"

The frog lanterns had big, silly, red mouths and prominent black and white eyes. Their legs were pulled by four strings which made the frogs jerk spasmodically as if they were in mid-hop. A red candle was inserted into the center of their open bellies. Contrary to the stupid frogs, rabbit lanterns had timid and docile looks. Two red eyes dotted their plain white bodies, bamboo sticks curved to a pair of ears on the side of their heads. Their mouths were circled with green slices signifying that they were having dinner at this moment. The most elegant was the lotus lanterns. Two lotus roots stuck out from opposite sides, lifting the pink flowers in the center which was supported by four green leaves stretching out in different directions. Within the pink bowl, bunches of yellow pistils plugged in the heart. Airplane lanterns flew on tall bamboo poles. The fuselages were in transparent red, green, orange and purple paper, shining from the sky.

"I am going to buy that lion lantern for the gang at home," Lishan said with apparent reservation. They went over. The lions were commanding the square with their bell-shaped eyes and wide open mouths. Their gigantic bodies were covered with gold foil and their curly hair dangled along their bulging heads. Too much to see and too hard to choose, the girls milled about. Finally Jianfei bought the frog, Huifang the lotus and each carried a lantern home to please their siblings.

"Look what I've got for you! A New Year's gift!" Jianfei knocked at Xiaoshi's door, the bottle in one hand and the lantern the other.

"Go away!"

Turning off the light, Jianfei lit the frog. The light flickered merrily, dappling the ceiling, and projected the body on the wall.

"The frog is hopping on the wall. Don't you want to see?" Jianfei tempted, "Sister has a frog lantern and a magic bottle, which one do you want?"

"Neither."

"Sister apologizes. Sister will bring you to the Confucian Temple tomorrow."

"Forget it!"

No lie had ever upset Xiaoshi so much; a piece of candy was enough to cheer him up. Jianfei wondered whether something else had popped up during her absence.

"What's bothering my little brother?" Jianfei knocked at the door again, "Please open the door."

The door was opened and there stood Xiaoshi, eyes brimming with tears.

"Did dad scold you?"

"No. Big Brother is moving away." Tears sluiced down, "His parents told him today."

"Where?" Jianfei felt short of breath.

"To a different compound."

"Which compound?"

"I don't know."

Jianfei blew off the frog and dashed to her room where she locked herself in, buried her face in the pillow. Her body shook slightly as tears stained her bedding.

Sunday afternoon. A loaded army truck parked at the east end of the building. A car was waiting beside. Neighbors gathered and waved goodbye to Commissar Yang. Yang Bing came to Xiaoshi and held him in his arms.

"Big Brother, when you find new stamps, would you please come over and show me? Big Brother, may I visit you and see your new collections of the lead soldiers?"

Xiaoshi's little fingers shook the big hand.

"You will still be around, won't you?"

Yang Bing nodded absent-mindedly.

"Where is your sister?" he heard his voice shaking.

"In her room crying."

Yang Bing lowered his eyes and looked away, and then he bent over and looked Xiaoshi in the eye.

"Please do me a favor; please tell your sister I said goodbye."

The engine started. Yang Bing hugged Xiaoshi once again. The car honked. He jumped into the car and waved. The car roared off. The truck dwindled into the distance and Big Brother was gone.

Part Two

Chapter 1

"Catch up with America in twenty five years! Surpass England in twenty years!"

Chairman Mao's ambition had fueled a patriotic fervor sweeping China. Following the Anti-Rightist movement, a national zeal for Socialist construction erupted. Everywhere people spoke excitedly of "catching up" or "surpassing", and these expressions set a rhythm for the train of Socialist progress that was steadily accelerating, about to enter the terminal where her two Western enemies loomed large, presumably lollygagging in their affluent flatulence.

On this train six hundred million passengers crafted their daily lives into short episodes of eating and sleeping and hours upon hours of vain attempts to forge steel. The whole nation was mobilized to collect bits of scrap iron and feed them into their own backyard smelting furnaces in the hopes of producing steel, steel of God-only-knows what quality. The target was set at 10,800,000 tons. Since the Chinese count large numbers in the tens of thousands, the number 1,080 was an ever present reminder, posted on streets and doors and factories, calling on everyone's mandated participation. All over the land, from the fields to the factory workshops, from the classrooms to the government offices, on the stages, in the public latrines, on the operating tables and the department stores were heard similar dialogues.

"Did you collect any scrap iron today?"

"Of course, I even donated my cooking pot."

"Let's take the sewage cover; it's iron, too."

"May I borrow your pencil sharpener? Mine was contributed to the school."

"Dad, may I take your razor?"

"I haven't shaved yet."

In the narrow lanes where dim street lamps flickered in the early spring breezes and were reflected in the bleary eyes of early-shift workers; in the lively market places where frugal morning shoppers bargained over celeries and lettuces down to the one or even half ounce mark on the scale; in the streets where scavengers halfheartedly swept with bamboo brooms, stirring dust onto pedestrians' shoes, while their hearts' other halves calculated what else could be contributed, besides kitchen knives and scissors, in order to fulfill the day's iron assignment; in the gymnasium where athletes started their day with a new speed target racing against U.S. imperialists—1,080 was a clarion call.

While the steel production campaign continued to combat China's external enemies, China had also designated four internal enemies: sparrows, they pilfer our grains; mice, they loot our harvests; flies and mosquitoes, they carry germs and sabotage our health. The whole country was plunged into a relentless battle to wipe out the four pests, lots of fun. Classes were half in session; the other half gave way to steel forging and pest extermination, two activities of the utmost importance.

Especially heart-stopping was the anti-sparrow warfare. Chairman Mao, the great strategist, advised the adoption of fatigue tactics: exterminate the sparrows by exhausting them, make loud noises to scare the sparrows until they were too weak to fly and fainted or dropped dead. The technique was simple and effective and had also proved to be the most efficient method in the history of sparrow eradication. Public park entry fees were cancelled, the grounds turned open for this special human-bird war. Girls were ecstatic when entering the battlefield with its picturesque terrain. Beating gongs, knocking on basins, shouting at the top of their voices, they witnessed their enemies, in a stupor, falling headlong, like downed aircrafts, plunging into the blue clarity of the lake. Some lay on green lawns, bellies exposed to the sun and were quickly added to the booty list.

"Number twenty six!"

A few, when tumbling from the sky, had the luck to fall into the massive foliage of a large tree. Their dead bodies hung on certain branches, hoping the dew and gusts would bring them back to life. It was a wonderful new game clearly stamped "Made in China." Lots of fun.

On the very blackboard from whence came the suitcase incident more than a year ago, a chart caught everyone's eyes: "Daily Collection Numbers". These daily measurements tracked the number of eliminated pests and the weight of collected scrap iron by each Young Pioneer Team. Statistics spurred the competition and boosted large figures. If Monday showed one hundred pounds of iron, Tuesday might jump to three hundred and by Friday, one thousand would be the promised delivery. Class versus class, school against school, individuals chasing after each other, the girls were writing history again and this chapter was called "The Great Leap Forward".

As millions upon millions engaged in the frenzy of the time, some talents found other means of self-expression. Dramatists devoted their spare time to propaganda, offering free shows in the streets, and finding themselves opportunities to satisfy their vanity. Some of the girls enjoyed themselves immensely. Theatre troupes mushroomed. Short plays caricatured the U.S. and its likes as paper tigers. Big noses and pot bellies appeared on the stage; accompanying derisive remarks triggered great laughter. The enemies were always portrayed grotesquely so as to stir up and deepen the hatred. From time to time, children picked up stones, aimed them at the big noses and let them fly. The actors felt greatly honored when struck in the nose with a stone, a sign of the effectiveness of their acting and their propaganda. A bloodied nose was borne with great pride.

Among the freshmen, ten girls were sifted out to stage a two-act play, *What is Taiwan Up To?* The leading role, Chiang Kaishek, was given to Jianfei; Song Meiling, his wife, was played by Huifang. Playing a beautiful enemy, a role that could spare a lady from making herself hideous, and shoulder to shoulder with Jianfei, her idol, was unanticipated bliss for Huifang. Jianfei's popularity, gained through active participation in political actions, had been Huifang's dream yet she didn't see how, from a blotched family, she could ever possibly become as popular as Jianfei.

Her affection for her family gradually subsided and spite began to blur her limpid eyes. The incident between Ms. Guan and the senior students had taught her to always give a second thought to what to say in public. Suffering helped her maturity. Innocence was leaving her day by day. Dad's sullen face greeted her at home, a different person from her childhood memory.

Chapter 2

General Liu looked at himself in the mirror, a sulky face. The uniform was an eyesore; the green was too green, no subtlety; and the epaulet, a pain in his heart. He saw a younger general, handsome, in a green uniform of a different shade, American style, smiling.

Peeling off the uniform was the first thing he did after work; the second, to repose on the couch, a cup of tea in hand, reviewing his old lessons that would warm his heart as well as tear it to pieces.

Smoke filled the cave, his headquarters. Cannons roared and rumbled over, shattering the earth into millions of crumbs. Bodies flew into the air with black flowers of mud and smoke. Limbs and torsos were scattered in the fields like freshly reaped crops. Another wave of heat gushed in, roiling violently through the dusty tunnel. The parched earth trembled under foot. Flames licked the burnt wall like hundreds of snakes attacking a helpless animal.

"Guard!" General Liu shouted at the top of his voice, "Call all the…" His guard was nowhere to be seen.

"Trai…"

His cry of "traitor" was stopped short as he spotted his guard lying lifeless at the entrance, blood splashed like a grotesque Pollock. General Liu covered his eyes. In the past ten minutes, his troops had launched their last-ditch struggle, only to face the fiercest counterattack. The enemy machine guns clattered, flames like red tongues, mowing down his soldiers in tens and twenties.

Is this it? April, 1949. Does this day mark the end of a dynasty? Communists! Have the Reds won? He began to prepare for his last moment.

General Liu started his military career at Huangpoo Military Academy, China's West Point, at the dawn of the Northern Expedition. Chiang Kaishek was its President and Sun Yatsen, the father of the Chinese Revolution, its founder. It was unimaginable to him, still to this day, that his political instructor Zhou Enlai would later become the Prime Minister of his enemy and many of the outstanding figures on campus thirty years later would turn into nationally renowned characters on both sides. The course of history was running contrary to his youthful wish and now his opponents had avalanched him. His allegiance to his leader collided with the will of the people; his exhortations to serve the country stranded in reality as he watched his dreams shatter. All the military knowledge he had gained in the Huangpoo classroom had turned out to be nothing but a piece of flimsy paper that wafted into the war fire, a transcript of ashes.

Suddenly, quiet. Everything had come to a standstill, no cannon, no explosion, no rumbling, no "Charge". He saw his father, bedridden for three years and passing the year before, waving at him with a welcome-to-join-me smile, his arms wide open. He was a rich merchant, transporting silk from Suzhou to Shanghai. Those delicate and exquisite silk goods: silk fans which helped to dry sweat from white and fine skins; elegant purses at night clubs dangling on the slender wrists of glamorous Shanghai ladies; silk gowns that brought the full display of female physical attractiveness; silk slippers only worn on waxed mahogany floors in concubines' chambers; silk curtains that shielded the grandeur of truly magnificent mansions. He was somewhat relieved that his father had expired earlier than expected so that he could at least save some human decency. *Who knows what would happen to those affluent families if President Chiang Kaishek tumbled down from his throne.* His wife, he should have spared more time for her. Too much concern and anxiety had aged her in the past two years. Students protesting against the government, financial scandals within the Party, unprecedented inflation, incorrigible corruption… all had weighed her down. As a teacher and the wife of a high ranking Nationalist, she balanced a lot in her head: the government; the whole nation whose destiny depended on her husband and his like; her husband's failure in fulfilling responsibilities and performing as a decent politician in the public's eyes; her husband's inch-by-inch loss of territory in the tug-of-war Huaihai Campaign between the two parties: the KMT, Kuomintang, the Nationalist Party, and the Chinese Communist Party (CCP). Her forehead wrinkled like a ploughed field, her eyes encircled with crow's-feet and her grizzled hair, all lied about her age. Suddenly his dark memories were brightened by a little sunshine face, tears gushed out. Four years old, she already knew how to follow the steps of *The Merry Widow Waltz*. He missed the five minutes of tucking her in during the last few nights he stayed at home, his kisses on her pink cheeks, her ringing voice when she babbled about a boy in her kindergarten, how adults jokingly put them together to play a bride and a groom. Her white complexion, brownish hair, red lips, twinkling eyes and dimpling smiles, all depicted a standard beauty, a princess. His heart, his life, his light, that was his daughter, Huifang, a name chosen to defy the precarious times in which they lived, Huifang, his dearest daughter, "amiable and fragrant," Huifang.

Very quiet still, only an occasional bullet sounded in the distance.

"Hey! Look what I have found! A big live fish!"

He heard a cheerful young voice. Instinct told him Colonel Wang was captured just outside the headquarters. *They are approaching, those reds, my old schoolmates!!*

Grinding his teeth, he squatted down, his body hunched into a pile of squalid flesh.

Pulling off his watch from his wrist and taking out the fountain pen from his pocket, he handed both to Lieutenant Xie, "Please tell Ms. Huang I am leaving one step ahead."

He took out his wallet, a gift from Mr. Smith, the Military Advisor, and took a look at the photo. He could not imagine that this was taken only four months ago. Though the President's compound showed no sign of retreat, the New Year's party had much more a sentimental than festive atmosphere making it more a farewell party. There, three of them, with Mr. Smith standing in the rear, put on the last show of a happy family. He took a last glance at the photo, then holding it to his heart with one hand, he reached for his pistol…

"Hands up!"

Thunder crashed over his head as a silhouette appeared at the bright entrance. The sunlight blinded him; he could not tell whether he was falling into the hands of a soldier or an officer. Cool-headed, he gripped the pistol and held it to his temple…

A puff of light blue, the bullet went upwards, his arm grabbed by the owner of the voice from above. He opened his eyes only to meet a chubby face and a naïve smile.

General Liu, throttled with rage, spat out "Congratulations!" to Chubby.

He was furious at the fact that no enemy officer was present at his capture. This is unfair! Head high in the air, accompanied by three triumphant soldiers, he walked towards the light at the entrance. Outside, a roar of cheers, an ocean of red, charred bodies strewn on the smoldering earth. He saw General Lee, his Huangpoo buddy; Colonel Wang and several other high-ranking colleagues. They were all crestfallen, their bodies like deflated tires. Seeing him, they all straightened up, a flicker of hope in their eyes.

General Liu was ready to face his death. An execution with a bullet or a swordsman's axe would make no difference to him. However, to his disappointment, he found himself returned to the same compound where he had lived for many years as a Nationalist officer. So narrowly escaped from death, it was beyond his comprehension that his career would continue here as a Communist officer.

Huifang's dinner table, like everyone else's, provided the forum for dad's didacticism on morals and sophistication.

"Sickness enters through the mouth; trouble shoots out through the mouth."

To which Huifang no longer turned a deaf ear.

"The mouth, the mouth, the entrance and exit of disasters, guard it!"

"But Lishan makes acid comments all the time."

She saw Lishan's jaw opening and shutting.

"Yes. She can, but you cannot," dad said calmly. "You don't have her father."

"It's all your fault, always taking the wrong side, choosing the wrong color!"

A fuse was finally ignited, without any regard to dad's ego.

"How come you joined the whites and not the reds?"

"One misstep and you fall into a pit."

A smirk hung on dad's lips.

"Life is nothing but a gamble, a matter of luck. History simply played a joke on me."

"No. It is a matter of right and wrong,"

Disobedience was rare in this house. Huifang was not Lishan. The situation worried mom who cut in, casting a quick glance to shut her husband up. Of course, all the books, radios, movies and newspapers agreed that the Nationalist Army never fired a single bullet when the Japanese devils looted our shops, burned our villages, bombed our cities, butchered our men and raped our wives and mothers. It did not take Huifang long to realize that the differences between her dad and Jianfei's and Lishan's dads were far more than separate compounds and free movie tickets. The truth was she would never become one of them no matter how sincere Jianfei's friendship was. There was an invisible trench lying between them, impassible, dividing them into two sides.

"Dad, I won't be home this Sunday. The school will dispatch six drama teams to perform on the streets. I have three rounds."

Huifang asked for leave. Dad had recently increased her Sunday working hours from four to six since her grades were going downhill.

"What does this kind of activity have to do with you, my daughter?" dad laid stress on the "my".

"I am playing Song Meiling."

A premonition rose. She knew things would be tough for her at home.

Dad raised his tone, "Oh? Since when has my darling baby become Scarlett O'Hara?"

The Hollywood name known to nobody except her parents was another shame on her. She kept her mouth shut, fearing other surprises would jump out of his mouth.

"What is your great performance about, may I ask, Miss?" dad rasped.

"To liberate Taiwan. To capture your comrades-in-arms!" Huifang clenched her teeth. In her memory this was the first time rage took full possession.

"Wow! Gre...eat!" A mirthless laugh burst out.

"Don't be so harsh on the girl!"

Mom came to the rescue of both.

"You know what schools are like nowadays."

Huifang was on the verge of tears.

"Ridiculous! Do you really expect to drive a Ford in twenty five years? As if Uncle Sam would sit on his fat ass waiting for us? Look at the liquid dross flowing out of the earthy furnaces! Do you really believe it can be turned into a cannon to shoot down Taiwan's reconnaissance planes? Ha! A pipe dream!"

He smirked again.

"Hush!"

Panicked, mom hopped over and covered dad's mouth, her frightened eyes searching outside the window while signaling Huifang to leave the dinner table.

Huifang withdrew to her room, tears trickling down. She was stuck between her own nuclear family and the larger family of society, neither of which could she tear herself away from. Her desire to make herself a worthy friend of Jianfei, wishful thinking at best, mustered up her courage and she said to her mom, "I am going, with or without his approval."

Mom stroked her hair, looked her in the eye and said, "Please forgive your dad." She sank into deeper thought. "It is not easy for him to adapt to…"

"You think it is easy for me at school?"

Silence fell. Mom cuddled her.

"Huifang, you will not repeat your dad's words in public, will you? Promise me. Look at me," profound concern and anxiety written on her face.

Huifang nodded, "I promise."

"One more thing," mom hesitated.

"Be very prudent with boys. You are no longer a child and you are very beautiful. Walking around in the streets might draw evil eyes."

"Where can I find a boy? I'd like to know. At a girls' school? I wish I could."

Mom stood up. She breathed into her cupped hand and then transferred the breath to the daughter's brow.

"Good night."

Chapter 3

The streets on Sunday were thronged with shoppers, eaters, strollers who, though on a variety of errands, shared the same goal, to watch the free show. Young ladies skimmed through clothing stores, trying on every piece but leaving with nothing, except the annoyed looks from the shop assistants. Old folks, not fully recovered from their winter afflictions, folded their arms and dug their hands deeply into the tunnels of their sleeves. Their grandchildren sat on their laps, fondled their beards, and scrutinized their fancy walking sticks, wondering how the dragons, tigers, orchids and birds landed on the gnarled handles. The old ones and the little ones were the earliest birds. Their stools and benches had secured their seats and they didn't want to be moved. In the breakfast eateries, men chatted, sipping steaming soy milk, dipping in their crispy fried Chinese crullers. Every few seconds their heads popped out of the windows, searching for the school banners.

At around ten, silk red banners fluttered into view. School girls wearing red ties poured into the stream of pedestrians, charging the air with their youth and exuberance. The stream thickened and swelled. Someone's toe was stepped on,

"Are you blind? Screw you!"

No one cared about the benches and stools. The grandpas and children had to use them as weapons to fight their way out of the crowd.

The young voices began to expound the Party's General Line, "Go all out! Aim high and achieve greater, faster, better and more economical results in building Socialism."

Old eyes looked at young eyes. Big ones stared at small ones. No matter what, their voices were pleasing, brisk like the air, clear as the sky. People nodded and smiled.

Jianfei's team was scheduled for three performances, two downtown, and one in the afternoon near the Academy. The morning shows were located in two different squares. All lanes leading to the squares were stuffed like sausages. Buses honked. Babies whimpered. And men were yelling and cursing. The improvised stage was assembled on two doors lying on top of four benches. The curtains were two bed sheets sewed together, held by two pairs of stage hands.

Opening Scene: The White House. Eisenhower, played by Wufeng, swaggers in. The American President is caricatured exactly as seen in the daily newspapers. A red, white and blue stars-and-stripes hat, huge nose and pot belly—a must!

Swaying her stick, the president picks up an imaginary phone, "What? China? In twenty five years?"

With exaggerated pompousness, "No, no, no," in English. "Impossible" in raw Chinese with an assumed accent.

Laughter rose. The audience rocked. Very good! Americans are stupid! They cracked seeds, narrowed their eyes, mocking and with spit hanging on their lips. Some watermelon seeds were spat at Wufeng's feet. She felt greatly honored. She knew that the moment was arriving for her nose and the nose was waiting in a tingling thrill. Children began scouring for stones. One landed on her hat, another popped on her belly.

"Stupid imperialists!"

"Paper tiger!"

Now Eisenhower paces to his desk and embraces the terrestrial globe with both arms and postures as if swallowing it up.

"This is mine! The world belongs to the U.S."

The globe spins under Wufeng's finger tips.

"Down with U.S. imperialism!"

Somebody thrust his fist. Others followed. Applause thundered.

That it was the most obscure and modest Wufeng wrapped inside the arrogant chauvinistic character made her fellow schoolmates bend over with laughter.

Huifang felt lucky that she did not have to risk her image or ridicule herself in carrying out the revolution. Her body was not subjected to baggy pants as Wufeng's was or the ill-fitting army uniform as was Jianfei's. Huifang was quite satisfied with her costume, painstakingly chosen from a large pile of dazzling outfits, which Jianfei's mother, a vanguard of fashion, had made available. Having modeled each and every outfit before her own critical eyes in the mirror, some of them multiple times while Jianfei patiently stood alongside, she had finally settled on a flattering black velvet cheongsam and a short, light yellow cashmere sweater with a 'V' cut. Out of a dozen fancy shoes, a pair of white high-heeled sandals caught her eyes. The shoes sported black bows at the toe.

Now the stunning Huifang ascends the stage in her elegant, steady gait; her prominent buttocks swaying left and right rhythmically; her legs moving agilely and the high heels squeaking all the way along.

"Bravo!" hooligans cheered. Some whistled.

Lishan noticed from the side of the stage how Huifang's breasts protruded under the thin, tight sweater to feed the devouring eyes of men. Lishan's nerves splintered and her stomach stirred at this sight. A feeling of betrayal filled her; Huifang was unveiling female secrets. Never had all the ins and outs of a girl's body been highlighted in such a shameless way. *I would rather deform myself than let men's eyes feast on my chest in such an obvious way,* she said to herself. Lishan was not one of the actors in the troupe. She was one among the overstaffed stagehands, responsible for taking care of costumes and make-up.

Huifang could have put on a pair of decent trousers to discipline her lustrous, plump hips, Lishan thought. *Yet she allowed this abundant pair of hemispheres to stick out into men's faces. And, good gracious! Look at the wide openings in her cheongsam revealing her marble legs!*

The indignation was in her eyes though she admitted that Huifang could not hide the natural growth of a healthy body, nor could the male audience watch the show blindfolded. Lishan doubted Huifang's acting talent but not her beauty. She was sinfully beautiful. *But why should I care? What do I really care?* Lishan dug deep into her rancor and fathomed that her jealousy was actually not sparked by Huifang's beauty but by her friendship with Jianfei. Playing her wife, Huifang in Lishan's eyes had become Jianfei's lifelong partner and this revelation set her on edge. Watching Huifang on the stage, she felt as alienated as a street orphan. Her pique extended to Jianfei. *Why should she offer Huifang such an opportunity and let her take advantage of her good looks and make use of the propaganda team to propagate sex? How can Jianfei stand her?*

Chiang Kaishek/Jianfei is wearing Lishan's father's uniform, a pair of cardboard Nationalist epaulets on her shoulders, Madame Song at her arm. He is examining the map of the world when the mimed telephone rings, a call from big-nosed Wufeng.

His sword dances in the air. "Our American friend is right. We should penetrate the mainland with more secret forces. Meanwhile we should molest their coast and dispatch warships to launch a surprise bombardment on the isles of Jinmen and Mazu. This way, we will foil their catching-up and surpassing dreams and prove ourselves to be Eisenhower's friend indeed. Charge!"

Chiang Kaishek was an out and out warmonger, and the play was nothing more than slogans and caricatures. However a message was delivered and the audience was now prepared for the immanent onslaught of Nationalist spies. Hands clapped and cheeks reddened with excitement. The applause refused to die down even though Chiang Kaishek and his wife, hand in hand, accompanied by their old friend Eisenhower, returned to the stage a third time.

Jianfei lifted her hat. Her silky cascading hair flew out and draped her epaulets and loose uniform. The male-female, evil-good conflicting images fanned louder cheers. Again, she crossed her legs and bent slightly, her hands waved in the air. As she was about to swerve back and end the fourth curtain call, her eyes met a pair of eyes. A face floated out from the ocean. This was the face that kept visiting her dreams and walking into her days, a face that spoke to her with a soundless voice, that lit her lonely hours, that accompanied her to the library and to her classes and prompted her poetic instinct. Five seasons had passed since that blue sweater vanished from the playground. After that, the sun seemed to dim, trees were no longer verdant, flowers were limp and birds had lost their voices. *Yang Bing, Yang Bing*, her eyes and hands calling him, waving and smiling.

He was with his family, all wearing glasses, an intellectual family that stood out from the medley of workers, shop clerks and peasants. He had grown into a man; a moustache distinguished him from the younger Yang Bing. His imposing stature and the composure of his carriage announced maturity. In three or four months, he would enter high school. All of a sudden, Jianfei saw the one-year gap between them widened. His mother and sister beamed, waving ardently. He nodded with a smile, almost invisible. She made another graceful bow and cast a meaningful look in his direction.

Chapter 4

Nothing could be more boring than standing guard. In the mind of this Shanghai high school graduate, Tang Wei, joining the army meant galloping on the prairie while whipping your saber across the enemies' skulls, enjoying the scene of beheaded bodies, or sailing with the wind across the Yangtze, stepping out of the bunk at the bugle call, and then, as the crow flies, storming the KMT President's Residence, as seen time and again in documentaries, or being a flag bearer while dodging sporadic gunshot at your back, hailing as the liberated wretched hailed. His dreams of driving the warship into the enemy and sinking together with them, or of swooping down onto a pack of U.S. helmets climbing up the hillside, and setting off a bundle of explosives cradled bravely in his arms in their midst, or the percussive rat-a-tat-tat of the machine gun firing into the fuselage, rapturous over the black cloud rising at the tail of the Jap's plane that plunged nose down to the transparent placid blue of the Pacific had long been crystallized by movies and novels. Tears rolled from Tang Wei's eyes whenever an imposing hero was pulverized and the mountains chorused his eulogy and pine trees reliably filled the screen as a symbol of his immortality, or when the vastness of the glittering blue sea bellowed, claiming the eternity of another buried seaman, foaming, surging, shooting up and slowly merging with a more boundless blue above it ....Patriotism and heroism were two words which, even without details, would fill his chest with a sense of obligation and a sublime feeling, pumping him up and setting his blood boiling, inspiring him to join the People's Liberation Army.

Standing guard had never appeared once in his slumber. Had he fathomed the significance of spending eight lonely hours guarding the walled compounds? In the past two months he had kept lecturing himself on the essentiality of this duty. Just as he was about to come to terms with the heroism in standing alone on the eventless shifts, he was switched to a different complex. His gallantry, valor and hankering for the romance of combat had turned into humor. Fate interceded to blacken this humor as he had become a protector of his enemy. The compound he was guarding was the North Pole, ex-KMT central.

Two faces floated into his head, like two balloons bumping against each other.

One balloon said, "There is nothing wrong in my scraping together my meager salary to send my son his favorites."

The other balloon scowled, "No, he is no longer your baby, not from the moment he put on this green uniform."

This balloon spoke the words of the Political Instructor, Li Yi, Enduring Strength Li, when Tang Wei's parcel arrived. Cheerful Shanghai White Rabbit candies and preserved plums had dropped out.

"Tell your mom to send you some revolutionary books. You are no longer a baby sucking lollipops but a People's Liberation Army soldier holding a gun! This army does not accept babies."

At the Political Instructor's remarks, Tang Wei was tongue-tied. But he couldn't alter mom's decade-long habit in a day. She had made it her goal to offer him a life equivalent to the one he would have had with two parents. He had never met his dad. He knew him from those yellowing pictures hanging on the wall, proudly dressed in the uniform of the New Fourth Army, the father of the People's Liberation Army, four pockets, a pistol in his belt. He was smiling out at his wife and his son who was born two months before he closed his eyes on the charcoaled field. It wouldn't be easy to forward the Political Instructor's advice to mom. It was not that the White Rabbit candies and plums were his favorites, but simply his mom's eyes, the eyes that wore fatigue from long hours at the factory, and from the sadness of her son's departure to the army and from the dread brought on by the foreseen loneliness that would reshape her life and spirits.

"I am anticipating the day of your return when you will take over my position at the factory," she wrote.

People coming in and going out registered their faces and backs. His eyes functioned as a camera, helping his mind restore every detail. An officer approached. Tang Wei clicked his heels and pulled his hand up

113

to his brow. The officer drew up a listless arm. His head stared at the pavement, not bothering to make a moment's eye contact. The deliberate haughtiness was a brisk slap to Tang Wei's cheek. Mute as a fish, he cursed loudly in his belly. *Go to hell! To salute the enemy is absurd! To salute every officer squarely without receiving an equal return was unfair!* Yet he continued to click his heels and raise his arm.

Just outside the gate, a young pioneer banner zoomed in. Soon a makeshift stage was constructed. One eye in, one eye out, Tang Wei caught glimpses of a pot belly and an Uncle Sam costume, a KMT uniform and the curvaceous body of a woman. Fragments of dialogue were audible along with laughter and familiar slogans that drifted over to the guardhouse. Tang Wei was a bit curious about the goings on.

Within a half hour, a female Chiang Kaishek, her wife and a third girl approached his post. Tang Wei recognized them. These were the three girls roaming from compound to compound, emitting laughter, trailing admiring eyes, officers' daughters. One of their fathers was an officer who passed by with an unwilling salute.

If my father were still alive, he would be striding shoulder to shoulder with their fathers. No, he would doubtlessly be a general whose shoulders were glistening with one or two stars. Then I would be on a bicycle, flying by these girls' without even looking back... On Sundays, I would join the loitering gangs on the steps of the auditorium, eyes searching for one of these girls... hanging around on the sports ground, playing psychological games with the opposite sex. I would kill the drowsy summer in the sparkling swimming pool and read away the drab winter in the sunny library...like a typical dandy.

His brain darkened on the sultry room he and his mother shared with a curtain hanging in between. His sweaty body printed distinctively on the board whenever he got out of the naked bed! The cling and clang of spatulas on woks and pans; the scraping, scratching and brushing inside the urine-coated chamber pots; the droning of the morning peddlers:

"Pan-fried cakes, sizzling hot!"

"Soy milk, ten cents a pot!"

The scolding of parents and screaming of children...a symphony of his bustling life in that sluggish lane of Shanghai echoed in his ears while Tchaikovsky's Four Swans danced from the compounds' loudspeakers. Brought up in that superior city and among conceited Shanghainese, he felt no superiority here. The gap between him and these three girls was boiled down to one word: dad. Dads determined your future. Fate.

They were all tall. Each displayed a discernable subtlety. Tang Wei analyzed the three physiques. One was tall and skinny; one tall and plump; one just tall. The skinny one was in her sagging uniform, under which her feminine developments were hard to assess, but the slender waist, long, athletic legs and stooping shoulders suggested a well-framed young lady. The mere tall one wore neither make-up nor costume but a sullen expression. Her pouting lips seemed to be grumbling all the time, announcing an unfair life. She must have had a rough day watching her friends displaying their talents while she waited in their shadow like a disowned dog. His observations moved to the plump one. There was something in her that brushed his heart slightly and made his throat tighten. Her blue-gray eyes were serene like the autumn sky. Her coy, lingering smile shone like a fading sun, in the shade of her friends whose laughter was hearty or cynical. Her white complexion and the high bridge of her nose rendered an exotic touch to her oriental feature. What distinguished her from her friends was her precocious body: firm breasts, solid buttocks and a pair of marble pillars revealed through the high slits of her Chinese gown which could arouse man's most fanciful ideas. Unconsciously, Tang Wei was dissecting her from the perspective of a lustful eighteen-year-old and not a disciplined soldier. For a moment he forgot what he was: a stoic revolutionary, a pure-minded People's Liberation Army soldier, whose hours, minutes and seconds were devoted to the noble cause which meant studying the red handbooks, jotting down notes, and recording any suspicious traits observed at his post. Gluing his eyes on a beautiful thing was taboo but his eyes were so tired of the green.

Huifang knew Madame Song could only carry her a few yards away until she took a turn and vanished into her building. The Cinderella was determined to stage an impromptu performance to fully utilize her costume and entertain the last audience who was now standing at her compound, providing protection. She felt the guard deserved an award, a bit of a free show.

Leaning against Jianfei with her arms hooked on her elbow, she knitted her brows and pouted, still in character, "My darling, I am dead tired.

Don't you wish you could carry your sweetheart home?" delicate as a glass flower.

Jianfei bent over laughing. *Huifang acts better now that the show is over.* Though Huifang's performance turned her stomach, Lishan cast a menacing look at Tang Wei. *Don't you dare to fancy my friend!*

Dragging Huifang by the arm, Lishan patted her on her back, "Straighten up!"

Huifang pulled herself up strutting by Tang Wei. Head in the air, she cast a haughty side glance at the guard with an exaggerated posture as if saying, "Who dares to harm the President's wife?"

Jianfei kept laughing. A faint smile flitted over Lishan's face. To Jianfei, Huifang's atrocious flirtation was simply amusing; to Lishan, however, it was blatant flippancy. *A girl from a good family never flirts.* Lishan's smile was soon overtaken by her grimace.

The moon splashed its silken light on the roof of the barracks. Thickets were dappled like crouching leopards. All the lights were off; even the political instructor's window, which at this time usually framed a head bending over reports, documents and theoretical works, was dark. Tang Wei lay motionless in bed. His brain however persisted in chasing the three tall figures who, for the first time, stirred up some excitement in his dull, motionless, lengthy sentry hours. Insomnia paid an unwelcome visit.

Rhythmic snoring and even breathing poured into his ears, exasperating his battle against the draining hours. The Gold-Purple Mountain loomed in the distance. Somewhere in its belly echoed a "cuckoo-cuckoo", the harbinger of the spring, bringing in his far away childhood! The stretch of yellow flowers on the green land, the "cuckoo-cuckoo" that played hide-and-seek with him in the woods, the jingling brook in front of the thatched hut, the savor of the freshly picked fava beans, all tickled the city boy's nerves as he enjoyed his spring break in his grandmother's rural nest. Tang Wei was the favorite child of his father's mother. "Cuckoo-cuckoo, cuckoo-cuckoo," patiently and peacefully, the bird chortled…Tang Wei's mind blurred amidst the bird's lullaby… A pair of eyes poked through the darkness. The light turned on again in his mind.

A pair of blue-gray eyes pierced through…unfathomable eyes, tantalizing eyes, bewitching eyes. Tang Wei replayed his day movie in his head searching for these eyes. They belonged to Madame Chiang. Alert, Tang Wei sat up, shaking his head to cast the eyes off. But the more he shook, the deeper they became engraved into the black slate, into his soul, more assertive, more persistent. With the eyes, slowly wafted in a face, soft like rice paper. Finally the body sailed in, round and full, lithe and supple, cut against the evening sky. Tang Wei became fretful. He was furious with himself.

Stop! Stop thinking of her! Think of your career!

A sudden premonition fell over him. Somewhere in his heart he knew he was destined to be his own enemy. Lying down again, his body was still fidgety and feverish. Frustrated, he went to the bathroom, showered his face with cold water and then returned to bed. His fever chilled and his mind murky. Day broke.

Chapter 5

Swallows migrated. They abandoned their houses during the dreary winter days and then, as the winds carried traces of spring, they dredged mud and carried it to their nests to renovate them. Maple leaves blew red and then green. Another Spring Festival had passed, and another April came. The North wind folded its razor blades, breathing over the earth, turning it green. Stretches of azalea dyed the hillside with pink vapors.

Head over heels, the three girls buried themselves in preparation for high school. Burning the midnight oil, skipping weekly movies, they found entrance examinations were no fun. The deflated volleyball lay in the corner of the classroom. Humor was smothered. The afternoon sessions were extended to eight o'clock in the evening, dinner finished at nine thirty. After dinner, books fought the eyes until the eyelids could no longer endure. Enigmatic equations that had been troubling them during the day became entangled in their dreams while chemistry formulas and physics definitions flashed in the darkness like random lightning on a sultry summer night. Three heads put together, surrounded by triangles, rectangles and squares. Jianfei's room was a cluttered battleground.

Huifang's father made the situation clear to her, "If you fail, you will be sent to the countryside to live with your uncle. I have already talked to him; they welcome you there."

In the fall, the three girls put on new badges. Jianfei and Huifang were assigned to Class A and Lishan to Class B. Upon entering high school, Huifang held her head as high as any of Jianfei's classmates, but her father's scheme was still an axe hanging even higher and would hold her hostage for the next three years, weakening her pride. From the start Huifang knew there was no way she could make it to college.

Mists filled the early morning air. Tiny beads of dew oozed from the waxy leaves. Blades of grass wet the shoes. The world was a damp and foggy place, in which buildings and earth were the only tangible objects and faces were floating phantoms, merely suggesting human figures, making Tang Wei's guard duty tough. He cherished the hope that the sun would show up and lift away the veil from one particular face when she turned around that corner.

She arrived daily at seven forty and then in twenty minutes a new soldier would salute to Tang Wei and take over the day shift. Tang Wei glanced at the ticking clock, still more than half an hour ahead of his precious moment. Seeing her was his most important daily duty and he would feel no regret returning to the barracks where he could kill the remainder of his day in fragmentary sleep, a distasteful lunch and feigned study of revolutionary works. His shifts varied from week to week. The rotation of the shift did not always give him the chance to glimpse that face whose appearance would accelerate his heart, pump his blood, ring in his ears and burn his cheeks, a guaranteed time bomb in his daily routine. Day in, day out, she nourished his body, fed his brain, lit his night and shortened his shift. In two or three seconds, she would be gone, passing his post, merging into the day's traffic, leaving him seared in her wake. At last, all the boredom and loneliness, along with the crazy thoughts and wild imaginations they had hatched, the hurt pride and disillusioned dreams were all worth it. They had only exchanged a nod two or three times since her spell was first cast more than two years ago. Before summer, the girl was so preoccupied, her eyes always glued to her flash cards and her hands always gripping her books. His urge to communicate was diluted and postponed. Her two month's absence at his post during the summer vacation had gnawed at his heart, fermented his desire. Occasionally he encountered the three girls back from the swimming pool, their hair wet and legs glistening with healthy tans. This image was the catalyst. September arrived. With it came the aching for her presence and a determination to start a long journey. The bomb had been primed.

In the past three weeks, he had challenged his masculinity by putting on an uncertain smile. Once he even tried a timid greeting. And, to his amazement and consternation, he received a similar cheek twitch and a murmured "Hi." Although he was instructed time and again that a sentry was a fish and not supposed to open his mouth, he defended himself that this was a necessary circumstance, reckoning it a revolutionary courtesy. By now he had already probed many of her secrets. He knew her name and age, her school and year, her friends, her family and its story.

Tang Wei glanced at the ticking instrument of torture: the two hands were almost sticking to each other, seven thirty. He shot his eyes again to the corner of the building where the red of the brick met the white of the pavement, for the thirtieth time, maybe, since dawn. He refilled his courage by picturing her face in newly charged radiance, her springy steps, and the happy-go-lucky air that enveloped her. Two officers were pushing along their bicycles. A maid was squatting in a small vegetable plot, filling her basket with dark green cabbages. The clock was ticking, so was the bomb in his pocket. He sighed, no sign of his girl. He rolled his eyes over to the corner again, humming in his heart a line from a song: "Straining my 'autumn water', no sign of my loved one." Autumn water. Lover's melancholy. Longing eyes. Two little boys dashed out, buns in hands, bulging cheeks still munching.

Tang Wei's hand dived into his pocket again, the thirtieth time, maybe, since dawn. His sticky palm clung to the slip. It was still there. He was aware this was another risky step he was taking in addition to the series of illegal smiles and greetings. He had foreseen the consequences of breaching discipline. The stringent discipline and severe punishment were documented and studied on a daily basis; the soldiers' performances were reviewed twice a day, in the morning opening assembly and at the evening closing rally, and the evaluations reported weekly at their squad meetings. Two and a half years in the army, he considered himself a veteran now; his temper was tamed, his anger tapered at the pompous enemy officers; his heart no longer cringed at the thoughts of a dishonorable discharge and his eyes no longer dodged the sight of his political instructor.

The letter in his pocket had been revised four times, word by word, avoiding frivolous terms. The first letter was a brief introduction of himself and his family, a son of a revolutionary martyr, ready to give his life for national defense, etc. He tore that letter to pieces, disgusted by his own uncouth image. The second time he made a simple confession, I love you. Sickened again, by his lust this time, he threw it into a manure pit.

The third time, he wrote a poem, the moon and the spring, the sun and a bird. It sounded phony, like an imitation of some third-rate magazine. The fourth letter he locked in his bag. On Sunday while many of his comrades seized the day to study the newly arrived *The Selected Works of Mao Tsetung*, and a few others washed their clothes, or played chess to strengthen their comradeship, he unfolded it. Taking his stool made of canvas and sticks, he settled himself behind a bed sheet on the clothesline. A book lay open on his lap, *The Youth of Mao Tsetung*, the letter spread on a writing pad suggesting he was taking notes. The political instructor Li Yi and his platoon leader Pan Weiguo strolled shoulder to shoulder in his direction. Tang Wei rested his elbows on the writing pad and scribbled from the book:

> To strengthen his learning ability, the young leader Mao
> Runzhi, later Mao Tsetung, stood at the city gate, in the
> thick of the hullabaloo of peddlers, artisans and peasants,
> to memorize classical essays and poems…

"Hi, little Tang! Aren't you a studious one? Your fingers are always on the run!"

His platoon leader Pan boasted about his soldier to Li Yi.

"Taking notes, eh?"

Li Yi nodded.

"Yes, sir. Chairman Mao has set a brilliant example for us Chinese youth."

Tang Wei stood up, saluting squarely. Li Yi and Pan Weiguo analyzed Tang Wei's sincerity and his loyalty was confirmed. They walked out of sight.

A month later Tang Wei was promoted to squad leader.

Tang Wei returned to his project. As his eyes went down the lines, his stomach began to turn again.

Dear Huifang:

> Pardon me for addressing you in such an intimate way,
> which, I hope, will not be taken as imprudence, but rather
> as friendship without ceremony. Ever since that fateful day

of our chance encounter, Madame Chiang's image has been etched in my mind. My life has become intertwined with yours. Hundreds of sleepless nights and restless days have convinced me that I am in love with you. Your eyes are a beacon illuminating my every night's voyage and the vision of your smile sets aglow my lonely post. I would be the luckiest person if you could take five minutes to respond to this pathetic soul of mine that is longing for your reply like a beggar…

He listened with abhorrence to this self-pitying groaning. *Your passion is a malarial fever and your confession is despondent and pretentious and therefore repulsive*, he said to himself. He folded it up. *What should I do with it? Shred it and dump it together with my remnant soup into the dining hall bucket? No, even the cooks are soldiers there.* The kitchen was all eyes. He crumpled the letter into a tiny ball and snuck it into his shoes next to his stinking feet, then walked to the sewage where he witnessed his love swirled down into the black filth. After two hours of pondering, his letter shrank to one line.

When Tang Wei shot one more glance towards the corner of the building, Huifang emerged into his vision. The figure that had been reviewed day and night was drawing nearer and nearer. His nerves taut, eyes straining, he pulled his hand out of his pocket. The letter was wet in his sweaty palm. The girl was wearing a short checkered jacket and a pair of well-tailored trousers in which her plump bottom became a pair of balls. Shrouded in the splendor of the morning sun which timely vaporized the mist, she was a gilded goddess. His heart melted into a pool of sugary water. Will it be a yes or no? Before his train of thoughts could continue, the pretty face was already in his face.

"Hi."

He stepped forward. His cheeks squeezed out a nervous smile.

"Hi."

She beamed.

No time to lose. No room for hesitation. He quickly unraveled his fist. A tiny paper ball flipped over and then landed right in front of her feet.

He demanded in a low voice, "Pick it up, it is for you."

His lips directed to her, but his eyes stared ahead, his neck was stiff and kept a straight line with the back.

It took Huifang several seconds to grasp the meaning of this order. She bent over, quickly touching her shoelaces while her deft fingers snapped the small ball into her shoe. Two minutes later, once blended into the rush hour traffic, she transferred the letter to her zipped pocket.

Chapter 6

To have your first admirer was a secret bliss and Huifang, though still in the dark as to what the note might hold, sensed that it must have something to do with a boy/girl affair. *The young man obviously has had his eye on me for some time. The way he scrutinizes me, his awkward smiles and clumsy greetings are all so obvious.* However to unfold the letter in public seemed to Huifang disrespect for a sacred secret. She kept the letter in her pocket warm like an egg about to hatch and then she would nurture the bird. She let her curiosity tantalize her. So the letter was hoarded away and the whole day, Tang Wei's somewhat childish face accompanied her with his imperceptible smiles and inaudible good mornings. From time to time, her fingers pressed the note like a child touching a candy that was saved for dessert. She realized that the green in his uniform, the red on his cap and the cold glint teal of the bayonet on top of his shoulder had long been the most attractive color combination and blended into the fabric of her school life. Once in a while, she pictured the silly Madame Chiang strutting by the gate and she asked herself whether her deliberate flirtation that day was emboldened by her costume or whether it was merely a whimsical idea prompted by the flattering male audience. She was never too sure, but as time went by, this distinction didn't seem to be of much importance. During the entrance exam, he was sort of obliterated from her mind as it grappled with math and chemistry. Now with sharp vividness he revived and loudly reasserted himself. Preserving his letter in her chest, her heart felt an urge to sing, to laugh, to jump, to dance, to embrace the tree, to kiss the sky, to stretch her arms welcoming the wind to comb her hair and the sun bathe her body...*Is this love? Is this what the Soviet, the British and American call "love" in their movies?* During recess, she narrowed her eyes at Jianfei, itchy to reveal her secret to her. Love needed to be shared. Yet at the last moment she checked herself. The sharp-eyed Jianfei had already caught her evasive, secretive eyes, her absent-minded classroom manner and her muffled ecstasy. She cast an inquisitive glance at Huifang in physics class. Huifang rounded her lips and breathed out a silent "What?" shrugging her shoulders and shaking her head. However Jianfei did catch two dimples as Huifang pursed her lips, sinking in her own thoughts. The self-smile told a tale.

Scraping the last rice grain into her mouth, Huifang excused herself and retreated to her room. Layer by layer, she unfolded the note like a mother unwrapping a baby. The letter was laid naked under the lamp, ready to reward her daylong patience.

"Cabbage, cabbage!" from the dining room, dad's explosion shook the walls, "Nothing but cabbage! Since when have these inedible leaves been promoted to a delicacy?"

His voice drawled on the last syllable, screeching, raspy and ugly. *Lord, why has it to be at this moment?* Huifang sat on the edge of her bed, picking up the baby and wrapped it again, fearing the storm might blow it away. She waited for the hurricane to die down. Dad had been complaining about cabbage for months.

"Shh…" mom's muffled voice crossed the floor, "newspapers call this 'temporary hardship'. Be patient."

"Ha! Newspapers! Liars! All they tell you is bumper harvest! Rocketing numbers! Thinking of those ridiculous production figures! Ten thousand jin per mu? Only God knows!"

"Well, Mao must like it," mom replied sheepishly. "I had almost convinced myself that revolutionary zeal could actually turn a fairy tale into reality and make magic happen. But today our neighbor upstairs showed me a letter from her father in the countryside. A horrible famine has claimed fourteen lives in a village with a population of less than six hundred."

"That's not too bad," dad complimented sarcastically. "The worst is this. When the county governor accompanied the central government officials to inspect those areas, the leaders of the People's Communes had the guts to boast about their Great Leap Forward. In one village, steaming hot, white buns were stuffed into the hands of corpses, allowing the officials to attribute the cause of death to excessive food consumption! What genius!" Dad choked with fury, "Look what is left after the open-door eating policy of our communes! The thick and hard cabbage leaves only pigs patronized a year ago! The so-called meat once a month in the dining halls is nothing but the canned pork liver taken from our soldiers' mouth! Soldiers guarding our borders in blizzards!"

Dad paused.

Nothing was heard from mom but sighing.

"Shame, shame on Mao!" dad started again but was cut short by mom. "Shush!"

The image of the soldiers her dad described touched the strings of Huifang's heart. She pressed Tang Wei's letter to her chest.

"And look at those Communist compounds! Things are no better. Cabbage commands their dining halls, too." Dad burst out laughing, amused by his humor. "Cabbage Commander, yes, cabbage commander."

"Hush! Thank God we still have rice," mom sounded really fatigued.

Dad's barrage of cabbage continued until the clang of the pots and pans put the dialogue to an end.

After the hustle and bustle of the day and the cabbage seminar in the evening, Huifang finally was alone with Tang Wei. She tiptoed to the door, clicked the spring lock, turned on the reading lamp which excluded everything but his letter. The small square of white paper showed a free and elegant scribbling. Heart palpitating, she read:

> Please meet me outside the back gate at seven o'clock this Sunday evening under the second willow tree to the left of the riverbank.

> It is important.

As if scorched, she dropped the paper on the floor. *Maybe this is just a snare to lure a girl to his lust? Maybe there is something seriously jeopardizing my family? Is he discharged?* She surmised all the possibilities. The day's feverish anticipation had suddenly hit a stone wall. The poem she imagined, the nightingale, a rose, a moonlit garden like in the movie *Eugene Onegin* had boiled down to two cold lines. She lifted the cold scrap and studied it. No passion, no tinge of romance nor tenderness, no streak of yearning, nothing but a time and place, cold as a slab. Huifang slumped back. All day long, she had been a girl hand in hand with a boy giggling in the fields, in the woods, sometimes chasing each other with hearty laughter just as seen in those Soviet movie screens. A gentleman holding a lady's face, drinking the honey from her lips like an education movie repeatedly played in her own mind... *My love started with a slab.* Had Tang Wei known a girl's heart better, he would have saved those painstakingly written sugary letters from the cesspool and the sewage.

Huifang knew Tang Wei would be there, the second tree...but she was wavering between providing great promise and great disappointment.

At this moment, on the other side of the compound where the guard platoon reposed, Tang Wei sat praying that his girl would bring his dream to reality, a transition which took him months of courage to put into action.

Chapter 7

Two faces stared at Lishan, Lermontov, the innocent-looking, melancholy-eyed Lermontov, the aristocratic Lermontov, and another aristocratic poet, Pushkin, curly-haired, askance and dandyish, whose life was cut short by love. *Stupid duels*, Lishan thought. The Chinese translation of their anthologies had largely enriched her after-school life. Patronizing the secondhand bookstore and probing shelves for valuable western literature and rare Chinese classics had become her hobby. Idling along the lanes walled by disfigured books, navigating in the forest and mountains reeking of the thirties or forties, she found the spring of her pleasure.

Leafing through Lermontov; a line jumped into her eyes:

> …
> Just like a beggar,
> Begging for your love.

With a heavy sigh, she jotted down the lines in her diary, not sure who she was lamenting for, Lermontov or Lishan. All the one-sided lovers were pitiable. She empathized greatly. The extremely intelligent Jianfei was simply dumb. *Can she catch a glimpse of my inner world which grows verdant with her sunshine and withers in her absence? Doesn't she know that without her, my life would be sailing without wind? Jianfei has insight into every heart except mine...she can't be so dense.* Yet the more Lishan reviewed her "Jianfei" lessons, the deeper Jianfei's apathy stung her.

Lishan's resentment germinated as high school started when she found herself tossed into a different class, torn apart from Jianfei. Surrounded by brand new names and strange faces, she felt stranded on a desolate isle infested with crocodiles and rattlesnakes that harbored in the shallow water, full of malice, and ready to hop out for a bite. The old happy days were like the wreckage of her ship, still visible and calling to her from a distance. With a sour jealousy, her eyes chased Jianfei and Huifang, in and out, shoulder to shoulder. Huifang, living in Jianfei's shadow like a bodyguard, seemed to have been instilled with her master's spirit and was always light-footed like a gust of spring breeze. Lishan wanted to grab Jianfei and own her as much as possible out of school but was aware that this all-evening-and-Sunday possession was beyond her reach. She also came to a sober realization that her desire was an obsession and this obsession was morbid but this morbidity was something she couldn't help. It had been embedded in her soul and was consuming her body every day. Prostrate in bed, her mind played back the childhood pictures, each with Jianfei's face: chattering, joking, gossiping, skipping.... With abhorrence, she reminisced how her seemingly naïve friendship had blazed into a bonfire of passion and how this friendship had metamorphosed from a beautiful butterfly into an ugly caterpillar with prickly skin and a wriggling body. Tossing and turning at night, she saw Jianfei floating like a piece of cloud. She woke up in a cold sweat. Going to school with a heavy heart, aching to see her face, to drink in her smile, but avoiding her as soon as she approached was a new pattern in their relationship. Lishan and Huifang had reversed positions. Lishan knew what she wanted: a whole Jianfei. It was this obsession that spurred Lishan to look deeply at herself and it was this newly discovered self-identity that shocked her and kept gnawing away at her heart. Once or twice she was overwhelmed by an urge to sniff the scent emitted from her youthful body by pressing it to her own, to fondle her cascading hair and kiss her oval-shaped rosy cheeks. This compulsion stunned her. Her eyes lingered on the two small buns in front of her until conscience signaled a warning and she averted them. She frequented the indoor pool to feast her eyes on the curves of her body. She let her fingers glide up and down Jianfei's naked back, tasting the creamy smoothness of her skin. She gulped down copious love stories and poems. Outwardly she maintained the friendship; inwardly she knew she was corroding it. The fact that she was infatuated with a girl and had absolutely no interest in boys filled her with terror. Boys repelled her. Though luckily she had never encountered one since middle school, the ones at home were enough to drain her endurance: boisterous, reckless, rowdy, crude, insensitive and worst of all, hostile to her. Growing up with a string of brothers, she could only picture herself to be one of them, sharing a boy's fantasy, interest and style. Her thoughts were preoccupied by the same sex since her early age. In a word, she was totally messed up, emotionally and physically.

A week ago, Sunday afternoon, Jianfei was washing clothes and her hands were covered with suds. She asked Lishan to take her handkerchief out of her chest pocket to be washed. Lishan's hand dug into her pocket and groped, and then, shockingly, lingered there longer than necessary. Pretending to tickle her, she let her finger flip over the warm and supple small lump and cupped it for a second. The circuit was connected in her body to allow a strong wave go through. She was stunned but felt quenched. Jianfei pushed her away, her face reddened with rage. Is this sin? She turned over and asked the tiger on the ceiling. Of course, the tiger seemed to wag its tail in the flickering light. Am I a pervert? No doubt, the tiger blinked. I must see her. What am I going there for? She felt she had been waiting for this moment since the day she was born. She was going to make a solemn declaration, to claim her new life, to reestablish her identity. A confession was on its way.

Pushkin in one hand and her diary in another, Lishan headed for Building Seven with a determined will. The moon displayed its roundness for the Moon Festival. The laurel was tinted with a dewy sheen. The air, charged with sweetness, seeped into Lishan's lungs. A teardrop stole out. *There is nothing to be ashamed of so long as the love is genuine.* Lishan dabbed it off.

Jianfei was reading. Lishan, sullen-faced, shuffled in.

"Tagore, 'Stray Bird'. My favorite poet. Meditative, philosophical, succinct and elegant."

Lishan closed Jianfei's book and opened her own.

"Look at mine."

A carefree Pushkin looked at Jianfei.

"Do you know who Pushkin's best friend was?"

Then Lishan answered herself.

"His childhood nanny."

"Interesting."

Jianfei was always a disciple of Lishan's knowledge.

"She was the first and the only listener to his…love stories."

To Lishan, "love" was a thorny word in Jianfei's presence. It pricked her tongue and it weighed a thousand tons. Lishan weight-lifted the word and tossed it in the air, then exhaled heavily.

A pause.

"Do you know who my nanny is?" Lishan asked, keeping her eyes on Pushkin.

"Who?"

"You."

Jianfei guffawed, "You? In love?"

She held her sides.

"I am more than willing to be your nanny. I am all ears. Go ahead!"

Jianfei's lightheartedness greatly irritated Lishan. She began to pace in the room, biting her lips. Her heart was a sail riding against the wind, swelling and bulging. But none of this registered in Jianfei's eyes.

"Come on," Jianfei narrowed her eyes.

Ferociously, Lishan's eyes drilled into Jianfei's marrow, sending down a chill.

"How do you like love poems?"

"I like Tagore," Jianfei said. "He brings you into the open field, the lingering clouds, and the glimmering stars. You smell the dewy grass blades, the vapory morning forest. You make dialogues with birds, with…"

"Are you listening to me? I am asking you how you like love poems! Answer me!"

Lishan's demanding and agitation, falling from nowhere, took Jianfei aback. She replied timidly, "Well, Tagore is very subtle; his love is insinuated."

"Then read this!" Lishan shuffled her diary forward.

"The Beggar," Jianfei read.

"Imagine the pain of the lover," Lishan said.

Jianfei went through the short poem word by word but failed to relate the beggar to anyone. Shrugging her shoulders, she returned the diary to Lishan.

"Well, maybe love is miserable."

"One-sided love is truly tragic."

Lishan's eyes were a pair of tiny flames, searing her friend. Just as fog gathered thicker in Jianfei's head, a tear welled up on Lishan, extinguishing the fire in her eyes

Out of the blue, the masculine Lishan was transfigured. Jianfei searched for words to comfort the heart-rending Lishan while grappling with Lishan's tear, probing the meaning of it.

"Come on. Tell me, I am your nanny."

Lishan shook her head.

"Who is this lucky guy?" Jianfei adopted a debonair tone.

Lishan shook her head. Embarrassment and smoldering rage turned to deep sadness; it was too hard to bring her heart to her tongue.

"Is there a boy?" Jianfei ferreted about.

"It's not a boy…" Lishan faltered, swallowing "but a girl." Eventually she sealed her lips, "no, I can't tell you today."

Steering her heels around, the iron-faced Lishan recovered herself and walked out.

Something is seriously wrong with both my friends, Jianfei reckoned the situation. Huifang's covert smile and Lishan's open tear indicated that childhood was left far behind and youth was in sight.

Chapter 8

Jianfei sat in her room and cocooned herself in a small collection of miscellaneous dog-eared books excavated from the second-hand bookstore where Lishan led her in a cruise of the ocean of authors disowned by society, chiefly for political reasons. Discolored and dust-bound, these books stood on the spider-infested corners draped in webs, waiting to be sifted out and taken home like orphans expecting to be adopted. A small volume of Tagore, *The Selected Poems of Ai Qing*, and a few other of her favorite poets littered her desk.

The poetry she loved inspired her to create a poem of her own: "To My Loved Poplar." To her, the poplar tree had become synonymous with Yang Bing. Yang— poplar tree. Whether he was in or out of sight, he was always there, engraved in her heart, persistently resurfacing from the jubilant night with the firecrackers' popping sound, from the silent movie projected from the opposite window, the oil paintings on the dinner table and the ridiculously unfair stamp trading to her favor. Her brother's stamp album was emblematic. The mini-Olympics was his souvenir. She was now knitting her own souvenir, line by line, with her signature, and someday it would be delivered to him and kept in his possession. Her first love poem was thus inspired by the secondhand books. A clandestine liaison was established between her and her love through her immature pen.

Tap, tap.

"Come in."

Jianfei was familiar with Xiaoshi's knock.

To her surprise, dad walked in, a bulging envelope in hand, on which Lishan's handwriting greeted her through his stumpy fingers. It was too late. Ai Qing, Tagore were laid bare in dad's eyes, and her own poem stood stark naked. She jumped up, blocking all the shady paper and suspicious books. Dad approached the desk, examining its content. Jianfei felt she'd been caught red-handed.

"You are an avaricious reader," dad said, browsing the books, "Pushkin, Lermontov, Tagore and…Ai Qing!! The celebrated rightist! Do you know what you are doing?"

"I didn't know he was a rightist," Jianfei mumbled.

So the secondhand bookstore is nothing but a dumpster!

Dad picked up a piece of paper and read, "To My Poplar?"

His voice rose, as did his brows.

Jianfei's cheeks were set ablaze; caterpillars began to crawl up and down her back. She snapped the paper back and concocted a story.

"I copied it from the magazine 'Poetry'."

Luckily dad dropped the topic.

Dad's fingers leafed through Tagore and read in a soft voice,

"Summer birds sing at my window and fly away.
Autumn yellow leaves have no songs; they fall with a sigh."

As if sipping scented tea, he licked his lips.

"Beautiful! Where there is beauty, there is a poem. And for Tagore, there is always philosophy. That's what fascinates me."

Holding Tagore, Dad was lost in his thoughts.

"I had poems published before the War. But do we dare to write like Tagore now? No. Beauty is no longer needed and literature is dangerous."

In a second, dad remembered himself.

"What I have just told you is strictly confidential. I have to protect my own daughter, do you understand?"

Jianfei was baffled. Her judgment teetered between the two dads, not knowing which to follow.

"I believe this is Lishan's handwriting."

Dad handed over the mail to Jianfei.

"What's enclosed? Is it necessary to waste a stamp? Odd!"

"This must be her report to the Youth League, the monthly ideological survey. The report needs to be revised. She is trying hard to get into the Youth League."

Jianfei put up a false defense for Lishan. She, too, felt odd. *What does Lishan the weirdo have up her sleeve?*

"And she could not walk two minutes and hand deliver it?" Dad frowned.

"She had too much pressure from trigonometry, Sine, Cosine…you know…"

"Trigonometry? What does that have to do with a two minute walk? Anyway, here it is."

The envelope held four pages, two parts: a letter and a poem.

Jianfei:

My intention is to clear my chest to you because my heart is brimming over with inexplicable feelings. A face-to-face confession would make our meeting unbearable. Writing will spare me the torment and embarrassment.

Yes, I am in love, but with a girl. That girl led me through darkness where I groped. She shielded me when I was under vicious attacks. She has constantly renewed our friendship and it is this friendship that continuously sheds light on my life.

This girl is you. You are the first in my life who, like a spring breeze, gently stirred up the ripple of love in my heart. I love you.

I know how this sounds to you: repulsive, abhorrent, despicable, abnormal, morbid, perverse…The motive of my confession is pure selfishness. I simply couldn't stand myself. I long for your presence yet I take another path when your steps draw near. Hankering and yearning versus avoiding and shunning; love one moment, resentment the next. Burning, chilling, the self-inflicted agony is crushing me. My grades are going downhill; my energy is drained. I am a parched blade of grass, a candle burning out.

No matter how sickening my love sounds, please
remember one thing: it is as serious as a boy's love.
I am at your disposal as I have always been.

Lishan

Jianfei pushed the window open, gasping to expel the stench in her
lungs. Though Lishan's diary filled with Jianfei's name had left a scratch
in her heart years ago, this sudden brazen confession thrown square in
her face as it was was totally unexpected. The confession was made in
such a stark shameless fashion. Lishan simply stripped herself bare. Black
and white, word by word, asserting a fact Jianfei had long suspected but
refused to admit. It forced Jianfei to review her friendship in retrospect,
to sieve out any iota that could have sparked Lishan's whimsical ideas and
led her astray.

Resisting the growing rancidness, her fingers picked out from the
envelope the second part. The poem began, "My love! My Nightingale!
My Serenade!"

Jianfei could never imagine that Lishan's passion for western literature
would carry her so far as to abandon totally Chinese analogies such as
the peony or phoenix and come to adopt fully the "nightingale" and
"serenade." *Am I reading Lishan or Pushkin?* Her eyes swam in "my light",
"my sunshine" and "red roses", roaming along the aisles of "your laughter is
the jingle bell" and "your eyes are the twinkling stars". The poem consisted
of twelve stanzas, each concluded with "my love" with an exclamation
mark slapping Jianfei's face. Jianfei didn't know who should feel ashamed.
Being someone's sunshine, star and light was so unreal! Jianfei saw herself
lying in a web, wings fluttering. *What a mess! Involved in such madness!
Stranded in a ridiculous predicament! Stuck between a girlhood friendship
and an indescribable, unspeakable, ignominious romance! Forced to be
somebody's secret lover!* And this was Lishan, who had shown no trace of
affection towards any human being, whose cold and indifferent carriage
and stone heart had quickly won her notoriety among her new classmates
none of whom befriended her. Sickness, mental sickness, Jianfei diagnosed
Lishan's symptoms and finally found a name for it: lunacy. The poem,
despite its perverseness, displayed a seamless imitation of a western literary

style. It could easily pass for a translation of Pushkin and this added fuel to Jianfei's rage. All of a sudden, Pushkin was found guilty of murder of an innocent child.

As if seeking a blood transfusion, Jianfei opened her own poem, a poem from a girl to a boy. Laying the two poems side by side, Jianfei's indignation thickened. *How dare Lishan compare her love to a boy's? To twist the definition of love! To confound the sick with the healthy, the decadent with the fresh, the despondent with the cheerful!* She started to revise her poem and then copied it down to a hardcover notebook where she collected all her childhood writings, which made her blush sometimes, like an adult looking at his naked infant pictures.

To My Poplar
(Dedicated to Yang Bing)

You are a young poplar,
Your verdant leaves,
Tinge my shoulder,
And I grow green.

Though inches away,
We are separated by miles,
You merge in the morning haze,
And in my heart you smile.

You entered my dream in fall,
And in winter we said farewell,
You gave to me your all,
For words that failed to tell.

I want to be a bird,
Hopping in your hair,
When breezes start to stir,
Together we drink the dewy air.

I want to be a little lamb,
Leaning against your trunk,

Like a shepherd's hand,
You stroke me in the twilight of dusk.

I want to be a cicada happy go lucky,
Smiling at the sun so bright,
Cuddling in your arms so cozy,
Chiming with a heart so light.

I want to be a butterfly,
To your chest I cling,
With wind howling high,
Your leaves cocoon me in.

The childish poem was a reflection of the poplar tree outside her window, the Yang Tree, rustling and soaring against the starry night. In the three years of his absence, the tree stood, filling her sweet reminiscences. Young and healthy, straight and upright, the tree established a firm image of human integrity. In the frosty, icy winter mornings, in the lethargic, sultry summer afternoons, the tree and Yang Bing merged into one, an invariable warm presence in her life.

From dad, she knew Yang Bing's father had been promoted to Vice President. The Yangs resided in a more exclusive area. Though out of sight, Yang Bing was omnipresent.

They were not seeing each other, yet they saw each other everywhere. Their occasional glimpses and chance encounters only served to increase the attraction.

Every day during rush hour her eyes skimmed the moving human ocean and scoured the flying bicycle stream for that one in particular. Once or twice, from his bike, he turned back to meet her eyes and she asked herself, "Is he looking for me or someone else?" The thought that he might be doing the same traffic survey thrilled her and set her face aglow the whole day.

In summer the blue indoor swimming pool where children swarmed provided Jianfei ample opportunity to fill her heart. Reclining on the wicker chair beside the pool, she allowed Lishan's fingers to flip and stroke, playing her naked back as if on a piano keyboard, hoping they were his. A sway of her silky hair brought her eyes to the boys' direction and she was always rewarded by Yang Bing's timely glimpses.

For his part, he didn't understand why he would sit on the tiled floor, making young spectators wait until she emerged and only then did he execute an elaborate dive from the springboard in the public eyes. Nor did he understand why his voice would rise whenever her blue swimming suit popped out from the medley of other colors, nor why her pattering feet sounded louder and her smiles shone brighter than others'. His eyes outlined her curves, but shied away at the buds in her front.

At the movie theatre, as long ago, Jianfei would loiter in the lobby. And Yang Bing was still one of the stragglers delayed by his never-hasty family. Then in the dark, her eyes alternated between the screen and the silhouette of the Yang family.

However above all these chance encounters, one stood out more vividly. They were both in the Youth League delegation at the conference room of the municipal government. She sat in the back watching him. His female schoolmates approached him, smiling, chattering. For the first time a new feeling visited her heart. In Jianfei's mind, he was living in a sexless vacuumed space; no girls had ever existed. The unfamiliar sour, bitter taste alarmed her.

They never exchanged a word again but the few words they had between them kindled the best memories when she was sick in bed and he was lighting the Spring Festival fireworks. Time and again, she reviewed and recited them like an old lesson, the words engraved in her heart. They were like a mysterious brook, murmuring, echoing from a remote mountain, lush and vital with forests and wild flowers.

Chapter 9

Huifang's self-protective instinct told her to say "no" to the first tryst in her life. Tang Wei, however, challenged and tested her determination with perseverant greetings and persistent smiles until Huifang's resolution began to thaw. A month later, a second note was dropped at her foot.

> I need to talk to you. It is urgent.
> The same place, same time.

She was more than eager to accept the date this time. As a matter of fact, she had grown fidgety as days passed without any trace of a disappointed reaction from the boy. If no further contact came from him, she would take the initiative herself to make up for the missed opportunity, despite her female pride.

The scented season again. Laurel was everywhere, permeating the air. Secluded between a shaded river bank and the red brick wall topped with barbed wire, was a path. The river severed the Academy from its neighboring villages, and the parallel path doubled the segregation. The path started from the guarded gate and extended to the bank of the narrow river where the wall ended at the edge of the water. The barracks of the guard platoon was in its immediate enclosure. In the morning, the path served as a drilling ground, bustling with thumping steps, exuberant with heroic spirits, and resounding with the syncopated cadences of patriotic songs and slogans. After the day started, it was usually abandoned and left in the hands of the guards. The post here seemed to guard against any enemy who dared to swim across the river, one meter in depth, five meters in width, to sabotage our national defense. The river was a tributary of the Yangtze. Meandering through the hazy city, it carried away sewage, falling leaves, papers and rags, like a mother tending to her pampered child. A mile of the walled academy had little waste to contribute; therefore the river water gradually cleared as it entered a more or less placid section. Where the wall met the river and the path ended, the river bank curved southward leading to the side gate which was out of sight from the path. On the opposite bank, a stretch of green meadow patched with various wild flowers in yellow and white merged with the Purple-Gold Mountain, presenting an idyllic scene to the eyes of the cadets who, except for the morning drills, seldom visited this backyard path.

Tang Wei could not afford a meeting place too far away, nor could he picture himself meeting a pretty girl in a dingy lane, a stinking market or a restaurant reeking of garlic. The library? A movie theater? No. Why waste time sitting absent mindedly waiting for the movie to end? Or pretending to show some interest in a book? Also, there was too much danger in public; familiar faces were everywhere. Romantic and private were the criteria that Tang Wei demanded in a meeting place, but above all, secure. He was looking for a spot hidden from public eyes, isolated and secluded, within no more than a ten minutes' walk, because every second of his absence from the barracks was risky. No furtive manners. No hangdog looks. The escalation path for a breach of discipline was well known: "Warning within the Party," "Serious Warning," "Record of Demerit," and "Expulsion from the Party." For a soldier, it went from confinement to discharge. This was serious business as any perceived infractions could mean the end of his career.

He decided the safest location would be right under the nose of the enemy. For days, he had racked his brains on how to sneak out under the vigilant eyes of his comrades-in-arms at the gate. The challenge was that he and she must not be spotted by the same guard. They had to elude the same eyes and one should pass during the afternoon shift, and one after dark. Since the sentinels switched posts at four in the afternoon and the earliest hour that darkness could cover the secret lovers was about seven, Tang Wei needed to fabricate something to bridge the three hour gap. It was a touching serve-the-people story that he made up: a high school student needed him as a tutor. He asked Huifang to bring along a math or physics or chemistry, whatever textbook, just in case.

The day they had been craning their necks looking forward to was finally here. Returning from his night shift on Sunday morning, Tang Wei lay down. Huifang's face kept shining through the curtains of his eyelids; her elastic body bouncing around; her bewitching eyes teasing him. He touched her silky, cascading hair, fondled her supple palms, somehow imagining her soft knuckles joined with lovely dimples like the ones on her smiling cheeks. At the lunch whistle, he hopped up, glad that the morning was over and he was halfway on his long journey to that ecstatic moment. He shoveled down some lumpy gunk, gulped down some slippery thing, not sure whether they were cornmeal buns or lily flower soup. And then he lay down for another pseudo-slumber till three o'clock.

The sun, fatigued from its long hours of combustion, narrowed its blazing eyes, and reclined on top of the buildings. Tang Wei was on his way, canvas stool in his left hand, Chairman Mao's Volume IV in the right. Tang Wei approached the gate.

"Hi, little fatty!"

Little Fatty, He Guangfu, Recovering the Light, another Shanghai soldier from a worker's family, eased Tang Wei's fidgeting. His chubby, rosy cheeks with their naïve smile loosened his nerves.

"Hello, Tang Wei. Where to?"

The baby face lit up with an ear-to-ear grin.

"Trying to find a quiet place to finish my monthly performance review, and then go to the village to tutor a student."

"Serving the people! I should learn from you!"

Little Fatty was generous with his smile.

"I bet I'll have to burn the midnight oil to complete my monthly survey for tomorrow's seminar," the chubby guard added

Little Fatty's eyes sent a farewell to Tang Wei, watching him entering the thicket a hundred meters away where he was swallowed by willows and maples while Little Fatty's mind began to sketch his own summary.

The dying sun projected three long shadows on the pavement that gradually entered the vision of the sharp-eyed guard, Xiao Ming, Xiao the Bright. He was a slim young man. The narrow shoulders and narrow body resembled a coat rack.

"Please sign out in the book," with stiff courtesy, Guard Xiao requested.

The girls stopped short at this unexpected intervention. Leaving a record would do Huifang no good. Huifang turned to Jianfei, who tossed over the rescue signal to the brave Lishan.

Lishan said diplomatically, "Yes, we will. But may I ask why, since this was never required before?"

"To make sure of your safe return, because of the river," Xiao replied in the same dry, professional voice.

The girls turned their faces to the river, shallow to their shanks. But Xiao Ming obviously meant what he said.

"We are big girls, not kids. And I don't see how the river could possibly inflict any harm on anyone." Lishan began to show her teeth.

Xiao Ming made no reply; he only shifted the weight on his feet.

"Look," Jianfei stepped forward, "we just want to take a walk and will return at a different gate. It will complicate the situation if we sign out without signing in. We would appreciate if you could override this unnecessary formality since this is only your personal concern and not a strict rule. We have in deed never been asked to sign out before."

"If you insist, I will turn back right now and bring the matter to my father's attention…" Lishan faked a VIP air.

Just as she was about to veer around, the hesitating guard opened his mouth, "All right, but please be careful."

The girls rewarded him with three blossoming faces and disappeared at the end of the path. As planned, Jianfei and Lishan continued on the curved bank that led to the side gate where they entered and headed home while Huifang started to count the willows.

Chapter 10

Seeing the three girls descending the slope, Tang Wei realized that even Huifang had sensed the danger. She was smart enough to bring along two accomplices to remove any possible suspicions that might be cast by a single, pretty girl walking alone along a desolate road. After all, she was not as carefree and happy-go-lucky as she appeared and her friends were indeed friends in need. By averting any questions that might be raised by leaving at dark, Huifang had gained two precious hours. It was only five o'clock. This thrilled Tang Wei.

Sparrows hopped around, their heads knocking incessantly on the ground, pecking out meager leavings from the mid-fall soil. A caterpillar dangled from the willow leaves and was gently rocked by the warm breeze. In its ecstatic swinging, the ill-fated worm was intercepted mid-air. Birds flocked together to help rend the delicacy into pieces. In the depths of the grove, an unknown flying object cracked a mirthful song, in concert with the gurgling water. A lonely cicada hidden somewhere in the dappled sunny treetops screeched a feeble dirge, bidding farewell to its lover, summer, eulogizing her glory and mourning his short lived friends who had screamed away the sizzling days.

Under the second willow, camouflaged by the lively green was the dull green of Tang Wei's uniform. Huifang walked over. Tang Wei sprang to his feet.

"You are... two hours... earlier," he stuttered.

The most important part "thank you" was forgotten. Not knowing how to continue, Tang Wei rolled up Mao's book and then unfolded it, rolled it up again.

"You are even earlier," Huifang upheld her female pride, "actually I plan to do some homework first."

She waved her geometry book.

"Me, too."

They both sat down. Words failed. Books won.

Stupid! Is this how you reward your painstaking arrangement of the meeting? Tang Wei cursed loudly in his head.

After one minute of feigned reading, Tang Wei laid down Chairman Mao on his stool.

"Shall we take a walk? Let's skip rocks."

The eager Huifang jumped to her feet throwing away the geometry.

Tang Wei collected flat and thin pebbles and said to Huifang, "Open your hands."

Huifang stretched out her fingers, fine and slender; Tang Wei's eyes fell on them, feeling an urge to touch them.

"Hold these for me. Now watch."

Bending over, he leveled out his arm and shot the pebble. The pebble skimmed over the surface of the water, bouncing, swirling, and swishing in the air. A string of circles blossomed on the placid sheet.

"Wow! Seven!"

Huifang clapped her hands. She picked up a piece and made a careful throw. The pebble sank like a plumb bob.

"It's unfair. Can you show me the trick?" she pouted.

Hands-on instruction was what Tang Wei planned; the student's suggestion met his expectation and made him tingle. With furtive excitement, he moved behind her, positioning himself close to her back. He brought his arm to join hers, leveled it at the surface.

"Now try. Rapidly and forcefully like whipping."

The flat piece scratched the surface and leapt three times.

"Bravo!" They both cheered.

The slight brush with her body made him taut. He tried again. She tried again. Their laughter echoed on the surface as the pebbles rippled along the river.

The mournful cicada gradually quieted its voice until its song completely died down. The birds, startled at the rapid enclosure of darkness, fanned their wings home and rested in the armpits of the trees, dreaming of tomorrow's caterpillar feast. The azure canopy drew low above their heads; the mountain and the river were getting blurrier. They sat down.

"You said you had important things to tell me."

Huifang cocked her head.

"Well, nothing in particular," Tang Wei confessed with rosy cheeks, "I just want to spend time with you, to have fun. It's stifling within the walls."

Tang Wei withheld his admission of love like a child denying himself a candy. The longer, the sweeter.

"I am from a poor worker's family, my mom raised me single-handedly."

His summary of himself followed the normal course, starting with his class stratum. Then his description became more detailed, his childhood and his grandma, the little cottage in the spring field, his mom, her textile factory and their one-room home, his high school, his dreams and his disillusionments. Huifang followed the pattern he had set, presenting her parents and friends to Tang Wei.

A bell rang in the distance from the temple. It rippled down the mountain and across the river, announcing the nightfall. The colors of the day became monochrome. Taps were at ten and Sunday's wrap-up at nine. The platoon assembly in the guards' dormitory was on its way.

Tang Wei gathered his stuff for a safe return.

"I'll take the south gate home. Don't worry." Huifang said, "By the way, the guard, the thin fellow, gave us a hard time today. He asked us to sign out which we never had to do before."

"That's Xiao Ming. He meant no harm." Tang Wei said.

He looked at her in the eye, full of gratitude. "May I see you again?" tentatively.

"Of course, next Sunday?"

"No, too soon." After a calculated discussion, they both figured out that the safest interval would be a month.

"Remember, the second Sunday of each month… Now we have to rush," Tang Wei said.

They stood up, face to face, breathing each other's breath. Four weeks! Four weeks meant a void in their life, a hole in their hearts. That meant thirty days, seven hundred and forty-four hours. That meant tossing and turning in bed, absent minds on duty and in the classroom, hungry eyes, scant appetites. Time would tick along. So would their hearts, one second, two…*Time, you enemy! You drag along in lovers' separation yet fly away in our union.* The tiny-footed, steady-moving time whose seconds they treasured a minute ago suddenly became their curse.

Tang Wei held out his hand, subconsciously two, for a handshake, "Till next time."

Confused with the two hands, Huifang accepted one, murmuring, "Till next time."

Chapter 11

The road was dimly lit. For four hours, Xiao Ming's eyes patrolled from his feet to the end of the wall, a total distance of one hundred meters, and then to the river and its banks. After two hours, as usual, his taut nerves slackened and his eyes no longer strained. He was tired of looking at nothing.

At around eight forty five, something emerged from nothingness, a shadow, an enemy. Xiao Ming tightened his grip on the rifle. His vigilance returned. As the shadow approached the gate, however, Xiao Ming relaxed again. The shadow was a package of three: a single body; a stool hanging on one side and a thick book swaying in and out of the street lamp, flitting between red, white and black. The enemy turned out to be none other than one of their own.

"Tang Wei! Squad leader! It's you! You are in my firing range!" Xiao Ming slung his rifle back, "What the devil are you doing in the bushes? I was about to record this on the log book as an unusual event on my shift."

"Relax, buddy," Xiao Ming got on his nerves. Tang Wei would never have addressed him as "buddy" if not for this imminent danger. "Don't make a mountain out of a molehill."

Tang Wei decided to socialize a bit. He produced a brand new cigarette box which he had prepared as a precautionary measure for an occasion like this.

"Cigarette?" he put it under his buddy's nose.

Xiao Ming shook his head, but changed his mind. He took one and plugged it into his chest pocket.

"The monthly summary is really brain racking." Tang Wei said with a deep sigh. "It took me three solid hours and I had to cut my tutoring short."

"With twelve years of schooling, you have more to contribute to the people," Xiao Ming said with earnest envy. "I dropped out in the third grade, too poor to finish my primary school. My old man needed hands in the field..."

"See you inside," Tang Wei cut Xiao Ming short and started to run. In one minute, Tang Wei was in line marching to the assembly.

Huifang's light fingers turned the doorknob, whose unexpected jarring click exploded into the apartment, triggering havoc.

"Where on earth have you been?" mom rushed out.

Turning a deaf ear, Huifang strode across the living room and darted straight to her own, her muddy footprints blossoming on the glassy floor.

"Good gracious! The floor was just waxed," mom knelt down and rubbed vigorously, in an attempt to recover the lost mirror, "You've made my three-hour labor fruitless!"

"Hold it right there, Miss!" dad barked from his study, "Stop abusing your residential rights in my house! Sit down and let us hear your story! Leaving at three thirty, back at nine thirty. Flying away like a butterfly, sneaking back in like a mouse."

"And you, leave the evidence!" he ordered his wife.

Huifang held her advance and mom's hands withdrew.

Seeing her husband in a rage, mom gave up on the floor and tiptoed over.

In a whisper, "Go to the kitchen. Dinner is on the stove."

"I am not hungry."

Huifang looked down. From her feet, spread a sheet printed with large yellow flowers on which her two heels, doubling their weights, carried two cakes of matted mud and green grass. In her haste, she must have stepped in a puddle. Now her crime was made palpable by these flowers.

Dad pulled up a chair and sank into it while he motioned his daughter beside him, "I am all ears for your explanation of how your shoes came to be pasted with this country road muck. All the Academy roads are decently paved. Are you going to tell us where you did your geometry?"

"I was with Jianfei and Lishan," Huifang's alibi was ironclad.

Dad showed no interest in checking her alibi. An invisible smile flipped over his face. He had no doubt that his daughter was caught red-handed. Gloating over the besmirched floor, dad's howling tuned down to sneering: "Leaving at three thirty for a movie which started at seven thirty? Or to the coop buying nougats yet coming back empty-handed? Or maybe to the studio to have your photo taken without bothering to brush your messy hair? How about to the library without borrowing a book? Or the swimming pool, returning home dry-haired? Which one?! Tell us now!!"

Dad shot an assured victorious glance at his daughter's shoes.

Unexpectedly, his volley of questions bounced back with a guiltless reply, "None of them. We took a walk along the river. That's all."

Huifang was unruffled. Her equilibrium shook her dad's ego.

"Very good then! I would like to have a serious talk with Jianfei to dig to the bottom of this six-hour walk."

Dad's confidence fizzled out. His victory was short lived. Huifang knew her dad only too well; he would do anything to shun the communists, even their children. When reaching a dead end, dad's retort, needed to save his face, was an empty threat.

Lying in bed, Huifang spoke to Tang Wei and Tang Wei smiled back. They played with the pebbles again. Layers of rings radiated from the skipping stone, creased the surface, and kindled the river. Her skin relived the tremor from his brush and touch, cautious or casual, still prickling and tantalizing. Like a warm liquid, the feeling permeated and finally flooded her whole body. *I'll bring my photo album next time… save some Sunday specialties from the lunch table for him…buy some milk candies…* Meanwhile she launched a battle against TIME, its unhurried ticking. She needed to kill each of these seven hundred and forty four ticks. Suddenly an idea struck her and it made the battle seem easier to win. *I can write to him every day and simply drop a note at his foot as he did to me. After all, the long, dreadful waiting does not have to be so excruciating as long as he is there in my eyes and I am able to pass him once a day, even if just for several seconds.*

The next morning at six thirty, Huifang left the house, a book in hand, a letter inserted in.

"I am going outside to memorize English vocabulary," she made an announcement this time, fearing dad might make a fuss again.

Her plan was to pass Tang Wei's post, deliver the letter and then return for breakfast. Not a soul was at the gate in the early hour, Tang Wei's red star and green uniform was a sweet reminder of yesterday. A small square of folded paper was flipped at her foot before she had the opportunity to drop hers. With her eyes rolling around, Huifang quickly bent over and pinched the square into her fist.

Outside the gate, oriental plane trees stood in a line like another platoon of guards, leaves rustling in the rising sun. Huifang took a left turn and wedged herself close to the gate between the wall and the soaring trees. She unfolded the square and read: "Please use a different gate next time." Her throat tightened. Her heart jumped to her mouth.

With her back pasted to the wall, Huifang raised her head and threw a question in the air, "Anything happen?"

From the other side resounded Tang Wei's voice, "No."

"Can we meet sooner?" her back asked again

"No!" firm as steel.

Huifang stepped out and returned. She flipped her own letter to the ground. It gave a lengthy account of how her parents interrogated her and about her harrowing, sleepless night.

At seven forty, she passed Tang Wei the second time. A second note fell at her foot which read, "Please don't drop any piece at my post. This is no place to play games unless it is extremely urgent."

Searching Tang Wei's face, she found no trace of affection, nor resentment. Fatigue and wariness were written on the cover of a book whose theme was love twelve hours ago.

How could you change so overnight? Don't you miss me? Huifang asked with her eyes.

Yes, Tang Wei's eyes replied, *of course I do.*

If only Huifang could read Tang Wei's mind!

Chapter 12

As Huifang merged her steps with those of the morning rush hour traffic, Tang Wei began to play back the Sunday night assembly.

The soldiers were housed in a large bungalow which contained several large bedrooms, one small bedroom for the Political Instructor, a multi-purpose long room with chairs and a table which served as a classroom during the daytime, an assembly hall in the evening, a ping pong room on the weekends, an exhibition hall, a theatre and in other miscellaneous functions when called for by their daily education. It was also an art gallery. Hanging on the walls were soldiers' drawings displaying their education: U.S. imperialists were nothing but paper tigers; the People's Communes were the sun, their members sunflowers; Mao Tsetung's thoughts were a beacon of light, illuminating the chartless voyage for the world revolution; the Communist Party was our mother, etc.…

At the assembly, three squads sat in lines on canvas stools. The second squad leader stood up in the front of one of the lines. He lifted his arms to his chest.

"Comrades, let's sing a song. 'Without the Communist Party, Without New China.' One, two, three!"

He tuned his voice and chose one note and then spat that note to his soldiers, uniting the voices. The jaws sitting beneath him opened. As his arms started paddling rhythmically, fourteen mouths worked in an assured unison. The resonance produced from these twenty-eight lobes of lungs lit the political instructor Li Yi's face with a simultaneous smile. The platoon leader Weiguo responded with a nod and narrowing eyes. The majestic voices prompted Squad One and Three to challenge each other.

The first song had hardly come to a full stop before the first squad leader, Tang Wei, rose to his feet, stretching his arms and throwing them at his neighbors.

"Squad One, did Squad Two sing well?"

"They did!" Applause exploded.

"Do we want a song from Squad Three?"

"We do!"

Peals of thunder cracked from all corners. The air was charged with the boundless energy of youth. The third squad leader, eager to make a show of his own team, sprang up, crossed his arms in front and began to roll.

"One, two, three; three, two, one. We the revolutionary soldiers are going to sing a song."

The short and stout third squad leader wasted no time to continue with the Revolutionary Song Relay in his sexy, hoarse voice, "My sword swung over the enemy's head!"

His soldiers bellowed and their chests heaved, earnest pride and glory decorating their red cheeks. Their song had shorter lines and the beats were faster. The cadence was a perfect match for their virility and valor.

"Wipe them out, wipe them out, wipe them out! Kill!"

In their heads, they saw their swords hacking up their enemies in unison, chopping off Japanese heads and mowing down their bodies. Their sabers whistled in the air as their song soared onwards.

Tang Wei hurried to his feet as it was his squad's turn to perform. He began to row his arms as forcefully as his predecessors.

"I sling my rifle…start!"

When Squad One finished their song, the platoon leader ascended the stage and erected his fingers against his palm, bringing an abrupt end to the competition among the three squads. Recreational activities were brief but had largely boosted the morale.

Silence reigned. The agenda was announced: first, appraisal of "good people and good deeds"; secondly, self-evaluation of the weekly performance; lastly, a survey by the political instructor.

Good people good deeds. Starting from squad one. Arms raised, soldiers enumerated, "Zhang Linyu helped cooking in the kitchen…"

"Sima gave his fellow comrades free haircuts…"

"Our deputy squad leader washed all our dirty shoes…"

Li Yi sat in front jotting down summarized meeting notes into his hard cover red notebook. Mao Tsetung's gold profile was etched on its front. The soldiers seemed to have quickened their pace to revolutionize themselves. This week's list exceeded last week's.

"I think what our squad leader Tang Wei did deserves the highest merits."

Little Fatty stood up, seizing the opportunity to repudiate the fallacy largely held by his comrades-in-arms that Shanghai soldiers were too rotten to be tempered into the hard steel of revolution.

"He devoted almost the whole afternoon and evening studiously studying Chairman Mao's works, holding it as a mirror to reflect his own behavior. He even chose a secluded place so that he could concentrate and write undisturbed. He also volunteered to help a poor peasant's child with his school work."

Little Fatty bragged on. Li Yi's pen raced with his mouth. Tang Wei was on pins and needles. *What a pain-in-the-ass his hometown brother is! That stupid, chubby face, his feverish cheeks, his peanut-sized brain, his well-intended betrayal!*

The speakers prattled on. To Tang Wei, their voices were as faint as mosquitoes. His head spun. His body hummed with fury at himself: *how could you be so muddle-headed as to choose your own gate for passing? In order to save time? For convenience? Now see what convenience has brought you?* He felt his nose becoming itchy. It began to grow like Pinocchio's. His thoughts swam randomly and then came to an abrupt stop at Xiao Ming. He quickly checked every detail of his brief encounter with him. *What will come out of Xiao's mouth? How far can a cigarette carry him?* Suddenly his name drifted to his ears from the ping-pong table.

"Comrades, Chairman Mao teaches us: 'The theoretical basis guiding our thinking is Marxism-Leninism'. I agree. What the first squad leader Tang Wei did is of the utmost importance. We can do hundreds of good things but remain blind. Our deeds carry far-reaching significance only if we know why we do them and that 'why' is hidden in this book!" Li Yi waved Mao's Volume IV high in the air and let it shine there for two seconds as if posing for a photo shooting. "I call on the whole platoon to learn from comrade Tang Wei. Let's bring our study campaign to high tide!"

Chapter 13

Lishan's diary lay open on Jianfei's desk. A slip of paper next to it read,

I beg you to read it. Words fail me whenever I see you. Shame, pain, fury, jealousy and passion consume me, burning inside me and nibbling at my heart. Please read it.

The epitome of swine. Jianfei put it down. Taking a deep breath, she was totally sickened. Leaning back against the wall, she watched a moth drawn to the lamp fluttering its wings which grew less functional closing to the light. It dropped to the night stand, blinded, gasping, flapping, and finally lay motionless. A sacrifice for the light, Jianfei touched the dead moth with the tip of her pen, tossed it into Lishan's empty pages and left a footnote, "This moth gave its life for the course of love."

The cruel humor poked a hole in the thickness of the atmosphere in her room, allowing Jianfei to breathe a bit more easily and brave the sordidness facing her. Jianfei reopened the brown cover and leafed back to the beginning to analyze how such a deformed seed could have germinated. The first few pages were already laden with her own name, showing the lonely agonizer on a hopeless journey into a dark night. She forced her eyes to travel down the pages.

December 2, 1957

Jianfei was sick today. There was a big hole in class. She is the spring of my happiness. I sail in her wind and moor in her haven. I suddenly realized how hollow the names around me sounded and how bleak their faces looked!

What do I need the world for if she is not in it! I blame Jianfei for all my miseries: tasteless food and impatient eyes. I counted every minute waiting for the bell to ring. Recess was again another torture. No one came to me and I talked to nobody. Time and again, I heard her footsteps and I turned to see an alien face. I hate Xiaonan whose back bears too much of a resemblance to Jianfei and I hate Wu Feng who bears no resemblance at all. I abhor Wang Gui's pathetic, trembling voice, calling out "stand up" with her ugly accent; I long for Jianfei's standard mandarin and self-assuredness calling to welcome the teacher.

December 15, 1957

I went to see Jianfei. She is an angel. Fever has colored her face. Her cheeks were peach blossoms; her lips were cherries and brows like painted black willow leaves. I excused myself and edged along her bed sitting next to her pillow. Our relationship has never achieved such intimacy and my body still shudders to think of it. I was appalled at my impulse to touch her. I debated whether I should kiss her good night and was glad I did. The sweet tenderness lingered on my lips; her scent accompanied me home and swept me into dreamland. My lips brushed her forehead! I felt we were one. She was part of me. Under the starlit vault, for the first time, I realized that my life could also be beautiful, as beautiful as my paintings, so long as I have my angel Jianfei near me.

December 26, 1957

Today is Chairman Mao's birthday. To me, however, it is a memorial day. Ms. Guan was taken away in handcuffs, in front of all her students. Jianfei watched me with secret concern. My enemies stole glances from all corners, finding relish in my grief.

Thanks to my dear friend Jianfei, I'll keep painting, the only way to commemorate Ms. Guan.

December 28, 1957

Look at our so-called "Communist Youths"! What crooked minds and twisted visions! They stirred up rumors and slandered my dear friend. My heart writhed in pain to see Jianfei's name abused on the board. They attacked me with their big character posters months ago, and now this. A bunch of mindless fanatics with low IQ's, lazy in class, but hurtling themselves into politics! I swear I'll do everything to protect Jianfei as she did three months ago for me. These Youth League members are malignant tumors of our society. I am not favored by the League, but at least my conscience is clear. I would never be so base as to vilify my classmate by lying. I draw a clear line between right and wrong, and will never confound white with black.

December 29, 1957

Contemplating the suitcase incident, I can't help but compare our Youth League with the Russian Youth League member Pavel. Like many of my contemporaries, I love *Gadfly* and *How the Steel is Tempered*. Sometimes I feel I am instilled with the spirit of a man and that I am guided by a masculine will. Pavel and Arthur have helped to shape my personality: masculine with a streak of tragedy. I envision an ideal human in mind when I think of them and I try to step into their footprints. Even their gallantry and daring style is my fashion. Such a driven man deserves a female match and my match is Jianfei who in my mind's eye alternates between Tonia and Gemma.

April 18, 1959

"Three Red Banners": the Great Leap Forward, the People's Communes and the General Line.

My motherland is turning into a waste land; our sports ground has become a dumping ground. Bricks littered, scrapes of iron piled up in all descriptions, pots and pans, scissors and knives. Newly-tempered steel like cheap jewelry displayed in the center.

Fanatic. However, Jianfei herself was a fervent participant in destroying her favorite place where she had won the championship in the one-hundred-meter dash and high jump. My heart led me to follow her, but I am not a blind follower.

Who is insane? I or Mao? I know this is called "counterrevolutionary" …better not to think about this.

During recess, Jianfei harshly criticized me for skipping last Sunday's rally to celebrate the newly smelted iron. I didn't feel like doing it, plus Sunday afternoon is my scheduled painting session. In my heart, she is my muse, a replacement for Ms. Guan. It is painful to see Jianfei getting involved, deeper and deeper, into those propaganda activities. The gap between me and my dearest Jianfei worries me.

October 11, 1960

God intervened. Huifang has found a boy. That soldier will eternally occupy her heart and Jianfei will be returned to me. Helping Huifang stow away was to help myself.

The People's Liberation Army is liberating Huifang. Long live the PLA!

Jianfei could no longer play dumb. For weeks, she had covered the morbid relationship with an innocent façade. The poem, the letter, now the diary had repeatedly proved that Lishan's love was saturnine poison. The shred of regret that lingered after she pinched the dead moth into Lishan's diary with that poignant remark was completely blown away. The moth was a vivid, woeful image of a pathetic love, flying into the light, fatally seared. She had no remorse for the prank. However she had no intention to see a friendship die, a friendship sprouted in their childhood. In her heart, she had long vowed her allegiance. Lishan's family was within easy reach and the two dads worked closely. Besides, Lishan, introspective and sensitive as she was, could be easily traumatized by any rejection, even in a very oblique and suggestive way.

The matter had to be handled with extreme caution, no rebuff, no encouragement, keep the surface calm. Let the friendship flow its natural course. A river can turn turbulent and treacherous but eventually will calm down and enter a placid section. Deal with the changes with consistency, this was Jianfei's principle.

Chapter 14

Winter passed unnoticed like a plain girl. Spring, beautiful and lively, passed as well. When summer arrived, people shielded themselves indoors. The scorching sun monopolized the outside world. By late June, days were already sweltering. The unremitting sun's rays poured down, baking the earth, parching the grass blades which gasped for relief. Trees vibrated with the hysterical shrieks of the cicadas. Even in the shade, the slate steamed. In the street, melted asphalt matted to pedestrians' soles. The invisible vapor of heat quivered over the roads, making the city appear a desert mirage. Too hot!

On a sultry Sunday afternoon, lethargy dominated the city. The Academy, too, wallowed in drowsiness. Jianfei was toiling over her trigonometry. Beads of perspiration dripped onto the paper. The final exam was imminent. A bamboo mat was spread on the floor. From time to time Jianfei rolled over the mat's sleek and cool slats to dry her wet body. Too hot to keep her shirt on, she was in a sleeveless silk vest.

Tap, tap.

"Who is it?" grabbing her blouse hanging on the chair, Jianfei asked.

"It's me, Lishan."

"Come in," Jianfei flung back her blouse and lay down on the mat, "Sit here, the chair is like a heating pad," Jianfei patted on the mat and Lishan slumped beside her.

"It is stifling," said Lishan. She began to unbutton her shirt and fan herself frantically with her English book.

"Open the curtain if you like," Jianfei shook her goose-feather fan. Tossing a palm-leaf fan to Lishan, she said, "I don't want to be seen dressed like this."

"Well, then keep the curtain drawn."

Lishan lay down beside Jianfei. Jianfei rose up and hopped back to her desk.

Sweat trickled down. The three-minute walk made Lishan perspire profusely. Her cheeks were ablaze. Lying still on the mat, she covered her face with the fan, pretending to doze off. Jianfei sat at the table, engrossed in her equation, her pen rustling on the paper. For a minute, no one uttered a sound.

Twenty minutes elapsed. Jianfei continued grappling with her sines and cosines and Lishan continued with her sham slumber.

"I want to show you something," Lishan mumbled under the palm leave.

"What is it?" without moving her eyes.

"Lock the door first," her voice muffled through the fan.

"What is it?" without raising her head.

"I won't show you with the door unlocked."

Jianfei shuffled in her slippers to the door. The spring lock clicked. Jianfei veered back. What met her eyes next was an appalling picture which made her cheeks burn for decades.

Lishan was sitting up. Her blouse was tossed aside. A bra was the only thing she had on above the waist. The bra cupped her breasts, black and white, a sharp contrast from her usual image in balloon uniform pants. The bra was brand new. Jianfei's feet were nailed to the floor, agape.

"I bought this..." Lishan stuttered.

"This is the first time ... I wanted to show you..."

"What are you doing in my room?"

Anger choked Jianfei. She flung Lishan's blouse at her chest and in a menacing voice, "Cover yourself!"

"I just wanted to show you this thing..."

Lishan regained her self-control and resumed her nonchalant expression. Shrugging her shoulders, she fumbled among words for an excuse.

"...nothing shameful wearing this...just a piece of clothing...we only see them in western movies..."

Her words like the intangible wisp that breathed outside the window somehow smothered in the heat. Lishan felt she was talking to nobody. Profoundly shaken, Jianfei returned to the desk, her ears blocked, head spinning. Tears, not of grief, but of rage and shame, welled up. Fanning, fanning, with a trembling hand, Jianfei shook the feather fan with vehemence, trying to thin the stench that polluted her study.

Jianfei sat there feeding the disturbed emotion; for how long she didn't know. Her body was a simmering volcano. She wanted to expel Lishan, to tell her she was most unwelcome and never to return, to advise her to see a doctor, but she was tongue-tied. Something swam in her lungs like saliva; she had to cough it out but she couldn't.

Two arms encircled her from behind. Jianfei felt her body was captured. Lishan's front pasted to her back like a pair of cakes to be baked.

"Feel me," Lishan murmured, shivering like a leaf.

Something was shattered, pulverized inside Jianfei, the pure, the innocent and the cherished. She blamed herself for her magnanimity and repeated forgiveness, for letting her friend nurture her whim and go so far and for allowing herself to wallow in such shit. She could bear Lishan's letter, poem and whatever confession in words and on paper, she could read her diary and return it with a smiling face. Yet the imposed physical contact was pushing her to the point of eruption. Her tolerance drained out; it was over.

She peeled off Lishan's arms and rose to her feet.

"Go home and never come back," word by word, straight in Lishan's eyes, no tears, Jianfei's eyes calm as an unruffled lake.

Lishan was flabbergasted by her own madness. To upset Jianfei, to see her in such anguish was not her intention. The heat! She cursed the summer, the madness of the sun and the cicadas. And the friendship! Friendship was the grain she must save from the diluted relationship.

Pulling herself together as if awakened from a sleep walk, she said, "I am awfully sorry."

Lishan put on her blouse and stepped out into the smoldering steam. Too hot!

Chapter 15

Tang Wei was promoted to Party Group Leader thanks to his role as a model student in the recent study campaign, a role foisted upon him by a lie which he accepted not without uneasiness due to the increasing pressure of gullible believers.

Every month, Huifang and Tang Wei varied their dating location, the time of meeting, and which gates were used to slip out. Tang Wei applied Chairman Mao's strategy of guerrilla warfare effectively: change your location when firing gunshots to hoodwink the enemy. While the second willow was still their stronghold and the last retreat in case of emergency, more bases had been explored and established: the wilderness opposite the riverbank, the stone steps sheltered under a bridge, the abandoned backyard of a small temple, a path hidden in the bushes, and the foot of the Purple Gold Mountain where the grass was taller and the thickets denser.

Six months had passed. Their encounters still remained within a psychological and emotional realm. They both became familiar with each other's history, family, schools, friends, favorite colors, dishes and clothes. They spoke about the movies and books they liked and disliked, and shared their excitement over music and sports. They learned each other's habits, normal and abnormal. They shared their dreams and nightmares, their awards and criticisms. They sang together. They both loved to sing. Tang Wei impressed Huifang with his wide range of knowledge: Shanghai and its material splendor; Beijing and its historical glory; Nanjing and its military strength; the affluent Jiangsu province and the poverty-stricken Northwest; Chairman Mao both as a politician and also as a poet and philosopher. Huifang saw a world beyond that of her three friends and her parents.

There was one topic yet untouched: why they kept seeing each other and what direction their rendezvous were heading. Tang Wei, fearing what he might not be able to control, evaded the subject of love.

On one particular Sunday afternoon, Tang Wei and Huifang escaped along the path leading to the mountain, which was draped in the pink and white of peach and pear blossoms. Bees were droning a lullaby. Huifang lay on the grass on her back, her head pillowed on her arms. Her corduroy jacket was hanging on a holly bush, shading her eyes from the blinding sun. Tang Wei sat at her side, chewing a blade of young, green grass, tasting the fresh and tender spring. Huifang's white blouse hugged her form in front and the open slit betrayed a piece of her marble flesh, round and smooth. Tang Wei's eyes were stung but he could hardly move them away. His throat tightened and his body heated. A sense of guilt emerged. He stood up, restless. He spat out the grass furiously, but shortly afterwards resumed his position next to her. His eyes swam into her blouse and dwelt there. His mind was in turmoil.

April was marching towards summer. The sun, governing the earth ahead of schedule, baked Tang Wei, who took off his long-sleeved shirt and bared his arms in his white T-shirt. From somewhere in the belly of the mountain, a brook gurgled as it skimmed over the pebbles.

The forest echoed an unknown bird's song. It started with a mournful, cooing alto but then soared to a gleeful, trebling soprano, "Weeeeee—go?"

"What amazing music! Do you know the bird's name?" Huifang scanned the blue sky, straining her ears.

"Weeeeee—go?"

"I don't, but I hear it every spring at my grandma's house. There were these birds and cuckoos."

"So sweet and yet so mysterious. Let's go and find it. Pull me up."

Tang Wei stretched out his arms and they both jerked up, bumping into each other's chests. They stopped, their eyes riveted on each other. They let their hands knot into one and their feet refused to step back. Her smell seeped into his nostrils, the familiar scent of a youthful body, warm and enticing.

"Weeeeee—go?"

They forgot the bird, forgot the brook, no chirping, no trilling, and no whispering of the mountain spring. An ecstatic dizziness seized

Huifang. Her head rested on his broad chest, a chest she had dreamed of for hundreds of nights, a protective, masculine chest. She nestled there and let him tenderly stroke her cascading hair. He held her tightly, feeling her elastic and supple body. Is this how it happens, no words needed?

Tang Wei was bewildered, though he had rehearsed for this moment hundreds of times since her smiles first intruded into his dreams three years ago. When their lips brushed against each other's cheeks, they both felt clumsy and awkward but quickly learned to press them against each other, thirsty, burning and now drinking. Avidly, they inhaled and tasted each other, the juice of youth, the spring of life. They forgot about time; they forgot their surroundings. How long they were locked in each other's arms, they did not remember. All they remembered was that for the first time in their life they had opened a new book, a book that had been forbidden them since childhood. Now they were going to read this book. Darkness engulfed them. They let their fingers carefully grope, exploring the virgin land. On that warm spring evening, beside the orchestra of a jingling brook, twittering birds, croaking frogs and timid, tentative crickets, under the serene, pale moon light, enshrouded in the pink and white petals, cradled in the silently growing bamboo shoots, newly emerged grass and fresh pine needles, two young bodies were reborn.

What was most precious was that they learned how to bridle the galloping horse they rode at the brink of a precipice as their burning bodies marched forward. They curbed themselves at the threshold. Tang Wei instinctively knew the fruit could be bitter if they picked it green. Even at the hottest moment, there was something that cooled him down. What it was, he could not define. Sometimes he felt that his body went further than his heart. This "something' at first was two dots flickering under the dim light of his mind; then the two dots grew into two shadows, looming up from the world beyond the two of them. As they drew nearer, he saw two officers, two fathers, looking at him from the forgotten battlefields of modern history. He recognized them as the two spirits that had been haunting their love since the very start. Tonight as his body began to blaze, his dad came to assert himself. The fatherless Tang Wei saw his father in his mind's eye. The story told by grandma, in that spring field colored by yellow and green, the childhood memories that had long passed, now came back to intervene.

It was a pitch dark night. The rain slashed the silent faces of the New Fourth Army soldiers. Winds whistled high in the sky. Dark clouds flurried overhead. Hasty footsteps splattered through the muddy road. Tonight they were going to be stationed in a small village until the rain stopped.

Day broke with sporadic gunshots. Dogs were barking, horses whinnying, men shouting and women screaming. They were surrounded. Soldiers sprang out bleary-eyed, and dashed for their weapons. Presently the scout rushed in, panting out the information: it was not the Japanese, but the KMT, two battalions.

Following a prelude of gunfire, a voice broke out, "Put down your arms and step out. Surrender is your only way out."

Commissar Tang had a brief meeting with the commander. They decided to have a short negotiation with the enemy in order to gain time for a breakthrough. To propagate the Party's policy and to unite all the forces that could be united to fight against the Japanese invaders was the Commissar's goal.

In the still interval, Commissar Tang raised his voice, "Brothers! The New Fourth and the Nationalist Armies are brothers! We have a mutual enemy, the Japanese. Chinese should not fight against Chinese. Our gun barrels should point outside and not inside. Brothers…"

Machine gun clattered, cutting him short. Red flames puffed out, licking Commissar Tang's body. He felt a thump in his chest as if hit by a rock and he lurched. No pain, but a bit of burning, then something salty gushed out from his mouth. He lurched again, stumbled and fell. Casting a glance at the world he had enjoyed during his thirty three years of life, Commissar Tang closed his eyes. The dark green pine trees, the dark gray sky and the dark blue mist, like a set of snapshots, were taken with him and printed on the faded apples of his eyes. In his chest pocket, people found a photo of a woman and a little baby, soaked in blood.

Lovers, when nourished by love, forget hunger. Tang Wei and Huifang met in the afternoon and usually skipped supper. Only after their desire for love was fed, did their stomachs grumble to claim its rights. One day after dark, Huifang suggested they go to a modest restaurant at the foot of the mountain.

"What if we run into some familiar faces?"

Safety was a never-ending bell ringing in Tang Wei's head.

"At seven o'clock on a Sunday? Who would be at a remote and shabby village? The closest northern compound is the administrative area and it is not a working day. I bet all the officers now are at their dinner table and in forty minutes' walking distance. As for your dear comrades-in-arms, they grudge every penny anyway."

Tang Wei was sulky, "What is wrong with a thrifty life?"

"Take it easy. I didn't mean to offend you. My point is that your soldier friends won't eat at a restaurant and we are safe." Huifang scooped out a handful of coins and bills from her pocket, "here, I have put aside some of my allowance, four yuan, enough for the two of us."

"I have my allowance, too!" as if slapped on face, Tang Wei spat out the words.

"I am sorry, but I am just tired of the boring food at home," Huifang stumbled at a different excuse, "cabbage, cabbage, cabbage leads the menu in all the dining halls. Commander Cabbage!"

Repeating dad's version of Commander Cabbage, Huifang was glad she could also offer some humor. She burst out giggling which, contrary to her intention to fan away the tension between them, added fuel. Without a word, Tang Wei walked away and sat on a newly chopped stump, his face turned aside, eyebrows knitted.

Unable to read Tang Wei's mind, Huifang panicked. She tiptoed over. Her hand lightly brushed over his shoulder and asked with extra caution, "Are you mad at me?"

Tang Wei stood up, his eyes sparkled, "Miss, we are lucky to have cabbages! Our Party and our country are facing challenges from all sides, abroad and at home, from natural disasters to the Soviet betrayal. What side are you taking? Look at the abandoned worksites, the half erected Yangtze River Bridge! Those are the projects started by our older brothers, the Soviet experts. Now they have been called back home. Which side are you taking? Your dad's side? The one who is watching our setbacks with a secret bliss and hoping that the Communists are incompetent and the situation becomes a failure?"

Dumbfounded, Huifang slumped on the grass as Tang Wei's voice softened, "As a Party member, I am not supposed to accept your complaining voice. Instead, I should help you to build up the faith in our ability to conquer all obstacles and go through this temporary hardship. Cabbage or no cabbage, the question is: can we, you and I, be on the same side?"

Huifang nodded without thinking, tears trickled down her pretty face. She stood up and threw herself into his arms.

"Of course, of course. Forgive me for my stupidity. I am a simple girl…"

Her words were choppy.

"Wherever you stand, I will be at your side. I just love you. I am simple-minded…"

Fearing further trouble, she muffled her voice with kisses, showering Tang Wei's face and neck. The storm subsided, yet Huifang was not completely appeased. She would never imagine that a simple meal could draw such a political lesson. Damn the cabbage! Tang Wei was also smoldering but allowed his arms to join hers and his thoughts to stay at bay. He felt sorry but could not help his anger. Now he had come to a painful realization that no matter how close their bodies were, their minds might always be miles apart. There was always another love above Huifang, his love for the Party.

Chapter 16

Swallows migrated from the south again. Dressed in tuxedos, they gathered under the eaves for another spring party.

This was their last spring at high school. Cloistering herself in her room, Lishan devoured Tolstoy, Gogol, Turgenev, Balzac, Mao Dun, Ba Jin, Luxun…foreign and Chinese, contemporary and classic, in defiance of the approaching college entrance exam. A recluse, Lishan had withdrawn from the girls and stayed mainly alone. Occasionally on Sunday afternoons, she would sit on the lawn in the rock garden by the auditorium, books and drawings in hand. Childhood laughter rose from the past. Her eyes softened, her thoughts roaming with the flying clouds to those days when the three of them whiled away their happy hours. To escape the growing heat, she sought shelter under the canopy of a huge elm tree and passed away the drowsy afternoon, watching the sun sieve through the leaves, dappling the green carpet.

"Gone, gone," she unfolded her dramatic life in her diary, "gone are the days when my life sailed with the wind, when we brainless kids were still a group of laughing fools, when my face was not yet darkened by loneliness. Gone, Jianfei is gone…Life is a cup of herbal medicine, and yet I am destined to drink it up no matter how bitter it is."

Despite what had occurred between the two, they could not completely avoid each other since they lived less than three minutes' apart and their parents exchanged greetings, news and gossip on a daily basis. The initial fury and disgust which had so consumed Jianfei could not be sustained for long. It was her nature not to nurse a grudge against Lishan, nor hold a special charity for her. If there was any debris left in her heart, she tried to erase it. The memories of that hot summer afternoon were quickly shoved to the back of her mind once the new school year got under way.

In September, she started to normalize her relations with Lishan. However, since that sweltering day, shame and humiliation had torn Lishan far apart and she became standoffish and was difficult to converse with. This made it especially difficult for Jianfei to break the ice. Jianfei turned to Huifang for help, but Huifang, head to toe in love, offered no remedy.

As spring came, their life entered a new phase. The approaching college exam made everything else trivial and insignificant. Jianfei was still on good terms with Lishan's parents who came one day to her, with a specific, pressing request: help their daughter in college preparation.

At the senior assembly, the principal bleakly depicted the seniors' prospects: only five to six percent of the luckiest birds flew into college over the past two years, which meant in a class of fifty students, the chance for a higher education was to fall to no more than three. Top scores were a necessity, yet an immaculate family background was always the decisive factor. If two examination papers with the same grades were placed in juxtaposition to compete for one spot, the one whose father worked at a cotton mill would most likely hit the ball. In a society where manufacturing workers were labeled as the leading class and the peasants, army officers and government cadres were honored as their "revolutionary" allies, the meager food supply always went to the workers' mouths first. Remember, they were red. Teachers, writers, journalists, actors and doctors…, intellectuals of every hue, their color was smudged in the spectrum, somewhere between yellow and green. The landlords, rich peasants, factory owners, businessmen, later joined by the Rightists were birds of the same feather. No distinction was made between their shades of blackness. Their offspring carried a "black caldron" on their backs, hobbling in every walk of life. Thousands of talented youngsters fell like autumn leaves at the entrance exams. In this way, the society achieved its law of the jungle. Talent or no talent, one's family was one's foremost talent.

Universities and colleges were categorized into three. Category one: science; category two: medicine; category three: the humanities.

Jianfei knew her opportunity would be scarce if she chose science. She would have to wrestle against a hundred including the most brilliant boys like Yang Bing, who was now attending a prestigious university in Shanghai. Her own classmates, such as Minming, even though they had insuperable math and physics scores, could hardly be guaranteed a place when the applicant pools from all the schools converged into one great examination sea. The second category was medicine. Jianfei had never put herself into a white garment, behind a mouthpiece that smelt of sterility, dealing with blood, excrement, fever, listening to the moaning and groaning, facing pallid cheeks and withering bodies. Besides, chemistry was her weakest subject. Jianfei measured her advantages and disadvantages and speculated her strategy. Among the seniors, fifty percent chose category one. Everyone craved a profession that would secure a job and a superior salary in a large-scale, state-run enterprise. Forty percent dreamed of white garments and saving lives. The remaining ten percent, the pathetic few, who lagged behind in math, physics and chemistry, who were left with little hope and scant choice, were forced into the narrow lane of the humanities. Among them, were a couple of weird geniuses, like Lishan, but the majorities were good-for-nothing leftovers. A talent for writing was the prerequisite in category three.

At the dinner table, holding a book, Xiaoshi, munching away, spoke to dad.

"Dad, listen. An ancient man had three horses. In order to win the race, he uses his slowest horse to race with the fastest horse of his contender, his second best against his slowest horse and his best against the second best."

Dad rubbed brother's hair.

"So he won two out of three? Eat your meal."

Jianfei put down her chopsticks. Her horse definitely belonged to category one. Her writing skill and high grades in all subjects could ensure her a seat in a prestigious university if she raced in the third category. *Why are so many talented girls trying to get through the main entrance and forgetting the side door?* But she soon realized that not many of them, among the brilliant scientific students, were gifted in writing, performing, painting and singing.

Jianfei's compositions constantly served as a model essay used by her Chinese teachers. They were read in classes. The teachers changed but the reading of her writing in class never changed; this was a family inheritance.

The English department, F. University, Shanghai, the goal was secretly set. It was secret because someone was waiting for her there. Shanghai was Yang Bing's city.

"Dad, what was your career before joining the revolution?" one day Jianfei asked dad.

"To become a poet."

"Poet? Were you confident that you could earn a national reputation?"

Dad nodded slightly, "if not for the Japanese invasion."

"Why didn't you pursue your dream then?"

"How could I? Ninety-nine percent of my poems were anti-reality and anti-government."

"Wow! You never showed me any of your poems."

"Come here." Dad opened one of the wooden boxes. The boxes had been sitting in the closet in oblivion like two criminals serving life sentence since the suitcase incident five years ago. "Here. Be my first critic."

They were two volumes of poems. The paper was flimsy and brittle, lines jumped into Jianfei's eyes. Some of them showed a different dad like this one:

> The moonless Moon Festival brings forth resentment,
> Separation calls for ten thousand mile's reunion,
> From the woods, crickets chirp in the falling leaves,
> When can we restore a mirror that has broken?

The broken mirror and the moonless Moon Festival, a symbol of separated lovers, created much pathos.

"It's beautiful and full of nostalgia."

Jianfei raised her eyes and looked at dad's grey hair, wondering what had been stored in his head from those remote and romantic years. She couldn't picture her dad consumed with his passions, seeing only his daily battles against his wife.

"You are my heiress. When I am gone, you will be their keeper."

Dad changed the topic, "Have you made a decision as to your college major?"

"Yes. English language and literature."

Dad stood up, squinting.

"Wrong decision. Wrong. Literature is not a toy with which you can play. You are actually playing with fire. Tons of intellectuals, the majority of them writers, come crashing down when one political campaign sweeps over. They are nothing other than autumn leaves in a storm. Put on a pedestal today, trashed tomorrow. That's the fate of our writers. Ruthless."

He paced.

"There will be no room for genuine literature as the revolution deepens…you must keep all these bottled up inside you."

"You just said I am your literary inheritor," Jianfei said.

"Do you know what it means to set your life in the track of literature? Plus English! You are playing with fire! I have repeatedly warned you against literature, yet you turned a deaf ear and fell in love with it regardless."

Dad quickened his pace.

"The twentieth century! The atomic age! The electronic era!"

"Your great epoch is irrelevant to my interest, neither the atomic bomb or radio or telephone. Look at your poems! That was where your passions lay thirty years ago. I am your daughter."

Ignoring her retort, dad continued with his train of thought, "Yet you'd rather go back to an age without light! What future do you see in the relics of an alien nation?"

"Interest and passion do not have to go with the tide. As a poet, you know that better than I do," Jianfei said.

"What about Yang Bing?" suddenly dad touched to the quick.

Her heart slipped a beat: *how did he know my secret?*

"What about Yang Bing?" she repeated, trying a tone as dull and indifferent as possible.

"This time last year, Commissar Yang's son made a smart choice; now he is studying architecture. Brilliant students make brilliant choices."

"Sure. But I am not brilliant and his interest is not mine."

At least one thing was confirmed: her father viewed Yang Bing as representative of the highest standard of educational success, hoping his daughter would emulate and surpass him, an achievement which would enable him to hold his head higher than his Vice President, Commissar Yang. Yang Bing's name in his mouth did not imply that he had the slightest inkling of his daughter's secret.

Not long after this conversation, Jianfei's father was appointed by the Central Committee of the National Defense to be the president of a scientific research institute, an institute with two thousand scientists and three thousand manufacturing workers, one of the most advanced research facilities of the nation. Maybe Dad had hoped I would join his staff and become one of the two thousand. Jianfei always suspected that dad's opposition to her choice had something to do with his own career.

Chapter 17

Lishan chose library science, determined to marry books. Her target was the nation's number one school, Beijing University. She had no doubt about her destined failure but didn't oppose martyrdom on the way to the best university. This was Lishan's way to die.

"Your application for Beijing University is suicidal," her dad stepped into her room one day. His fingers climbed to his forehead, furiously adjusting his crooked spectacles, "You must adjust your absurd plan!"

"I am not getting anywhere anyway." Lishan said, turning her back to dad, "What do you care? How often do you ask me about school?"

"Change to art, forget Beijing!"

"No."

"Never mind," out of breath, dad bellowed, "I will talk to your principal!"

In May, Lishan was summoned to the principal's office. On the colossal mahogany desk, her application form was shoved in front of her nose across the ocean of paper.

The principal was in her mid-forties. While grizzled hair and a creased forehead spoke for a seasoned educator, a pair of bubbled goldfish eyes together with two grayish slate cheeks effaced any female attraction. She and Lishan's dad were alumni of the same university.

"Lishan," her voice was as flat as her face, "you have to believe that your dad is really concerned about you."

Unfortunately the principal's intention to bring the parent closer to the teenager immediately pushed Lishan in the opposite direction.

But the principal knew how to win her back, "Would you reconsider your application? I will help you with a new strategy based on your strong points. You are still a very hopeful candidate for any art school. You don't want to squander your chance at a higher education, do you?"

The soft, caring and persuasive voice made it hard for Lishan to throw a "no" at her face as she did to dad. With the aid of an almost invisible smile, she continued, "Your talent in painting was discovered by a teacher..."

As if punched in the chest, Lishan felt short of breath. A bittersweet feeling surged up and swept all over. Ms. Guan stepped into her head, a specter suddenly resurrected from her past. She saw her strutting. She saw her own painting on her desk. Any subject related to her painting was a reminder of Ms. Guan. The principal had touched to the point. Using a counterrevolutionary as a lever proved the principal's desperation.

"Your dad is not the only one. Your teachers, the current and the past..." Ms. Guan was on the tip of her tongue, the principal continued to beat around the bush, "They all pin their hopes on you. Please cherish the artistic value of your works and do not fall short of your teacher's expectations. My heart aches to see a talent wasted."

Her words touched something deep in Lishan's heart. Lishan wiped her eyes. Her frivolous attitude towards her college application was not really the indication of any enmity between her dad and herself. It was merely a symptom of her anguish. Subconsciously she realized her rejection of art school was not just a gesture of rebellion against her parents' vanity but also, and more importantly, a protest against the unjust arrest of Ms. Guan, the only one who had kept an eye on her work and fostered her art talent. For Lishan, to engage in the ferocious battle to enter college would be for her to embrace an institutional cornerstone of society, a society which had robbed her of her ardent passion and brutally removed from her life someone very dear in her heart. Ms. Guan, if only she were still here, was the one who could easily reverse her college decision. Now Ms. Guan's name, which everyone had evaded for many years, was alluded to by the Principal. The mere suggestion of Ms. Guan brought back memories of the painful past which had long been buried deep in Lishan's breast. Sitting in the principal's office, these repressed images burst open the floodgates of her heart. She began to sob.

The principal seized the moment to secure her victory, "Now, now. Take this form home and give it a second thought." She said with a big smile, "You would make our school shine if your name shines."

Lishan, overcome with sudden uncharacteristic emotion, also broke a small smile through her watery eyes.

"The deadline is in a month."

A week later, a revised application was placed on the principal's desk. A college of fine art was Lishan's first choice.

When asked about her college application, Huifang's replies were invariable, "I have to ask Tang Wei."

Huifang's dependence on Tang Wei exasperated her friends, "Tang Wei, Tang Wei, don't you have your own will?"

No. Huifang did not. As a matter of fact, her infatuation had carried her to the point that everything and everyone else had faded into oblivion. The entrance exam seemed to her just another quiz. Her future career? Seldom did she give it a thought. The first category was not in her range since math was always her headache and she had hardly even passed physics. The second category? Chemistry? A little above average. The third category? She was not gifted in anything. A survey of her grades showed that in all her subjects she fluctuated above and below a passing grade. Jianfei was out of her reach; even the acrimonious Lishan had something special; she was queer but talented. *How do I picture myself?* She ruminated. *Engineer?* She shook her head affirmatively. *A writer or a professor? No way.* After several headshakes, she timidly suggested, *"How about a doctor?" White, pure, hygienic, elegant and with a high status. Tang Wei would like the image.* After consulting her boyfriend, Huifang's eyes slowly nailed on the second category. Her parents also agreed that being a doctor, one could afford a life away from the political maelstrom. Deep in her heart, she was prepared for a fruitless battle. College or no college, Tang Wei was her college. She was prepared to accept that destiny. *I may not be a college candidate but I am very well qualified to be a sweet lover.*

Something else diluted her confidence, the indifference of her parents.

If the offspring of the Communists could hardly hold a seat in their own universities, where could we, the old foes, find room? She is fighting a lost battle just like I did fourteen years ago. The idea was like a bee droning in dad's mind.

Soon Huifang began to adopt her father's attitude although no words had ever been exchanged between the two. *A Nationalist officer wearing a Communist uniform, that's what dad is, a wolf in sheep's clothing. What do you expect from me at the entrance exam? Even the red Jianfei and Lishan are fighting an impossible war. This time, unlike the movie tickets, their social privilege is too meager to provide them with much sustenance, let alone to be shared with me.*

Huifang had never felt so lonely.

Chapter 18

Summer vacation began. The whole school evacuated, leaving the graduating classes behind burning the midnight oil. The University Entrance Examinations were a sword hanging over every head. Despair and confidence, hopefulness and hopelessness, pessimism and optimism, assurance and doubts, staunchness and vacillation… alternately weaved into the daily emotional pattern, like the summer sky one minute sunny, the next rainy, making the routine preparation even more strenuous. Teachers of all subjects patrolled the ocean of open books, fearing that any essential points might be overlooked. They carefully planned how to make the students' deliverance safer, how to obtain a higher percentage of passing grades, who they should let slide and who should be fed with extra nutrition. In their heads, a few stood out while the majority faded away whom they knew they had to let go. From time to time, the homeroom teachers came in with a bucket of cold water into which the girls dipped their sticky faces. Milling around with a broad fan in hand, the teachers stopped behind each student fanning a bit, drying a bit. Soon the sweat beads were transferred from the younger faces to the older ones. Everything was scorching, the chair, the desk, even the wind puffed heat into faces. When someone stood up, two vertical dark lines were printed on her chair and two horizontal dark lines stained her desk, those were her legs and arms. Windows were wide open, sucking in temperatures of one hundred ten degrees. Languid leaves steamed in the sun. Cicada shrieks tore apart the leaves, pierced every eardrum, adding fuel to the fire. The city fell victim to the relentless summer for which Nanjing was notorious. At dusk, the sun gradually withdrew its shafts after inflicting long hours of torture. Gliding over trees and buildings, the broad face narrowed its eyes but its orange glory promised another sizzling day to come. The girls, their slender shadows projected on the parched earth, dragged themselves home. The earth was blistering, the river boiling. The streets paralyzed in the still air. Buses gasped by. With hoarse voices, they blasted unsurely, blowing blue hazy winds from their rear.

All the graduating students had been regrouped according to their examination category. Lishan and Jianfei were placed in the same reviewing class. These full-day-study sessions on the eve of their epic life-and-death battle provided both of them with numerous opportunities to attempt a recovery of their lacerated relationship, if that was what they mutually desired. However the ugly scene had left a deep gash between the two, mocking their childhood friendship: one was rejected, one repulsed. They each saw themselves as a puppet whose strings were in the hands of the other. One sharp tug of the string, intentional or unintentional, by either hand, might reopen the old wound. Fortunately, Jianfei's thoughts held no space for everlasting, dark memories; dad's "Xu Huai Ruo Gu" was her motto. But Lishan, whose passion had fermented her own tragedy, was different. Not until Lishan's parents made urgent calls for help and Jianfei tried several smiling approaches, did Lishan thaw and emit a wispy smile.

"You are a natural born artist, not a librarian," Jianfei said. "I am glad you have changed your application."

Lishan shrugged her shoulders. Acid was about to return to her lips.

"Can I help you in any way?" Jianfei meant academic tutoring.

"Yes. I have a favor to ask," Lishan hesitated, "I have to submit my latest painting to the college I have applied for. Do you mind if I paint you?"

"At your service," Jianfei said readily.

"Thanks a bunch." Lishan said, "Please join me at the rock garden on Sunday afternoon. Wear your red silk dress, please, the one you only wear on weekends. Bring your books, you still can review."

When completed, the oil painting was entitled "Comfort." A stretch of green lay out the backdrop, contrasting with a red and white centerpiece. The red was a girl; the white a birch tree. Jianfei was leaning on the white trunk reading, an apple in hand. The girl's mouth was slightly open, the apple held midair. All was frozen in a moment of absorption. The only perceptible object in motion was her eyes which dragged the viewers' eyes in along her line of sight to share with her her focus of interest. A lock of hair was slightly pasted on her forehead; the short, red dress was unbuttoned at the top; her sandals were kicked off and sat beside her bare feet, seeking freedom on a sweltering day. The shade of the birch surrounded her figure creating a frame within a frame, a world within a world. The book was her comfort. On her face, serenity blended with blissfulness. High above, through the silvery, pale green leaves, the blue sky peeked in. Leisurely, white clouds drifted by. In the distance, the sun splashed gold. Even the girl in the shade was slightly gilded. Obviously, a painting submitted as part of a college application must have a political dimension. Lishan wanted to make sure that the girl engrossed in her studies pleased the examiners. Comfort. The book was a comfort; the shadow was a comfort; the bare feet were a comfort; the tree was a comfort. Lishan's brushstrokes rendered comfort. What remained secret to outside eyes was that, for the painter, the girl she had painted was a comfort.

Jianfei scrutinized herself, and her admiration was resurrected. Lishan's talent remained intact, only more assertive. After five years of hibernation since Ms. Guan was taken away, her artistic instinct seemed to have fermented and mellowed. A long lost smile appeared on Lishan's face. Art revived Lishan, and Jianfei was her inspiration.

In the youngsters' heads, heaven and hell was only one step away. University drew the demarcation line. An ascent or a descent at the age of eighteen meant a step up to the tip of a pyramid or to the trough of a pit. Whether the timbre of one's sixty or seventy years of life belonged to the highbrow elite or the mundane plebeians was decided at the age of eighteen. On the one side were professors, doctors, engineers, architects, writers, government leaders, army officers and artists; on the other, factory workers, peasants, scavengers, shop assistants, bus drivers, and peddlers. Applicants fell at the entrance exam like flies dropping dead from DDT. Many faced the misery of cloistering themselves at home for yet another year, waiting to try their luck again. Others threw themselves into the labor stream and made scant but immediate income to shut up their nagging parents. The community picked up college leftovers wherever there was a job opening. They might be sent to assemble toys or machinery parts in a dingy workshop, or be seen at a market behind the meat counter, their aprons stained with blood, bickering with buyers over an ounce, or be found in a restaurant, shuttling between tables, memorizing different complicated orders...Yet these were the lucky ones, for the majority, the opportunities were awaiting in the countryside.

To be a peasant, for a high school graduate, was the greatest waste: playing in the mud was something children could do. So-called technical jobs which required a high school diploma were nothing more than repeating the weather report over the P.A. system or copying documents by hand.

The peasants' domain was the green fields. In spring, they transplanted the rice seedlings in the rice paddies. Their feet and ankles were soaked red and swollen in cold water, causing serious menstrual pain and other related female diseases. Sometimes their young calves were visited by bloodthirsty leeches.

In summer, they were favored by mosquitoes that, tired of rough meat and stale blood, swarmed in, humming to taste the fresh blood and sweet meat from the cities. Their dinner tables were frequented by uninvited, droning, flying guests from the nearby cesspool. As refrigeration was still decades away, leftovers were kept covered or put in the cupboard, but still remained the happy breeding beds of countless flies. It was not unusual to find maggots wriggling out from yesterday's pork. Seeds of malaria and cholera were sown everywhere.

In fall, they doubled their bodies, cutting, bundling, transporting rice from the paddies to the threshing grounds, one hundred jin on each shoulder pole, panting, groaning and stumbling all the way along.

After the bone-breaking harvest, came the winter, with it, the long, dreary but somewhat entertaining slack period. Mountains of documents and countless meetings marked this season. Day in and day out, they sat with peasants, blabbering away for hours. Young mothers, whom they watched with humor and shame, unbuttoned their jackets and blouses and scooped out, in front of all the revolutionary commune members, their breasts sucked long by their sucklings. They let the little crying thing hang in front, nuzzling for their milk, and then freed their hands to engage in knitting and sewing. Middle-aged wives made shoes. They first sharpened their long needles by scratching them in their dense hair, and then pulled out a long, homemade cotton string and threaded through the thick sole pasted by many layers of homemade cloth. All these were performed with an amazing elegance. With the threads and the needles set, their mouths began to work feverishly. Jokes, stories of ghosts and monsters, legends, tales, gossip breathed out without much thought.

Men and women called each other names.

"Hi, you little dick, I waited for you last night. My man found our back door unlatched and he beat me!"

"Liar! Liar!" the man rocked and smiled.

Laughter burst out.

Men were not so open about such things, they muffled voices and replied, "You, little bitch, wait till I slash you with …!"

"Ha, ha, ha…," reddening the faces of the educated city youths.

The village head shouted to his lewd villagers, "Folks, folks, watch your tongues!" When the laughter showed no sign of abating, he mumbled, "Give me one minute, folks, I am about to wrap up…"

The students are abashed; this was the bulk of their reeducation.

All these helped the high school graduates reassess their educational level; they soon were to realize that they were no better than those semi-proletariats, with their collective laughter, their quick-witted, tit-for-tat verbal fights, vulgar jokes, and their stuttering readings of the central government documents.

"The countryside is a vast realm. There, youth has the opportunity to achieve greatness!"

The younger generation, bearing Mao's words in mind, was ready to utilize their knowledge to build a new countryside. It was a mixed feeling. On the one hand, they could not wait till they severed themselves from their sullen-faced parents. They wanted to feed their mouths with their own hands. They were sick of the stench, the cluttered cities reeking of tobacco and garlic. They craved the open field and the green air. On the other hand, the flies and mosquitoes, the meager rice and scant vegetables boiled in well water or fried without oil, the cesspools and the malaria abhorred them.

"Go to the countryside", a veiled threat, hung over all the heads as the exams approached.

Jianfei and Lishan were no exception. For Huifang, it was a vast spider web in a bright living room that enclosed her tighter and tighter in the three years of high school. Now the spider was making its move.

Chapter 19

At this juncture, an unexpected incident altered Huifang's fate. She suddenly became a boat with a broken mast, her voyage to college turned adrift on the currentless water.

One Sunday afternoon, Tang Wei helped Huifang grapple with her chemistry problems. The hours ticked by and their stomachs began grumbling. They decided to feed themselves at the small eatery Huifang mentioned before. The so-called restaurant was nothing but a shack, sitting at the end of a country road. The simple and uninviting façade was however overtaken by a staggering backdrop, the Gold Purple Mountain. Its white wall and black straw roof stood silhouetted against the dark grayish, greenish and purplish towering peak, making an ideal subject for an aspiring painter's canvas. They headed to the place, bringing the shadow of their previous quarrel with them.

"You go first. I'll enter separately," Tang Wei slowed down his steps.

Huifang was a bit tickled. *This is a drama of an underground liaison, as seen in the movies.* A few scenes went through her mind's eye. She managed to stifle her laugh, remembering the trouble it had brought to her before.

The restaurant, though weather-beaten and ramshackle, had an enticing name, "The Apricot Blossom Village." It was engraved in red on a faded white board, quite eye-catching.

The name was borrowed from a Tang poem:

May I bother to ask where I could find a wine shop?
The little cowherd pointed far at the Apricot Blossom Village.

Huifang stepped in. The Apricot Blossom Village consisted of four naked, worn out tables, each surrounded with four narrow, long-legged benches of the same status. A slovenly middle-aged man was dozing off at the counter, saliva drooling about his lips significantly.

"Hi," the man grunted through the drool, "Want to eat?"

The liquid hanging in front of the man largely sabotaged Huifang's appetite. She looked around. The wood floor squeaked happily under every step. The red paint had been washed away through mopping, though the floor was still sticky. The walls were scratched with white paint, yet mostly smoked gray. Chairman Mao's portrait was hanging squarely in the center; the other three sides had windows wide open. A family of chickens was leading a peaceful life outside, pecking and cackling. Without any screens in the windows, flies had free entrance.

The only diners there were a young couple who had just exited, their table strewn with white scraps and drippings. The man at the door began to move his bottom. Stretching and yawning, he shuffled over to clean up the mess.

"Want to eat? Take a look," his chin pointed at the wall.

There was a small blackboard; the day's menu was scribbled on it, barely legible:

Slices of dried tofu fried with cabbage; shredded pork fried with cabbage; tofu dregs with ginger and scallion; sweet and sour cabbage; egg soup with cabbage; pickled cabbage.

"OK, at least they have pork and egg in addition," Huifang dug into her pocket.

Whether her fair face or the bills showing from her pocket brightened up the situation was unclear, but the man, who served as the receptionist, waiter, cashier and cook, began to scurry.

"Comrade," a belch escaped, he smiled an apology, "what would you like to order? We are closing in half an hour."

Tang Wei stepped in. Huifang steered around. Her eyes skimmed outside. The young couple had dimmed into the twilight. In the village, smoke puffed out of thatched roofs, thinning into the swarthy-faced mountain. Not a soul was in sight. Evening was closing in. Safe, they exchanged an acquiescent look. Tang Wei settled himself at a window seat with a view of the backyard and the chickens. A wooden board vaguely read: "East Wind People's Commune, Chicken Field." Tang Wei smiled and shook his head.

"Should we eat separately?" without raising her head, Huifang asked.

"No. Not at seven thirty," Tang Wei dug out some money from his pocket.

"It is a shame that tofu dregs are served as a restaurant dish now; they used to be thrown out before..." Huifang checked herself just in time; Tang Wei was glaring at her again. The lecture over cabbage by Tang Wei still echoed in her ears with acute pungency.

"Comrade," Tang Wei beckoned to the only man in the restaurant, "one pork and a tofu dregs, please."

The waiter, now the cashier, swept his fingers adroitly on the abacus, "Two yuan for the pork and fifty fen for the dregs."

"A pork and a tofu dregs," the waiter twittered to the audience and himself. Tossing the greasy towel on his shoulder, he whirled into the kitchen.

Tang Wei shook his head at the waiter's back. "Do you remember the movie *Guerrillas on the Plain*?" Tang Wei smiled faintly. "Two guerrilla soldiers stayed in a small restaurant when the Japanese surrounded the area. The waiter sang the menu loudly, dropping a warning code." A bitter smile emitted from his drawn lips. "It seems that a high-pitched voice and a dirty shoulder towel are the trademarks of all the waiters. Look at us," Tang Wei chuckled, "I hope we are not surrounded."

"But we are guerrillas," said Huifang. They looked at each other and burst out laughing.

"What luck! They are still open."

A voice brought in a young man and an old woman. The man was of medium height but extremely thin, practically a stick figure. A pair of narrow eyes was a perfect match to the one thin vertical line of his torso that ran up like a coat rack in the middle and the two thin horizontal lines stretching out as his shoulders ready to receive someone's overcoat. His eyes, nose and mouth were assembled in a compact way, leaving spacious room for the vast cheeks. A pair of ears was planted widely under the stubby hair, like an infant's open palms, a perfect illustration of the

Chinese expression "wind-catching ears." He was wearing a short-sleeved white shirt. The shirt was tucked into a pair of green trousers.

Checking the hygiene of his chopsticks, Tang Wei moved his eyes to the incoming voice but immediately dropped as if scorched. His hands gave a spasmodic shake and the chopsticks slipped to the floor. Tang Wei bent over and burrowed under the table, trying to pick up the chopsticks, but couldn't return to his straightened posture. All he wished for at this moment was to dig a hole and bury himself in it. The newcomer was none other than his comrade-in-arms, Xiao Ming.

Still crouching under the table, he tapped slightly on Huifang's skirt, wishing that she, too, could vanish with him.

"What happened?" without a clue, Huifang shouted, drawing arrows from all corners.

A thief caught red-handed, Tang Wei sat up, lowering his eyes on the table.

"Hello! Little Tang!" Xiao Ming walked over, smiling from ear to ear, one hand stretched out for a shake. "Didn't expect to see you here!"

The three of them in an instant recollected the same scenario, the three girls and Xiao Ming, face to face, trying to give each other a hard time. For Tang Wei, the lie about tutoring was as fresh as yesterday.

"Hi," though on pins and needles, Tang Wei managed to squeeze out a surprising smile and put on a carefree face, "Little Xiao, good to see you too. Coming out for a breath of fresh air?"

Never on earth would Tang Wei have dreamed of running into his fellow soldier here!! And Xiao Ming, who had already had a dramatic encounter with both of them, was destined to be the one!!

"Yes. This is my mom," the old woman looked woodenly around, "I went to the railway station to pick her up, the train was half an hour delayed. By the time we arrived at the barracks, the dining hall had long closed. Here, mom," he waved at the old woman, who waddled over on her bound feet, fanning herself forcefully with a palm leave fan.

"You'd better order food first, they are about to close," Tang Wei could not wait to extricate himself from the precarious dilemma. A premonition began to envelope Tang Wei.

The supper was completely ruined. The pork was dished out in an extra-large portion due to the late hour since the restaurant had no other means to store the leftovers except to keep them in the cold well water overnight. The plentiful, shining, enticing pork lost all attraction which, on any other occasion, they would have wolfed down to their heart's content.

Tang Wei and Huifang dipped their hangdog faces into their bowls, their minds shifted from one question to another. *What will come out of this chance encounter? Will Xiao Ming tell tales? What kind of person is Xiao in nature? A snitch? How should we explain our relationship? Why is it this face again? Damn the fate!*

For Tang Wei, there were more questions. *Will I be demoted? A warning? A serious warning? Expulsion from the Party? Discharge?*

Question marks studded their minds and answers were quickly fabricated.

Tang Wei coughed, empty and dry, to cover his voice, "Remember, you are my cousin, working in a store nearby."

"Impossible," Huifang muffled her voice into her handkerchief, "I see him as often as I see you. I told you about him the first time we met."

Of course, to stand guard was everyone's daily job. At his wit's end, Tang Wei had forgotten this simple fact. Now the conversation with Xiao Ming under the dim light was rekindled, with it, the cigarette, the third-grade dropout and the tutoring… No. No escape.

It was not until the four of them finished the dinner and stepped out into the dimly lit dirt road that Xiao Ming had the opportunity to show his courtesy to Tang Wei's female companion.

"You are… You live in the North Pole Village, don't you? I am Xiao Ming," the "wind-catching ear" extended his hand. "You were with your friends at my post last year."

Why did Xiao Ming mention the incident from eighteen months ago? Tang Wei's nerves tingled.

"I am Huifang. I need Tang Wei to help me prepare for the college entrance examinations." She waved her books.

Huifang surmised that a candid, matter-of-fact answer would be smarter than a poor lie.

"You chose the right one." Xiao Ming smiled—*the right teacher and the right lover, how convenient.*

The heat had abated as the night progressed. Faint breezes timidly kissed their cheeks. The four of them sank into embarrassment. They walked in silence until the academy gate loomed in the dark.

Huifang turned to Tang Wei, loud enough for Xiao Ming to catch, "Could we spend another five minutes to go over the details we have studied today?"

She needed an urgent instruction how to deal with the unprepared predicament.

"Sure, but first let me say good night to my friend," Tang Wei laid such stress on the syllables of "friend" that even Huifang was disturbed by the pretentiousness.

Tang Wei turned to Xiao Ming and pulled him aside, "We are friends, aren't we?" Tang Wei's imposed friendship amused Xiao Ming.

"Another cigarette?" Xiao Ming replied, looking into Tang Wei's eyes, an imperceptible smile swept over his face.

"Is she the one we all believe you have been tutoring? You did the right thing, Party Group leader. Serving the people, eh?"

He started to move, but returned with a blink.

"Don't worry."

Without another word, Xiao Ming turned to the academy, leaving Tang Wei behind to chew on his words. The ambiguous tone of Xiao's remarks, somewhere between mockery and flattery, lingered in Tang Wei's mind. His worry carried him so far until he convinced himself that they were just another token of honest worship from his illiterate comrade-in-arms. However, subconsciously he was haunted by the step-by-step realization that Xiao Ming had already gained the upper hand politically.

"How is this Xiao Ming?" Huifang blurted out, her pretty face half eclipsed in the situation.

"Ambitious yet limited by his education. We are buddies. He replaced me as the squad leader after I was promoted to the Party group leader. He was also nominated as the activist in the study campaign."

Now the eclipse was completed.

"Is he trustworthy?"

"I think so."

Tang Wei did not want their last five minutes together overshadowed.

Tossing and turning, Huifang flailed in a muddy torrent. Some black dots drifted towards her, up and down the surface. Straining her eyes, Huifang attempted to discern the nature of the dots. The dots touched her face, they were dead fish. Their mouths wide open and crooked to one side as if smirking. Their eyes leered at her, yet their puffy bodies showed the sign of decay. Their flesh was peeling. Clouds were gathering, winds howling and the water roaring. The fish, the sky and the water wove into a murky night. The liquid formed an enormous box, engulfing everything, including Huifang. Her limbs thrashed, and her head bumped on all four sides trying to poke a hole in the unbreakable box. Breathing was getting harder. She opened her mouth and shouted "Tang Wei" but no sound came out from the dark cave of her mouth, no word, not even a syllable was produced.

"Huifang!" a faint voice scratched the air, wafting over. "Huifang!"

It was Tang Wei. He was near but far. Her eyes exerted their efforts but no one came into sight.

"Huifang!"

She swam to the voice but was devoured by a towering wave that went down smashing, snapping and snatching. Down, down…inside the box the water was silky and beguiling, like a profound sleep.

When she finally pumped her body upwards, the surface turned crystal clear. The clouds dispersed to reveal the bluest of skies. The rising sun greeted her with a fresh smile. She smiled back. A second look at the sun brought her a broader smile. The sun that shone in the sky turned out to be Tang Wei's cheerful face. She smiled and smiled, laughed and laughed…

She heard a giggle and opened her eyes. Huifang was wide awake now. She sat up and turned on the light. *What was the interpretation of the dark water and clear water? Was it auspicious or evil? And the red sun and the dark sky, what omen? What did those dead fish try to tell me? What did the torrent stand for?*

"Huifang, are you all right?"

Light seeped through.

Mom's voice.

"Yes."

The light went off.

The rest of the night proved restless. She sat in the dark until the dawn light sifted through the window and brightened her room.

Snatching a bun, Huifang darted out and rushed towards the gate. There he was, green uniform showered in the morning sun. She must see him and make sure that her absurd dream was nothing but a dream.

As she drew near, Huifang's feet nailed to the ground. The green uniform clothed a different face. Tang Wei was scheduled to be on guard, she had no doubt about it. She searched her memory again and again. *Yes, he told me he would be at the post this time.* Tang Wei was nowhere to be seen. Nor was he the next day, nor the day after that...

Huifang was in deep, dark and troubled waters as the dream showed her. She flung herself on her bed. Tears came in a deluge. Her textbooks were discarded. The Entrance Examination was here.

Chapter 20

"Zhi-liao, Zhi-liao!"

Hundreds of cicadas, peeping through the sycamores, the willow trees and the maple trees, peering through the windows at the black sea of desperately racked brains, emphatically shrieked, "Zhi-liao, Zhi-liao!" homonymous in Chinese with the words "I know, I know!" Nature seemed to mock human desperation. Inside the classroom, hundreds of heads synchronized their response with "I don't know, I don't know!"

On this red letter day, examinees from different high schools were concentrated on several college campuses. Each one stared at the paper in front of him, seeking to answer questions far beyond what any of them had prepared for, bleary-eyed, cotton-headed in the boiling temperature, greatly exasperated by the mocking "I know" chorus emitted somewhere among the massive foliage.

On the third category campus, parents gathered on the shaded, well-trimmed lawn, gazing at the two hands of their watches, counting every second. Time had stopped; the two hands never seemed to move. They shook their wrists to make sure the watches were still ticking. They were. Ticking, ticking, light-footed time thumped in harmony with the thumps in their hearts. To share their hopes and their fate, that was why these strangers converged here. Now they were all willing to open their hearts.

"My daughter did not sleep a wink," a pair of glasses initiated.

The parents craned their necks.

"My son set the alarm clock at four this morning," a dull face responded.

"Your boy is good. Mine hadn't touched a book until two weeks ago. Last night he tried to burn the midnight oil, I told him..." one potbelly chuckled.

"I tossed all night myself," a mid-aged tenor chimed in.

"They say this year the rate is one to forty," a heavy man breathed laboriously.

"No, no! One to sixty," a scrawny fellow whose son was at the top of his class was indignant at the lowered rate.

"Yes, yes, harder, much harder," echoed unanimously, heads shaking. It was excusable if their children fell victim to the examination system.

"Are you sure?" a beautiful skirt questioned. "That means less than two percent get to college? How can that be?"

Her eyes traveled from one face to another, seeking salvation.

"Let Heaven decide," a pockmarked fatalist yawned.

Faces scattered. Yes, who can beat fate?

Jianfei's mom took a day off and was now sitting on a shaded lawn talking to Lishan's mom about removing the "rightist" labels from some well-behaved, nationally-known intellectuals in the correction camps. Xiaoshi was making new friends. A group of twelve to fourteen year olds were bicycling along the concrete paths.

Hours of waiting brought the parents' their long-waited news. When the bell finally rang to loosen and tighten their taut faces, into their arms flew their tortured offspring, some jumping in the air, some blossoming with an uncertain smile, more drying eyes, wringing hands, wiping clouded faces, drooping heads and slumping on the lawn. Laughing or sobbing ensued accordingly among the parents. Both Jianfei and Lishan's mothers received sunny faces on their shoulders. The composition, the first examination and the heaviest stone in everyone's heart, had now been uplifted.

"What was the title?" was everyone's first question.

"As I Sing 'The Internationale'".

"That's about the Soviet revisionists."

Mom hurried to interpret, looking around.

"You are supposed to denounce them and repudiate their fallacies."

"Of course."

Jianfei, though immersed in triumph, was a bit annoyed to hear mom raising her voice among dozens of parents who were in the midst of intense emotional fluctuations. "And we have practiced similar titles at the review session, such as 'As I sing 'The National Anthem'".

"Arise, ye prisoners of starvation; Arise ye wretched of the earth…"

The scrawny fellow broke into song trying to distract his crestfallen son. Other parents nodded to the rhythm. The song was imbibed in new China by millions since birth if not before.

The two girls had surmounted the most formidable obstacle on their journey to college. The most monstrous iceberg had passed them without inflicting too much damage. Yet the tension had just started. The admission letters wouldn't be sent out until a month later.

Chapter 21

The girls awarded themselves three full days of sleep. On the fourth day, Jianfei and Lishan met to see Huifang who had grown somewhat estranged due to her affair with Tang Wei.

Huifang's mom, teacher Huang, was bustling about in the kitchen. Rubbing her hands anxiously on her apron, she poured two cups of cold tea from the water bottle. This math teacher had been battling to restore her family's order. Her husband had built a nagging habit during his fourteen years of superior life as an inferior officer. From Beijing to Nanjing, from the emperor to the dinner table, from uniforms to schools… nothing met his standards. And now, after nearly two weeks, the daughter too had become equally obstinate. She had locked herself up, rejecting everyone and everything. She ate only once a day when the bathroom wall vibrated with dad's snores after midnight. Seeing her daughter's friends, teacher Huang grasped them as a drowning person clings to a branch. The rescuers had finally arrived!

Holding Jianfei's hands in her own, Ms. Huang whispered, "Do something! Both of you, she just won't talk to us, for two weeks now!" Her head shaking like a toy drum.

Jianfei and Lishan exchanged a glance. It was indeed two weeks since they last talked to Huifang.

"How was your exam?" Ms. Huang handed over the tea, "you were in the same examination site, right?"

"The same classroom. I guess I have borrowed luck from Jianfei." Lishan said.

"How did Huifang do?" Jianfei gulped down the tea, soothing her parched throat.

"Chemistry, good; math, good. Everything seemed better than usual... You know how we worried...of course, the countryside is not necessarily a bad choice and we have relatives down there..."

"Mom, shut up!" barked from a room.

Mom was subdued. On the way to her kitchen retreat, she said, "I'll leave her in your care; see whether you can get her out of that room."

Huifang's door clicked open. Swollen eyes and puffy cheeks were the new image of the well-known beauty.

"My God! What happened?" Jianfei stepped forward.

"Nothing. My period and abdominal pain, that's it." Avoiding Jianfei's eyes, Huifang's legs turned to cross towards the bed again.

Jianfei cast a significant look at Lishan who rolled her eyes.

After thirty seconds of silence, a cold, curt greeting was released from Huifang's back.

"What brought you two lucky birds here?"

Aloofness and apathy had been Lishan's copyright. Huifang was quick in adopting Lishan's patent. They were so used to Huifang's happy-go-lucky, merry-go-round style. The only tones they recognized from their carefree friend were amiable, tender, submissive and helplessly sweet.

"Cheer up. You aren't me," Lishan softened dramatically, "Let's take a walk to the river..."

Jianfei squinted and frowned slightly. Lishan sensed a change and checked herself. The river, where Huifang and her lover met, might be the source of her trouble. No one was able to bring about such a metamorphosis in the debonair Huifang, except one, the one who dwelt in her head, the one who took possession of her soul, who nibbled her heart at night and refilled it with fresh blood every morning, the one whose smile was the sun in day and beacon light throughout her dreams, and whose appearance at the riverside had turned a new page in her life.

"Let's go to the rock garden," Jianfei suggested as she pulled up a white shirt and offered it over to Huifang.

To their surprise, Huifang leapt up and began to dress. She had not learned Lishan's full bag of tricks yet. Jianfei smiled inside. She still lacked a bit of Lishan's stubbornness.

The cadets were all gone for the summer vacation. Faculties worked half days but the Academy Cooperative was a beehive. Children buzzed around, ice cream and popsicles hanging on their lips. Jianfei joined the little army and quickly streamed back with three ice cream cups.

They settled down on a bench near the gate. Two guards were saluting each other, changing their posts. Cautiously, Jianfei avoided the topic of soldiers.

"How were your entrance exams?" Jianfei started with an assumed safe subject.

"I don't know." Huifang looked to the ground.

"I heard this year the second category had an easier examination, is that true?" Lishan followed up prudently.

"I don't know."

Huifang's indifference agitated Jianfei.

"What do you know then?"

"I don't know."

Huifang kept her equilibrium.

"How was the chemistry paper? Was it difficult?" Jianfei persisted.

"Leave me alone! I told you I don't know!"

The sudden eruption startled the three; Huifang rose to her feet and walked away.

Jianfei chased after. Lishan stayed behind and watched as her two friends suddenly stopped in the middle of the road, face to face, necks sticking out like two ruffled roosters. One slowly sat down on the curb. Her ice cream dropped on her white sandals which she kicked off in a rage. The other stood by, with folded arms, looking somewhere over her shoulder.

"What's going on between you two?" Lishan loitered over.

Silence.

"Jianfei, what's wrong with Huifang?"

"Ask her," Jianfei snapped.

Huifang slumped on the lawn behind Jianfei, silent tears trickled down.

"Tell me!" Lishan yelled.

"She...ask her..." anger choked Jianfei, "she did not go to the examinations!!"

Lishan, jaw dropping, could not believe that the most optimistic and obedient girl would have the guts to defy the nationwide university entrance examinations. Abandoning the exam was tantamount to abandoning life.

Chapter 22

Standing in line, his jaws mechanically moved along with "without the Communist Party, without New China". Tang Wei's mind flipped from Xiao Ming to Huifang and Huifang to Xiao Ming. The restaurant at the end of the lane marked the beginning of the end of his career.

"How is this Xiao Ming? Is he trustworthy?" Huifang's questions hovered in his head.

The cigarette he bribed Xiao Ming with and the brazenfaced lie about tutoring (serve the people!) made him fidget. He saw himself walking in the dimly lit road, his arms wagging along his side to exhibit Mao's book under Xiao Ming's nose like a third-rate, overacting performer with no stage experience. And then what had ensued surpassed his expectation and fed his vanity: a model soldier in the study campaign, the promotions... He rocked his head to shake off the shameful memories.

You are stupid.

A voice teased him in his head.

Stupid to let an animal's desire replace a hero's dream, stupid to lie, causing irreparable damages, stupid to eat in a public place. Now what?

As if to reply, the Political Instructor summed up his speech:

"...As an Activist nominee for the quarterly study campaign, Comrade Xiao Ming has set a brilliant example for us all. Not only did Xiao Ming overcome the study barrier and gain literacy, but he digested Chairman Mao's works word by word. Beyond these, he showed his mastery of revolutionary theories by dissecting his own thinking and expose those he considers bourgeois or petty bourgeois to the Party organization. Comrades, only those who dare to lay bare their shady souls have the hope to revolutionize themselves. Even on Sunday when his mother was with him, he spared some time to have a heart-to-heart talk with me. He surveyed his performances and invited my opinions. His self-criticism was a good lesson for me and I'd like to share it with you. He regretted that he had spent money dining in a small restaurant with his mother while millions upon millions of poor peasants in the country, in his home village, cannot afford rice. Comrades, plain living is our glorious tradition and this tradition needs us revolutionary soldiers to carry on…"

Thunderous applause brought an abrupt end to Li Yi's conclusion. Tang Wei was slapped in the face, yet automatically his palms joined the synchronized clapping. After the meeting, he was told that his night shift would be replaced by the second squad leader. No explanation was given.

Tang Wei was granted eight hours' sleep, but his mind was in revolt. *Why should I be stripped of a soldier's basic duty?* Tang Wei would be particularly stupid if, by now, he still could not see the connection between the two incidents. He should have realized that his extra hours of sleep had everything to do with his dining out. It was to be a lifelong payment for a momentary luxury at the rickety "Apricot Blossom Village." Xiao Ming was a puzzle. Ming, brightness, carried everything his poor father could hope for in an uneducated child. A peasant's son with only three years of schooling, logically, according to Tang Wei's beliefs, he should not be a snitch, since ignorance breeds dumbness, hence loyalty. But people change due to circumstance. Temptation could be found almost anywhere, even in mundane daily events. Simple attainments could have glorious ends particularly when all sorts of titles were bestowed and handed out: activist, model, hero, leader: who would want to lag behind?

Xiao Ming caught up fast. Within three years, he could read Mao's works without much stumbling. With Tang Wei's recommendation, he became a glorious member of the Chinese Communist Party; he was elected as the squad leader, stepping into Tang Wei's shoes. He addressed Tang Wei as "old brother"; he accompanied Tang Wei to the clinic after he got injured in a basketball game; he brought meals to his bed after his night shift. "Friendship" had been the source of these kindnesses in Tang Wei's mind. Now he began to assess Xiao Ming's deeds in a different light. Suspicions crawled in from the dark.

A pair of eyes followed him, inquiring as to his whereabouts, waiting for his return. He shook them off. *Huifang, I am sorry.*

On Monday morning, the agenda was announced over breakfast: Self-study: "The Speech at the Yenan Symposium of Art and Literature", one hour; group discussion chaired by each Party group leader, topic: "Standpoint and World Outlook", two hours; cleaning up the dining hall, one hour.

Li Yi clapped Tang Wei on his shoulder as he was slurping up porridge, "I need to talk to you. Please come to my office. Your group discussion will be chaired by Xiao Ming."

Tang Wei nodded. *So this is it, Xiao Ming has got what he has been seeking. An usurper.* Tang Wei planted his face in the bowl, cracking a mirthless smile. The steaming porridge bit his tongue. *Are you sure? You're oversensitive!* Tang Wei clung to a glimmer of hope. *Maybe it's just a confidential meeting about recruiting new Party members. Yes, it could be, it must be...* Abundant evidence seemed not enough to convince Tang Wei: this was it. Smart people grew dumb when they blindfolded their eyes to plain facts. Anyway, the thought of recruiting new Party members suddenly became very convincing and cheered him up. He wolfed down the buns with a much lighter heart. He even hummed a song from the Soviet movie *The Forty First*, a song Huifang hummed all day long the day before. Eyes turned to him. His western song was completely out of place in this proletarian army dining hall. He looked around and started to tune the Soviet song to "the Commune is evergreen ivy and the members are its melons". His notes jumped from the likely western, re, fa, la to the Chinese do, mi, so, making him sound like an off-key singer. What a chameleon, he cursed himself.

If not for Huifang's friends, he would never have had the luxury to watch the so-called "teaching material," *The Forty First.* It was a controversial movie, banned everywhere. Tang Wei sent Huifang into the theatre with his eyes and he himself entered only once the lights had dimmed as the cast list slowly scrolled down and the droning theme music began. The movie was poisonous, so the audience had been warned. What the "Soviet Revisionists" advocated here was peaceful coexistence between the two antagonistic camps, Socialists and Capitalists. It was a love story between a captor and her captive, the Red Army female and the White Army male. They were cast on a remote island, a symbolic Eden where love germinated and bloomed between the two human bodies, a revisionist Adam and Eve. For this, the Soviet filmmakers were bombarded with severe criticism for their "bourgeois sentimentality and humanitarianism." Their intention was to create an idyllic society, pure and innocent, to prove that human nature could, and should, transcend the barriers of class. The Chinese repudiated this idea. How could it be possible? Where there were humans, there were classes and class struggles. The "revisionists" returned to Marxism only at the end when the Red Army soldier lifted her gun barrel, aimed it at her lover who was hailing down the warship of his own army, and fired, marking on her record the forty first enemy she had shot dead. Was it logical? It seemed possible. By killing the impossible love, the movie redeemed itself; class instinct eventually conquered human nature. But in China, the very notion of mixed-class love itself was absurd and therefore could never occur. The movie's music and cinematography were presented on a grand scale, larger than life, overwhelming the woebegone subject with a beautiful sentimentality and a romantic pathos so intense that the majority of viewers, of either sex, harbored a secret wish that the girl would fly away with the man to the White Army's ship. But to what end? The girl would get killed. The movie would have to end in a death, him or her, the White or the Red. Death was inexorable.

Tang Wei stole a glance at Huifang, who was sobbing incessantly, his own eyes moist. But the tears were forbidden here because Chairman Mao had made it clear, "There is absolutely no such thing in the world as love or hatred without reason or cause."

Tang Wei blinked to mask his half-shed tears. He touched Huifang's hand. *Here is my White Girl!* This thought struck him like lightning, leaving him senseless. His grip loosened and his hands withdrew. On the screen, the White officer staggered a few steps and then lay dead on the sand. A white spray of the sea soared into the sky as the wind wailed a dirge. Huifang wept and Tang Wei tried to remain immune.

That was a month ago. They never had the chance to talk about the movie until yesterday.

"I don't understand the girl. Does she love him?"

Huifang knitted her brow, her hands combing Tang Wei's hair as he lay on the meadow.

The peach trees offered a piece of shade; their pink petals had just turned to tiny green nuts.

"Yes, but when the personal and class interests clash, the class instinct will ultimately overcome the other, because a human being is, in essence, a class being." Tang Wei was always a glib talker.

"What are you talking about?" Huifang mumbled, "Love is love, a male and a female, that's it. Simple and clear." She stroked his hair tenderly. "She should have joined him on the ship." She looked at the mountain in the distance.

"Then what? Get herself killed?"

"So it is the human instinct of self-protection that comes first, and not the class instinct."

Huifang's sudden sharpness made Tang Wei speechless. His tongue returned momentarily, making a wittier remark, "No, because she chose death by staying behind alone on that isolated isle rather than living among her enemies."

"You are bad," she purred like a kitten.

"Well, well, whatever." Tang Wei rose to his feet and planted a kiss on her lips. It took the edge off her anger.

The theme song of *The Forty First* played over and over in his mind like a droning airplane. Knowing that at this moment, Huifang would be passing the guard, and knowing that she must be devastated at his absence, Tang Wei felt like a caged animal dashing at all sides for a way out.

Chapter 23

A capital day! Mailmen with admission letters would be dispatched. On this day, fate would be sealed in sealed envelopes. The younger generation would regroup. Yesterday's friends might bid farewell for good because their divergent roads might bring them together only once in the next thirty years. Their value and approaches to life would also be spread wide apart. Yesterday's strangers might dine at the same table, toasting to each other's successes, networks built over glasses... The admission letter, a ladder leading to an ivory pagoda would descend to a few prosperous courtyards to help renew the hierarchy while the notice of rejection would also be delivered to the families of the condemned.

Ten o'clock, the decisive moment, the moment the mailmen set out, was drawing near.

Since early morning Jianfei sat in the shade near the mailbox, a book and a cup of cold tea beside her; her eyes strained; her neck craned towards the direction from which the mailman, the King of the Day, would appear with the ringing of his bike. She tried a few lines of Luxun's "A True Story of Ah Q" but found the reading exasperated her patience.

> ...Ah Q peeled off his own lined jacket and searched all over...but only found three or four lice and they popped faintly in his mouth. He glared at Beard Wang: one after another, in twos and threes, the lice made explosive sound in his mouth... Ah Q was indignant...

The laughable paragraph failed to ignite any reaction in her. Jianfei looked at her watch. It was 9:29. She put down the book and tilted her head. Thirty minutes to go. She kicked off her sandals and began to pace the grass. From time to time, Xiaoshi and the maid came out popping their heads, adding fuel to her fire. 9:40, Jianfei calmed herself down and returned to Ah Q:

> ...Revolution is coming...then the sons-of-a-bitch of the Wei Village will have to kowtow to Ah Q: 'Good Q, please spare my life!'...treasures...go straight to open the suitcases. Money flushed out: shoe-shaped gold and silver ingots...the bed of the scholar's wife must be moved to my temple...Little D has to do the job, and must be quick. If not, slap his face...

Ten thirty now. Jianfei flung the book on the lawn and ran to the road. Not a soul. Magpie, magpie, show me a sign; crack a song to report the good luck! Raising her head, her eyes ransacked the surrounding trees for the auspicious magpie. No magpies. Even the cicadas sounded faint today.

Eleven o'clock...Eleven thirty. Tears trickled down, so that was it? That was it? All these years! The dream of a university badge, the passion for a foreign language and literature... just drivel? Xiaoshi and the maid withdrew to the house, sharing a pain that might convert to a deluge of despair and humiliation.

Twelve fifteen, Jianfei's heart sank. As she dumped the tea on the grass and dragged herself listlessly inside, a strange phenomenon occurred. A visitor slowly crawled into her vision. A spider, of a modest size, timidly edged over from the pavement. Jianfei spontaneously stepped aside to make room for the felicitous creature. She laid her body flat; her eyes chased the tiny moving object on the green blades. She vaguely remembered the maid had mentioned that a spider crossing the water casts a propitious omen. The spider was in no rush. It zigzagged along the green carpet. Come this way, Jianfei patted gently on the wet grass. The spider surmounted peak after peak, took a breath and landed on a dry peak. This way, keep moving, Jianfei wagged a long stem, beckoning at the spider. The tiny thing recognized its ultimate goal and regained momentum on its long march. Jianfei held her breath and clung to the spider that was laboriously trudging over the dry land and then waddling across the wet land. Almost simultaneously, Jianfei heard the ding-ling-ding-ling of a bicycle. It startled her.

There standing in the blinding sun, silhouetted against the azure vault of the summer afternoon sky, was the mailman, a letter fluttering in his hand. Transparent beads of sweat stood out on his forehead. Jianfei was slow in responding: too good to be true!

"Congratulations! I am the harbinger of your university!" the mailman beamed into her wet face, "What? Are you crying? Celebrate! I deserve a jin of milk candy! Pedaling in the sun, threading through hundreds of lanes!"

Jianfei snatched the envelope and tore it open: F. University, English Department. Laughter broke through tears.

Her bare feet splattered into the kitchen. "I made it! I made it!" the paper danced in her hands.

Xiaoshi shot to his bicycle, "I'll go tell dad!"

The maid took the opportunity to free herself from the kitchen. She wiped her hands on her apron and joined the neighbors who swarmed in. Tongues clicked; eyes danced; exclamations flew in the air. The mailman gloated as if he were the one who hit the ball.

"Remember the candies, tomorrow!" he mounted his bike and waved to Jianfei.

As crowds thinned, a face floated into her mind and said, "Welcome to Shanghai!"

And she replied to it in her head, "Yang Bing, I am coming!"

The idea that they would be studying in the same city, and away from home, thrilled Jianfei. *I have to let him know.*

Jianfei rushed to Lishan's building. Halfway, Lishan ran up to her, her letter in the air. They threw themselves into each other's arms, "We made it!"

Chapter 24

Huifang's fate had already been sealed since the moment she decided to skip the exams. Actually her fate had been sealed in her cradle, with or without an entrance exam, and she knew this. Too worried to leave her alone on such a day, Jianfei and Lishan felt obliged to go and check things out. Their admission letters were heavy in their hands—never in their life had there been anything heavier.

Jianfei looked at herself in the mirror: the brows arced on her forehead, the eyes limpid as the sky in fall. Drooping shoulders, willowy waist, Jianfei was like an elegant tree. She dressed up to visit Huifang and to celebrate, but the grooming embodied special significance. A wisp of hope, vague and faint, sneaked into her heart. She was looking forward to a chance encounter. Maybe a magic wand would bring Yang Bing to her eyes somewhere some time. *It is summer vacation and he is home!! What will he think of me now? Will he think of me at all…after five years? Five years!*

During her long college preparation, the blue sweater had nearly retreated into oblivion. Now, only after the success, did she have the luxury to dwell on his face, his glasses and his blue figure. During his absence, she had built an interest in dad's photo albums simply because Yang Bing's father was among several photos though the rest were all senior officers, potbellied, unattractive and uninteresting otherwise. She had intruded into Xiaoshi's drawer to view his small collections; she donated her old stamps, placing them side by side with the Olympic Games. Touching Xiaoshi's marbles, coins and figurines, old days came tumbling back with acute vividness.

She asked the girl in the mirror, "Has your inferiority vanished? We have come across each other in the past; fate will tie us even closer in Shanghai."

An ocean blue silk shirt, a black silk skirt and her mom's black leather sandals enhanced her festive mood. Jianfei joined Lishan on the way to Huifang's.

Lishan was also in her best, a white silk shirt and a brand new purple silk skirt, long enough to cover her shins: a novel look for Lishan, a temporary reprieve from her sarcasm.

A twenty minute journey in the sun seemed like hours. They took shelter in the shade of a massive willow where the three of them had the saddest moment four weeks ago.

"Huifang's father might be at home!" Lishan suddenly recalled. Huifang's father could be as nasty as a hyena.

The cooperative was nearby, a beehive. Children rushed in and out with ice-lollies in colorful wrappings. Teenage girls clustered in front of the photography studio, chittering and chattering over the displayed photos. A flock of small boys flew towards the trees nearby, long bamboo sticks in their hands. Tiny balls of wet starch were stuck to the tips. These sticks were cruel tools applied on the arrogant cicadas. The boys tiptoed to the tree trunks, their eyes sieved through the dense foliage searching for the shrieking, black dots. Then their poles lunged out, the starch glued to the arrogant dots whose "I know…I know" instantaneously faltered. Their gauze wings fluttered, quivered, making last-ditch appeals, "I know"— until they realized their pathetic plight and made an abrupt stop.

It fascinated Jianfei, "Let's go look at what those urchins are doing."

They stood up, but the shoppers thickened the road, and they waited in the middle.

"Hello, isn't that Jianfei?"

She heard a voice. She turned her heels. What entered her vision immediately made her heart pump fast. She felt her chest tight and her breathing heavy. A group of glasses, just like five years ago, the Yang family always strung together. Yang Bing, his college badge shone in front, was facing her direction. The speaker was his younger sister, Xuezao, the Snow Date. As she waved at Jianfei, the whole family was waiting nearby, expectantly.

"Long time no see!" Jianfei said, cheeks reddening.

Yang Bing blushed too, worse than a girl. Jianfei's eyes skimmed over him. A striking feature about him was his beard, which aged him and cast some sort of maturity on his whole being. "My!" It was beyond her knowledge that a beard could be planted on such a young face. She could hardly match the beard with the blue sweater skipping rope on the sports field.

The awkwardness lingering between Jianfei and Yang Bing seemed eternal and neither could quite regain their equilibrium. All of a sudden, the hullabaloo around her died down. The busy pedestrians vanished and the world was left with only these two.

The boy she had been seeing in her dreams stood close to her, face to face. Her eyes evaded his and passed to his sister.

"Ask her about the letter, the enrollment announcement," Yang Bing wasted no ceremony and pressed his sister Xuezao for the priority of the moment.

Xuezao parroted back, "Have you received the college admission letter today?"

"Yes," doubly entranced by the college admission and the chance encounter, Jianfei gave the simplest answer, forgetting the details.

"Ask her what school," Yang Bing urged again, in a low voice impregnated with anxiety.

"What school?" Xuezao echoed again.

"F. University," Jianfei continued her passive and foolish role.

"Ask her what department…" in a bit of laxity, Yang Bing turned to his sister the third time.

The repeated indirect speech in the face of the interrogated object obviously pushed the brother into a deeper awkwardness and made him realize that soon it might shed a light on his secret in front of the family. Turning the indirect into direct speech might be the only way to save face and himself from suspicious eyes.

He said in a way as casual as possible, "What department?"

"English," turning to his sister, Jianfei replied in indirect speech, as if seeking retaliation.

Satisfied, Yang Bing tied his tongue again but turned to his parents to say something appropriate who then offered a very reserved "congratulations" and continued to scrutinize a blanket they had just bought. The color matched their son's silver-gray shirt and suited the mild climate in Shanghai.

Jianfei cast a sidelong glance at Yang Bing as if saying, "We are in the same city now, just you and me, and no more parents!"

Chapter 25

Huifang was lying on a bamboo couch in her room.

In the living room, her father was noisily blowing the tea, skimming over the tea leaves, his other hand patted vehemently on the newspaper headline, "Ha! A Sino-Soviet Cold War! Another editorial attack on their old friends. Endless debates!"

He mumbled and chewed the tea leaves, sipping loudly out of his cup. The two girls, guilty over their mutual success at the college entrance exam, facing the clattering, slashing tongue of a grumbling father whose ill-fated daughter had fallen victim to Darwin's "survival of the fittest", walked in, single file, passing Huifang's father.

"Wait a minute!" the man stopped sipping. "Sit down."

Folding up the newspaper, he turned to Lishan stern-faced, "Tell me how you got in. Through the back door?"

Attacked by surprise, Lishan's heart leapt. Hyena, she addressed him in her heart. Her feet nailed to the floor, she was completely in the dark as to what the hyena was talking about. Perspiration beaded her forehead. She stood aghast at this bellicose ex-KMT officer accusing her of impropriety.

We are not here to subject ourselves to your castigation. Jianfei came forward, "How is your daughter? May we see her?"

Huifang rose from her couch languidly and dragged herself into the living room. She glanced at dad. A cold glint flashed in her eyes, "What else can you do except grumble? Who's a loser? A laborer in the countryside or a captive in the battlefield? Same old mumble jumble, like father like daughter…"

Lishan and Huifang had traded their personality in less than two months; Jianfei could not fathom all these inexplicable changes in Huifang. She was a complete enigma now.

Huifang's dad was profoundly ruffled. He paced mutely. The soft sole of his slippers left no trace on the waxed floor on whose mirrored surface his white silk shirt reflected back and forth, back and forth.

"How much better is Lishan's score than my daughter's? Jianfei, you are off the hook. As for your admission, I hold no grudge. You deserve the best school…"

He laughed eerily, turning to his target again.

"Lishan, tell me, is it that you have a Communist father, who has a classmate who happens to be the principal and who has a husband, who happens to have the power in the higher education bureau …"

As if opening boxes wrapped one inside the other, he unfolded his clauses within clauses. Slowly but emphatically, he spat out every word, snarling each rabidly. The redundant use of "have" and "has" was to deliberately build the links leading to Lishan's back door.

Humiliation and resentment drove her tears out. The mauled Lishan dashed into Huifang's bedroom. Huifang followed and shut the door on dad's face.

So the principal's husband played an unspeakable role in my admission? So I am still a loser, only shielded by my ignominious privilege? Did my dad strike a dirty deal behind my back? Am I just a plaything in the hands of the powerful? As if splashed with cold water, Lishan suddenly abandoned her brainless happiness.

Her anger bottled inside since they entered the house, Jianfei decided to confront this ex-enemy. *It is unfair to attack Lishan since she has no knowledge of what was going on under the table. It is unfair that you should compare your daughter to us. Do you know your daughter skipped the whole exam? In the final analysis, what is your background, your color? By the way, why do you hold such animosity against our Party's international policy? Once an enemy, always an enemy!!* The word "enemy" flashed in her mind.

"Uncle, why don't you ask your daughter about her score?"

Without another word, she joined her friends.

Huifang was biting her lips, "I am sorry. I am a black sheep. He hates you because he hates me and he hates everything."

Jianfei saw their already frayed bond about to break apart as it nearly had during the anti-Rightist movement six years ago.

Lishan was stone-faced. She was determined to dig to the bottom of the enemy's accusations against her dad. A storm was brewing at Lishan's house.

The blazing white, sultry afternoon faded. The sun dragged itself down from the sky. The earth was warped and cracked, like a freshly baked enormous cookie. Yet the heat showed no sign of abatement. Dinner was moved outside. A small table was set on the lawn. Mosquito incense was blinking like a firefly.

Lishan was the first at the table today. The brothers, her nuisances, had just returned from the swimming pool, their hair matted on top. Two of them were clipping their dripping T shirts on the clothes line.

"What brought the last diner first to the table today?" one of them patted Lishan's head.

She dodged and barked, "Leave me alone!!"

"Easy! Sis," the boy stepped back, as swift as a lamb at a wolf.

"College student!" another brother allied himself with the other, "Take it easy! It is your red letter day!"

"Did mom prepare a 'congratulations dinner' for us?" the youngest chimed in.

"Shut your mouths!!" the Queen of the Day put up a sullen face.

"Watch your tongue, sis!" the oldest put his hands around the youngest's shoulders. "How did we offend you?"

Dad shuffled his feet to the table, "Congratulations!"

No response.

"Congratulations!" dad said condescendingly.

"Dad, I have a question for you," the surly Lishan was well prepared.

"Boys, boys," Dad gestured, the boys scattered away.

"Did my principal and her husband have anything to do with my college admission?"

Lighting a cigarette, dad was in no hurry to settle the account with his angry only daughter. He puffed, circled his lips and exhaled a thin blue line, watching it twirling into the twilight, "Why?"

"Don't ask why, just answer!"

Dad's indifference broke the dam that struggled to hold the sluice.

Mom carried a bamboo couch for dad. It was a rare happening at home that her daughter initiated a conversation with her husband.

Dad leaned back. His eyes squinted at the steel blue sky, and then took a comprehensive glance at his daughter. With a taunting voice, he ensued, "Bothered by jealousy, eh?"

"Bothered or not bothered, is it true?"

Lishan glowered at dad, standing staunchly. Puff, puff. The red dots fanned Lishan's fury.

"True or false?"

An evening breeze gusted. Dad flicked his ashes, "Ahhh, Cool!" He took a deep breath as he raised his face to welcome the wind.

"So it is true, isn't it?" Lishan stood up, tears brimming up.

"Sit down," dad sat up and patted the stool beside him, "Listen, all you want is the result and not the means, the 'what' and not the 'how'."

Lishan stomped her feet. "Back door…snake! Cheater! Shame on you!"

Betrayed, she was betrayed by her own father. Lishan dashed inside. The door banged closed behind her.

Part Three

Chapter 1

"The ninth passenger train bound for Shanghai is leaving in thirty minutes…" the broadcast gathered the passengers quickly.

On the platform, Jianfei hauled her gigantic wicker suitcase, "Xiaoshi, lend a hand!"

Xiaoshi hurried to take over the suitcase.

A hand whose palm was gemmed with calluses and ornamented with greasy black lines grabbed the handle, "Fifty cents to the train." The unkempt head turned to show a pallid face. Without any response from the suitcase owner, his legs were already on the move, the suitcase hoisted on his shoulder.

"No," Jianfei and Xiaoshi had to make a tug-of-war to retrieve her suitcase. "No help is needed."

The man spat on the cement, rubbing his palm indignantly against the fabric on his side whose color faded into an unknown age.

"Mom, I told you the suitcase was oversized. Even Xiaoshi is staggering."

The young lady strutting and swaying her silk skirt drew curious eyes among hordes of seasonal peasant-construction workers migrating from the north who lingered on the platform. Her standard Mandarin dialect, her exuberance and youthful beauty served in the villagers' eyes to mark her as an urban abnormality. In dismal contrast were their tattered bedrolls, sordid clothing and wooden looks. Besides the dainty young lady and her neatly-dressed young gentleman, obviously her brother, there was this middle-aged, extremely proper, well-mannered lady who apparently knew little about the luggage and its size. Peasants observed the family of three as if at some animal show. Out of place, these aristocrats, they thought. Some of the peasants had turned the platform into their temporary living quarters until the day the police might come to patronize them.

Presently another aristocratic family walked into the show.

"Xiaoshi, it's you!" A young voice, but thick enough to be taken as an adult.

Jianfei turned to face the familiar beard. Again her heart gave a leap. Yang Bing passed his canvas bag to his younger sister beside him and moved the suitcase from Xiaoshi's hand into his own. A smile creased mom's face.

"Big brother! Haven't seen you for ages!" a squeal of delight escaped.

Xiaoshi patted Yang Bing on his shoulder. Surprising ecstasy lit Xiaoshi's eyes. The two men locked in each other's arms.

"How I miss you! You are a man now!"

"You, too. You are almost my height!" Yang Bing hugged his little friend again.

Thrilled, Xiaoshi cast a glance at his sister. The days of stamp-trading reappeared in Xiaoshi's mind. Not until he reached his sister's "stamp-trading" age, did he possess a vague notion of what the unfair trade meant to his sister and his Big Brother. The favored part was not him, but her.

"You two must be taking the same train to Shanghai," Xiaoshi's finger shuttled between the two.

Mom came forward. Like any mother, her first concern was the safety of her daughter who would be traveling alone.

"Please keep an eye on Jianfei. A fledgling flying away from the nest, it's her first time to leave the house."

"Mom!" mom's forward sentiments turned her stomach and made her lose face, "What do you mean 'keep an eye on me'? Am I a piece of luggage or something?"

"I will," Yang Bing replied regardless of the protest.

The siren called for boarding. Mom hugged Jianfei, eyes moist. Xiaoshi waved, face beaming.

The train slowly accelerated, opening the new page on Jianfei's life. The wheels rolled. The earth swirled back. Click, clank, click, clank..., a boring lullaby. Jianfei's eyes chased the flipping landscape. Green, green, yellow, yellow, blue, blue. The blue was the small ponds reflecting the sky. Ducks and drakes swam wing to wing, living an unmolested life, proud of their fidelity. The yellow was houses, mud walls and straw roofs, short and stout, like old men squatting in the sun watching the modern monster roaring by. Electric poles and soaring trees flashed by. In one pond, naked little boys ducked in on one spot and popped up twenty feet away, their self-made fishing rods and bait containers abandoned under the canopy of the weeping willow. Their siblings toddled, watched in the fields, giggled as they giggled. Their moms, lunch baskets on arms, waved at the men hoeing in the fields. Jianfei was absorbed in the idyllic picture. All of a sudden, slogans jumped in, making incoherent notes, breaking the pastoral harmony.

Long live the three Red Flags!
Long live the People's Commune!
Long live the Great Leap Forward!
Long live the General Line for Socialist Construction!

Bumpy big red characters were scrawled on the mud walls of the unsteady huts. Jianfei moved her eyes away to the whirling green. Every inch of this land seemed to be saturated with politics and the countryside was no exception.

Her mind wandered back to the railway station. Mom and her brother continued to smile and wave, one with red eyes. Dad was assiduous in the preparation for the new semester, and he was the one Jianfei really wanted to be there. All the bickering at the table over clear soup or golden chicken ponds suddenly appealed to her. She was leaving all this behind. Everything in Shanghai would be novel, except perhaps for one thing …Yang Bing. The thought of her childhood admirer alerted her and she straightened up. *Will he come to my compartment to "keep an eye on me"? My God!* Nervous at the thought, she stood up, looking towards the door. And then she sat back down again. Her head lolled against the window frame. The monotonous drone of the wheels soon rocked her into semi-consciousness. Like a slide show, she saw the blue sweater running up to her, in the snow…click, clank…the street show, the female Chiang Kaishek, a pair of glasses were watching, she saw her own figure responding to the curtain call, a bow and then…meeting his eyes…click, clank…stamps of The Olympic Games, marbles…click, clank…

"Excuse me, Jianfei," the stamps opened their mouths.

She opened her eyes and a pair of glasses shone above her. She rose to her feet.

"Sorry, it's so hot and boring," Embarrassed by her disorientation, Jianfei rubbed her eyes.

"Do you need anything?"

He is indeed keeping an eye on me, Jianfei thought. She shook her head.

An enormous yellow pear was held to her face. Its enticing aroma wormed into her nostrils.

"Have some fruit then," he said.

"Oh, no, no," she shook her head. He would not put down his hand and the pear dangled as the train rocked. But her head continued to say no.

"Then I will leave the cold tea with you," Yang Bing passed over an army water bottle.

"Big Brother", she called him in her heart, a warm gratitude rose up.

"I am in Car 9, Seat 11, in case you need me. I will meet you at the exit when we arrive." He was my bodyguard now, Jianfei smiled, shaking her head.

Shanghai—a city of skyscrapers, of bustling shops, of lanes jammed with soy milk and cruller stands in the morning, of alleys filled with the echoes of scrubbing brushes on chamber pots, of boisterous streets with strutting westerners whose memories of the horse races of the thirties were still fresh and who returned to seek their past adventures. Junks lay moored languidly on the Huangpoo River. High rises jagged the city's skyline. Unlike Jianfei's hometown, the old dynasty capital, which was notorious for its unbearable summer heat, where the suffocated earth languished and gasped for breath in the burning afternoon, where cars and pedestrians panted heavily in the sweltering sun and dragged themselves along at a snail's pace, here in Shanghai the ocean caressed the city and the air was circulated fresh. The elastic briskness of people's gait and the verve of the city made Shanghai seem much younger than Jianfei's city. Life seemed lighter and easier here. Unlike the tree-lined streets of Nanjing, Shanghai streets were lined with shops. The humility, rigidity and serenity of her hometown, only four hours away by express train but now far in the back of her mind, contrasted with the glamour, flourish and splendor of this modern international metropolis staring her in the face, eliciting a moment of wariness and reluctance in her bosom. Timidity quickly gave way to excitement however. Around her, stylish ladies in sleeveless blouses and permed hairdos were seen everywhere. Indifferent to any stunned provincial eyes that happened to be staring, these elegant ladies cocked their heads, threading between towering buildings as if no one else existed. The fashion and mode were daring here; her old Nanjing was far too conservative. Shoppers buzzed around. Northerners or "outsiders," as the natives derogatively addressed them, tried to blend in with their newly-purchased dresses—a charade that could continue so long as they did not open their mouths. Shanghai's renowned chauvinism was written on every native face.

"I love Shanghai!" Jianfei responded to the ocean of the fluttering university banners at the reception stations. Her face radiated.

"I will bring you to my grandma's and show you around the city," Yang Bing was also affected.

"F. University" caught Jianfei's eyes and she walked over. Yang Bing followed, carrying her enormous suitcase.

A woman in her late twenties stepped forward, stretching out her hand, "You must be Jianfei. I am Zhang Yue, Yue as in moon, the political instructor for freshmen from the English Department. Welcome!"

Political Instructor? Jianfei digested her title. She could be a fashion model! Never in her life had Jianfei seen a political figure with such style and elegance, although she had grown up in an environment teeming with politicians. Clad in a russet one-step skirt, a skirt so tight that could allow the wearer take one step at a time, a beige V-cut silk shirt and a pair of mid-heeled leather shoes, Ms. Zhang presented herself with unique taste. Jianfei smiled to meet Ms. Zhang's outstretching hand meanwhile having a hard time adjusting to her shoes; she could hardly put the Political Instructor and the mid-heeled shoes together. *There must be something special about this lady if she dares to wrap herself up in such a conspicuous way and still be the representative of the Party and the voice of political propriety.* Neither her shirt nor skirt met the Chinese taste. They were too foreign, in color, in cut, and in style. And yes, just as Jianfei had conjectured, she held a Ph.D. in Russian Literature. Ms. Zhang had just returned from Moscow two weeks ago.

Jianfei was quite aware that the first day at school with a boy acquaintance would not go unnoticed. However she was so carried away by the new city, the ebullient surroundings and friendly schoolmates and especially by the longed-for companionship of Yang Bing that she continued to let him walk beside her, a peccadillo which would later prove to be a painful mistake.

"We will send you to the dormitory," Ms. Zhang's hospitality was not just out of duty but bore the graciousness of a hostess. "Where is your luggage?"

"Here it is. I can help. I am Yang Bing. I am Jianfei's neighbor." Yang Bing did not know what to add next to his self-portrayal, "I am Yang Bing from the University of …" A redundant and feeble excuse, he hoped it could erase the suspicious impression on the Political Instructor as he knew well what that title meant.

"All right, you go with them," Ms. Zhang waved to a chubby face who grabbed the luggage from Yang Bing, and the three of them boarded the school shuttle.

Colorful banners bordered the green lawn; drums and cymbals joined in to provide a festive concert. The blue sky, clear as if washed, was etched with red slogans:

Welcome freshmen! Celebrate the new semester!
Long live the Party's education line!
Take the revolutionary road! Be revolutionary!

Loudspeakers played the theme song of "The Young Generation," "We young people have ardent hearts…" At the entrance to the university, a group of sophomores rushed from the reception station and took hold of the suitcase, leading the way to the girls' dormitory.

Seven smiling faces turned from the desk where they had been sitting around and chatting as Jianfei and Yang Bing appeared at the door.

"Hi, my name is Jianfei," smiling, she held out her hands.

"We have been waiting for you long," seven voices proffered greetings in a unanimous Shanghai dialect.

The strange language made her feel somewhat discomfited in her new home. Seven pairs of eyes rolled from Jianfei to her male companion and then rolled back towards each other. She was shown to her shared bedroom. Jianfei looked around. The room contained four bunk beds. A large desk with eight separate drawers stood in the center. The windows were wide open. The lawn, sprawling and well-manicured, bordered with large gold and red chrysanthemums, stretched from Jianfei's dormitory building to the one next door. On one side of the building was a small volleyball court lined with poplar trees. Poplar trees! The sophomore boys invited themselves inside the girls' dormitory room, taking the quick opportunity to check out all the new faces in their department, making sure they met its reputation for beautiful girls. They then politely said their goodbyes and left with the satisfaction of having accomplished their secret mission. Yang Bing was the only male remaining. He stood at the entrance; his feet shifted left and right, unable to find his tongue.

"I am leaving for my school then."

The girls, bidding him farewell with silent, inquisitive eyes, smiled meaningfully at him. Jianfei suddenly longed for his presence. There was too much to catch up on, yet she could not spare a moment of her precious time on this first day of her new life recollecting her past. She left the room, feeling obliged to walk him downstairs.

"I don't want to cause any misunderstanding of our relationship in public eyes," Jianfei faltered. "I am…uh… frightened of gossip. Please do not come again," almost inaudibly, she politely suggested, feeling short of breath.

"I understand."

Yang Bing's face displayed his guilt as he should have known better. He held out his hand. Their hands touched each other, though Jianfei gave only a cold, casual brush. The eyes of her roommates barbed her back, reducing the fresh excitement of the day.

"May I write to you?" Yang Bing groped tentatively.

Jianfei nodded an uncertain consent. What else could they do to prevent the rekindled one-day-old relationship from elapsing for another six years? Do they have to go through the agony and yearning again?

However on her way back, her uncertainty grew greater. The day's events resurfaced in her mind and she began to reassess them in a different light. A series of decisions which she made that day cast a shadow on her judgment. First, she should have parted with Yang Bing before they entered the Shanghai station; secondly, she should not let Yang Bing show up in front of her political instructor and then later in front of her roommates; thirdly, a verbal warning would not be enough to effectively ward him off; lastly, she was not sure whether encouraging or discouraging him was the wiser strategy. And to make things worse, her ambiguity would help only to drag the relationship into an uncertain future.

The atmosphere of the university seemed to have completely reversed her course, veering from seeking love to making revolution in just two hours. This was a place where everything was supervised and nothing counterrevolutionary could hide. Remember, though notorious for its capitalist and bourgeois way of life, Shanghai was also known in contemporary history as the birthplace and a leading city of the proletarian revolution, a stronghold of the iron and textile industries. An open city, its ins and outs hid no secrets. And F. University was itself in the grips of revolution, out and out, being the core of the nation's higher education. Ms. Zhang had just returned from the USSR with a Soviet Ph.D., a qualification for a revolutionary.

Chapter 2

Unlike Jianfei who was the last to show up, Lishan was the first to arrive at her dormitory. Her dad's presence was a permanent torment to her. Likewise, she was an eyesore in his eyes. She vowed never to return home again.

Her school was in her hometown. Situated on a hilltop, hidden behind dense foliage, the cloistered art school provided a perfect reclusive life for Lishan who had become more and more a hermit and enjoyed her own companionship immensely, a nun ready to give herself to the celestial life. She immersed herself in the symphony of nature played by the saxophones of the grazing cows of the neighboring peasants, the violins of the "weaving-girl" flies and the pianos of the forest brooks. At sunrise, when the hilltop was hidden in a pink vapor, and the twittering birds started their alarm clocks, Lishan opened her eyes to greet the splendor of untainted nature. She sat up, took out her painting kit and blended the world into her canvas: the lotus pond with all its rich reflections of blue, russet, yellow, red and green, the fuzzy thickets and the pasture embellished with variegated wild flowers. From time to time, her eyes glided with the white clouds and her thoughts wandered away.

How is Jianfei? How does she like that disgusting metropolis? Will she be popular? Will she be spoiled by friendship, genuine or false, as she used to be? Jianfei was absent from her life for the first time in eight years. She saw a void, a hole. An acute need for daily companionship took her heart in a tight grip. She took out paper and a poem began to flow from her pen. I must mail it to Jianfei before others show up.

Finally, one by one, the other seven roommates made their appearances and brought an end to her reclusive pleasure.

"That's a great painting!" Lishan heard a ringing voice and turned her back from the window. A slender girl stepped forward, long braids dancing behind, adorned with pink bows at the ends like a pair of lilies. The voice continued to ring, "Stand there, don't move!" the newcomer said, "Inside the window frame are leaves sparkling in the sunlight. A girl stands in the center, silhouetted against the shining green. The bright backdrop centered on a dark image is a perfection of contrast!"

Lishan frowned, "You certainly have a dark imagination but I am not a dark image!"

In a second, she realized she needed to pave the way herself now that her baby sitter Jianfei was in Shanghai, so she extended her hand, "Lishan."

"Hi, my name is Juhua Lu," the ringing voice had a childish face and a naïve smile.

"Juhua, Juhua," masticating the name, Lishan asked sarcastically, "Juhua like chrysanthemum flower or Juhua like orange picture?" Her old smirk crept over the corner of her lips.

Juhua replied in earnest, "Ju as in chrysanthemum, hua in China. I apologize if I offended you but it indeed created a striking artistic contrast when you stood inside the window frame with the sunlight in the background."

"Thank you," Lishan walked out, uninterested in the topic.

None of my new classmates can be compared with Jianfei, not even close. With this thought, she strolled along the wisteria-covered veranda to the lily pond. The ideal of hermitage strengthened her repugnance at mingling with her peers. She decided from then on that her painting brush would be her only everyday companion; no more human being would intrude into her heart. Every memory of Jianfei, even her harsh words, her frowns and scowling countenance, brought with it agony as it affirmed her absence. That night she wrote a long letter to Jianfei, and from then on the frequency of her letters to Shanghai was once every two days.

Lishan's standoffish and disinterested manner gained her a nickname, "Dark Image". It did not take long for this name to begin to circulate among her roommates except for Juhua, the inventor of the dark image, who felt responsible for the confrontation at the start of school and carried her guilt everywhere, begging the other six girls to give up this nickname. A loner, a thinker and a cynic, Lishan cocooned herself in the library or studio. Sharing quarters of less than twenty square meters with seven roommates was no easy job. It required the talent to sound cheerful when you were actually upset because someone had used your soap or toothpaste without telling you and the prowess to be an enthusiastic gossip effortlessly bringing up such newsworthy items as "I noticed that Professor Li had his eyes on…" and "how can boys draw a naked girl?" Propriety demanded that one put on some semblance of interest during the Sunday night fashion show after the girls returned from shopping downtown, followed by some smiles in the morning to comfort some grumpy ones due to a sleepless night, and then a nod of acknowledgement in response to some vivid account of an eerie nightmare…

Lishan abandoned any efforts at courtesy from the very beginning. She refused to endure the torture of the three meals while the rest sat at the same table sharing stories and gossips. She shrank in the corner, buried her face in her bowl, oblivious to whatever she was eating. But she had to bear her suffering when she was forced to sit next to someone to finish a certain project in class. Her presence, too, had become loathsome in others' eyes. Growing up behind the walls of a vacuumed army complex, shielded by Jianfei, Lishan's socialization was comparatively retarded. Jianfei was a walking stick without which she could hardly stand on her own feet. She had no clue how to converse, how to make herself acceptable. Even deciding how to walk had troubled her. *Should I hang my head low or hold it high?* She had no inclination to improve the situation because she was in the dark about what basic skills were required. She became frustrated with her own ineptitude.

At ten thirty, all the lights in the dormitory were turned off. To avoid the inevitable chatter that occurred just before getting into bed, Lishan usually stayed late until the murmuring tapered off and then stole back into her upper-decker in the dark. One night as she tiptoed in the hallway to her room she heard her name dropped in conversation. Her steps halted.

"They say Lishan's family has some connections in the bureau of higher education and that's how she got in." A hoarse voice.

It was Hu Jie, a basketball player on the university team. She was also late, having just finished a game. Rubbing her wet hair with a towel, she crept into her mosquito-net-wrapped bed. Lishan stepped back into the corridor and pasted her ear near the door.

"Oh? That dark image?" Hu Jie's buddy chimed in, "You have ears all over the school."

"Well, the basketball team has ears everywhere, not me." Hu Jie said.

"Would you please shut up? I was just falling asleep!" an angry voice cut them short.

Silence reigned. Lishan's sleep was blown away; just as she turned her heels, the silence was broken again.

"Why does she hate us so much?" the previously angry voice got even angrier as if Lishan was the one who sabotaged her sleep, "She seems always in a rage. She is arrogant, unreasonably arrogant."

"Unreasonable? She doesn't think so...Look at her collections of paintings, Russian, French...She is an alien." Another voice said calmly.

"All right. Let's be quiet. We'll have to get up at six for the military drills, remember," Juhua raised her drowsy voice which eventually hushed up the gossip.

Lishan sat on the hillside until midnight. Like a yacht, leisurely and elegantly afloat, the crescent moon sailed high above in the silvery, serene sea. A veil of clouds dangled on its hook. Hundreds of fireflies holding tiny lanterns twinkled mid-air, illuminating their own microcosm. Dew drops oozed from the blades of grass; giant fingers covered with moss stretched out from bulky trunks as if wearing gloves. Lishan, the midnight intruder, found more friends here than in her own room. As she raised her eyes to the moon, the Song poet Su Shi's lines popped into her head:

人有悲欢离合，
月有阴晴圆缺，
此事古难全。
但愿人长久，
千里共婵娟。

People are tearful and joyful, parted and reunited,
Skies are cloudy and clear; moons full and crescent,
Since ancient times, nothing is perfected.
May people last long,
Sharing the moon's beauty from a thousand miles apart.

Raising her head, Lishan asked the moon, "Are you shining on Jianfei? Will you convey my message? Tell her I miss her."

Why am I here? Why must I fake a smile and force myself into a friendship? She sighed. It is too late to return to the team now. She knew she had messed things up from the very beginning at university and there was no return. Her roommates had already shut the door on her.

Days passed. The crescent moon closed into a full circle. The wax and wane brought in a round-faced moon which ushered in the Mid-Autumn Festival, a festival for family reunions. Girls could not wait to get out of the dormitory. Lishan could not wait to resume her hermitage. Her hangdog countenance could be given a temporary relief. The dorm was a sanctuary for Lishan only on weekends and holidays when her peers were out of sight. The network of connections and favors her dad had exploited to get her into college had completely shattered the father-daughter relationship. Although enticing memories of past holidays at home tempted Lishan to join the family, she could not bear to be with her father. Her self-imposed isolation would continue without regard to the calendar.

Not far from the school gate, peddlers' stands flickered with gas lamps. Five spice tea eggs, fried tofu soup with soybean sprouts and vermicelli noodles, scallion pancakes, sesame biscuits, sunflower seeds, boiled salty peanuts, roasted walnuts...The appetizing aroma of the frying scallions filled the air and drew a dozen or so eaters. For those students who spent the festivals on campus for whatever reasons and could not control their pangs of homesickness, the urge to pamper themselves with a bit of luxury at such stands was quite overwhelming and the wily peddlers knew well how to lure more coins into their pockets.

Fifty cents in hand, Lishan strolled to the lights. A distinctive aroma sizzled in the air. Her nostrils followed it and quickly detected what it was: deep fried stinky tofu, her favorite. The peculiar addictiveness of this salty-spicy-fermented flavor was hard to resist. Every day she restrained her cravings, for fear of mocking eyes. Her classmates would never let her know a moment's peace if she were to return to the dorm stinking of putrid tofu. *Imagine the "dark image" eating stinking tofu! A laughing stock before my dear roommates!* Now, with most students away, without any hesitation, she approached the stand. Watching the man string the pieces of fermented tofu on bamboo sticks and dip them into boiling oil until the delicate smelly pieces shrank and turned golden yellow with a crispy crust greatly whetted her appetite. The peddler sprayed them with soy sauce and hot pepper.

Just as her hand stretched out to take them over, she heard a voice.

"Hi, Lishan!"

Quickly withdrawing her hand, she turned around. Juhua was dismounting from her bicycle. Mortified, Lishan rapidly thrust the fifty cents into her pocket and stepped away from the stand. Lishan was not used to being addressed in so friendly a manner. A first name without the last name signified intimacy. The outside world had already shut up on her. Lishan lived in muteness. Juhua's unexpected greeting poked a hole in her blank existence. It was an alarm. She was vigilant.

Not knowing what to say, she stammered, "Ah… hi… it is…er… cool out here."

"With all the stoves and frying pans?" asked Juhua, unaware of Lishan's awkwardness.

At this point, the peddler called out, "Stinky tofu!" The peddler waved, "Hey, your stinky tofu! Twenty five cents!" One hand holding the bamboo stick high in the air, the other wiping perspiration with his dirty apron, the peddler asked Lishan for payment.

Caught red-handed, Lishan cast an apologetic, shameful smile at Juhua, "Do you want to have a taste?" The tofu was still sizzling on its string.

"No, thank you," Juhua shook her head, smiling but took a step back from the happy sizzling stick, "I have had supper already." Juhua kept the smile on, trying to break the tension built by the pungent tofu.

"Listen, I know you plan to spend the festival alone. I have brought you some moon cakes." A nylon net with a box of moon cakes was hanging on her bicycle handle.

Tormented by her own family dilemma, touched by the sincerity and thoughtfulness of Juhua, regretful of her former rudeness, Lishan was choked with words, "Oh, no, no," she pushed the box back.

"Lishan, the Moon Festival is meant for family reunions. I am coming to invite you to join my family's moon party."

"No, please go home; be with your parents," Lishan was on the verge of saying "leave me alone" and "I enjoy myself better than with any companion", but she held her tongue.

"You should at least take one cake then, please," Juhua was a bit upset now.

Lishan was afraid that further refusal might make Juhua turn her back again.

To save further embarrassment, Lishan picked one cake symbolically and said, "I appreciate your invitation, but I really enjoy being alone."

Juhua hesitated and said, "I understand your situation," she paused, "but family is family, please forgive your dad."

"Don't ever mention my dad," Lishan burst into rage.

An awkward silence. Juhua mounted her bike.

Lishan then said almost inaudibly, "Please do not breathe a word about the stinky tofu."

"Don't worry," Juhua waved her hand and rode away.

Juhua's dad sat on the balcony with two students from his department whose homes were too far for a one day holiday trip. The history professor considered it his responsibility to provide a domestic environment for students from remote regions.

The moon carried a wisp of clouds, swaying in the sky. Its gleam sprinkled on the trees and houses, shrouding the world in silver. Watermelon and moon cake slices were displayed on a small round bamboo table. A white porcelain vase holding chrysanthemums stood in the center. The petals had two colors, yellow on one side, dark red on the other, arousing curiosity.

Juhua stepped in, flinging her bag on the sofa.

"Will Lishan join us?" dad turned his head.

"No," a bit crestfallen, Juhua answered, "she seems to enjoy her own company. She took one cake."

"That's good," dad said. "Juhua, remember to invite her for the next holiday. On special occasions like this, you should always take the initiative to improve the relationship. The holiday provides a chance for making up. You should grasp the opportunity and create a healthy environment for yourself and your classmates."

Chapter 3

Three-star General Du was Jianfei father's war time superior, now Shanghai Area Military Commander. Through thick and thin, battling in the south and the north, the two had forged not only a shoulder-to-shoulder comradeship but a blood tie of brotherhood. Holding a prominent and crucial position in China's strategic city, Commander Du was the spotlight of the media. His photos often occupied the front page, sitting in his wheelchair next to the mayor and distinguished foreign diplomats. Now the sixty-year-old father of three had assigned himself a new mission—to assemble the offspring of his friends, mostly high ranking military men, who came from all over the country to attend college in his city. He hosted the weekend entertainment. The young people called it "Uncle Du's Club." The members of this club were a handful of elite from prestigious universities in Shanghai. There these privileged youths were provided with the trappings of an affluent material life, and in exchange, were showered with the preachings of the veteran who believed he was speaking for their fathers. To keep the younger generation red was his obligation in this city, the dyeing pit and melting pot of capitalism.

On the third week Jianfei received a letter from the General, inviting her to his house this coming Saturday. Attached was her father's letter with an account, not without pride, of his daughter's current status at F. University: two weeks ago, Jianfei was appointed by the Department Party branch to be the Chairman of the Students' Union of sixty three freshmen.

Saturday afternoon was the scheduled time for weekly dorm cleaning. Jianfei stood by the windowsill, wiping the glass panes, trying to render them invisible. She wanted everything the best in her bedroom.

"Letter, Jianfei!" A thick envelope was tossed over.

"A thick one!" voices rose, a bit saucily.

"You are blushing!" a voice persisted, "Is it from that boy?"

Yang Bing's handwriting again! Her heart raced like a rabbit. She thrust it into her pocket, savoring it for a solitary moment, and continued with her cleaning.

By late afternoon everyone had left for the city. Jianfei walked to the school gate to catch the bus downtown, the letter still in her pocket. The jingling trolley bus leading to the heart of Shanghai was a shared memory of generations at this historic university. It jingled at the dawn of the century and rang into the thick of it, winding, wriggling, jostling, cutting through bustling streets. Saturday carried a thicker stream of traffic. Workers rushed home. Shoppers strolled in the city streets with bulging bags in hand.

On board the trolley, Jianfei took a seat by herself. Her hand reached the letter which had been nursed for hours. She unfolded it. A line jumped into her eyes, "I love you…since childhood." It was a song repeatedly sung in her heart hundreds of times but only confirmed now, a line familiar in their hearts yet fresh in their mouths. For the first and the last time, she had confirmed, after hundreds of cycles of denial, doubt, confirmation, denial, confirmation, during these six long years. The rest of the letter was a blur. Neon lights and shop windows flew by. The evening was settling over the bustling weekend. She saw nothing but, "I love you… since childhood."

The trolley jingled along. Passengers chatted. All she heard was, "I love you…since childhood."

Jianfei pressed the doorbell. General Du's house was a Tudor style house with three gables, situated next to the former American residence. Many of the houses in this neighborhood had been built by westerners. Two round windows, their glasses stained in blue, yellow, red and orange, glared like a pair of giant eyes. Enclosed behind a tall gray wall, hidden among the dense green leaves, the house emitted a streak of mystery. Outpouring light from the house shed on the garden and the well-manicured lawn bordered with furry bushes and dwarf pine trees. A pond issued little bubbling sounds in the center; lotuses and lilies lifted their pink and white crowns, listening to the murmuring water. A shoal of goldfish, red, yellow, orange, white and black, stroked their tails leisurely like a group of ladies and gentlemen in promenade. A huge miniature mountain towered from the bottom of the pond, on which a dwarf laurel tree prospered, perfuming the air with its magic.

A soldier saluted Jianfei and led her through the garden to the dining room. Jianfei's body still hummed with, "I love you...since childhood."

The dining room was in a rotunda. An elaborate plaster medallion molded with an acorn leaf pattern was attached to the center part of the ceiling from which was suspended a large crystal chandelier reflecting the glory of western life decades ago. In the center of the room stood a huge round Chinese mahogany table with twelve dinner place settings neatly displayed. Five young people were already seated. They were sipping tea, chatting with the General.

"Welcome! Welcome! Jianfei's father is a professor of philosophy at The Nanjing Military Academy."

The General rolled his wheelchair towards the new arrival. He grabbed Jianfei's hand and buried it in his own solid palm. His young guests eyed her from head to toe, measuring her social standing. They were three boys and two girls. The girl with a round face patted the chair beside, motioning Jianfei to sit down.

The general nodded, "Go over sit next to Ye Lingling, Ye as in leaves, Ling, bell, the daughter of the Commander of ... Girls, introduce yourselves!"

Jianfei looked at the round eyes and round nose tip on her round face; everything reminded her of a bell.

"I am a freshman at Shanghai Medical College," Lingling said dryly.

A pointed chin turned to Jianfei, "My dad used to work in The Nanjing Military Academy. Two years ago he was reassigned to the Department of National Defense in Beijing." He nodded and extended his hand, "I am a sophomore at the Commerce University."

The other two boys had recently moved here from the neighboring provinces when their General fathers were appointed to positions near Shanghai. The other girl was a journalism major; a daughter of some commander. Jianfei felt no inferiority, she was sure her dad was a more learned and knowledgeable man and she was in no mood to count the stars on each father's shoulders.

"We are still waiting for one more guest." General Du looked at his watch and beckoned to the maid and his family.

At seven, the clock and the doorbell synchronized. The last guest stepped in. Sitting with her back towards the entrance, Jianfei could not see the face but her ears received a name that had never left her since afternoon.

"Yang Bing, you are punctual!" the general wheeled to the door.

"Sorry for making you all wait," Yang Bing walked to the table. "The Youth League meeting lasted till six and the traffic was heavy."

"Come here, I want you to meet a new friend," the general skated his wheels on the waxed floor. "This is Jianfei. Your fathers work at the same academy. You might know each other."

Jianfei's heart began to accelerate, her cheeks burning, her eyes averting his. "I love you...since childhood," the song soared over from her heart again. *How should I meet him? As a stranger or an old acquaintance?* As if stepping on eggshells, Jianfei rose to her feet and slowly edged forward.

"Hi," she murmured. But in a second, a decision flashed: we must hide our relationship.

"Jianfei, a freshman at F. University, English Department."

She held out her hand, and then with knitted brows, she asked, "How come I have never met you on campus? Which compound is your family in? How long have you been in the Academy?"

By bombarding Yang Bing with a volley of questions, Jianfei gave him enough time to adjust his distance. He quickly mastered the situation and cooperated, "Strange we have never met, sorry."

Their hands touched; so did their hearts.

The maid dished up the first course. Jianfei and Yang Bing felt they were off the hook.

Jianfei stayed at the General's overnight. After breakfast she strolled outside the compound.

A few yards away, separated by the wall and the massive trees lining the street, was downtown and its boisterous streets. Fashionable stores filled with Shanghai sweaters, emblematic of the city, attracted thousands upon thousands of women from all corners of the country. Hundred-year old silk shops with dazzling scarves and beddings, authentic Jiangsu-Zhejiang restaurants with their steamed dumplings and wontons permanently fogging the front windows, coffee shops, the medley of refreshment stores, pastry and candy shops smelling of chocolate, toffee and other dairy products, all together transformed Huaihai Road into a never resting ocean, surging day and night, making Shanghai Shanghai.

Returning from the street to the garden, where the club resumed, was a bizarre contrast. It was early fall. Everything in the garden was tinged with gold. The dense but obscure laurel and the sparse but conspicuous lotus blended to perfume the air. Maple trees had dyed their fingers red, painting the landscape. From time to time, a frog hopped out with its hoarse voice, breaking the tranquility. Jianfei went into the house to grab a book and quickly returned downstairs, joining the group.

General Du was holding dried insects and feeding the fish. Tiny, round circles bubbled on the surface, fighting for a nip of the droppings. Jianfei craned her neck over the water. Other young companions circled in.

"What are you reading?" Uncle Du asked, glancing at the book in her hand.

"O. Henry, an American writer."

"How are your classmates? What is the percentage with capitalist family backgrounds? This is Shanghai, not Nanjing, you know. One is known for its money, the other for its army. In the old days a lot of the fathers of your schoolmates owned factories. And of course they were not happy after 1956 when the government took over their businesses. Happy or unhappy, the same to us. We simply reduce the recruitment of their children."

General Du touched the fish with a short-handled net; the fish were unmolested in their food competition.

The other young people were disinterested in the topic, their eyes watching the orange and red in the pond.

Yang Bing shook his head and made an eye to her: you don't have to answer. But she replied, "I am not quite sure about the percentage, three to four, I guess."

"How are the professors in your Department?" Uncle Du continued.

"Very strong, quite a few from Oxford and Cambridge of Great Britain."

"Don't scare me with names. I don't care whether it is Oxford or Sheepford."

A fish was biting the net. The General jerked the handle up and a white fish followed flying in the air.

"Bravo!" everyone applauded.

But General Du's mind was hooked on Jianfei and not the fish, "By the way, you don't have to use the word 'great'. England is England. We don't call ourselves Great China, do we?"

He smiled at Jianfei from over the surface and it was a brilliant smile. The other two girls nodded in unison, "Right, right, America, England, China, we are all equal. Uncle Du is correct!"

Jianfei felt embarrassed and baffled.

"And, what do you mean 'strong'? I am not asking about their academic credentials. I am talking about their political standpoints," Uncle Du was persistent.

"Well, one was a nationally known rightist; his label has been recently removed."

A new arrival, Jianfei was still foggy about the class stratum in the department.

"What is his name? ...Oh, I know, I know, everyone knows this name. What a character! Is he tamed yet?"

The General was pressing down a stubborn fish whose head kept popping up from under his net. Jianfei quickly associated the word "tame" with "the shrew," but the professor was an old, benign gentleman.

"I don't think so."

That she seemed to be the sole target of Uncle Du made her a bit resentful. She wondered whether every newcomer would have to go through the same entrance exam.

"What is the symptom of his disobedience?"

"He used to teach the seniors Shakespeare, but now he has been demoted to teach us grammar lessons. He can be very grumpy."

"Don't drop foreign names around here, Ox, Bridge or Spear," all of a sudden, Uncle Du became quite rhetorical. Young people laughed agreeably. Uncle Du was humorous!

"What did he say in class that was suspicious?"

Jianfei recalled the past three or four weeks, reviewing each grammatical example he cited and then came up with a case that aroused her political vigilance, "Once he compared the suffix of the adjective 'audacious' and the noun 'audacity'. He digressed. He said, 'Audacity, audacity, and more audacity. That is all that revolution requires.' He was quite carried away by himself and all the boys applauded, the whole class was boiling."

"Audacity against our regime," the General was a quick learner, "this professor has made a rebellious call."

The General lifted the net and let the fish sway away. He rubbed his hands on the wheel chair and glided around the pond.

"This is our university, not theirs. You are the leader, which is good. Your department did the right thing. The leadership should always be in our hands. It is your responsibility to see that the bourgeois viewpoints do not penetrate our young minds. Hold our fortress!" He paused, "You too, Yang Bing, and you, Lingling, and you, you, you. You all need to be more politically sensitive."

Jianfei looked at Yang Bing who lowered his eyes and said nothing.

One of the locals said, "Shanghai is our headquarters!"

Again Jianfei raised her head to Yang Bing. The native Shanghai did not echo.

Uncle Du coughed slightly. A nurse rushed to roll him away, "The General is not supposed to talk so much."

Never had it occurred to Jianfei that her English classes were a battlefield and that she was destined to be a commander there!

Chapter 4

In Li Yi's bedroom office, the interrogation started casually enough, "Comrade Xiao Ming's mom was here yesterday, a modest, respectable working woman. Did you have the chance to meet her?"

"Yes," as soon as he gave an affirmative answer, Tang Wei knew his fate was sealed.

"Where?"

"In the small restaurant outside the Academy."

Li Yi stood up. He lit a cigarette and handed one over to Tang Wei. The luxury of a cigarette marked the opening of this unusually grave meeting. Tang Wei shook his head. Li Yi began to leaf through a book on his shelf, on which a dozen works of Chairman Mao, Liu Shaoqi and Marx were exhibited. The Political Instructor's office consisted of a desk, a bookshelf, a bed made of a single board, a quilt folded in a square and a pillow covered with a white towel on which was printed "carry the revolution through to the end." Two minutes elapsed; Li Yi was making room for Tang Wei in his carefully strung web.

"Who was with you at that time?"

Tang Wei began to falter, though he had rehearsed ten times for an aboveboard reply in good conscience.

"A girl…" in the past twelve hours, he had reaffirmed his belief that a candid answer would help to clear his name. After all he had done nothing that would eclipse his reputation. Lying would be in vain since Li Yi obviously had been fully equipped with the information.

"Comrade Tang Wei," the Political Instructor laid stress on the two syllables "comrade" to reinforce the fact that so far, they remained comrades. "Who are you? And who is she? Think. Think hard!"

He left the shelf and began to pace up and down along the walls whose periphery was ten feet by ten feet, sparing the center for Tang Wei to think hard. He dragged his tones on a very sincere and heavy "you" and "she", creating something touching, making Tang Wei's eyes warm and throat tight.

"A revolutionary army officer, a son of a martyr who shed his blood and laid down his life for everything we enjoy today. Yet his son mingles with his enemy!!"

A blow to his chest, the "enemy" shot directly into his heart. Tang Wei saw Huifang, her eyes happy and limpid, naïve like a baby's. He saw her ransacking every bush, eyes exhausted at the turn of the building seeking his presence and yet he had no inkling when his post would be given back to him, maybe never. Finding that the news had circulated at such lightning speed and the investigation had been conducted overnight, Tang Wei slowly began to nurse the smallest morsel of a grudge against his worshipper Xiao Ming, yet still deep in his heart he held out hope that it was not the case. All he wished was to wake up from this nightmare and walk into a new, sunny day. He was treading on eggshells trying not to exasperate his interrogator.

"A confession will lighten your case; resistance will only aggravate it".

The Party's strategy in dealing with "problematic" personnel had proved to be the most efficient and had ensured repeated victories in our numerous political campaigns. The slogan shouted into the enemies' ears was now repeated gently to Tang Wei who had mastered this tactic in his own practice. No rebuff, no denial, Tang Wei advised himself.

"And you know what?" Li Yi leaned across the desk, narrowed his eyes and nailed them on Tang Wei's face, "It began to dawn on me that all those late nights studying Chairman Mao's works was nothing but a camouflage for a secret tryst. Right or wrong?"

A caterpillar wriggled up and down Tang Wei's spine. He yielded an automatic faint nod.

Li Yi, satisfied with his own cleverness, continued to rattle his tongue, "That is an insult for our study campaign! An insult for our beloved, respectable leader Chairman Mao! I could easily label you as an anti-Chairman Mao, anti-Mao Tsetung-Thought counterrevolutionary."

A roar filled Tang Wei's head. Something turned in his stomach while Li Yi continued to unleash his tongue.

"How the Party has trusted and honored you! And yet how you have laughed in our face! Betrayal, the cruelest betrayal! Do you deserve glory?"

At this, his torrent of invective turned to the floor and sprayed it. Li Yi scrubbed the spit vehemently with his sole to cooperate with a good effort of effacing the titles, "Activist! Party Secretary! Party member! What an activist! You are very active in love affairs! And with our enemies! Liar! You have cheated on the Party! Here, read this yourself!"

A pile of paper was shoved in front of his eyes. Guilt-stricken, Tang Wei's brain was ready to absorb any accusation. By now, he was convinced he was an out-and-out, despicable traitor, as seen in countless movies. "Recollections of the Standing Guard in October." It was signed by Xiao Ming, a recount of Tang Wei's first late appearance at the gate more than two years ago which was, at that time, reported as studying Chairman Mao's works. In juxtaposition was another statement of what had happened the previous evening. Staring at Xiao Ming's signature, Tang Wei was petrified.

The Political Instructor resumed his pacing. Then he stopped by Tang Wei's side, pasted his lips to his earlobes and, with a grin on his face, blew in them these words,

"Did you pay her?"

"No!"

Tang Wei jumped to his feet. His face reddened, rage and sadness attacked simultaneously. *Huifang was no whore and this was not a flesh trade! Do you know anything about love? Have you ever loved anyone?* However, he managed to swallow up these words; instead, he stared at his comrade-in-arms blankly. He was looking into the face of an utter stranger. This was the man who had been his superior, who had been representative of the ethical military life, who had set examples of probity, decency, honor and glory which Tang Wei strived to imitate, who had won the young soldier's trust and his love. Tang Wei now looked on him with absolutely no recognition. In the blink of an eye the man Tang Wei thought he knew had vanished.

Li Yi rose from his chair and said matter-of-factly, "Temporarily Xiao Ming will take over your responsibilities including secretary of the Party branch leader."

What a good stepping stone, you fool! Tang Wei cursed himself.

Li Yi paused to test Tang Wei's military discipline.

"Yes, sir," Tang Wei saluted to Li Yi and was ready to turn his heels.

"Wait a minute," the Political Instructor said, "I am expecting a self-criticism with a thorough confession of your relationship with that bourgeois lady, a thorough confession, no later than by tomorrow morning. Well…you know what I mean, well…" For some reason the Political Instructor blushed, "thorough… thorough relationship…which includes physical contact, to what extent…"

Blood began to run faster in his veins. Tang Wei couldn't stand it one more second.

"From now on, you are not allowed to leave the compound."

Tang Wei tried hard to hold himself straight.

"Yes, sir."

Turning his heels, he let the tears spill out. *I am suspended, permanently.*

Huifang was sick. In a month, her life had taken a precipitous dip. Her two good friends were out of reach; Tang Wei had simply vanished. Her body ached. Insomnia brought her an excruciating headache. Her dad's accelerated nagging hammered her temples, a ticking time bomb.

"Countryside, that's where you'll go someday! Shame, shame on you and shame on me!" the officer knocked his pipe. "Look at Jianfei's dad, showered with congratulations. Colleagues lined up to dine with him and his classy daughter. Young cadets covet her as their companion. And you? A wasted beauty! The countryside is a vast field and you can contribute your talents there, as Mao has said."

Dad's sarcasm only served to widen the father-daughter gap.

Huifang retorted poignantly, "You are absolutely correct, I am trash. Feel free to dispose of me!"

"Have some noodles," mom snuck in beside her daughter's bed. She put the noodles down and stroked her hair.

The noodles were thread-thin, two tantalizing fried eggs with crispy laces lay on top, young scallion chopped even thinner sprayed decoratively, complementing the white strings and yellow circles. Huifang sat up. Tears streamed down her beautiful cheeks.

"Don't take to heart what your dad said. College is not for everyone." mom touched her forehead, "My! Your head is scorching!"

"No. It's not dad," she swallowed one mouthful and stopped. Huifang began to sob.

"I know. Try next year, the opportunity is always open for those who are willing."

"You forget your husband's history," a sardonic smile hung on her face, "plus, who could be so indomitable to go through the torment of examinations year after year? You want me to end up like the old crazy Fan Jin in *The Scholars* struggling to pass the imperial exams?"

"Forget that novel and Fan Jin. Your dad has been complaining about everything ever since the retreat, you know that. He is not necessarily targeting you."

"I said it's not dad," Huifang looked at her mom with watery eyes.

"What is it then?"

Wringing her hands, Huifang murmured, "There is a man, Tang Wei. We are in love. I haven't seen him for months." Huifang could no longer hold her tongue now that her friends were out of sight, leaving her with no one to talk to. A story of a three-year-long love came out pouring to mom's ears who listened with astonishment. There had been no hint in her daughter's affair.

"What is your plan?" Mom asked, her head was foggy.

"I want to marry him," Huifang said unflinchingly.

"Has he mentioned marriage?"

"No."

Mom breathed a long sigh. She rested her elbows on the windowsill. Holly leaves rocked in the breeze, glistening like shattered glass. In the distance, the sun brushed a last orange stroke on the dissipating blue. Buildings and trees gradually became paper cuts in the thickening twilight. Somewhere among the lit windows wafted the scent of aromatic fried scallions. Behind these windows, families gathered; senseless bickering and laughter broke out. But her family was quiet, her husband reading, her daughter continually wringing her fingers.

Mulling over Huifang's case, mom drew a conclusion: *this is a fruitless love. Even if Tang Wei gets out of his present dilemma, the two families are still foes. The barrier has two layers.*

"Listen, don't let Tang Wei wear away your health. Nothing is wrong."

But her heart said the opposite. She had no doubt that Tang Wei was already in deep water.

Mom tiptoed back and waited till her husband put down his book. She whispered into his ears, "Huifang is in love."

"What? With whom?" the husband was quite agitated.

"A soldier."

"What the hell...Where is he? What is his name?"

"He is a Communist Party branch secretary. Tang Wei, in the platoon, standing on guard."

"Here? Under our noses? Great! Another mess...enough spice for our boring life!"

The armchair groaned as he slumped into it.

"I should have frightened her...she is too pig-headed anyway..." he muttered and lit a cigarette, "fruitless, a fruitless affair."

Mom mustered her courage and buzzed at him like a gadfly, "Listen, you have plenty of time to complain but Huifang is heartbroken. She said the boy simply vanished from his post two months ago since they were spotted eating together in a restaurant. You had better find out what happened to that young man."

The tormented couple stayed awake until the two fingers of the clock closed in the center, making a variety of assumptions as to what the future could have in store for their daughter.

"A discipline violation," dad's eyes chasing the gray veil of his cigarette as it floated upwards. Through the whorls of smoke, he pondered the nature of this love affair, "And perhaps a political incident. If worse comes to worse this could be a discharge."

Chapter 5

The small park three blocks away from General Du's mansion had become Yang Bing and Jianfei's secret dating place, two hours before the club on Saturday and two hours after it on Sunday.

"Talking love," the Chinese term for courtship, was quite common in overpopulated Shanghai even among the lowest Shanghai locals. Jianfei hated it because it smelt of vulgarity and she wanted nothing to do with this fishy, fleshy phrase. However the wording matched exactly what she and her boyfriend were doing, "talking of love." The past returned to their lips like an echo from a distant mountain. Old lessons were reviewed.

"Tell me, why did you make the stamp trade absurdly unequal?" Jianfei just wanted to hear the answer from his mouth, knowing the key herself for all these years, "a whole set of sixteen Olympic Games for one of my brother's tattered stamp?"

By now Yang Bing had abandoned his abashment, he replied with a smile, "As the Chinese saying goes: the drunkard's mind is not on the wine. In my case, the stamp collector's eyes are not on the stamps!"

They both burst out laughing.

"And what made you choose Xiaoshi as your faithful playmate, a child of six who shared no interest, whatsoever, with a thirteen-year-old middle school juvenile?" Jianfei slanted her eyes, teasingly.

"The same reason," Yang Bing said.

"Why did you give us extra movie tickets since you knew all the officers already had more than enough for their families?" Jianfei closed her eyes, raising her head, waiting to taste the same sweetness in his repetition.

Yang Bing gave up the game and came up with a master key to all the questions, "For you."

"Why did you squander one hour of your study time with Xiaoshi every evening?"

"For you."

"…?"

"For you, for you, for you."

Jianfei stopped her questionnaire and said, "You know what? In those days, your blue sweater served as a flag in my life. It summoned me to follow your discipline, and helped to shape my character."

"Don't make a big deal out of my running. The morning exercises were just another scheme to catch your eyes."

"But not in the snow and rain! I compared you to Pavel and Arthur."

"You are flattering me."

Jianfei giggled, "I used to watch the shadow show on your window."

"Shadow show?"

"Yes. You and your family. I turned off the light and sat in the dark watching every movement in your room."

"You bad girl!"

Yang Bing raised his hand. She jumped out of his reach. Her laughter rippled like water skidding over pebbles.

From her bag, Jianfei pulled out a thick package, "Here, read my letters. All these years, I cherished a hope that someday my letters and poems would find their resting place. They are yours now."

Yang Bing placed them on his heart. Her smile adorned her face, splendid as the dyed fall.

Yang Bing said softly, "You know you are beautiful?"

The leaves rustled with their laughter; the surface of the pond reflected their faces; the setting sun painted their youthful figures. They ambled along the path threading through bamboo thickets and miniature mountains. They were enthralled by the past and present. Six years of pent-up love finally found a release. They detailed each other's experiences after their separation, gave accounts of their families and friends, and together described a future they were preparing to share, each filled with the careers they had dreamed of and the successes they had imagined. Life spread before their eyes like a spring meadow blooming with unknown flowers and growing colors, waiting for them to explore, hand in hand.

In Shanghai where forests of buildings occupied the city's every inch and boxes of residential dwellings were crammed to the ceilings, lovers were literally given no room for touching without being ogled or caught red-handed. The park was an overcrowded sanctuary for urban lovers. Oppressed by skyscrapers and the throngs of shoppers who filled every street and alley, stifled by the heart-stopping stench of night soil, salted fish, dried giblets, and unwashed shoes which hung on bamboo sticks and sunned in the sunless sky, sharing one bedroom with four or five siblings, bathing in public baths, under the same roof with their parents, terrified of being bumped into by awkward parents when half naked, totally revealed in their bras and underwear, adults in love frequented parks for a change of pace. Here they drank the air fermented with laurels, roses and lotus flowers and fed their eyes on the rich verdancy. They hid themselves behind bushes, their thirsty lips searched and then quivered upon each other's. Their itchy hands explored and then fondled under the fabrics until their lines of defense were broken. Yang Bing and Jianfei, red-cheeked, passed these flagrant scenes. They looked at each other and then averted their eyes. Talking was everything; their thoughts were redolent of childhood. They clung to it and never allowed themselves to drift astray. Once or twice, their shoulders brushed against each other but they conscientiously adjusted themselves to maintain a safe distance. Occupying the other's presence and enjoying each other's voice were all they had dreamed of and they were complacent. The four hours together were sufficient for their rumination during the whole of the following week.

Had Jianfei ever dreamed of being kissed? Was she longing to be cuddled and caressed? The physicality portrayed in western movies that once accelerated her heart beating and put her in the movie now came to tantalize her senses. Her shameless imagination was an unbridled horse, galloping into the wilderness of love. In the ninth grade, she was profoundly shaken by the brazen display of sex in the Soviet movie *The Silent Don* based on the novel of the celebrated dissident Sholokhov. On the screen, the protagonist Gregory climbed to the top of a haystack and spread his callous palms over Natasha's arched breast. It fascinated her though she overtly condemned it as "vulgar" in front of Lishan and Huifang. Now she was appalled by her own vulgar wish.

Still, talking was the only activity. Talking, talking, they had six years of the past and twenty, thirty years of the future to talk about. When love and idealism were woven into youth, the three produced the most attractive picture.

Situated in a secluded residential area, the park enjoyed more tranquility and less obscenity. An iron fence surrounded the park, dividing it from the streets, buildings, and houses only a few steps away. As dusk set in, visitors began to thin. Yang Bing and Jianfei decided to show up at General Du's separately.

They strolled to the gate. A black Benz was sliding outside the iron railing. A minute later, the same car circled back and slowed down as it passed.

Yang Bing said, "I wonder why that car drove by twice."

Jianfei stared at the car and the car shot away. Strange, Jianfei shrugged her shoulders.

They never took a look at the license plate. The first two letters clearly indicated that this was a military vehicle.

Chapter 6

The frequency of Jianfei's letters thinned. Her babbling about her blazing relationship with a boy in her letters soured Lishan with its excess. The boy whose three-jump performance had won cheers on the playground six years ago aroused in her a feeling close to animosity. He quickly became Lishan's number one rival. Jianfei's weekly correspondence was cut down to bi-weekly and then, monthly, far from sufficient to feed Lishan's emotional appetite, like a sparrow in an elephant's stomach. Now Lishan saw a void not only outside but in her heart.

Three months had passed since the moon festival, yet the sweetness of the cake still clung to her palate. She could still smell the long departed laurel flowers, a fragrant reminder of the moon festival. The full moon, the golden twilight, and Juhua's suavity had woven a therapeutic picture in her loneliness. Sometimes Lishan wondered whether it was a smart thing to give up the whole world and withdraw to her own mute isle. How long could she stay in a world of isolation? After all, her world used to be made of three. How long could she remain oblivious to the pleasures of youth and collective enjoyment? Patching things up with Juhua would be the first step if she wanted to edge into a world with sound. She was waiting for the chance to knock at her door, too proud to be the first to reach out. And this time, she would grab it without delay.

Juhua followed her dad's advice and sent another invitation to her offended roommate whose resentment lasted until the New Year. "Please join my dad's party. Only two or three of his students will be present. You will like it."

The invitation card was a self-made work of art with a New Year's greetings on it. Lishan's heart gave a twitch. Among her peers, Juhua was the only one in Lishan's mind who could be placed on the scale for a comparison with her Jianfei: responsible, talented, caring, daring to go against the tide, striking up a friendship with a loner whom everyone shunned, and defying gossip. In her heart, Juhua was slowly moving into Jianfei's spot and Lishan felt no remorse. After all, Jianfei was the one who had found a substitute first. Juhua had always held some respect for this queer loner whom no one bothered to exchange words with and whose versatility in literature and art was obliterated in public eyes. If not for the catastrophic beginning, they could have been friends. The invitation was not just a passive response to dad's help to ease the bumps on his daughter's college life but Juhua's own will to delve into a heart, abundant but mysterious.

"Well…I'll see," Lishan was Lishan, she was always a bit arrogant, "I think… I have time." Her face began to feel warm, for the first time since college.

My! She really has a splendid smile! She could smile, just like any of us! Juhua exclaimed inside.

"Thank you for the card," Lishan said slowly. "Actually this reminds me that I need to buy some New Year's cards, too. Do you mind going with me to the bookstore?"

What a surprise! Juhua nodded. The two walked out with goggle eyes at their tail.

The streets took advantage of the holiday to sell revolution. Slogans jammed the streets promoting thrift and frugality, curbing the tendency to indulge during the holiday season. "Usher in 1964 with New Spirits" hung from the sycamores, spanning the boulevard. Buildings overlooked the square, capped with loudspeakers which sang: "We are marching on the broad road, the sun is shining, and the red flag soaring in the sky…" The New Year once again promised an optimistic beginning. Optimism was much needed as the past three years had been fraught with natural disasters: droughts, floods, pests; only now did people's pockets begin to have a bit of spare change.

The two girls sauntered into the bookstore. Lishan bought the cards and returned to the art section where Juhua was browsing *The Art of Qi Baishi*. Contrary to Lishan's western taste, Juhua had an insatiable craving for the succinct and explicit strokes of traditional Chinese paintings. Hours in the library immersed in the great works of the Chinese masters gave her immense pleasure. Now the old man Baishi's works once again captivated her. The intertwined pumpkin vines, the chrysanthemum clusters on fresh or withered stems with curly leaves, the fine gauze of a cicada's black wings and a mantis' pale green wings, the delicate fibers and tissue on the pink lotus petals, a shrimp pedaling its swimmers, the crabs' menacing claws launching a war against anything in their way, the freshly hatched chicks… she was enchanted.

"Amazing!" without raising her head, Juhua smiled, "you don't look but smell, listen, taste and feel the paintings. Your nose, ear and tongue are called for participation to comprehend his paintings. They actually emit, suffuse and echo. They are living papers!"

His paintings recorded the chirping of the insects, the warbling of the birds, the cheeping of the chicks, the croaking of the frogs, the quivering of the wings, the rustling of the leaves and the snapping of a twig. You touched the cool, the hot, the scorched, the hard, the rough, the silky, the slippery, the furry, the sleek, the slimy and the flimsy. From the pages of the art books they hopped, flew, crouched, scratched and hoofed. They lived in the paintings.

Lishan's head joined hers, her hair touching Juhua's cheek. A warm fluid seeped all over their bodies. Juhua's interest seemed to be diverted a bit—she did not expect such closeness but the hair was tickling her and she let it be. Lishan stole a glance at Juhua who apparently enjoyed the strand of her hair leisurely wafting to her face and was continuously charmed by the old man's magic brush. Her skin was fine, her two braids quivered as her fingers leafed through the paintings. Her face lacked the striking feature that would catch an immediate second look but her smile significantly enhanced the grade of her looks. Lishan recalled a line she had come across somewhere in a nineteenth century Russian novel. Turgenev's *Rudin* perhaps? Its criterion of beauty depended on one's smile. If the smile added positive points to a face, then the face belonged to the good-looking side and vice versa. There Lishan decided Juhua could belong to the first category. Something long forgotten began to awake.

"Imagism. Yes, imagism," Juhua was again oblivious to Lishan's existence. Her eyes skimmed over the critic.

"I want this book. Lishan, the money is in my upper pocket; take it out for me."

Juhua's hands were occupied with the thick book. Her eyes refused to move away. Lishan reached into her pocket and the old trick was reminisced. Her fingers stopped as if scorched. The elastic and supple cashmere, no, her chest, was cupped in her palm like a rubber ball. Lishan had a clear concept of what she was experiencing. She was holding a breast. It was only one second but it felt like a year. Her own body responded with a tingling and a ringing in her ears like the alarm clock that woke her up every morning, her heart palpitating and temples throbbing. Juhua's hands loosened her grip on the book. Her eyes raised from it, alerted like a frightened chicken. Blood rushed to her head. Lishan's fingers extracted the crumpled bill. She felt like a real pickpocket.

The twenty minute walk back to school was an embarrassing silence especially for Lishan who had not yet given final acceptance to the holiday invitation. A step had been skipped. Recollection of the old days set new shame and agitation against Jianfei who, under the same circumstances, simply pushed her away as her fingers fumbled in her upper pocket. *She spared me a push*, Lishan was grateful for Juhua.

In Lishan's retrospect, another shameful movie was now playing on her murky screen. She saw her own shadow dip and rise on the wall. She saw two small buds. She saw her elbows bent behind her back and prop up a sticking-out chest, projecting two triangles on the wall until her slakeless thirst was quenched. Her own body, a female body, fascinated her. Next, she saw herself secretly penciling the curve on the wall and covering it with white paper. Every now and then, she uncovered the paper and remarked the growth of the twin peaks. After that, she tacked the paper up again. No one knew of the curve on the wall. It was the ignominious record of a pervert.

Juhua was totally, totally knocked out, like a first time drunkard. It titillated her physically but enraged her mentally. The taste was quite similar to eating stinking tofu, repulsion and addiction co-existed. She wanted to turn her back and say goodbye to this eerie artist. However she had to deal with the aborted New Year party which she and her dad, with great expectation, had painstakingly planned and she would have no explanation to offer. Her left breast felt warmer and more swollen than the untouched one, a constant reminder of the shameful incident. Soon her whole body rose in response to the upper left part. Strange to say, it asked for more. The left breast now demanded larger coverage and rougher contact. Mental versus manual, Juhua against Juhua. Some guilt? None, but confusion.

Halfway back to school, Lishan regained her confidence. She reckoned that Juhua's reticence was permission for her physical invasion. She was glad that Juhua was not Jianfei who might deliver a sound slap or a thick wad of spit in her face. For Juhua, there could be some ambiguity between friendship and ultra-friendship. By the time they reached the dormitory, an unspeakable wish reinvigorated the abated thrill.

Chapter 7

Two New Year cards arrived from her friends, old days rekindled. An idea struck Huifang. Lishan's father should have the authority to dig out Tang Wei's whereabouts. Returning a New Year greeting to Lishan, she asked the favor. Lishan traded with her dad as a prerequisite of homecoming.

The news was devastating. Tang Wei was confined in the barracks since summer. His freedom was limited to three meals and one sleep under supervision. Stripped of all duties, his daytime was packed into "helping meetings" held respectively by the Party branch, Party group, platoon leaders, squad leaders and the entire platoon. Enraged by his ignominious conduct, his buddies launched an anti-Tang Wei campaign and drove it to full swing.

The meetings were conducted among roaring voices and the pounding of tables with an occasional fluctuation of shoulder patting and heart-to-heart brotherly consolation. The sincere wish to pull a fallen comrade out of a quagmire was demonstrated in heart-rending sobbing, scolding mixed with love and hatred, deep sighs, explosive slogans and an emotional chorus of "Sing a song to the Party, I compare the Party to mother…".

Sizes and goals varied from meeting to meeting, each meeting carrying its designated mission. In Tang Wei's reflection, all these varied meetings were patterned like a Chinese banquet.

The ceremonial singing and quotation reading served like a cup of tea to open the attendees' mouths; the chairperson's reading of the agenda were a few cold cuts, proceeding to appetizers of curt questions; then a solid confession from the offender dished up as a main course such as a chicken; the barrage of criticism, topic one: family background—fried squid; topic two: exposure of a study model—could be something spicy, beef; topic three: sleeping with the enemy—General Gao's chicken or egg furong; topic four: cheating on the Party and Chairman Mao—a squirrel fish...and the dessert of sweet words to wind up: "we welcome you back with open arms so long as...", "we believe you can...", etc. etc.. Each theme was well-proportioned; flakes of adjectives and adverbs sprinkled like chopped onions and ginger; oyster sauce, sesame oil, peanut butter, garlic and pepper were ready at hand.... Oh lord, Tang Wei lamented, since when have all my comrades become such culinary masters!

Every evening, the meeting opened a new chapter of a thick book. Tang Wei read it. Chapter one, a revolutionary martyr, Tang Wei's dad; chapter two, a venom-dripping rattle snake, a sugar-coated bomb, Huifang; chapter three, a good comrade, Tang Wei; chapter four, a traitor, a hypocrite...the closing chapter: what lesson should the revolutionary soldiers draw from the Tang Wei phenomenon ... Each of his comrade-in-arms was given an assignment and every brain had claimed its authorship. Tang Wei felt he was laid on the conference table, peeled off, cut open, examined, x-rayed and diagnosed. His comrades took pride being heart surgeons with scalpels in hand watching blood gushing out. After all, killing on the table and in the field were not very different.

Supreme instruction:

> After the enemies with guns have been wiped out, there will still be the enemies without guns.

Li Yi carried his red book as a gun, "Comrades, as we analyze Tang Wei's deeds in the light of Mao Tsetung thoughts, once again we are convinced that class struggle is ubiquitous, even in the army. Under no circumstances should we slacken our vigilance! Comrade Tang Wei," his gimlet eyes drilled into Tang Wei's face, "you are at the brink of a precipice; it is high time you reined your horse!"

With the cigarettes reinforcing the zeal and heavy breath manifesting the dignity, the room was quickly fogged and the windows blurred. This was the smallest meeting so far, only the core of the platoon. Xiao Ming took the lead after Li Yi:

"Comrade Tang Wei, if you still deserve this sacred title, Comrade," he stopped, making sure each syllable vibrating the air would also vibrate

Tang Wei's heart, "and prove yourself not incorrigible, that's why we are here, by the way, you should make a full confession. Spill your guts!"

My old heaven! Tang Wei stared at his successor, what an elaborate opening! Xiao Ming proved to be a genius; his rhetoric ability was far beyond his education.

"Is this girl pregnant?" the second squad leader was a farmer.

"No," He had never ploughed that virgin land but Tang Wei managed not to answer too promptly, having learned to curb his temper. He felt his loins seared and the burning soon expanded all over his body.

"Did you... have... sexual intercourse?" blushed.

"No," Tang Wei didn't blame his comrades: the barrack life was finally given a legal vent for sexual yearning under the banner of Marxism. Every heart was itchy.

"Did you pay the girl?" a Party group leader asked. Tang Wei wondered whether he was coached or it was simply a business man's instinct.

"Why?" finally Tang Wei felt he needed to make some adjustment, "I love that girl, we love each other."

The use of "love" sent a shocking wave over the meeting: startled faces turned to the chairperson, who took time to simmer his anger before opening his lips:

"Love, love...doesn't it give you goose bumps? Love belongs to the bourgeois sphere."

Xiao Ming, the snitch, the interim Party group leader, Tang Wei's destroyer and the initiator of this criticism campaign, rose to his feet, starting the second round:

"Love, love...there is no such a thing as love! Have we ever heard any peasant, worker or soldier use that noun? We Chinese are not Westerners. China's population never declined without that word. Parents have strings of children and yet "love" is still a foreign language to them. Do we need that bourgeois diction? No, we don't!"

Who can say Xiao Ming is wrong? Tang Wei was almost convinced that in his motherland, perhaps "love" was redundant.

The eloquence from the half-illiterate garnered a series of nods. The third squad leader took over the relay baton and added:

"We say 'to have feeling for' or 'to like someone', verb, object."

"True, true!"

Heads nodded like chickens pecking for food.

"Comrade Wang has some feelings for comrade Li, Mom likes dad, etc. You have not learned how to speak our language yet, comrade Tang Wei."

"Exactly," Li Yi confirmed, "Love and hatred are both subjected to a class definition and impregnated with class content. Chairman Mao teaches us, 'there is absolutely no such thing in the world as love or hatred without reason or cause'. Comrades, please turn to Talks at the Yenan Forum on Literature and Art, page 809, last paragraph, line 6. Let's read together."

"In a class society there can be only class love; but these comrades are seeking a love transcending classes'…" they chorused.

Li Yi began to pace, his worn-out army overcoat draped over his shoulders in imitation of the way commanders wore their uniforms in the movies. His sunken eyes from lack of sleep also resembled the movies. A study-campaign banner for his platoon was almost in his hand but suddenly snapped away by Tang Wei, a black sheep who now haunted his dreams. He was angry also because his favorite trusted martyr's son had just recklessly joined the Soviet renegades, become a spray of water in the adverse current against Communism, a saboteur under his own eyes. Li Yi truly believed every detail in daily life had harbored international motive. He saw Tang Wei shaking hands with Khrushchev and himself shoulder to shoulder beside him. *Such a scandal, my fault.*

"Let's dissect Tang Wei's love. His love is dedicated to, tragically, a girl whose father once pointed his gun at us, whose father's hands drip with the fresh blood of our revolutionary martyrs …and…"

Silence was profound. The political instructor sat down, his hand covering his eyes.

"And who is a martyr? Think, Tang Wei!"

The words fell like a hammer. The modulation of his tone thickened the pathos. The meeting approached its climax.

Outside, the wind was howling dramatically, a sobbing widow, quickly turning imagination into reality.

"God only knows whose bullet shot your dad!" said the second Party group leader. "Could it be the girl's dad? Possibly! Did this ever go through your mind? I feel the pain here!" his fist pounding his chest.

The Political Instructor escalated the meeting by making a proposal.

"Let's have a moment of silence for those who laid their lives for new China."

Tang Wei hung his head.

The third Party group leader was a man of few words, "How can someone love his murderer?"

Tang Wei did not know what to think. The logic missed a link here.

Of course no one loves a murderer, but the daughter is not the father. Even the ex-KMT officers were given a chance to teach in the Communist academy. Is the policy wrong? Did Chairman Mao make a mistake?

The thought chilled him.

Just as he lost the train of thoughts, someone offered brotherly fraternity.

"Comrade Tang, comrade, comrade! How we wish that you could return to our big family!"

Touched by his own sincerity, the speaker was choked by his words. Forgiveness made him magnanimous and lofty. Heads beckoned, hearts melted and eyes moistened. The overflowing sentiment made Li Yi frown; it was too soon to pardon him. The first squad leader sensed the nuance and stood up to harden the untimely tendered hearts.

"Millions upon millions of our female comrades play active parts in our society."

His words immediately dispersed the warm air, reestablishing solemnity.

"They are workers, peasants and woman soldiers, yet Tang Wei's eyes turned away from the fair faces of our class sisters to the stinking bourgeois lady, raising another question: what is beauty? In my eyes, plain clothes and rough skin are the most beautiful!"

"Good point!" Li Yi knuckled the desk, "Aesthetics, another class concept. What looks pretty to one might appear ugly to the other. Tang Wei, we view things from different angles. White skin, delicate hands and slender body are the symptoms of a parasitic life out of the sun. Field work brings about a robust waist, stubby figures, knotty fingers, callous palms and bushy hair, all the elements for beauty. Tang Wei, you set different criteria."

Thunderous applause! Comrades looked at each other and nodded, their faces radiating.

Do I have to marry a stranger? Do I have to wander about in the factory workshops, farm land and drilling grounds to search for my spouse?

Questions filled his head, yet he managed to open and close his hands, making the same exuberant sounds of his comrades.

Eleven o'clock, the howling wind had died down, a whining baby. The snow began to fall silently, painting a white world. What a profound lesson! What a great school, the PLA!

Chapter 8

For two weeks Yang Bing did not write and the club dimmed without him. Devastated, Jianfei sent letters but received no reply.

November came, and with it the annual Autumn Harvest event. Every year the freshmen were sent to different People's Communes to help gather crops. It was a two-week curriculum for Political Science. To mark the annual departure a great celebration was held with music and a parade, the university's top leaders waving while marching alongside of the marching band. Under the festooned poplar trees spanned the slogan

Intellectuals must Identify with the Laboring People!

No English vocabularies, nor stern-faced professors and their sudden attacks. What went through the freshmen's minds was the fun waiting for them in the green fields and the rustic life represented by the thatched roof and straw-laid beds that smelled of sunshine.

Ms. Zhang was wearing a faded short jacket; her hair was freshly bobbed, giving her a sprightly look. She had prepared herself by reducing any encumbrance which restrictive clothing might provide.

"By the way, everyone please check and make sure you have brought 'Talks at the Yenan Forum on Literature and Art' with you and never go without it," Ms. Zhang reminded the class.

The bus shot ahead, first through the forest of high rises, then out through the greenery of the countryside.

An English song soared up:

> Red sun rising from the sea,
> Sets aglow the new era of the liberation.
> Look, the passing world is disintegrating,
> Miseries of the poor have come to an end, come to an end!

...
Imperialists and their dogs, ghosts and goblins,
How could they stand the rising, stand the rising tide?
Fearless before the paper tiger,
We are to puncture it,
Get it blown down, get it blown down!

Jianfei's mind flipped between two faces, her father and the Ph.D. from Moscow. Ms. Zhang's way of political propaganda bore similarity to a man's, her dad's: beautiful and hard to refute. Dad's preaching was also camouflaged in philosophical profundity. Marx and Confucius held hands. Ancient proverbs and fables, analogies and metaphors ornamented his advocacy. To read dad's letters is to read poems. As Ms. Zhang's words merged into her daily life, she found her mind filled with revolutionary romantic images such as sea waves pounding the cliffs, a blue sky with soaring eagles and a red sun nurturing flowers. *Always be one step ahead as a student leader... I have submitted the Communist Party Membership application twice.* Suddenly an image intruded. *Where is Yang Bing? Could his school's sophomores also be joining this education campaign? Will it be possible that his figure appear in the streams of laboring college teams? How can his letter reach me?*

The bus lulled on, and finally stopped in the rice fields. Golden paddies converged with a blue vault, stalks laden with swelling ears. Some patches had already been cleared making the landscape look like a half shaven head. Stubs were strewn about. Children with bags hanging on their necks roamed about gleaning the remnants. There were also ample empty plots waiting to be planted. The sky was washed clear with a leisurely cloud wafting in the breeze. Yellow leaves and red berries reflected in the ponds; a brook murmured on.

As the students marched into the village, thatched roofs met their eyes. Although the thatched roof was a long-accepted picture in the bucolic life, they were not prepared for the weather-beaten facades long lost of their original characters, a good match for the wrinkled, worn-out face of the brigade leader, who stepped forward stretching out his coarse fingers and callused palms. Little children who had been chasing the intruding bus stopped awestruck in the distance. Ms. Zhang bent over and smiled into their multi-colored cheeks, encouraging them to edge forward. Some were picking noses, others sucking fingers, their rosy cheeks crusted with tears, mucus, and all shades of deposited muck from the fields where they tailed their toiling parents. A few wore shoes, toes peeping out through the holes; the majority went barefoot.

Students milled around. Unadorned muddy walls were everywhere, yet the doors were embellished with proud couplets squarely pasted in front "Rip off the heavens and turn over the earth!" accompanied above the door header by "Miracles are performed by people; a happy life is not bestowed by God!"

Another read, "Nightingales sing, swallows dance—another spring; Peach red, willow green—another village," followed by a footnote, "Rivers and mountains are charming."

Students browsed the doors, taking notes. The rustic talents never entered their minds. Pleased to see the youngsters' sensitivity in learning from these semi-proletariats, Ms. Zhang seized the opportunity to order a ten-minute break.

The loudspeaker crackled to life.

"All commune members, please gather on the threshing ground! Gather on the threshing ground. The students are here! The students are here!"

The emphatic urgency reminded the Shanghai students of a fire alarm.

Intermittent gongs and drums were audible in the air and drew nearer. Children flew away again like scared sparrows. A jarring voice in an attempted Beijing dialect shouted with a strident southern accent, "Learn from the college students! Welcome the revolutionary little warriors!"

Presently, a few commune members showed up, mostly the older members, because the younger women were all using this public time to do their personal chores, cooking or washing, while the men, tired from their field work, were stealing a nap. A handful of curious young members shuffled over, telling lewd jokes, scolded and spanked by the elderlies. The straitlaced students tried to turn a deaf ear to the rude intimacy among the poor and lower-middle class peasants since, despite their bawdiness, they were the major revolutionary alliance of the Party.

Chapter 9

Cotton petals on the earth and the cloud speck in the sky mirrored each other. Girls moved slowly among these white flowers. The cotton bags tied to their bellies were quickly bulging, making them look like pregnant women. Sweet voices swept over,

> "Green mountains soaring to the sky,
> White mountains winding their sides…"

The challenge for the boys was twofold, both from the crops and the people. They worked shoulder to shoulder with peasants who, with dubious eyes, evaluated each hand for its competence. Standing aside their pale faces and slender shoulders were the two mountains of bundled rice weighing two to three hundred jin. Whether they could solidly package these loose stalks without scattering them on the long-distant transportation and dutifully deliver them one mile away across the field strewn with rice stubs was a titillating question in each head. The peasants were stingy in offering help—after all, it was the students who were helping them. They were the ones to be hardened, toughened and tempered to meet the mettle needed by revolution. Besides, who had the time? The students found themselves left on their own with collected stalks, at a loss as to how to sheave them, to estimate the weight on each end for the shoulder-pole balance, and to skewer them before painfully tottering to the threshing ground. The peasants had picked up all the old ropes for themselves, leaving the shining and inflexible new ropes for the new hands, making the bundling more burdensome: the ears kept popping up and the sticks refused to bend. As if from a mirror, they watched each other and saw their own clumsy performance: grappling to discipline the stalks that persistently stuck out or slipped away; moving a handful from the left to the right pile and then moving back a quarter of that pile to achieve balance. Then they lurched clumsily, like a departing train on its way, extending one hand backward to hold the ears, trying to ease their bumpy journey. The feet that had been comforted by Shanghai's asphalt boulevards and the university's cement paths now said hello to raw yellow earth. The clammy ridges gave way to their feet, creating miniature craters with each step; between the furrows, the sunken ditches sucked their feet into accumulated rain water. Walking on egg shells, they avoided the stumps that shot out like evil fingers to grab their ankles and to trip them up. Their movements were stiff and robotic, a bit like a puppet show, amid which these English majors covered the distance until they slumped to the threshing ground, three piles in one lunge, two of rice and one human, panting like a wheezing horse, thick vapors steaming out from their dilated nostrils. Once someone's load fell from the hoop and the loose grain scattered everywhere, jamming the traffic. The young commune members snickered behind their bundles while the older ones could not conceal their scowling faces.

But the mockery quickly gave way to respect. The peasants watched the college boys firmly grasping the stalks and throttling them with the two dead knots, adroitly sliding the poles in, breathing evenly and producing rhythmic sounds to lighten the labor: Hai-yo, hai-yo. By noon of the third day, the college boys managed to keep abreast with the natives. To make the competition more dramatic, the city boys created a labor song:

> Hai-yo, hai-yo, leap forward;
> Hai-yo, hai-yo, look at the peasants;
> Hai-yo, hai-yo, our old brothers;
> Hai-yo, hai-yo, catch up;
> Hai-yo, hai-yo, learn from them;
> Hai-yo, hai-yo…

On the other side, echoing from their brother peasants:

> One two, one two, look at the students;
> One two, one two, good boys;
> One two, one two, speed up;

One two, one two, finish the damn rice;
One two, one two, go home and eat rice;
One two, one two…"

On the fifth day, Ms. Zhang called a meeting for all the student leaders. They sat on one side of the furrow forming a circle. The competition between the peasants and the students was in full swing on the other side of the furrow. The soaring enthusiasm of her students greatly affected Ms. Zhang, a scene from her dreams. A reporter from the Department of Journalism had written an elaborate article about the English freshmen on the university newspaper with a picture of Jianfei and other girls picking up the cotton. The newspaper had just arrived which prompted this meeting.

Holding the newspaper in hand, Ms. Zhang said, "We are on the front page. Jianfei and her group are in the pictures." The Political Instructor made a significant pause, "However, ideology cannot be remolded in one step. Working hard in the fields is only half of the procedure because we intellectuals harbor a petit-bourgeois kingdom in our souls, as Chairman Mao warns us. Are we sharing their weal and woe?"

Ms. Zhang reached to her bag for the book, "'Everything reactionary… if you don't hit it, it won't fall. This is also like sweeping the floor; as a rule, where the broom does not reach, the dust will not vanish of itself.' Do all of us put ourselves wholeheartedly into the ideological remolding campaign? Is there any dust that our brooms have not reached?"

The first Youth League group leader cleared his throat, "Some of our classmates have been seizing the time, five or ten minutes before going to sleep—by the way, the peasants prefer us not to use electricity, they themselves go to bed right after dinner—to study English. Some even brought their books to the fields."

The secretary of the Youth League branch nodded, "It was appalling to see Charles Lamb's *Tales from Shakespeare*, *Oliver Twist*, and Mark Twain's *The Prince and the Pauper next to the shoulder poles* laid wide open in the eyes of the poor peasants who could not afford the luxury of writing their own names in their mother tongue. What are we doing here? Flaunting our education? Advocating privilege?"

Jianfei said, "we should make it a rule that Chairman Mao's works are the only books allowed in the harvest season…"

Carrying a bulging bag, the mail girl approached. Jianfei's mind went astray.

"Jianfei, letter!"

A thin piece flew over and landed on her lap. She knew the handwriting and her heart gave a thump. Feeling dizzy, she grabbed the envelope and hid it under her jacket.

After two minutes, she decided that she should find a place to read.

"Excuse me." She stood up. Eyes riveted on her, including Ms. Zhang's. She rushed to the nearest hut, feeling needles on her back, and stopped at the turn where no vision from the meeting could reach. The envelope was torn open in such a haste that the letter dropped out. The flimsy piece whirled in the air and landed at her foot. With a numbness in her heart, she stooped over for the letter. The mystery of Yang Bing's sudden disappearance was about to unravel.

Four scribbled characters jumped into her eyes, hardly legible.

"No. I cannot."

Cannot what? Continue to write? Or not to write? Above the enigmatic line were three crossed-out lines blurred into blossoms and creased. Yang Bing, crying? Jianfei held the paper to the sunlight. Under the scratching pen, all she could make out was, "My dearest, dearest Jianfei:" No signature, no date.

"No, I cannot," echoed with "I love you, since childhood." The paper laid bleak and despondent, just like her face. Time and again, Jianfei held the letter to the sun, but nothing more filtered through. The mystery deepened.

Cannot what? Cannot continue or discontinue the relationship? Something must have happened.

She reviewed every detail of their last meeting. *Was there anything I said that offended him? No. they separated happily.* She slumped over on the edge of the irrigation ditch. The dazzling water gurgled forward. The "dearest" warmed her heart. Everything proved his love unchanged, but the crossed-out lines indicated some decisions had been forced on him.

Something died inside her. The sun dimmed; and winter seemed to be approaching. Tears rolled in her eye sockets and finally snatched out. Is this the beginning of the ending? She sat there till her eyes dried. Then she walked back and regained her seat in the panel.

Her telltale eyes did not escape Ms. Zhang, who whispered into Jianfei's ears as she bent over to sit down, "Is everything all right?"

Jianfei nodded, keeping her eyes on the ground.

The Political Instructor continued, "Please do not let your personal affairs tarnish your performance."

Personal affairs? Tarnish? She nodded.

What Ms. Zhang said next was a peal of thunder, "It is Yang Bing, isn't it?"

How did she get that name? Her mind probed in the dark wilderness and found the answer easily. It was her first day at school when Yang Bing helped to carry her luggage to campus. She nodded, then shook her head. *Caught red-handed! Denial and admission, what difference now?*

Mao's words entered her empty head like water splashing on a stone:

> "'Our point of departure is to serve the people wholeheartedly and never for a moment divorce ourselves from the masses...'"

"Look at Little Third's fat ass, swaying left, right, left, right, like a dribbling basketball with no target to deliver," a middle-aged peasant said avidly.

"Shut your stinking mouth!" Little Third jumped on the man, stuffing his mouth with a handful of mud, "Don't you ever dare to comment on my ass!"

Blushing, she giggled and cast an apology at the college students, "Don't lose face for us poor, lower-middle class peasants!" Whacking the man's bottom.

"Men all covet your ass!" the man paid his last tribute and fled to the farther side. Laughter roared.

"They are the mainstream of our society and the core of the revolutionary forces," Jianfei reminded herself, "and I want to become a glorious Communist Party Member like Ms. Zhang."

On arriving at school, Jianfei wasted no time trying to unravel the mystery, but her letter to Yang Bing went unanswered like a stone sinking into the ocean.

Winter vacation was on the way.

Chapter 10

The train slowly jerked to a stop.

Stepping out on the platform, Jianfei flew into Huifang's open arms, "We missed you so much!"

Jianfei looked at Huifang: sadness and sentiment could not hide her beauty. Crowds passing by turned back for a second look at this rare beauty. A white satin scarf clouded around the neck, contrasting her rosy cheek, outlining the oval face and pointed chin. She was wearing a light brown woolen jacket, a pair of plaited black trousers and black leather shoes. After months of drab clothing, finally she had found an excuse for herself to dress up today. With the attire, she stood out among the other three. Three, because of a new girl, slender, two braids swaying behind.

"This is Juhua, my classmate."

Lishan extracted one hand out of her lower pocket. The new uniform trousers were her dad's latest tribute to maintain his painstakingly procured father-daughter relationship. A smile, almost invisible, hung on one corner of her mouth, to which Jianfei turned a blind eye. "Nice to meet you. Lishan wrote about you in her letter." Jianfei produced a diplomatic handshake.

In Jianfei's eyes, Juhua was the new product of Lishan's old trick. To Huifang, this new friend of Lishan's was innocent as any of them. The matter was transparent only between Lishan and Jianfei, therefore Lishan's insinuating smile was meant only for Jianfei. On Juhua's side, she had given little thought to Lishan's old friends. The only thing unbreakable was her bond with Lishan.

Lishan, Lishan, the sunken-eyed Lishan, nasal-voiced Lishan, cynical Lishan, unfathomable Lishan and never-changing Lishan. Jianfei smiled, too, shaking her head inexplicably, meeting Lishan's eyes.

Lishan began to wag her sharp tongue, "So tell us about yourself. Has Shanghai cultivated a snob?"

"Snob or not, you have two weeks to judge."

Tit-for-tat, she threw back a question, "So you're still wearing your dad's trousers?"

"Why not? The old man was eager to have his daughter back home. This is a token of his repentance and redemption."

That the uniform pants kept her in a man's role among the girls was obvious to Huifang since middle school; but to the extent to which Lishan emulated a man, she was in total dark because when Lishan was courting Jianfei, she was head to toes in love with the PLA boy. Juhua, listened to their conversation and giggled, triggering laughter among the rest. The old days were rekindled.

"How come you only have two weeks of vacation? We have three." Lishan stopped in front of a fruit stand and bought four oranges. She handed one to each.

"The third week is dedicated to political study." Jianfei said, "The student leaders are summoned back for a study sessions of the editorials of the People's Daily."

"You mean the Comments on the Soviet Communist Party? I study the editorials every weekend at Juhua's house."

Lishan and Juhua exchanged a significant smile.

"By the way, Juhua and I are going to an artist's salon tonight. Juhua's father has some connections in the Artist's Association. It's an opportunity we cannot afford to miss. There are quite a few nationally known artists attending."

"I thought we could all dine at my house," Huifang pursed her lips. "I've told mom."

"Why can't we all go to the salon?" Juhua proposed.

"You are all college students. Who am I?" Huifang looked at their badges in front, mumbling.

"Don't worry. We still have a few hours to kill. Let's walk over to the Cock and Crow Temple where we used to go!"

The street was lined with dimly lit shop windows, a sorry assortment of "New Year's Groceries" hung perfunctorily: moldy, greenish ham; soggy, salted pork; "thousand-year-old eggs" with pulverized husks falling off the shells; and discolored sausages. Images and advertisements were no concern for the business because even these pathetic exhibits would be gone in less than one month when the Spring Festival arrived, regardless of how unappetizing they looked, and because the government-issued monthly coupons would have expired. Where else could they turn for the celebration? A household of six to seven was allocated two to three pounds of pork, a dozen of eggs, one pound of sausage and two pounds of fish in addition to their rice allowance. Hungry stomachs could not be too picky. A little mold and a few worms were welcome regardless.

"How can you afford such high-class clothes, all wool, when everyone is scraping every grain of rice into his mouth?" Lishan said, her lips tilting.

"High class? These are my mother's old clothes before liberation. When the political winds shifted direction, she had to hide them away. I just dug them out to brighten up this special day. Actually they are old fashioned, have you noticed!"

Lishan sniffed, "Sure enough. Your whole body reeks of mothballs."

"Could you put away your waspish tongue for a moment, at least for the sake of Jianfei, if you don't care about me?"

Huifang was on the verge of tears.

"You don't know what I have been through since summer. No job, no school, no friends, all I have is a nagging dad."

"I don't care about you?" Lishan hopped up and barked, "I would not have humiliated myself, I would not have bothered to make good with my old man, and you would have still been in the dark about his whereabouts, if not for what I did."

"Oh, yes," Jianfei said, "In your last letter you said he was confined to the barracks. You've got to do something. You cannot stand by and look on."

"She told her mom she wants to marry him!" Lishan said.

"Are you serious?" Marriage for Jianfei was something decades away.

Steel-gray slates led up to the hill top where the stately temple towered to the sky. Behind the temple was the city wall overlooking the lake where once upon a time thousands of young Socialists launched a war against the pestilent sparrows by beating anything they could and shouting until the enemies dropped into the placid, silky water. The drama seemed like yesterday. White walls flanked the steps, on top of which black tile mosaics blossomed in floral patterns.

"When was the last time we were here?" Huifang touched the naked gingko boughs, "Remember? On our way back from the Sparrow War, we came here and knocked down so many gingko nuts with bamboo sticks."

"And the nuns came after us," Jianfei laughed, doubling over.

"And we barked back as the dog yapped." For the first time in more than six months Huifang laughed heartily. The hillside echoed with ringing voices, the leaves covered yesterday's footsteps.

"Where did the gingko tree go?" Huifang scoured in the woods.

The leaves were shedding; bald trunks were easy to distinguish.

"Here it is." Huifang's fingers caressed the slippery gingko bough. "It's been nearly six years!"

"My, my," Lishan shook her head, "girls, you are getting really sentimental!"

The wind whooshed after them. The sun was vanishing.

The entrance hall to the temple swarmed with pilgrims. In front of the threshold, round straw mats received prayers' knees while their torsos bent over kowtowing and muttering: "Merciful Buddha" and "Amitabha." Two enormous bronze vessels stood on guard. In each, bundles of burning incenses were planted in ashes. The vessels glimmered with two looped handles and three legs in the sun which quickly moved behind the dark clouds.

At the long altar, people raised the incense with louder wishes as everyone wanted to be heard by the Buddha, "Amitayus...May Buddha protect us..."

"Please send my son back; please make him happy and healthy at your side..."

"May my piglets be sold at a good price..."

"Please stop the leaks..."

"May Buddha remove the tumor and save my mother..."

Buddha, with a smile on his face and a lotus flower inserted between his tilting fingers, sat twenty feet tall, inspecting the hall. An assortment of little benign figures nestled in his bosom, each with a name, also smiled at their worshippers. Wisps of burning incense carrying wishes rose to their faces. Fortune was deposited and auspices invested. Promises bounced from the air:

"Have mercy on the wretched souls…"

"Good deeds will carry you to heaven…" Beggars lined the steps as the pilgrims proceeded to the sacred hall.

The four girls found a quiet corner in the *Buddhist Delicacy* and began to scan the menu. The restaurant run by the temple commanded a magnificent view of the lake and mountain. The lake stretched out in all directions from the foot of the Purple-Gold Mountain. From the open windows, the flying eaves of the temple were silhouetted against the sky, sometimes blue, sometimes gray, as the setting sun fought a losing battle with the clouds. Pine needles shivered in the whistling wind, making the sound of sifting sand. Autumn carried itself into winter in its remnant foliage, dying the hillside in warm tones of yellow, orange and red. As the girls marveled at nature's wonder, the wind began to gather clouds, preparing for a storm. In a wink, thunderclaps rolled overhead like trucks driving by, tearing the lead gray with orange fingers, the rain slashing down.

"What evil weather! Thunder in winter?" an old man rushed in, stomping his feet, shaking off the raindrops.

His left shoulder slumped down with a tattered blue bag on which two characters announced his profession: "Fortune Telling". A piece of a bamboo stick in his right hand said, "Palm Reading." His scrawny body and gaunt face resembled an apparition. Squint-eyed, he hunted in the dining hall like a hound. Finally he paused on the four girls. Lishan shivered.

"I say, sisters, marriage, money, fortune, job, children… Whatever you want."

The man produced a book as tattered as the bag.

"All hidden in my book."

Lishan turned her head away. Jianfei let her chopsticks work incessantly. Juhua folded her arms.

Huifang tugged Lishan's sleeve, "Let's see what the old man says about my marriage…"

Lishan flipped her hand, giving an adamant "no." Huifang looked at her other companions and decided to go by herself.

Jianfei picked up the conversation with the two artists, "So what do you do in the salon?"

"We have weekly seminars. Last week Lishan made a speech on nineteenth century Russian oil paintings." Juhua was eager to drag Jianfei in. "Today a lecturer from our college will make an introduction to French impressionism. Have you heard of Monet?"

"No. I know little about Western painting. Xu Beihong's horses are my favorite," Jianfei said.

"Is that so?" Juhua was glad someone could share her interest. "I am going to talk about Qi Baishi next week. Would you like to join us?"

From the corner of her eyes, Jianfei caught a view of the fortune teller's yellow teeth and jabbering jaw. He waved at Huifang whose steps faltered, "This lovely sister, come over and let's chat."

Timidly, Huifang said, "I don't have money."

"Free, free. A piece of tofu from your dish will help this humble, hungry, old man."

Sadness and fury filled Jianfei—a beggar practicing ancient superstition now was luring the desperate Huifang into his snare. The old man rattled a bundle of bamboo sticks in a tin can and asked Huifang to pick out one. The sticks clanked for five seconds and stopped. Huifang's fingers fumbled in the can, picked one and handed it over to the fortune teller.

"High stick," he examined.

His crumpled, callous hand swept over his book.

All of a sudden, he cried out, "Congratulations! My finger was directed to the character 'happiness'. You have a noble man assisting you in your life. Congratulations! Now give me your hand. No, the right one, the left is for a man."

The old man put on an air of authority, holding Huifang's palm under his nose, scrutinizing every line, flapping the palm back and forth, and then knitting his brows, "However, the circle is not completed, the 'happiness' is not doubled."

With these words, the old man sealed his lips.

"What does that mean?" Huifang was on pins and needles; she knew this was about her and him, Tang Wei.

"Miss, it is heaven's plan, and I have no freedom to interpret it on my own."

As Huifang was still mulling over the prophecy, the unkempt old man moved to the table to claim his payment from Huifang's tofu plate. As he grabbed the dish with his coarse hand, the old man edged to Lishan's side. A stench oozed out from his disheveled hair and rags. Loathsome, Lishan honked through her nose. The man turned his eyes to the prompt reaction. His gaze froze on Lishan's face. His eyes dilated with fright. The tofu slipped back into the plate.

"What?" his cryptic look sent a chill to Lishan's marrow.

"Nothing," the old man murmured as if to himself, but his eyes remained glued to her face.

"Let's go," Jianfei was becoming very uncomfortable.

The rain had stopped but the wind was still blustering. The sky put on a scowl as clouds raced to muster for a new insurgence. The four girls stood on the balcony, leaning on the carved banisters.

Lishan shook her head vehemently as if just woken from a nightmare.

"What an eerie old man! For a moment I thought I was seeing a ghost," Lishan grew pale.

Thunder pealed with a flash, setting fire on the gray prairie.

In their consternation, they found that the old man had tailed them out. This time, he headed straight for Lishan:

"Miss, your face is overcast like the sky. Look, look at the sky, this is your face on which I read Death."

Thunder cracked overhead, striking everyone dumb.

Ashen-faced, Lishan reached her pocket and shoved ten cents into the man's dirty palm.

"Go away!"

Chapter 11

Huifang was missing. The panicked mother went to Lishan and Jianfei for help.

"Check the guard platoon's current events," the cool-headed Lishan said.

A farewell party for the discharged soldiers two days ago crossed teacher Huang's mind. She had never made a connection between the two events. The brawl in the dining hall was unrelated to her family, with a husband whose career was eternally fixed. Thinking that it was just one of the many celebrations at the end of the year and another excuse for the officers to get drunk, she gave no further thoughts to the foggy kitchen and the dimmed dining hall. Inside, red paper flowers blossomed on green uniforms, consummating the year with overflowing glasses in the clink and clank of 'bottoms up.' They patted each other's shoulders in the thick of jokes, guffaws and refills until they belched, drooled, staggered and waved their fingers to deny their tipsiness. Although wallowing in liquor may temporarily make them oblivious to their lofty defense mission, on holidays and special occasions a blind eye tended to turn to such infractions. Gaudy and slightly fat wives usually were allowed to stay sober at home, but wasp-waisted, nimble-fingered, supple-shouldered young ladies were not spared. They sailed in and immediately engaged their straight-backed, dreamy-eyed cadets in a fox trot or a Viennese waltz, reminding Ms. Huang of the days with her husband in the KMT. Bon-cha-cha, bon-cha-cha, the rhythm remained the same

None of these parties had ever born any significance to Ms. Huang until now. Her daughter was missing and the party was to blame. She vaguely remembered, as she passed the dining hall, the soldiers' faces were lit with pride. Red paper flowers hanging on their chests, they pledged to "build the hometown," "to contribute my youth to Socialist construction," so on and so forth, and then were cut short by thunderous cheers.

Many soldiers were leaving and her Huifang was missing. A mother's instinct rose suspicion: where was Huifang? She must be with Tang Wei… So long as Tang Wei is safe… her taut nerves relaxed. Mom was correct, Huifang was in Shanghai.

The next day after the farewell party, the discharged soldiers were transported to the railway station. Tang Wei was escorted by two soldiers to a Jeep, whose mission it was to ensure a lonely journey for Tang Wei, a journey without a female companion, as if they had predicted Huifang's move. Huifang took a bus and followed the Jeep.

Huifang's appearance startled Tang Wei, first in the square of the train station where she waved from behind a sycamore tree, later in the dining car several tables away where Tang Wei's two escorts were ferociously stripping the meager meat off the pork ribs. His heart ran wild like a bunny on seeing his dream girl. Are you crazy risking the danger? I love you. His eyes said. She shrugged her shoulders: what can they do? Arrest me for taking the same train? Discharge you? Go to hell! She smiled. My Love! He quickly lowered his head, his eyes riveted on one face then the other, showing total devotion to his two comrades. The six months had dug a deep hole in his soul. All his attempts to contact her had given way to waiting, yet the six months of waiting rewarded him with a discharge and an escorted trip home, leaving no chance for farewells. His dwindling hope was relit when his name was announced in the discharge list. He could write to her and come back to see her. Now here she was, safe and sound, in flesh and blood. He kept his eyes on the two uniforms.

Huifang streamed out of the Shanghai station following Tang Wei and the two spies. She waited till the two escorts left for the return tickets at the window and Tang Wei was finally left alone.

"Follow me," said Tang Wei, without raising his eyes, in a muffled voice, his hand covering his lips.

He entered a public latrine and reappeared in civilian clothes. His uniform, now stripped of its red star and red collar badges, was folded into a canvas bag in his hand; only the army cap was left on.

"Now I am a free man!"

Tang Wei opened his arms. Huifang edged over with caution, fearing the eyes of this strange city.

"Let's go to a park," said Tang Wei.

Their lips trembled to meet. They tasted, drank and breathed each other. His fingers fumbled, her body felt familiar and yet somehow estranged. They reviewed each other's body like an old lesson. The pine needles rustled around singing a gentle lullaby, sha, sha, sha... No language was needed. Darkness snuck in and engulfed them. Nestled in Tang Wei's broad chest, Huifang held him tightly, no storm would ever snatch you away from me again, you promise.

Thousands upon thousands of cocoons danced in the water, like marbles rolling back and forth, on top of which silk threads spanned out to the ceiling where the weaving machines hung, rumbling in deafening chorus. In this stronghold of the silk industry, silk worms were nurtured in the huts near the mulberry fields in the suburbs of Shanghai. Their cocoons were collected by manufacturers from whose hands strands of silk were extracted, reeled, dyed, woven and soon were displayed on elegant figures while their larvae sat on banquet plates as a queer delicacy. The metamorphosis of these squiggly worms into the most beautiful fabric not only prospered the East of China and made it the avant-garde of the modern civilization, but also pulled thousands upon thousands from destitution when they gave up their land to seek employment in the metropolis.

Tang Wei's mother was one of them. Rumbling, rumbling. Her wrinkled face wore fatigue and told no tale of her true age. Instead, it had won her the ambiguous title of "Mother Tang", Tang Ma, an honorific that reflected the indeterminacy of her age, anywhere between fifty and eighty. In reality, she was only forty four. She could not remember ever desiring anything else since the day her young husband closed his eyes and his blood soaked this yellow earth, other than to see her only baby grow up to be like his father. Her earlier years passed like the breeze sweeping over the field, noiseless and unnoticeable. Her life was cut into two parts, as day and night, since his death. Throwing herself body and soul into the cause she believed he had left behind, her life was blended into a world of red flowers: the red flower as she was elected the chairwoman of the Workers' Union... the red flower on her son's green uniform...the red flowers of the former factory owner whose handing over the property to the government was highly eulogized as "entering Communism" ahead of schedule. There were certainly a few black pictures in her memories, such as the series of midnight meetings labeling the factory owner as "capitalist" who had since hung his head low until he gave up his factory. She, a timid, grieved woman, had gradually sharpened her tongue and become a public figure. Tang Ma still saw herself, almost a decade ago, taking over the deed and announcing that the workers and the capitalists could build Socialism shoulder to shoulder. There were always red flowers. Red flowers and red flags, drums and cymbals, songs and slogans wove into her recent years and along with them, her career and her solid image as the epitome of the proletarian class to whom her husband was overlooking smilingly from heaven.

Tang Ma's life was woven on the weaving machines, whose monotonous droning never dulled her hearing nor numbed her nerves. New designs, bright colors, the factory's turnover and the market needs filled her daily concerns. The void in her personal life did not eclipse her happiness since her whole existence was to bring to life the sacred cause for which her husband had laid down his life. Men were totally out of her life, except one, her son—her laughter, her tears and her light who had already stepped into his dad's shoes.

Her son was coming home today. As the siren called for the ending of the day, Tang Ma left, for the first time on time. She hurried to the market, got the special items for her son and hurried back to her small apartment. Chopping, cutting, mincing, rinsing, her single room buzzed with joy.

Chapter 12

Something was missing in her son, the red star on his hat. She noticed this as soon as the door opened. His color should be red and green. The brown corduroy jacket and the navy blue pants portrayed a stranger, one from a different social stratum. The colors worthy of her pride were gone; the colors that had brought the mother and son admiration and respect along the shop-lined Nanjing Road and made obsequious the standoffish shop clerks turn were gone. For Tang Ma, seeing brown and blue on the body of her son was like watching a black and white movie in a Technicolor era. The contrast was too sharp to accept. The blissful mother-son reunion was eclipsed from the beginning.

The girl was another surprise. This must be Huifang. Tang Ma had already got familiar with the name from her son's letters. Her beauty struck her. There was no indication of her visit in his last letter. Although holding a grandchild and enjoying the filial piety from a daughter-in-law had been her dream, something about this girl just did not fit her ideal, like her son's brown and blue colors. Her beauty was a bit beyond what plain living could afford. Tang Ma's eyes measured this candidate, taking in her height and weight, from the economic and political angles.

"Aunt Tang, how do you do? I am Huifang."

The girl stretched out one hand, the other handed out a nylon bag.

"Here are some red dates, good for the cold winter, especially for women."

Okay, a thoughtful gift. Tang Ma's heart gave the daughter-in-law an A.

"You didn't have to go to this trouble."

Shaking her head, Tang Ma took over the gift.

Though a bit too glamorous for an ordinary family, the girl showed good upbringing, she knew the procedure of meeting a would-be mother-in-law. In her mind, Tang Ma began to list the criteria for her son's future wife: her dress, her gait, her tones, her dialect, her smile, the volume of her laughter, the number of teeth showing through a smile, her table manner…and first and foremost, her political standpoint. Every detail was crucial in advancing one rung along the arduous proletarian ladder. From the threshold to the bed, every step counted, and any misstep could send one falling down, perhaps irretrievably.

The dinner that cost Tang Ma two months of her savings was laid out. Having eaten little since the previous night and in the past several months, Huifang's stomach finally found a home. Her chopsticks targeted the jade-white tofu, whose flavor was greatly enhanced by a spoonful of chicken soup; the egg rolls whose golden brown crispy skin made mouths water; and the fish, a symbol of abundance and indulgence. Huifang did not remember when she had had such a sumptuous meal. Eating was only made flavorful with a settled heart. Her eyes concentrated on her chopsticks, incessantly visiting the plates.

Huifang was not herself at the dinner table tonight. At first, she was struck dumb by the fact that Tang Wei was sent for from another city, and then, she was exhausted from the nerve-racking detective work following him to Shanghai. Once in Shanghai safe in Tang Wei's arms, her body and mind experienced a new hunger. She was determined to make up for many months of starvation and eat to her heart's content. Tonight she ate like a hard-working farmer. This was home, she kept telling herself. *I have a new home now.* Her cheeks were bulging with rice. She skewered two pieces of fish and wolfed them down.

Tang Ma frowned. Picking up four pieces of fish perfunctorily, she landed them in her son's bowl.

"Son, it took mom two hours standing in the freezing wind to procure this fish. Aren't they tasty?"

Huifang's face reddened; her chopsticks took a retreat in their incessant attack of the fish. She had already graded her future daughter-in-law. Table manner: failure.

Tang Wei, however, transported the four pieces into Huifang's bowl and said, "I am forwarding your kindness to my friend; she has not eaten the whole day. I am sure you would not mind."

Tang Wei frowned; Tang Ma frowned and so did Huifang.

"No food the whole day? How come? I thought the Shanghai express was only three hours."

Tang Ma snuck another piece into her son's bowl, hoping that diverting the conversation would cover the movement of her chopsticks.

"Mom, your chopsticks have eyes. They see what you have in mind as to who to serve."

With these words, he flung back the fish into the plate and left the table.

"Yes, she had no food the whole day. How come?" Tang Wei made himself a cup of team without answering his rhetorical question.

Sinking in his seat and sipping the tea, he returned to his mother:

"Because I am discharged and under surveillance. Huifang followed me secretly all the way from the barracks until my two companions left the Shanghai station."

The devastating news struck Tang Ma, her lips wide open as she echoed her son word by word, "Discharged?" The fish slipped back to the plate. Tang Ma put down her chopsticks.

Eight families in each single room resided on the second floor of the workers' dormitory where cooking was done outside the door. Along the walls, eight stoves stood, sizzling, babbling and simmering, soy sauce, oil and spilt soup greasing and discoloring the corridor. Eight tables with cutting boards, knives and pots and pans stood on guard at each door; on top were short storage cupboards used for keeping leftovers. Vegetables, sagging and limp, lay in baskets leaning on the leg of the tables. Garlic and red pepper strung and hung on the wall like household emblems. All these were there to guarantee that the families, varying in size from two to six people, could move around in their fifteen-square-meter rooms.

Huifang's eyes looked around Tang Ma's humble room seeking her own lodge. A single wooden bed, a multipurpose table, two benches and a chest were the complete inventory of this mother-son bedroom. Chairman Mao commanded the central wall, conducting all the family activities. On one side, a man in a faded, yellowish uniform was smiling at his wife and son. Certificates and awards wreathed him. The shame and embarrassment at the dinner table capped off an exhausting day, Huifang now only hoped for a bit of privacy. She also wanted to leave some privacy for the mother and son.

Tang Ma read Huifang's mind.

"Son, you sleep on the bed, I will put the stools and the chest together to provide myself a comfortable bed. For Huifang, I could easily make a more decent arrangement in the workers' dormitory since the girls have left for the Spring Festival. I have the key and the beddings are clean. I am sure they won't mind. It's just downstairs."

Carrying a thermos bottle, Tang Wei went downstairs with Huifang. The room was small but cozy. Huifang nestled in Tang Wei's broad chest.

"Imagine this is our own room!" Planting a kiss on Huifang's forehead, Tang Wei said, "I want to marry you. I am going to clear things up with mom: I am discharged. I want to marry you. It's time for her to have a grandchild."

"Hush, no speaking. Just like this," Huifang closed eyes, her finger crossed Tang Wei's lips. In a dreamy voice, "Being with you is all I want."

Kissing Huifang good night, Tang Wei went upstairs for a surprisingly unpleasant talk with his mom which lasted till late in the night.

When Huifang boarded the Shanghai-bound train, her decision did not prepare her for a life without parents. Eating at a restaurant would drain her pockets in a couple of days leaving no penny for the return ticket, but yesterday's dinner had made it clear that free food was even more costly. The twenty yuan she had grabbed from the smashed ceramic pig before catching the bus was dwindling rapidly.

Tang Wei was given a job by her mom's factory and would start working in two weeks. He had never breathed a word about his late night conversation with his mother and Huifang was in no hurry to fish out the details. Every morning Tang Wei came downstairs with a bottle of hot water and a plan for the couple's day: to "The Big World", an amusement plaza with the all kinds of tempting foods; to the Shanghai Library; to the Bund where lovers strolled and kissed; to the Luxun Museum; to Nanjing Road for window-shopping or to the more sophisticated Huaihai Road; to Long Wind Park where there were boats to row on the lake; to the street vendors for their dumpling samples; to a movie house… In one movie they watched a bride and a groom kowtowed, the bride's head covered with red silk, the groom's neck stiff in a black satin tunic, their hands locked together in the dark, their lips brushing over each other's faces. Their hearts beat rapidly as if watching themselves on screen. Occasionally, they would sit at a restaurant window, enjoying the pedestrians scurrying by in a misty drizzle. They laughed in tears when the red peppers in their noodle soup scorched their palates. More often, they joined the army of lovers on the Bund, like sparrows perched on a telephone line, facing the calm or turbulent Huangpoo, their bodies burning in the vows of a love as long as the river.

In their endless window shopping, something caught Huifang's eyes. It was a navy blue woolen scarf dotted with white stars, thick, soft and with a fine weave.

"I need a scarf. Mine is ten years old." Huifang dug into her pocket.

"A perfect match for your light complexion and only twelve yuan," the clerk sauntered over, "Across Shanghai, you won't find such a deal!"

Her eye brow knitted, she only had eight yuan.

Tang Wei paid and turned to Huifang, "This is my Spring Festival gift."

Huifang and Tang Wei had no access to the rooms during daytime. Tang Ma took away both keys, fearing that her first grandchild might be illegitimate. But soon she was forced to give up after hearing repeated complaints that it was too cold to stay outdoors all day long. Cocooned in the fifteen square meters, Tang Wei and Huifang feasted on each other's body meanwhile taking precaution. To redeem and prove herself a qualified daughter-in-law, Huifang did all the house chores, laundry, cooking, cleaning. She was working her way hard to move into the house of the factory's celebrity. Every evening, steaming foods greeted the fatigued Tang Ma.

Sometimes Huifang caught Tang Wei's dazed look; she also noticed that fewer and fewer words exchanged between mother and son. Soon she was vexed by the question whether their estranged relationship had anything to do with herself. However her light heart easily managed to brush away the dark clouds. *It must be the discharge.* She'd rather focus on today and not worry about tomorrow because only love was real, only Tang Wei mattered, and their happiness was ephemeral. When she and Tang Wei first met and skimmed the stone over the water, their only hope was to see the stone jump to the opposite bank and not to sink midway.

Chapter 13

One day after the Spring Festival, Huifang said, "Let's go visit Jianfei. I remember her winter vacation was one week shorter. She must have already returned to school."

The idea of visiting China's number two university and seeing how her self-disciplined friend had adjusted to Shanghai's glaring life thrilled her.

"I wonder whether Jianfei is as popular as in the old days. I bet she must have strings of boys on her trail like stars around the moon."

"College life is not just boys and girls," Tang Wei said.

Jianfei was at a meeting. As they toured the campus waiting, they came across a long wall alongside the main thoroughfare displaying a blackboard used for the publications of the Students' Union. The university's biweekly journal, fifty meters long, two meters high, was read by everyone on their way to the classrooms.

One headline struck Tang Wei's eyes, "A Discussion of Campus Love Affairs (continued from last issue)".

....College is the prime of our life where our brains are the sharpest, our memory the longest and our intelligence the highest. Squandering our time and energy in love affairs is simply throwing away our talent. We have fifty to seventy years ahead, so why be in such a rush? Scoring high, focusing on your career, paving your way, maximizing your contribution to our great cause of Socialist Construction, this is the correct choice. Any rational brain would think this way...bourgeois ideology can easily lure us into a quagmire, as Chairman Mao said, it is a tug of war...

"Come over and read this," Tang Wei waved at Huifang. University ideas always fascinated him. His eyes moved on:

> Some are parroting the westerners, arguing that love is the sole motive in human activities. No, this is a bourgeois cliché. It is high time we brush aside this corrupt notion. A creative mind lies in career building and not in sensual indulgence…

Next to it, another article wrote:

> To love is strong and healthy, not to love is weak and sickening! True, youth is the best time to study, but who can deny that it is also the best time for love? If you believe you possess a sound mind and solid body, your answer to this question will be, and should be 'yes'. Say 'yes' to love, fellow schoolmates! Love is the quintessence of human life just like air and water. Love is the heart of all hearts. Love shows human souls. To be a revolutionary, you need to be a normal human being first! Let us seek happiness in true love! Grow up, fellows, let your heart and not your mind lead you! Build up your maturity, be brave and embrace LOVE!

"My!" Tang Wei waved at Huifang, his chest heaving, face radiating. *He is speaking for me…for us!* He looked at Huifang, feeling an urge to hug and kiss her. *How come I never had the guts to admit this? Why do I have to make myself a thief of love? Of course it is a discipline issue but love itself is no sin.*

Love, love…there is no such a thing as love! Have we ever heard any peasant, worker or soldier use that noun? Love belongs to the bourgeois sphere.

The words of his comrades-in-arms, the professors from the great school, the PLA army all echoed in his mind.

Army is army. College is college. The two schools have different curricula. What did our great leader say about our universities? Our schools are "dominated by the bourgeoisie". The two schools continued to debate in his mind when a voice interrupted him:

"So you are here! Enjoying my journal?"

"I thought you were a leader of the English Department," Huifang asked.

"Not any more, I was elected as the vice chairman of the Student's Union of the university, in charge of the Propaganda Department."

"So you are a VIP now. Any suitors?" Huifang made a face, giggling. Tang Wei swerved around.

"So all these are your idea?"

"No. It's from above, the Party Committee."

"So the Party is behind all the controversy?"

"Yes."

It was lunch time; they chose a small restaurant near the school gate. As they settled in a cozy corner, Tang Wei resumed his topic:

"So what do the passionate lovers get from your school? Expulsion?" His thumb pointing at his chest. Huifang took his hand in hers.

"No. The authority tends to turn a blind eye. But the gossip, lewd jokes, oblique criticism, and the impediment to the entrance of the Party," she paused, "or the Youth League…is even worse, making the lovers feel inferior, second-rate, branded. They either go underground or simply break up…"

All of a sudden, Jianfei stopped short, her voice choking. She excused herself and left the table.

Huifang felt guilty for dragging Jianfei into a topic she was so uneasy to talk about. When she returned, to their surprise, her eyes were red and sparkling

"All your fault!" she scowled at Tang Wei who looked blankly.

"Are you all right?" Huifang pulled Jianfei aside. "Something is bothering you. Do you want to talk?"

Jianfei shook her head.

"It must be serious. You never cry," Huifang said.

"Nothing," Jianfei sat down, regaining her composure.

Determined to create some laughter, Tang Wei opened his arms and said, "Look at me! An out-and-out proletariat, nothing to possess, nothing to lose. Nothing can hurt you if you have nothing."

Tears broke loose again.

Seeing his advice offered no solution, Tang Wei leaned forward and whispered, "Trouble with the authority? No, you are a favored child."

Huifang tugged Tang Wei's sleeve and whispered, "Stop! She must be in love."

Tears trickled down Jianfei's cheeks, her head shaking like a rattle.

Tang Wei tried in his desperate humor, "There, there. We are a gang of three now, birds of a feather. The only difference is that we are seasoned," his hand draped on Huifang's shoulder. "You are still a green hand."

Jianfei kept shaking her head.

Two weeks, fourteen days, had finally come to an end. Tang Wei and Huifang locked in each other's arms until the whistle blew. Dabbing tears from Huifang's cheeks, Tang Wei held her hand to his lips. The train jerked and accelerated to full speed, Tang Wei ran along with the train.

"I will write to you!"

Huifang waved as Tang Wei stumbled alongside the train, rumbling rhythmically as it accelerated to full speed. She leaned on the window watching at the figure waning to a dot and finally erased at the curve in the cold blue glint. The rail stretched backward, stark like a dead limb. Huifang cried her heart out. Her sobbing tapered off as she took some comfort in the thought of Tang Wei's discharge. *It is a fresh start for us, a transition from underground to above board. He is free! I am his and he is mine. I can see him any time I want and he can visit me in Nanjing.*

She saw her head covered in red silk and Tang Wei in a black silk tunic kowtowing like in the movie. She brushed her chin tenderly against the blue woolen scarf. Tang Wei, Tang Wei. Calling his name, her heart melted.

Chapter 14

Jianfei's memory of that winter was nothing but a nightmare. It was a page in her life she never wanted to look back on because the scar left in her heart was never fully healed.

Jianfei's family had relocated because her dad had been appointed the Political Commissar of a scientific research institute.

Xiaoshi jumped out of a walled compound and gave her a hug as she approached her family's new home. The compound included a two story house and a big yard, the Zhao residence. A pine tree canopied the patio, white capped. Winter dominated the compound but summer lingered. One rosebud, too late to prosper, drooped out of the rose bush, brooding over the glory of her deceased sisters. In the backyard, a plot of green vegetables invigorated the landscape, heads puffed white. Cabbage and spinach braved the elements; some had become dinner and were showing bare stumps.

"Cool! A vegetable garden! Who is the gardener?"

"Dad," Xiaoshi said, "I am his left hand."

"This is a big house."

"Big? You haven't seen the big ones yet. Dad had the chance to choose one in the secluded area where the governors, provincial department heads and generals reside. Some were left behind by foreign diplomats and tycoons of the KMT regime. Manicured lawns, heating systems, fish ponds, miniature mountains... the old man bluntly turned it down. Even this house was forced on him. Old fool! With his seniority, he is already over-qualified for these mansions," Xiaoshi stomped, kicking the snow.

"It is his house, his choice. We have no right to complain. This is good enough."

"I agree, well, partially. I despise those privileged dandies pampering themselves under the eaves of their fathers. But our dad goes to the other extreme. With the wound in his chest, he certainly deserves more."

Xiaoshi led the sister up and down the stairs.

"You know what? I think dad will eventually give up this house. It is too far away from the factory, too far from the workers, severing ourselves from the masses... stuff and nonsense. 'I don't feel comfortable with this wall'... I am afraid someday he is going to tear down the wall and we will have to bare ourselves to the street. He insists that we, you and me, should mingle with the children of his manufacturing workers."

"And," his hand flapping in the air as if swatting a fly, "The folks haven't stopped fighting since we moved in, quite a scene. One calling the other an 'ossified country bumpkin', the other yelling back 'corrupted capitalist'."

"The old story, a post chicken-war..." they bent over laughing.

They entered the sprawling living room.

Xiaoshi slumped into the couch, "This room is all chairs. Dad has turned it into a conference room. Meetings always go past midnight."

Tea tables stood before the couch, each holding a plate with a covered tea cup. The air was still tinged with overnight jasmine.

"This Scientific Research Institute has been playing a leading role in defense research since dad took over. Dad's competence has caught the eyes of Beijing. The Central Committee of National Defense will hold a meeting here as a sample of management for all the leaders all over the country in this field. They've struck a gold mine here." Xiaoshi said somewhat gloatingly.

"How did you dig out dad's secret?"

"Dad keeps a low profile, but mom told me that his name is on the front page of the Inside Reference Information and his institute has been named a 'Model Unit' by the Central Military Committee." Xiaoshi shook his head, "I have never seen dad so head to toe in his work. Policy, ideology, worker's education, gas pipe installation, intellectual-manufacturer relations, products, quality ... dad is unique, with his education. A genius. Though I hate to see this house be given up, I have to admit he is right, and the old man holds much higher standards for himself and for us. Mom is mediocre; dad is superb. Five thousand scientists and manufacturing workers work under him!" Xiaoshi said smugly.

"Be careful," his sister dragged him back, "don't let dad catch you like this. Arrogance is his sworn enemy...There he is!"

The gate clicked.

"I have asked the army to donate four hundred pieces of old padded clothes. Allocate them immediately to the neediest workers. This must be done before the storm hits us." Dad was on the phone.

We have a telephone now. Jianfei rushed over.

"Ha! My baby girl is home!" Dad threw down the telephone and opened his arms, smiling from ear to ear.

Dad, dad, my dear father, Jianfei scrutinized dad through beaming eyes. His hair was a bit grizzled, his back a bit bent, diluting the sweetness of the daughter's homecoming.

At the dinner table, dad asked Jianfei, "Do you have any specific plan for the two weeks?"

"Not really, visiting friends and having fun."

"How about having lessons with me?"

"What kind of lessons? And where?"

"At home, from seven to nine in the evenings. Topic: *How to be a Good Communist Party Member* by President Liu Shaoqi. You told me you have finished the reading, right? Good."

"Professor: father; student: daughter." Mom clapped her fleshy hands like a child, "May I attend your lecture, professor?"

Dad knitted his brows with a faint nod.

Chapter 15

"A good Communist is a submissive tool in the hands of the Party. She does whatever is required." Dad's tone was placid, flipping the pages of *How to be a Good Communist Party Member*.

Jianfei's pen glided swiftly on her book, underlining Liu Shaoqi's words.

Mom nodded emphatically, "Yes, loyalty, absolute loyalty is the first and foremost characteristic of a good member."

Dad frowned.

A photo flashed in Jianfei's mind. It was a young, slender dad, in the New Fourth Army uniform, very suave and amiable, saying "Be the Party's submissive tool" as was written on the back.

"Dad, when did you first read this book?"

"During the war."

"Was that when you put the motto on the back of your picture?"

Mom became very enthusiastic, "How that picture attracted me! A young Political Commissar, handsome and charismatic. That was when the "submissive tool" picture was taken."

"Forget the photo." Dad cast a long and unblinking look at his wife who made a timely retreat to her listener's position.

Dad continued, "Mencius says,

'Thus, when heaven is about to confer a great office on any man, it first exercises his mind with suffering, and his sinews and bones with toil. It exposes his body to hunger, and subjects him to extreme poverty. It confounds his

289

undertakings. By all these methods it stimulates his mind, hardens his nature, and removes his incompetence.'"

"A Communist Party member is a chosen one, made of special material, as comrade Stalin put it, born for hardships and sufferings, his heart must be hardened, his body tortured, he is destined to sacrifice. Are you ready for all this?"

She was raised to be a good Communist. This was the noblest calling she could imagine. It was a calling restricted to the most honorable, the most virtuous, and the most righteous. She longed for the challenge, to play a role in bettering the world and to help further the liberation of mankind from the cruelty of class enslavement. Yet this lifelong goal continued to elude her. Her application for the Party had repeatedly been rejected, the reason being "petit bourgeois sentimentalism," a character flaw Ms. Zhang warned her against in their heart-to-heart talks ever since Yang Bing's letter arrived untimely in the field, tarnishing her unblemished image in the eyes of her Political Instructor.

The chosen one! The entrusted mission!

She looked at dad in piety. Dad had mingled the Chinese sages with their young descendants and crossed a German beard with a Chinese goatee, making Stoicism an aromatic potion to take.

"Eat bitterness," mom hastened to put a footnote, "that's a more common term."

"Jianfei's intelligence is far beyond the common. Please do not throw in your random interpretation." Coldly polite, dad gave his unwelcome teaching assistant a verbal warning.

Friday was the last session.

Dad said, "Righteous, outspoken, aboveboard, a Party member keeps no secret. Everything he does is open to public eyes because his heart is pure and conscience clean."

Father closed the book and Jianfei capped her pen. Philosophical profundity, artistic presentation, poetic diction, logical exposition, eloquent argument and the wide range of knowledge collected from ancient and modern times made dad outshine any of her professors of political science.

Jianfei cherished the aesthetic as much as the cultural value in dad's lectures. She found her heart followed dad more willingly than in any classrooms. She felt she was embracing a noble ideal, to emancipate the human race, to build a brighter world. A lofty life free from vulgarity unfolded in front of her.

The room was heated. Dad poked the fire. An orange flame shot up into a mirthful dance, reflecting Jianfei's pensive face.

"Now, tell me, what do you think of 'nothing to hide from the Party'? Are you ready to act like a Party member?" Dad put on a smile, a typical benign smile, "Is there anything bottled in your heart you feel you need to pour out?"

"Like what?" a ringing in Jianfei's ears, her nerves taut.

"…eh…friendship…friendship with a different gender…"

Silence reined. The fire cracked merrily.

"It is time we put theory into practice," dad continued to drop his hints. "Dad knows his little girl will follow the light of truth and perfect herself. Some day she will be a glorious member of our Party."

What is dad suggesting? Yang Bing!! The siren blasted in her head.

Communism's grand view—to see the whole human race liberated, and the red sun illuminating the globe!

"Two thirds of the world population is still living in misery!"

"To deliver them from deep water is your mission!"

"Save the wretched laboring people from the iron hoof of U.S. imperialists!"

These daily bromides, drawn from the paper, the loudspeakers, the school assemblies, and the radio, all came to her mind to reinforce dad's philosophy and poetry. Her personal affairs were indeed incomparable to the sacred cause; they were trivial and insignificant.

Tears gushed out. Mom looked at dad, asserting her role as a trustworthy ally. Both the parents waited cool-headedly. Only Jianfei's composure was shattered.

"Do you mean Yang Bing?" Somehow Jianfei managed to transport that difficult name out of her mouth, but she sounded faraway to her own ears.

"Oh? Yang Bing? The son of Commissar Yang? What about him?" It didn't occur to Jianfei that dad could be acting.

"I am in love. We are in love," Jianfei totally lost her equilibrium. She shamefully burst into profuse tears.

Dad began to pace and exchanged a glance with mom, "I will be back."

Glad to be the interim professor, mom seized the opportunity to salvage her image in this household, "To what extent did your relationship reach? I mean…did he touch you?"

She made an incomplete gesture; one of her hands spread in the air in front of her chest and made an ambiguous circle. Jianfei tightened her fist in her pocket. She wanted so much to punch her mother's stupid pretty face!!

Dad returned from the closet, a letter in his hand.

"Your relationship was confirmed by General Du. He had spotted you and Yang Bing together more than once in private. Being my old superior and best friend, he showed genuine concern for your callowness. It is like seeing a green fruit picked by too eager hands. Commissar Yang, on receiving General Du's letter, made a special trip to Shanghai and put a timely stop to his son's irresponsible actions."

So that was it! Of course! It suddenly dawned on Jianfei that the black Benz was actually on an espionage patrol, and it belonged to none other than that stately mansion of the army commander! This provided a key to Yang Bing's mysterious disappearance. *Betrayal*, she thought. *So the whole fuss was generated by General Du's letter! Thank you, dad. Thanks to your glib tongue, I can hide nothing from the Party. Thank you for your ceaseless similes, fables and symbols that help to strip me naked.* At the same time a stronger force was pulling her closer towards that remote but bright spot called Communism and away from her personal feelings.

Jianfei looked at her dad. To her shock, an imposing figure suddenly loomed up from her earlier years, Cardinal Montanelli from *The Gadfly*, who turned his patient ears to his son's confession and had him arrested. She was agonized juxtaposing these two figures, after all, one was her beloved dad. *One is the enemy of revolution, the other, the leader.* Her love for her dad quickly erased any iota of doubt or resentment. As quick as her temper rose, it diminished. Her worship for dad and the faith he represented overpowered her insignificant self. Be a Good Communist!

Mom went to the kitchen and returned with a teapot and three cups. A serious talk was about to unfold whose prelude was composed by the ticking on the wall, the sobbing and soon the sipping of tea. The two hands of the clock drew to its center; night deepened. Dad waited till Jianfei's emotions subsided and silence filled the interlude between the two sessions. Five minutes passed, dad cautiously blew the scorching surface and took a careful sip. He then stood up and went to the window, gazing long.

"In summer we had so many gorgeous roses. They were red, pink, orange, yellow and white; and in full bloom. The garden prospered."

Jianfei pricked up her ears to see what was up dad's sleeve. Dad paced in front of the windows. Outpouring light fell on withered stems and shriveled leaves. Standing in solitude, braving the winter, was the last rosebud, the outdated lady that was lamenting over her sterility. Jianfei was highly alert, not knowing what dad was about to philosophize this time.

"Some buds failed to open, like this one. I saved it as a reminder of how beauty could be wasted, for you. As a reflection, a lesson that you need to constantly review, take a look."

Jianfei's eyes followed while her ears received more from dad:

"I examined these buds and found that worms had wriggled their way into their hearts. I picked out the worms and in a couple of days, those infected buds all caught up and showed the prime of their life, except for a few."

Dad paced back and his speech took an abrupt turn, "You have a worm in your heart—desire." Dad took Jianfei's hand and patted it tenderly, "Dad wants to see his little girl grow into the most beautiful rose. She will catch up; she will never allow the worm to dwell in her budding body, will she? Our society will prosper only if you prosper."

How correct dad is! Jianfei nodded through tears.

Revelation and relief soon changed to gratitude. Jianfei looked at dad, totally enthralled.

Mom gazed at her husband with the same eyes that had looked at the "submissive tool" picture twenty years ago.

"I have chest pains on rainy days," dad was producing more riddles for his daughter to solve. "Everyone likes a sunny day. Chairman Mao compares young people to 'the morning sun at eight and nine o'clock.' No one wants to see the sun covered by dark clouds. But my little girl's youth has been darkened, eclipsed, because of the love affair in the early morning of her life. Dad wants your days to be spotless, bright and sunny. I want to see you, like the sun, reach the midday and contribute the most light, heat and energy to the earth! Our society is the earth and you are the sun. Let the cloud pass and the sun shine brilliantly!!"

What a lecture!! Jianfei looked at dad in total awe, respect, worship, trust woven in her heart with a bit piece of uncertainty. Her eyes were brimming once again. Shame filled her.

"How to make the sun shine, and the rose blossom? You might ask, but the answer should be from your own heart."

Dad took a long sip, stirring the leaves from the bottom. Jianfei knew she was given an examination paper, but she was not quite sure what answer dad was expecting.

Mom chimed in sweetly, "Jianfei is a girl with correct decisions…"

Dad screwed her with his eyes.

The clock was ticking. The testers were waiting

Finally Jianfei croaked out an answer, "To stop the relation."

Dad made a slapping sound on his lap, "Correct!! The answer lies in this book, simple and easy." Dad wagged Liu Shaoqi. "Send him a letter, now. Make it clear to Commissar Yang's son that love at this age is damaging and destructive!! The letter must show no shred of regret."

"Yes, before it is too late…" mom's vulgarity gained her more white eyes from her daughter.

Mom brought in paper, uncapped the pen and then stood by watching Jianfei, willingly yet not without confusion, composing the letter, parroting dad's rose and sun metaphors. By two o'clock, the letter was scanned by both parents and sealed for the morning mail.

Jianfei cried till dawn. Seven years, purely platonic, was blown off in a whiff of a scented breeze. Her heart was heavy as well as light; she had said good-bye to her petty bourgeois kingdom. She was reborn. Dad had married her to the noble cause.

Two days later at lunch time, the telephone rang.

Dad picked up the phone, "Yes, she is in… A meeting for what? Does your father know about this?"

Jianfei put down her chopsticks. Mom and Xiaoshi held theirs in the air.

"You can return her things through the mail…No need to see her …Explanation? To clarify something?"

Jianfei rushed over, "Please, dad. Please. Give it to me."

The phone halted in the air for two seconds and then was passed over.

"Hi…" Tears choked her.

"I've received your letter," said on the other end. Silence ensued. She heard heavy breathing.

"Please do not cry. I owe you an explanation of my last letter…"

"I know everything now," Jianfei wept, "but how come you never wrote again? I sent you so many letters."

"I was in the hospital for a month. I couldn't take it…"

"Hospital? For what?"

"Insomnia."

On different ends, they cried into each other's ears. The lunch table was quiet.

"No matter what, the first love will last forever," Yang Bing said.

The phone clicked. Jianfei dashed into her room where she buried her head in the pillow until dusk.

Chapter 16

Breaking up with Yang Bing was not the only event that made that winter indelible. There was another breakup, the one with her best friend Lishan, for the second and the last time, for which she would blame herself for the rest of her life.

When Lishan and Juhua invited Jianfei to their circle, she had no heart to socialize. Juhua kept postponing her presentation until one day Jianfei grudgingly said yes.

The salon was in a professor's house. A white concrete driveway led the visitors to the hilltop. A black iron fence inserted in a cement wall enclosed the two-story brick house and its discolored lawn. Rambling along the wall was wisteria, stripped naked leaving only the sinewy vines to grapple with winter.

"Good gracious!" Jianfei laid in juxtaposition the celebrated professor in Nanjing with the three-star general in Shanghai, amazed at the same splendor.

"The husband is an English professor, a Ph.D. from America, and the wife is a nationally known pianist," Juhua said. "They are my father's closest friends. The house was bought in the forties. Amazing how it withstood the ravages of the war."

"Hard to say how long it might stand," Lishan said, picking up some withered leaves from the ivy. "Who knows what is in store for this couple in the next few years. A tall tree catches wind. A privately owned house like this is a conspicuous eyesore to some people. Anyway, you should see their son, our classmate. Quite a character! Born in America, he can't speak a word of English. We call him 'American Baby'. Naïve and innocent, he is still a child." Lishan shook her head, slinging her backpack.

All the guests gathered in the living room, some snuggling in the sofa, some lolling against the wall. Two females, six males, among whom two had made a special trip all the way from Shanghai. The room was warm. Red charcoal glowed merrily in the fireplace. The high ceiling was lined with brown molding, the walls wainscoted with mahogany panels carved with roses, orchids, goldfish, birds and butterflies along the border. Two built-in bookcases stood facing each other on each end by two columns. On the entrance hall a huge silk tapestry overlooked the audience, on which two iridescent peacocks were strutting leisurely, numerous blue eyes fanned out on their tails, grass blades glittering at their feet and pine needles soaring above their crowns. A piano stood in the center of the adjacent room.

"Hi, guys! The old folks were invited to a Spring Festival party hosted by the municipal government. The cat is away; the mice will play. Help yourselves to all the goodies!"

The voice ushered in a lanky fellow with a giraffe's neck. A pair of eyes shone like two commas, ears spreading out like miniature fans. A pouting mouth and a hook nose worked together to portray the ugliest features in the world.

"This is our American Baby," Juhua introduced apologetically, "but everyone likes him."

The American Baby whirled around with a ceramic plate in hand abundant with red and green treasures like fried peanuts, sesame candies, peanut brittle, toffees, nougats, mountain walnuts, pine seeds, ginger wafers, preserved apricots, dried peaches, fresh golden kumquats… A girl sashayed beside him with another exquisite tray carrying an equally exquisite teapot and teacups. The scent of jasmine seeped into every nostril. Her cascading hair swayed along with her graceful gait. Eyes moved from the tray to the hand, to the face and then rested there enjoying the view.

"That's his sister, a gifted music student. Like mother, like daughter. What a pair!" Lishan said in her usual nasal tone.

True, as if to sharpen the contrast, the siblings now stood shoulder to shoulder facing the guests. Though bearing a striking resemblance, each let his or her unique feature stretch to the extreme. Weihua and Meihua, Great China and Beautiful China, were their names. Though the brother perhaps did not accurately represent greatness, the sister truly deserved the epithet beautiful.

"Guys, don't thank me, thank the government, these are their special gifts for the renowned intellectuals," Great China said. "Thank you, our dear Party! Amen."

Laughter broke out as he closed his palms.

"We are indebted to Socialism," a man held up his teacup. "I propose a toast to our Party!"

Sarcasm could not escape Jianfei's ears. She felt uneasy. There was something missing in the atmosphere, something she was accustomed to from her usual surroundings. *The love for our Party was missing here.* Jianfei turned her eyes to the one proposing a toast: long hair, handsome pale face, navy blue jacket, a pair of shining shoes. *Leather shoes!* A loud shout in Jianfei's mind. Leather shoes were a bourgeois emblem.

The agenda was announced:

A piano solo by Meihua	**Beethoven's "Moonlight Sonata"** **Dvorak's "Humoresque"**
A talk by Juhua	**"Imagism in Chinese Traditional Painting"**
The annual art survey **Dance.**	

The salon was an eye opener for Jianfei, a liberation from her four months of boring lectures, backbreaking labor in the fields, weekly political discussions, mountains of newspapers and oceans of meetings, responsibilities that could not be shirked from the students' union... all had dulled her college excitement. The salon seemed to have rendered a touch of freshness to her life.

Juhua's viewpoint that Qi Baishi's paintings marked the beginning of Imagism in modern Chinese art and worked hand in hand with imagist poetry dating back to the Tang dynasty ignited interest and triggered discussion.

Then each artist displayed his or her masterpiece from the past year. Jianfei noticed all the guests carried a canvas bag like Lishan's. In a minute, the living room and the music room were converted into a small art gallery.

An oil painting with a green frog crouching on a lotus leaf caught Jianfei's eyes. "Sanctuary" was the title; a canopied pond filled with still water was the scene. Verdant weeds floated leisurely. Dragonflies fluttered, their dazzling orange wings looking for a landing spot. The frog's chin was sagging. Red and black fish patrolled underneath, their tails like satin ribbons. A pair of butterflies flapped their wings streaked with black and yellow, kissing the fishes. A lethargic and groggy turtle lurched to the top of a rock and dozed off there. A gigantic tree, or a formidable cliff, unknown in the painting, provided this shadow with profound coolness and stillness, called "Sanctuary." The corner of the pond, though somewhat murky, was invigorated with a detailed depiction of humble lives. In a distance, however, was a stretch of blurred pink blossoming lotus flowers. Blinding sunlight suggested a sweltering summer. The concrete details in the shade and the abstract impression in the sun struck a contrast. The near and the far, the dazzling and the obscure, the distinctiveness and the ambiguity of the two worlds delivered a set of comparisons. Escapism was obvious. Jianfei was able to read the mind of the artist. The painting was familiar.

"What a title!" a voice drew more spectators to the painting.

Jianfei moved her eyes to the bottom searching for the painter: Lishan. As always, Lishan had an eye for the insignificant and unnoticeable. The painting appealed to the spectators because of its embodiment of the humble. It was a work of character, speaking for Lishan's mind and imbued with her personality.

The artists milled around to the corner where another painting absorbed glances. "Reading" showed a girl reclining on a white sheet, reading. Her elbow propped up her head, a lamp spreading red sheen over her naked body. Yes, the girl was stark naked. The rest of the painting disappeared in a background haziness. The light was adopted in a way so that the last shred of shame was lifted, revealing the audacity of a daring artist. The girl was obviously modeled on Juhua except the face, half covered in her palm, half lowered over the book. Jianfei was head to toe immersed in rancidity. Her instinct told her to leave. However a second thought nailed her feet to the floor. She refused to admit in the face of the social elites that not only was she an idiot, knowing nothing about art depicting the human body, but she was an out-and-out old fogey rejecting new ideas.

In the thick of admiring gasps, clicking tongues, 'thumbs up' and feral grunts of praise, the artists feasted their eyes on female flesh. Jianfei's stomach churned. The sheen on the marble limbs, the red tinge on the torso, the tilted small and firm mounds, the youthfulness exuding from the whole being, the girl's complacence in reading, the enveloping darkness and the simplicity in color adoption...all spoke for a matured artist as if Lishan was tired of complexity and was experimenting with a more succinct presentation. Jianfei, while cursing her best friend for being vulgar, recognized Lishan's intuition for beauty and her talent to fathom and pin down the nature of things.

But, wait a minute, she warned herself. *These good-for-nothing, out-of-date arts are not what our society needs. They are opium. The more beautiful, the more poisonous for our socialist cause. What message do these paintings deliver? Stop building industry and agriculture, come enjoy the female body? How frivolous! How decadent!* She looked at Lishan. She was chatting with men. Not a shred of the old bashfulness could be traced on her face.

"All our literature and art are for the masses of the people", echoed Chairman Mao, confirming her political correctness. *Is it pure art? No,* she argued with herself.

"There is in fact no such thing as art for art's sake," again Chairman Mao reinforced her with a tit-for-tat repudiation of the bourgeois fallacy.

There were several outstanding pieces. "Prometheus Bound" showed the gory picture of the human liberator's torture: his liver was being pecked by the vulture. Quite dramatic: precipitous cliffs, overcast sky, and the glinting eyes of the vulture.

"Diqiu, Autumn Flute..." Jianfei chewed the name, "Who is he?"

Lishan pointed her chin to a handsome pale face with long hair. "Quite a genius. Suffered a lot because of his dad, a labeled rightist, who has just been released from a labor camp and resumed his position at the Writer's Association."

Everyone agreed that Lishan's "Sanctuary" was the champion piece.

Lights were turned off and candles lit. "The Merry Widow Waltz" swirled in the air. Weihua and Diqiu walked to each other. Weihua pressed one hand to his heart; another stretched to Diqiu who slipped into his embrace, his fingers poised on his shoulder like orchid petals. In a second the two men locked together and sailed into the center. Tripping, circling, spinning, pirouetting, sashaying, the couple proved to be masters of Viennese waltz. There was something odd about the pair, Jianfei thought, *is Diqiu playing a lady? And no one taunts them?* As if answering, one by one, the artists paired and waltzed in. Not a single couple was of mixed sex. The nature of this salon suddenly dawned on Jianfei. In the dim murkiness, hands groped, cheek pressed on cheek. Ineffable disgust set in and rage surged up. Betrayed, she felt like a fool. Excusing herself, she hid in the bathroom waiting for her stomach to erupt.

In a minute she was out. Her heart was lightened by the small victory of not having said goodbye to Lishan. A new-year's resolution of never seeing her again was sworn. *So they lured me to their den!* In her humiliation, a scene from *Strange Stories from a Chinese Studio* entered her mind. A young scholar on his way for examination stayed overnight in a temple. At midnight he was disturbed by some sobbing. He traced the sound and fell in love with a girl stricken by misfortune. Day broke. There was no girl, no temple. What was left behind was nothing but a fox burrow. The girl turned out to be a fox spirit. Jianfei looked back. Hanging over the smudge of plane trees and an ocean of roof tiles, the mansion loomed large. She began to wonder whether the house was real.

She felt her head spinning, ears tingling and nerves humming. Night air dabbed her cheeks rendering comfort which she inhaled and exhaled avariciously. The stench was bit by bit expelled and her intestines were getting cleansed. Night yielded watery sheen, trees and buildings were shrouded in silver. *Life is still beautiful. I just had a nightmare.* Young people passed by, exchanging Spring Festival greetings. *I belong to the normal majority.* She clung to her sanity. Red flags worked shoulder to shoulder with loudspeakers on top of the buildings. "Socialism is Good" and "The Revolutionaries are forever Young" permeated the air, pumping blood to her vessels, regaining valor in her heart temporarily intimidated by a pack of foxes. Firecracker explosions did not cause trepidation but reminded her to keep abreast with the Socialist New Year. Slogans were another reinforcement:

Make your New Year another progressive one.
Carry out the proletarian revolution through to the end.

This time Jianfei would sweep away all the remaining shards from three years ago. *Don't blame me, Lishan. Three years ago, on that summer night, you draped your shameful naked arms on my shoulders, begging for physical love. Now this! You are the one who shattered our friendship.* Thus thinking, she headed home without looking back.

Chapter 17

An ambulance whistled by, a red cross like a huge butterfly in the winter gray. Sadness, guilt and anger, as if spilt from a saucepan, simmered in Tang Wei.

The Party secretary sitting next to him whispered, "What triggered her heart attack? Your mom has hardly missed a day in fifteen years."

Tang Wei nodded and shook his head, a dazed look on his face.

"What induced her heart attack?" the doctor, brows knit, asked the same question, "Who was with her at the time?" his eyes shifted between the young and old faces.

"I," said Tang Wei, "I am her son. We had an argument." A deep regret and a loud self-defense rose in his heart simultaneously.

"When did this happen?"

"Last night…then this morning," Tang Wei lowered his head.

Pain and injustice that had been bottled inside now began to swell.

"*Whom to choose?*" loomed up and tormented him again, a question that had been haunting him day and night for the past month. *A mother or a wife?*

At first Tang Wei had no intention to let his mother know every detail about Huifang. A sketch should be enough— *I have a girlfriend, high school graduate, pretty, living in the Military Academy. Family background? Teachers, dad teaches at the Academy, mom at a high school.* Yet the lingering humiliation from the skirmish over the fish hastened his determination to lay his cards on the table.

The first night after Huifang went downstairs, the mother and the son lay still, one in the bed, one on the chest. Tang Wei's quilt, puffed up in the sunshine, was now being heated up with a bronze hot-water bottle while mom's decade-old quilt was cold like a piece of iron for which both the mother and the son had been fighting for since the bed time just like the chest.

"How come you are not wearing your uniform?" mom did not beat about the bush.

"I have been discharged. I have told you already," knowing how this would crush mom's vanity, Tang Wei tried to sound calm.

"You still can wear your uniform, though," Mom clung to the green image.

"Without the red star and the red collar badge? Green without red means nothing, anyone can wear it. You are obsessed with green."

"For years since you joined the army, what I have been expecting is your promotion: platoon leader, Party secretary, Political Commissar, stepping into your dad's shoes." in a deductive way, mom was portraying an officer, "...and I truly believed you will win these titles, being your dad's son. Are these all lies? Aren't you an activist in the study campaign and a Party group leader? Explain to me!!"

A tear could be detected in her voice.

"Love affairs are forbidden in the army. That's it. I didn't do anything shameful."

"So you let your career go to the dogs, for that young lady? Ha!" Mom raised her voice but immediately muffled it, fearing the building was not soundproof.

"I breached the discipline but that does not mean I have disgraced myself or you." Tang Wei felt he had finally found a channel to clarify himself, "On the contrary, my love is serious and I will marry her. The punishment is temporary but my love is permanent."

"Marry her?" The chest creaked, mom sat up. Silence fell.

In the distance, machines rumbled to meet their annual goal. Tang Wei could hear mom heaving a sigh in silhouette.

"I grew up with this factory through thick and thin. I know the days without food. If she snatches pork, skewers four pieces of fish at a time, how can I, a manufacturing worker with a meager salary, feed her?"

"Mom, enough. She wouldn't need you to support her."

"Well then... who is going to support me, your aged mother, if you move out with her? A mother, a single mother who painstakingly brought you up, who cried her eyes out for her husband first, now the son..." mom began to lament on fate:" All hopes have turned into a pipe dream. What an unfortunate soul I am!" The daily anguish that had been covered by political routine had finally broken loose.

"She is expensive. She is ill-mannered. She has nothing in common with this family. We cannot afford such a beauty. There is something in her upbringing that tells me she does not belong to this family." Tang Ma lay back on her makeshift bed, determined to dig out more about the girl.

There was some grain of truth in what mom said, yet Tang Wei was in no mood to fight. After all, it was not easy for a widow to bring up a child single-handedly.

Tang Wei's memory played back to the old days. *Fish, skewering four. Yes, food was always scant and money short. The two symbols of social status. How mom grudged every grain of rice and hoarded every piece she thought as treasure.* Once, a relative from the village brought her a piece of homemade ham during his Spring Festival visit. Mom hung it on the window frame for a whole year. When Tang Wei came back the following Spring Festival, he found that some parts of the ham shone with green phosphorescence, other parts were coated with frosty mold. Black-haired worms and white maggots squirmed cheerfully in the sun through tunnels and holes, entering and exiting for their own Spring Festival banquet. Repulsed, Tang Wei could barely keep balance on the chair where he stood to release the ham from the hanging strings. He bluntly refused to touch the ham no matter how mom insisted that the worms were actually harmless and the meat tasted even better because it had been preserved longer.

"Why didn't you eat it when it was fresh?"

"How could I have enjoyed it without you?"

Day broke. Tang Wei went downstairs to his sweetheart, smiling.

"Look at her scarf! One hundred percent wool. Who can afford that?"

A week passed with the bedtime routine discussion between mom and son on the future daughter-in-law. Tang Wei was optimistic and hoped that his mother might begin to look more favorably on his girl who had been making every effort to prove herself qualified to join the family. However her hard work had all turned futile. Although his childhood memories kept coming back to revive the relationship, memories such as mom shoving every bit of food to the son under the pretext that none was her favorite dish, the evening conversation would refreeze the thawed memory.

"That's my new year's gift."

"Oh?" mom shook her faded scarf on the pillow, "mine is almost ten years old, you never…"

"Mom…be reasonable…please," Tang Wei pleaded.

The scarf, yes, he remembered mom's scarf. In his junior year, mom had won the title of "model worker" again. A scarf was delivered into her hand on the stage by the factory director amid thunderous applause along with a certificate of merit. The red scarf, embroidered with the brand name "Glory," packed in a delicate box, was the product of her own factory. She put it on and looked at herself in the table mirror, her face radiated. Tang Wei was doing homework. He stole a glance and caught her coy, ecstatic smile. A sense of pride filled his heart. *Mom is still pretty.* However what mom did next completely confounded Tang Wei. With great care, mom folded the scarf as small as a book, then opened her chest from which she dug out a bundle and hid the scarf at the bottom of it. The bundle, which Tang Wei called "the bundle of war," contained a yellowish diary of his father's, a photograph of the same color, a cloth badge of the "New Fourth Army" and her faded red wedding gown. All were wrapped in a piece of home-woven, coarse cloth. Now the brand-new red scarf was interred in this glorious reliquary. When summer came, mom took these items out to be aired and sunned. The red scarf, reeking of mothballs, showing tiny holes, was only put into use after three years.

"She is expensive. She does not belong to this family," mom repeated, "She is a snake with a beauty's head!"

"Why can't you share my happiness? We are in love. Our happiness will last forever, just like you and dad."

"Don't you dare mention your martyred father!" Mom threw her padded jacket over her shoulders and turned on the light before winding up her speech in cold premonition:

"In the end she will trap you up in her coils and squeeze the life out of you, just like in the folktale."

The traditional image applied to Huifang as a seductive and murderous woman stabbed Tang Wei in the heart, blowing off his memory of mom struggling to raise him single-handedly. *How could such a loving woman let such venom drip out of her mouth?*

"Mom, you've gone too far! You have no right to speak about my friend in such a manner!"

In a minute, his rage subsided but soon would soar up again as mom's tongue continued to rattle, "Now, answer me, to what depth did your friendship go?"

Tang Wei could not believe his ears. Why is emotion always associated with flesh? And why do they all want to dig into sex? He turned off the light with such vehemence that the string snapped in two, leaving the switch out of reach when mom tried to turn on the light back again.

"Did you sleep with her?"

The words sent prickles down his spine. Tang Wei sank into a profound sadness. To him, discharge was liberation. Now he had to go through the interrogation once again, from his own mother whose love he had clung to during the six confined months. *What went wrong?* As the years passed into manhood, trouble seemed to increase. *Did mom change or I?*

Familiar phrases poured out of his mother's mouth in a torrential flow, communism and capitalism, proletariat and bourgeoisie, class and class struggle. Tang Ma's bedroom was turned into another classroom. Home became the barracks. A chill went through him in companion of a thought: *I have not even mentioned Huifang's father yet.* The pain was a double-edged knife. On the one hand, the legendary mother-daughter-in-law animosity was enough to disillusion a sweet home; on the other, mom's new cross-examining persona was identical with that in his army and this was something unforeseen from the son's perspective. "Bourgeois humanism", "abstract love", "sugar-coated bomb"…mom suddenly showed her true features as an eloquent Marxist theorist. Tang Wei was awestruck. *Where is my mom?*

Snatching his coat, Tang Wei darted out into the dark corridor. Unspeakable shame and fury drove tears out. He lit a cigarette and paced up and down noiselessly. *Neighbors!* He had the neighbors to consider. He returned to the room. Mom was sobbing. His heart melted. The last thing he wanted to see was mother's tears. When he was a little boy, he would cry whenever he saw his mom crying.

Dear mom, please, please put yourself in my shoes.

What changed my baby?

Never in her life had she imagined such disgrace. In her mind stood two Tangs: one braving the rain of bullets and forest of bayonets, laying down his life; the other, never having even sniffed the smoke of war before stripped of his uniform and live in sordid disgrace.

"A sugar-coated bomb," as Chairman Mao put it.

Yes, that is Huifang, and this is class struggle. Class struggle is ubiquitous. We must sharpen our eyes. The girl does not belong to this family. Look at the fine texture of her white skin and her striking facial features; her pleated trousers and shining shoes. No, no working class has that kind of offspring. And the way she walks, the tilted finger tips holding chopsticks, the showing-no-teeth smile...

After Huifang returned to Nanjing, Tang Wei felt obliged to give mom a complete portrait of Huifang, the future daughter-in-law. The topic would certainly touch a raw nerve in his mom, but uncovering the painful truth was only a matter of time. This was what happened the night before.

"There is something I need to make clear because I don't want to keep anything undercover for the future. I told you Huifang's father was a teacher, but that is only a partial truth. The whole truth is that he is an ex-Kuomintang officer, captured in the battlefield. But he is now serving the Communist Party with his warfare knowledge and command experiences."

He took a seat beside mom.

Ashen-faced, Tang Ma, for a moment, was tongue-tied. She was altering Tang Wei's padded jacket. From time to time, she sharpened the needle by scratching it against her hair. On hearing KMT, her left hand automatically rose to her heart and rested there as if her husband was dwelling right there and then, listening. Her right hand halted midair.

She asked, word by word, "What did you say? Her father is a Kuomintang?"

"Was," Tang Wei corrected.

"Is or was makes no difference," mom put down the jacket. "You don't need to remind me who murdered your dad!" Hatred set aglow her lusterless eyes.

"But I am not going to marry the father," Tang Wei hated to lecture his mom on the ABC's of marriage.

"Sit down!" Her tone sent a chill down his marrow.

Tang Wei resumed the seat at her side.

"Marry? Don't you dare to bring the enemy home!!"

"Eventually we will have to be together," Tang Wei wavered, feeling weak in his legs.

"Marry?" mom repeated the word, "I didn't take it to heart when you first mentioned it, are you serious?"

"Yes," Tang Wei mustered up his courage.

Mom raised her head. Her hoary hair and crow's feet took the edge off Tang Wei's anger. His thoughts drifted. He saw mother and son eating at a restaurant, mom ordering a ten-cent bowl of noodle soup for herself and a large plate of three-yuan dumplings for the son... mom shaking head pushing back the dumplings as the son shoved to mom. A pang swelled up. Tang Wei averted his eyes yet her eyes drilled into his and then moved away. With her eyes glued on the jacket and hand shuttled on the needle, her lips sealed with an inscrutable snort.

"What?" Tang Wei asked timidly, his anger greatly abated.

"Nothing," mom would not even look at him this time. She was her old tranquil self again.

"Talk to me."

"If you marry that bloody enemy, you are not my son and I am not your mother. Well and river water do not mingle."

"Then what?" Tang Wei's voice rasped.

"Her or me, you choose."

With these words, mom sank into complete muteness. This was the night before.

Day broke. After a sleepless night, Tang Wei was preparing for his first day of work. Hoping to start his day without mental turmoil, he left a note on the table for mom, "I am sure the three of us can live together peacefully. I will take care of you but my life cannot be without Huifang."

Mom rose from bed but dropped back again, her face white as the sheet which lay beside her like a murder weapon.

The doctor handed over the prescription, in the bottom was written, "Doctor's recommendation: part-time work only."

"Genetic heart disease induced by fits of emotion, that's your mom's situation. Young man, fluctuation must be avoided at home, unconditionally." The doctor then turned to the Party secretary, "Overworking has consumed her health."

Tang Wei's starting day at the factory marked the ending of his mother's career and the beginning of her semi-retirement. Tang Wei's self-reproach was beyond words.

Tang Wei was asked to help in the Union. A year later, he replaced his mother. The new face in the union, young, male and handsome, helped him to win the election due to the favor of the majority of the workers, most of them women.

"Hi, Chairman, may I talk to you about my subsidization?"

"Hi, Chairman, join us at lunch! We are saving some dumplings for you!" the girls giggled like bells.

"Brother Tang," some brave ones went even farther as to call him brother, insinuating an extraordinary intimacy, "I have some spare tickets. Let's go see a movie."

Girls circled him like bees around a flower. At home, they went up from downstairs, and swarmed the tiny room under the pretext of taking care of Tang Ma, seizing every opportunity to approach Tang Ma's unmarried, attractive son. Girls, girls, the textile factory had plenty. A smile creased Tang Ma's face. *These are our class sisters, our proletarian family!*

Huifang was a topic cautiously avoided between the mother and the son. Juggling with his routine responsibilities in the workshop, in the union and at home, Tang Wei's only hope was to see mom pass another day safe and sound without an episode. He prayed that mom would live long, no matter what the cost.

Tang Wei wrote to Huifang regularly, once a week, then every other week, but never heard from her. The fruitless correspondence dwindled.

None of them had any clue what had happened to their letters. They were intercepted, one by the mother whose fast-paced life came to a sudden halt, allowing her ample time to scan her son's personal belongings and decide what should be confined in her chest which was well-secured underneath her body; the other by the security guards at the North Pole New Village whose mission it was to confiscate any suspicious materials in the ex-KMT's mail.

Chapter 18

One day four months after Huifang had returned from Shanghai, two visitors appeared in her living room. One, in his fifties, owned a weather-beaten swarthy face and a pair of restless eyes. When he smiled, his yellow teeth and thin lips puffed out a strong odor of cheap cigarettes. His marvelous tiny ears were a fine replica of those of a mouse. A brand new dark blue cap, a typical 'cadre's cap', popular among low country officials yet discarded in the city some ten, even twenty years ago, crested on an abundant growth of unwashed black hair circling a barren spot in the center. A brand new blue suit, of the same color and fashion as his cap, stiffened his whole upper body making his movement a bit like a robot. He took over the teacup with such caution not to allow the first crease on his sleeve. A pair of military sneakers, also de rigueur in fashion among the political elite, worked foot in hand, to complete the portrait of one of the countryside politicians, perhaps a people's commune brigade leader or a Party secretary.

The other man was wearing a light brown traditional tunic. Hand-winded frog-shaped buttons lined down and sealed up all the way to his chin. A piece of unkempt cloth was carelessly wrapped around his waist both to preserve his body heat and to announce his defiance of the city fashion. With a tea in hand, he unbuttoned his collar revealing a rough neck encircled by a dark brown homemade scarf. His attire represented the downstream Yangtze countryside. The two pairs of muddy shoes brought the country road straight into the living room, smearing its underfoot mirror as if the floor was newly constructed in an abstract pattern. Although too late to rescue the mirror, Teacher Huang rushed over, taking off her own slippers and carrying her husband's.

"Here, here, slippers, slippers," she thrust into both hands, "They are comfortable. The floor is too cold."

Two bags made of reeds hung conspicuously in their hands. One contained two fish, gills red, eyes glassy, freshly killed; the other, two chickens, one recently plucked, freshly killed; the other, feathers still gleaming, also freshly killed. The sacrificial offering was squarely placed on the table, awaiting an exchange of a city meal.

"Have some tea, please," mom rubbed her hands on her apron, dragging the country sacrifice to the kitchen where it belonged.

"I thought you would have come during the Spring Festival. We prepared dishes for you."

"Couldn't get away, couldn't get away," the blue suit put on a sincerely busy look, "The whole village depends on the Party, you know that, Comrade Huang. Party documents, newspaper editorials, they are important, very important, and needed to be delivered without delay. The masses enjoyed the meetings; they love us. A roomful of gifts poured in, fish, duck, chicken, beef. The countryside still has these things on occasion."

"Mouse Ears" smiled, revealing a gold tooth.

"Cigarette?" He produced a packet from his pocket, shook out one to Huifang's mother, who politely smiled with a headshake.

Click, click. The gold tooth clicked a metal lighter. Narrowing his eyes at the flame, he said, "See this? A young man gave it to me. They all respect the Party, competing to offer me gifts. I hardly need to buy anything."

The traditional-tunic fellow took out a long-handled pipe and began to ladle down into his tobacco purse. Mom lit up his pipe timely and called to Huifang, "Huifang, say hello to your uncle."

She turned to the tunic, "do you remember Huifang? It must be more than ten years."

Huifang stepped in from her room. The gold tooth nailed her with his eyes, sending chills down Huifang's spine. She stared back at him until he looked away.

"You don't remember me but I remember you," uncle put up his hand, "you were this tall, to my waist. You and your dad came down to see grandma. What a beautiful big girl you have bloomed into!"

"How is your life in the country?" Huifang asked.

"Hanging in there. Hanging in there."

After dinner, mom kept the guests in the living room chatting while dad motioned Huifang to her own room.

"This month the city has planned to send down more educated youths. The reception teams from the neighboring counties are here to bring students to their villages. As I have been telling you for the past four years, university is not for everyone. Even if you try again next year and reach the qualified scores, with your dad's stained history, you are destined to be an outsider."

The day dad had threatened her with had finally arrived. Like so many others, it was now her turn to move to the countryside.

As the days passed by without Tang Wei's letter, Huifang found herself sinking deeper and deeper into a lonely abyss. At home, every free meal went down with increasing burning in her stomach and every idle hour she was on pins and needles. Her daily thoughts were focused on nothing but when she could board the train like four months ago. Without school, without a job, she felt she was gradually becoming a fossil of her past. Happiness was yesterday and hope no longer a tomorrow. If total emptiness yielded nothing, at least the countryside would open a door. Away from free meals was what she urgently needed, and then labor might earn her another railway ticket to Shanghai.

Across the nation, armies of 'educated youths' marched to the open fields because they truly believed Mao's words "The countryside is a vast realm. There youth has the opportunity to achieve greatness," and that Chairman Mao welcomed them there. Page-sized photos occupied the local newspapers: red flowers, elated faces, bustling stations, tearful eyes of glory-loving parents. Like trains in wartime loaded with soldiers, the railroad cars were now carrying students, idealistic, ready to sacrifice, with the same boiling blood and steaming energy. The trains rocked, roared and rolled towards the battlefield called Building the Socialist New Countryside. In a few days, Huifang would converge with this stream, flowing into the unknown land on the rumbling train, together with thousands of willing or reluctant builders. The tidal wave was here, in the living room now, ready to sweep her away.

Her father continued, "I invited your uncle and the brigade leader to come up with the reception team so that they will have a better picture of how you live in the city. Your uncle will keep an eye on you and the brigade leader promised to take special care of you. Things shouldn't be too bad. Life in the Jiangsu countryside, even in a fishing village, is better than in the cities up north, especially along the coast."

He paused, and then added, "Forget that Communist boy. The two of you are not meant to be together. Different classes never mingle. If you do, the fruit will be bitter. Believe me. I have passed more bridges than you have walked roads."

His usually harsh words had toned down a bit.

Huifang bravely squeezed out a sentence, "I wrote dozens of letters…"

"Forget him. It is a moon in the water."

Her mind wandered back to the temple four months ago, the cryptic fortune teller and his creepy premonition: the circle was not complete and the happiness was not doubled. Double happiness meant marriage. Her heart quaked at the fleeting thought that Tang Wei and she were finished. Before she could utter another word, dad led Huifang back to join the guests in the living room.

"Mouse Ears" or "Gold Tooth" or "Blue Suit" patted her on the shoulder, belching liquor and fish into her nostrils.

"Don't worry. I am also your uncle. I will protect you."

He belched again sending another wave of fish, spirits and garlic up to her nose.

Waving on the billboard, Chairman Mao smiled with his fatherly instruction. Loudspeakers burbled with the increasing statistics of hourly dispatched youths alternated with selected quotations from the great leader.

"'The world is yours, as well as ours, but in the last analysis, it is yours. You young people, full of vigor and vitality, are in the bloom of life, like the sun at eight or nine in the morning. Our hope is placed on you…The world belongs to you. China's future belongs to you.' …Our great leader pins his hope on us the younger generation…Long live Chairman Mao!"

The standard Beijing dialect was broadcast over the square in front of the railway station, a virtual ocean of red flags and red flowers. The air was charged with a duality of emotions, an itchy desire to plunge into the green fields, and the reluctance of tearing away from parents and painful letting go of fledglings into the blue sky.

Huifang looked around. Tears escaped again. The one who should be here was not here.

"Does Tang Wei know you are going away?" reading Huifang's mind, Lishan tried to offer a morsel of comfort through her usual coldness.

"No. My letters have never been answered, nor returned. Four months, forty letters, I guess."

"Do you think there is another girl, maybe? Shanghai is Shanghai, you know," Juhua cut in bluntly but was checked by Lishan's eyes.

Although tears were profuse here, Huifang's carried different significance.

"I don't believe so," Huifang said, almost inaudibly.

"Something must have happened to your letters and his," Lishan said, "Have you talked to your parents?"

"They both swore there was no letter from him."

"A whisper in the wind, a moon in the water," Lishan said as if with a light heart. "You have to let him go."

"Dad used the same analogy in persuading me to give up the relation… Now I believe in fate. Remember that old man in the temple?"

"Sheer nonsense," Lishan sneered at the image, "So you think I am a zombie?"

Juhua bent over with laughter, holding her sides.

"How is Jianfei? You said you saw her in Shanghai." said Lishan indifferently.

"Something was not right. She was crying all the time we were there."

"We invited her to our salon. She has simply evaporated," Juhua's eyes were like a pair of saucers, "and no good-byes. You are right, something must be wrong."

"Don't make stupid connections. Her vanishing had nothing to do with her tears." Lishan snapped.

The mere thought of Jianfei set Lishan on fire. Though Juhua was her everyday companion, she could hardly fill the void.

"Did she tell you why?" jealousy was like vinegar in Lishan's heart.

"No," Huifang's pain seemed to be diverted. She dried her eyes. "No, she didn't."

Relieved, Lishan suggested that the three of them take a picture and Huifang should mail it to Jianfei.

"I took the old man's camera."

Lishan waved at Huifang's mom and handed it over to her.

"How is your dad? Do you still live on campus?" Huifang asked.

"Yes, indubitably."

As the train gained momentum and built into a droning rhythm, a new ebullience entered the car. Tears gave place to laughter. Some prompted self-introductions while others timidly shook hands. The youngsters exchanged graduation photos, traded an apple for a pear or shared their snacks. The small tea tables were quickly spread open for playing card games. New friendships were quickly forged. Girls left their seats and stood along the passageway to catch boys' eyes. Boys began to casually scan the faces. Away from the stifling city, free from the parents' nagging and the parasitical lives! A new life was unfolding in front! A promising land! Self-reliance! New concepts filled the car and prompted songs.

"The revolutionaries are forever young, like the pine trees, four-season green…"

Girls leaned against each other, boys humming.

Maybe it would not be that bad after all, Huifang thought, and soon let her optimism go far. *Tang Wei might even be able to rid himself of the suspicious eyes and come down for a visit, so long as I can get hold of him. The sky is high and the emperor far away, as they say. The countryside should be more distant from politics than the city.*

In the lullaby of the droning train, her drowsiness soon sent her to a sandy beach outside her lovely, small wooden cabin where she and Tang Wei sat head to head, shoulder to shoulder. A golden disked moon was hanging above in the sky; its reflection quivering on the unfathomable ocean like quicksilver. Home-brewed rice wine, dried fish and shrimp, drunken crabs, mountain nuts and crimson-skinned peanuts rewarded her hard labor. In the twilight, she saw Tang Wei holding her hand, both heads covered in red silk, she in a red wedding gown, he in a black tunic. She giggled and woke up. *Wedding, is the dream propitious or a bad omen?* She closed her eyes and again she saw her in his arms, they chatted the whole night until the awakening sky enveloped them in its opaque orange. The splendor of the sunrise in her dreams thrilled her. And again, she measured the hidden meaning. What was in store for her was still uncertain but she was tempted with its bright promise, just like the sunrise. She could not have known that she was flying into a storm, feathers still downy and wings not tested.

Chapter 19

Thunder cracked over the thatched roof; lightning swam in the dark sky like a serpent, taking snapshots of the swaying willows and water lilies. Raindrops sloshed down. Frogs and toads croaked a concert, making the pond a festival market. Unknown insects hurried to catch up. Crickets joined in, their timid voice like the piccolo in Beethoven's Fifth. Hundreds of fireflies rallied, floating in the air, holding their tiny lanterns like the contestants at the lantern festival. It was only early June, but the sultry summer had hastened to their stage.

The village had long sunk into a profound slumber. The hustle-bustle of the spring season had fizzled out and a brief interval followed before the summer harvest began. This was the season when the villagers went to sea, leaving this amphibious village in the hands of women.

It was nine o'clock and darkness had just set in. The other two city girls were sound asleep on the west end. Their evenly-breathing sleep was decorated with a slightly girlish snoring. Huifang's room was on the east end of the house, one of the four rooms that made up this little house. Her window was composed of two wooden panels which, during the day, were unlatched and slid separate to let in fresh air, leaving four removable bars to fend off intruders. Outside the window was a patch of rice paddies with their shoots now covered in water and a small pond canopied by weeping willows. In spring, the massive apricot blossoms reflected in the water and painted the pond white; in summer, lotus flowers put on their pink tips; in fall the pond was dyed orange and red. The kitchen and the dining area separated the two bedrooms in the middle. A huge kettle sat on a brick stove. A small wooden table and two benches were provided in addition by Gold Tooth, attesting to the Party's concern for the educated youth. Gold Tooth had kept his promise and Huifang was enjoying special favors from the brigade. She had everything of her own, including a bedroom shared with the house owner who was never there. The bedroom shared by her two housemates faced the tool shed where sickles, spades, pickaxes and shoulder poles lay perfunctorily with no romantic view. A sty where pigs nuzzled their smelly food and waddled in the black slime of mud, rotting vegetables and their own excrement was exposed to the open next door. Despite this outrageous inequity, the three high school graduates lived in harmony. Huifang's easygoing way and kind nature defused their anger and jealousy and smoothed the bumps. The house was full of sisterly care for each other.

The owner of the house was a single woman in her mid-fifties who had gone to live with her daughter in a neighboring village. She was half-paralyzed after a stroke and had been bedridden ever since. This was the last house on the border of the village. From the rice paddies outside Huifang's window there was a meandering path leading to the sprawling village, where the brigade office stood in the center.

More than a year had passed since Huifang said good-bye to Nanjing. Life was not too bad in this remote fishing village if not for the absence of Tang Wei. Here the sky was bluer and higher, the moon rounder and clearer and people cruder but nicer. There were no weekly political studies as Lishan and Jianfei had been subjected to at universities. Nor were there slogans and banners except for a broadcast box hanging languidly on a tree reminding people of seasonal projects and the changing weather:

Load up the dried fish this morning. The truck will be here at ten.
A thunderstorm is on the way. The fishing trip is canceled.
The third team needs to reap the sesame today.
…

A ten-minute walk would bring Huifang to the sea. A stretch of bright green grass extended to the water where colonies of crabs scurried to their hiding holes at human footsteps. Nonetheless barefoot children never returned home empty-handed from the shoreline. Their ill-fated captives soon received a special treatment with mellow rice wine. Submerged in the wine jar, their eyes half closed, senses began to leave their bodies. They were rocked into a blissful and sweet drowsiness, permanently drunk and later promoted to the wealthiest banquet tables. Huifang enjoyed being one of these children. She brought to dad a wax-sealed jar of drunken crabs which dad treated his buddies with. They all asked Huifang to bring them the same gift. A relief came to her heart that the free meals had been paid off and she was no longer an open-handed beggar at home.

Tang Wei had visited her parents once, but was disappointed to find his girlfriend had moved away. "Address?" Her parents gave an evasive answer.

Huifang decided to go to Shanghai in a month. She was now writing to inform him, though fearful that this letter, too, would end up unanswered, like her numerous letters sent out in the past year.

The rain was still rampant and the wind howling. The willow tree at her window bent over like a dancing girl with broad long sleeves.

Huifang sealed the letter with a few grains of cooked rice and once again was lost in thought. This was the tenth letter in sixteen months. What has happened to him? Tang Wei had become her constant worry. The days at the Academy, like rice wine, mellowed in her memory— the murky Purple-Gold Mountain, the echoing unknown birds, the murmuring brooks, the glassy boulders, the pink and white clouds on the hillside, the paths resonant with lovers' laughter and trees that witnessed their kisses…. *Are they gone forever? Are they now merely the relics of our dead love?* She decided this would be her last letter. She would get up early to catch the mail six miles away in the nearest town.

She unbuttoned her shirt and examined herself in the mirror. The face remained the same, complexion a bit dark; the shoulders were rounder, arms more sinewy and skin was tanned. The fieldwork had unleashed her body. She closed her eyes, *Tang Wei, Tang We*i. His touch was still vivid and acute.

"Tang Wei", she moaned.

As if to answer her call, a willow branch cracked. She opened her eyes and saw a ghost…A flash of lightning whitened the dark willow tree. A face among the shadowy leaves was reflected in her mirror. In a wink the sky darkened and the face vanished. Huifang's face turned ashen gray. One of her hands quickly moved up and covered her body; the other reached up and snapped the string to turn off the light. The room sank into complete darkness. She slid the two window boards together, buttoned her shirt and rubbed her eyes. *Was it a phantom or a man?* Tiptoeing, she edged along the wall to the window and peeped out through a chink between the panel and its frame. *Am I delusional?* Penetrating the night, she saw nothing but the seedlings in the paddy grappling with the wanton storm like the unkempt hair of an angry man. The willow tree continued to dance with its leaves thrown into the wind like a dancing girl's sleeves. Nestling in the armpit between its branches where she first saw the phantom, there was no one now but darkness. *Am I seeing things?* Sitting in the dark, she tried to catch her breath meanwhile straining her ears. The pond symphony; the rampant wind and the splashing rain tried in turn to squeeze into her head, leaving no room for additional sound; no breaking of the branch. Had she seen a face in the mirror? Had she heard a breaking branch? Now she was not sure. Her eyes slit again through the crease. *Nothing, not a soul.* Half an hour passed, then one hour. The clock struck eleven. *I must report this to the brigade leader the first thing in the morning.*

The storm subsided and the moon swam out, breaking the dissipating clouds. The pond was playing the Sixth Symphony now, a joyful ode to summer. Stars blinked into the water from high above. Not daring to turn on the light, she groped to bolt the window. Somehow the latch was not in its usual place. Alarmed, she searched the kitchen, the courtyard and every corner of the house, but the latch was nowhere to be found. She searched in her head. Yes, it was placed on the windowsill this morning as a regulation after she opened the window, where it stayed until the bed time. *How could it possibly be missing? How and when was it removed?* There was no house between her bedroom window and the pond, the only thing existing there was a path trodden by the owners, and the owners alone. She shuddered. *Spooky.* First the face in her mirror, now the latch. She tied the two handles with a rubber band and sat on the bed dozing.

Something bounced on her face, cold and elastic. Huifang opened her eyes. The rubber band flew over and lay beside her.

Before she could grasp the situation, a hand covered her mouth and a muffled voice threatened, "Be quiet or I'll strangle you!" A familiar voice sent chill down her spine.

The moon seeped through the peaceful willow, its pale face lit a blotchy face decorated with a glistening tooth. The brigade leader, her protector! His eyes were bloodshot. A heavy gurgle rose from his throat, delivering straight to her face his patent stench of liquor, garlic and fish. In a second, her buttons popped off and her blouse was ripped open. Grunting like a pig, saliva dripping from his chin, he nuzzled Huifang's neck; his coarse palms fumbled.

Huifang dodged his smelly face and groaned.

"Quiet, bitch! What is your beauty for?"

A crumpled rag was stuffed into her mouth. Huifang flailed her arms and kicked about frantically. The predator crushed her with his stumpy limbs.

"It's payback time! The lily pond, the apricot blossoms, the room and the light fieldwork! Nothing is free!"

Huifang groaned.

"Hurt? I will cut a woman out of you!" the man sniggered at his own lewdness.

The dream to achieve greatness in the green fields was torn to pieces.

As he rose, he puffed into her ears, "Don't you dare to breathe a word! Or I will guarantee you will be stuck here forever!"

The moon was swimming in the watery blue. The summer orchestra continued their rehearsal. The willow was weeping, echoing Huifang's wrenching pain. Huifang scrubbed and scrubbed. She knew the filth had seeped into every pore, every cell, and washing made no difference in her heart.

She got up late and stayed at home. Pushing the window open, she stared at a white water lily stained with mud. Tears trickled down. She tore her letter to pieces and scattered them around the white lily. Tang Wei was gone, and forever.

Part Four

Chapter 1

Red Storm

Step by step, history entered 1966.

June then July… The red flood showed no sign of ebbing. Red sky, red earth and red people. Mouths wide open in unison: "The East is Red." A mammoth parade and a jubilant party of the proletariat. Mao had gathered thunder and lightning to wake up the nation from decades of slumber and rip open the dark curtains that shrouded any plots and schemes against Chairman Mao. All the filth and sewage will be disposed of, all ghosts and goblins eliminated…so were the Red Guards told by the newspapers and broadcast. Red arm bands and green uniforms came into vogue. Majestic pictures of the great leader stood everywhere, commanding school campuses, factory yards, hospital wards and city squares.

Tiananmen Square hosted mass rallies. Jumping, jumping, jumping, the Red Guards craned their necks from different corners eager to catch a glimpse of the giant above the ocean of heads. Coming, coming, the young hearts beat faster as the grand figure finally emerged! The Red Sun was rising from the Tian An Men rostrum! Beijing, China. The center of the center! The eye of the Red Storm! "Long live Chairman Mao!" soared to the sky from forests of red books, shaking the world.

Chairman Mao slowly waved his green cap to the green ocean down below and responded with a solemn and sincere voice, "Long live the people!"

"Down with the bourgeoisie!"

"To hell with the authorities!"

"Whoever stands in the way of revolution, let's kick them over into the garbage can! If the enemy refuses to surrender, we will smash the dog's head!"

Seeing the great leader, though a blurry outline from hundreds of meters away, fueled the revolutionary zeal.

Loudspeakers sang, debated, shouted, cursed and applauded.

"Fuck your bourgeois mother!"

"Crush Khrushchev's skull!"

"Down with the Soviet Revisionists!"

The proletarian young warriors were in a constant indignant wrath! *The whole world is upside down and we are the only sober ones.* During the Cultural Revolution, whoever happened to be young could consider themselves the luckiest. The old all turned a bit wary.

Whips worked together with the drums. Whip, whip!

Whips fell on the hangdog's skull, "Speak out! When did you join the Kuomintang?"

"Confess, you bitch!"

Slap, slap, slap, clear and crisp. The bitch hung her head.

"Are you a counterrevolutionary? Are you? Are you? No?"

Slap.

"Where is the blacklist? Hand it over! No blacklist?"

Whip, whip!

In the sun, sweaty beads oozed out. Questions were posed with belts and were answered with bloody welts. Cheers roared. In the city of Beijing, the shining scalp of party secretaries quickly came into vogue as "shorn heads". *How wonderful to be young and correct! Today we dig their graves, tomorrow we send them to hell!* The belts proudly spoke the new revolutionary language. Besides skinheads, the Red Guards popularized a new hair style: "Yin Yang Head", half hair, half bald—black and white, leading the fashion. Whoever could not stand the new mode only proved their bourgeois vanity. And if their humiliation drove these narrow-minded ones to hang themselves or jump from the fifth floor, they were welcome to do so!

In the great tradition of the guillotine, revolution proved to be the mother of invention. Another nationwide invention had acquired a modern name, "flying the airplane." The aircrafts were provided by the passengers themselves with arms pulled back like trussed chicken wings and bodies pressed down to the lowest level serving as the fuselage. Every day, professors, party secretaries, principals, presidents, managers, doctors, scientists, actors, artists and directors stood on their self-made airplanes flying through the clouds of fabricated stories, interrogations, slogans and "down with's." Although this nation was never short of great inventions, the compass and gunpowder paled beside the modern marvels. The traditional tortures, 'mo,' skinning of the face, and 'bi,' cutting off the nose, were so much less civilized. *If these social leaders failed to comprehend their charges, don't they deserve harsh words from revolutionary foaming lips? Should their hair not be pulled back to show their spastic faces in the ugliest contortions?*

Some perverse human nature is fed in inflicting miseries on others.

All the streets were renamed. Old signs were trampled under feet.

Plum Garden?

Smash!

Let's call it "Anti-Revisionist Road"? Temples, bodhisattva statues, Guanyin, Buddha, why do they deserve to be put on a pedestal?

Smash! Smash!

White pagodas, stone horses and Ming or Qing tombs…

Smash, smash!

Feudalistic landmarks!

Smash! Smash!

History needs to be rewritten!

His Majesty had claimed the patent in his youth:

> A revolution is not a dinner party, or writing an essay, or painting a picture, or doing embroidery; it cannot be so refined, so leisurely and gentle, so temperate, kind, courteous, restrained and magnanimous. A revolution is an insurrection, an act of violence by which one class overthrows another.

Among the Red Guards, an assortment of groups mushroomed with significant titles: "Red Detachment", "Little Eighth Route Army". Some romanticized their teams with poetic names: "Sweeping the Remnant

Clouds"—a reference to one of Chairman Mao's poems; "East Wind Strong"—borrowed from his quotation "The East Wind is prevailing over the West Wind"; while others were more straightforward: "Iron Fist"; "Avalanche", "Thunderbolt", again inspired by Chairman Mao:

> The Communist ideological and social system…sweeping the world with the momentum of an avalanche and the force of a thunderbolt.

Big character posters, Da Zi Bao, modern China's long-used weapon, walled the schools and factories. Exclamatory marks punched like iron fists. Day and night, pens and brushes worked incessantly, manufacturing new bullets. Genius Marxist theorists came into beings like bamboo shoots sprung after a spring rain. School boundaries no longer existed. Red Guards visited each other, parroted and transferred outstanding essays to their own schools. The camaraderie and affection were immanent; brotherhood was cemented. All served to make the revolution hotter.

They also ensured that no corner over the nation was left in dark. The great leader offered free train rides everywhere to help set the country ablaze. *To hell with railway tickets! Jump on the trains! No seats? Never mind, we can sit on the floor smeared with muddy footprints and strewn with papers, banana skins and watermelon rinds or we can simply stand in the restroom where the toilet bowls are filled with unflushed shit. If anyone covers his nose, he is a bourgeoisie and deserves an immediate criticism! Long live revolutionary tourism! Tai Mountain, Huang Mountain, Lu Mountain, The Shanghai bund, The Yellow River, The Pearl River and the Yangtze River! The beauty of our great motherland had been reasserted. Patriotism was greatly bolstered. Long live the free trip!*

A sultry day, still air and listless leaves. The sun silently baked the city of Nanjing. The temperature had shot up to 103 degrees. Everyone stayed at school. Summer vacation was forgotten.

A truck rumbled by, tooting its horn. Someone on the truck shouted, "Revolutionary artists, please take a look at this bunch! They are wolves in sheep's clothing."

Crowds streamed out. Sandals and slippers flip-flopped, trotting on the searing pavement.

"Let's go take a look." Juhua dragged Lishan and they converged with the flow of excited revolutionaries.

The truck was of medium size, not as large as the tall military trucks that could demonstrate the criminal features in a more lucid way. The canvas covering the back had been removed. Standing in the open on the truck platform were four human beings. Four Yin Yang heads shone in the blazing sun like four half-moons, one female.

"Down with bourgeois monsters and demons!"

An artist was obviously enraged at the ugliness; her voice became a tremolo like the next door music student who practiced soprano every morning on the hill.

The masses threw their arms high. Their unison proved how deeply they were affected by the indignation carried in the leading voice.

The Red Guards on the truck with bursts of laughter saluted like actors on call. One held a microphone in her hand.

"My goodness, they are from the Artist's Association!" Juhua was greatly alarmed.

"How do you know?" Lishan searched each face under the big banner which read,

"Down with the reactionary artists!"

Before her eyes could reach the bottom for identification, Juhua's panicked voice blew into her ear again, "That's Autumn Flute! My goodness!"

Lishan raised her eyes. Sure enough, there he was: head hung low, arms straightened along his gray pants, perspiration trickling down his handsome face. His dark blue silk shirt was painted with white circles deposited from rounds of sweating, his gray long pants drenched from the same source, streaked with a darker gray. The scorching sun had tanned him into a swarthy peasant. Sweat continued to ooze out and beaded the tip of his nose.

"I wonder how his friend feels. Where is Weihua?" Lishan nudged Juhua and whispered. Their eyes scanned the audience but there was no sign of Weihua.

Hanging on Autumn Flute's neck was a piece of white cardboard on which black characters were crossed with red X's:

Anti-Communist Party, Anti-Socialism, Anti-Mao Tsetung thought; the Remnants of Kuomintang.

Juhua was confused by the string of adjectives, "Kuomintang? Autumn Flute is too young to be a KMT."

Lishan was cool-headed, "You don't get it. 'Remnant' does not necessarily mean a KMT."

"What does Autumn Flute have to do with KMT anyway?"

As if unraveling Juhua's puzzle, the Red Guard with the microphone raised it to her mouth and looked into Juhua's face, "Revolutionary Red Guards, while millions upon millions of us follow Chairman Mao marching on the broad Socialist road, a handful of bad elements shrink into the dark corners, grinding their teeth and sharpening their knives. Look!"

Out of the blue, an oil painting was released from a pair of female hands, "'Prometheus Bound', is the title of this gruesome painting. Some of you might never have heard of the story. Nevertheless, take a look at the vulture's eyes, ferocious, malevolent, penetrating, with a cold glint…"

"I agree." Lishan murmured into Juhua's ear. "I always believe it is the vulture's eyes that made Autumn Flute a real artist."

"What is the vulture doing?" The Red Guard asked herself, looking at the painting in her hands. "It is pecking the liver of the fire carrier, the great savior of the human beings! And think, comrades, think, who is our savior?"

"Chairman Mao!" replied in one voice.

"Yes." The Red Guards were proud of their hundreds of unanimous voices.

"My God!" The chorus of the masses sent a chill down Lishan's spine. *The connection is too farfetched. It is very harmful and dangerous.* With these thoughts, Lishan cast a grim look at Juhua whose head had been lowered in the past five minutes.

"As the Chinese saying goes, 'the wolf's ambition is apparent'; Autumn Flute's ill intention is known to all. The villain's desire is disclosed. What are our enemies doing, comrades? They are crouching in the dark, leaping for an attack. Pecking our great leader's liver, draining his blood! Can we tolerate these bloodthirsty artists?"

"No!!" thunderous, again, in unison.

What is she talking about? Who wants to peck Chairman Mao? Autumn Flute wants to suck Chairman Mao's blood? Lishan blinked, trying to make sense out of the speech. It took her several minutes to come to a conclusion that this was nothing but another daydreamer sleepwalking with her lunatic ravings. *An illogical, absurd and spurious analogy that tries to put a ridiculous label on Autumn Flute. Any idiot could tell that the logic is absurd. If the painter is our enemy, there should have been no parallel of Prometheus with Chairman Mao. And why should Autumn Flute portray himself as a hideous predator? Ludicrous!*

That night, Lishan wrote down in her diary "A Defense of Autumn Flute".

At this point, the woman beside Autumn Flute suddenly collapsed. Her listless body slowly coiled into a shapeless heap. She was in her fifties. The sign she was wearing on her chest indicated she was the Party secretary of the Artists' Association.

"Pull her up!"

"Drag up the corpse!"

"She is playing possum!"

Someone broke a pine branch and lightly tapped her half bald scalp as if beating a drum. Instinctively the woman lifted her palm to her head. Laughter burst out. Red Guards on the truck felt firmly supported. One came up with a bright idea:

"Let's finish the job and give her a complete haircut."

"Yes! Let the bulb shine!"

"Go ahead and turn it on!"

"Bravo!"

The woman was hauled away from the truck, her feet dragged through the parched grass.

"I'll go get the scissors and the razor." One activist volunteered.

The turmoil lasted for about thirty minutes. When the woman was jostled back onto the truck, her head was a grapefruit. Lishan's eyes moistened. Juhua lowered her eyes to fake a reading of her red book. Her tears dropped on Chairman Mao's photo and smeared the page.

Lishan raised her arm and covered her forehead, "I am afraid I am having sunstroke."

"Sunstroke?"

"Yes. We must leave the sun."

They sat on a wooden bench in the shade, overlooking the drama in the distance.

"I don't understand," Juhua said. "The woman is a cadre of the Communist Party. Does Chairman Mao know this?"

"Communist or capitalist, they are all human beings," Lishan said drably.

Chapter 2

Red Ocean

After a sleepless night writing Da Zi Bao, Juhua could not wait to go home. She could smell her foul breath and feel her lids heavy like lead. The dormitory was like a morning teahouse, no one could treat it as a sleeping place any more. It had long been turned into a battlefield, headquarters, office and workshop. People slept through whizzing bullets and cannon smoke. Tanks rumbled past in their dreams. She was appalled by her own radical words against the professors. A premonition crept in: what will become of my father? During the past month of upheaval, a portentous silence enveloped her family.

She and Lishan shoveled down some porridge and left the school.

The streets swarmed with Red Guards, bubbling over in jubilation. The city was an ocean of red: arm bands, banners, lanterns, flags and books. The red ocean was strewn with green uniforms like flowers and their leaves. "Down with" and "long live" rose and fell, popping up from all the streets and corners like New Year firecrackers. "Beloved Chairman Mao, you are the red sun in our hearts..." sung from nowhere and everywhere. The modulation, the passion and the sincerity floated in the blue sky, touching every heart. In the square, people milled around in front of Da Zi Bao that hung two to five meters long from the department stores and bank buildings. Clumps of people gathered here and there like lumps in porridge wherever small spontaneous debates were held. The morning sun glowered ferociously over the drooping leaves among which cicadas shrieked in their hoarse voices. The asphalt pavement began to yield to the burning sun and softened under treading feet. And this was only the morning.

In front of the *Nanjing Daily*, some old men were "flying the airplane". Their hair was pulled back, faces uplifted. Lishan and Juhua turned away and elbowed their way through the spectators. Just as they slipped out, bursts of laughter rose from their back. They turned around; another man was shoved to the center of the stage. He was wearing something on his head, a tall funnel on which black characters revealed his identity, "Secretary of the Propaganda Department of the Party Committee..."

"What is that ugly thing on his head? A wastepaper basket? A spittoon?" A woman cracked a sunflower seed, giggled to her partner.

"A tall hat, made of newspapers." The man put on a serious, authorized air.

"Smart! The Nanjing Daily staff not only prints newspaper but makes good use of them also." Cracking another seed between the two rolls of white teeth, the woman scrutinized the tall hat.

"Let's squeeze over and take a good look at his crimes written in smaller characters," the man said.

By now the anxious Juhua was on pins and needles: if the Communist cadres had to go through such an ordeal, what will dad encounter? This thought accelerated Juhua's walking pace into a scurry.

The seed cracker was not accurate to say that the journalists were smart. When Juhua and Lishan entered the campus of the university of Juhua's father, a line of tall paper hats were already on display on the rostrum of the sports ground. Of course, college students' whimsical ideas always fed revolution; their potential and enthusiasm should never be underestimated, especially when presented by the students from a prestigious university. While the paper hat was still a novelty beyond the campus walls, it was already a bit out of fashion here. What people saw nowadays was only a modern version healthily evolved from its primitive stage when first introduced by its promoter half a century ago in his "Report on an Investigation of the Peasant Movement in Hunan." Revolution advanced. Its tools and appliances were renewed daily.

"Down with reactionary academic authorities!"

White banners with black characters flew over the classroom buildings. Huge red crosses straddled over the phrase "academic authorities". Juhua's heart jumped to her throat. She could hear her eardrums beating.

"I must find my dad." Juhua stomped her feet, her palms rubbing against each other.

"Calm down. Don't panic," Lishan said. After a short pause, she added, "Sooner or later your dad will have to go through the same ordeal. Let's go over and check things out."

Juhua's feet were nailed to the ground; she simply could not budge an inch.

"I'll go check, you stay here," Lishan said. Somehow Juhua managed to move her feet.

On the stage, five professors were temporarily freed from the funnel hats but their necks were shackled in I.D. plates stating each one's counter-revolutionary deeds.

"Stop your petty bourgeois whining! Down with the anti-Socialist poet XXX!"

The poet owned a head of silvery long hair which used to be combed backwards sleekly and had earned him admiration even in his mid-fifties. But now the once amorous eyes turned away when the gray tresses were matted by dirty sweat that kept filtering through his scalp.

"I have read his poems. Extremely talented." A girl said to her friend who followed:

"Oh, yeah. An old child, romantic and naive, living in his own dreams, knowing nothing about the world except moonlight and the singing creek."

Some boys sat in the shade, paying no heed to the speaker on the stage. The girls' conversation interested them more. They listened attentively.

The second one was a sort of stout old man. His identity was also showing on the neck placard accompanied by angry words, "Step down from our socialist stage! Down with the feudalistic playwright XXX!"

"He has the best attitude." A boy nearby cast a glance at the two girls, intending to strike up an acquaintance, "Look at his back, bending so low, almost doubling himself."

"Ha, ha, ha…" the girls laughed, "he is a hunchback. We love him in class because he is always so humble."

"Are you from the Department of Chinese Literature?" one of the boys leaned over.

"Yes, we know them all."

The third one had messy hair. He stumbled to the center when his name was called. His glasses dropped. His hands groped the ground. A revolutionary foot trampled on it.

"Crush your glasses so that you will never be able to produce more poisonous weeds."

Chairman Mao's term "poisonous weeds" was applied to the professor's works adequately.

Another quotation quickly followed the first, leading another pair of glasses, "'Oppose the red flag by raising the red flag!' Down with the anti-Marxist literary critic XXX!"

The next two professors were a bit pompous. They maintained their upright posture, held their heads high, rejecting the stormy voices, "Down on your knees, you pair of parasites!"

Sinewy arms pressed their heads down and then jerked them up, pulling up their hair from behind. One of the faces sent a chill to Juhua's marrow.

She tugged Lishan's sleeve, "That's Weihua's father, the celebrated English professor, a pillar of the academic community and my dad's best friend."

The meeting served as a fine example of successful cross-departmental revolution. And it was soon to reach its climax, surging, swelling and bellowing like a tumultuous ocean.

"Crush their arrogance!"

This was said while pointing to Weihua's father, who kept his back straight and refused to bend his legs. The ocean was boiling.

"Kneel down!"

"Kowtow to revolution!"

Some revolutionary iron hooves kicked the counterrevolutionary calves from behind and succeeded in forcing them into a pair of capital L's.

"Crush your capitalist arrogance!" the red arm band waved over his head.

"Down with U.S. imperialists!" another voice shot out through grinding teeth.

Slogans mingled with curses. The other professor clumsily hurtled forward after being pushed from the back and knelt down. As he tried to rise to his feet, fists showered him. All of a sudden, a bottle flew at him splashing black ink on Weihua's dad's white shirt; a flower blossomed on his left chest.

"Ha, his heart is black! Look!"

Two pairs of hands like pliers captured the renowned professor's shoulders, a third pair holding the ink and brush began to convert the flower into a heart.

"Down with the black-hearted academic authority!"

By now the meeting was a bit out of hand. Seeing the black mess, the chairman announced, "We will take these professors out from campus and parade them in the streets. We will show the whole city what kind of poisons our university has hoarded as treasures. Chairman Mao teaches us, 'The phenomenon of bourgeois intellectuals ruling over our school must stop.' It is high time!"

Crowds applauded. The broadcast was turned on, "Sailing the seas one relies on the helmsman; thousands of lives depend on the sun…"

Raging, the black tide of heads and green streams of uniforms poured towards the gate into the streets, slogans erupting as they marched, while the professors, listless, shapeless, sweating, gasping, eyes blurring, bones aching, hearts palpitating, too frightened to use the bathroom and eventually pissing themselves…were hauled ahead along blazing hazy streets like walking corpses. The sun's rays beat down relentlessly.

Chapter 3

Red Guard

Dad was nowhere to be found. Juhua shuttled between the sports ground and the auditorium like an ant on a hot pot, not knowing what to do.

Lishan said, "Don't you want to go home?"

"OK." Juhua nodded absent-mindedly.

In the walled compound of the professors' dorm, big character posters cascaded from the buildings, like funeral shrouds on the façade of each family, forecasting the doom of the intellectual class:

> XXX must make a full confession!
> Spill the beans!
> XXX, what did you do in the forties?
> Peel off XXX's mask as a Marxist theorist.
> Down with the worthy progeny of capitalism!
> …

Every single character stabbed Juhua's heart. Her eyes browsed them all, hoping against hope, seeking her dad's name. Finally, pasted on their apartment door, she found a small Da Zi Bao with her dad's name on it:

> To Professor Lu:
>
> We demand a clarification of your recent lecture on the International Communist Movement.

Juhua exhaled deeply. That dad's name was not terminated by red crosses as seen with other names everywhere else was a surprising relief. The language was pretty mild. A pittance of respect could still be detected between the lines.

"Thank God!" Juhua put her hand on her chest, "This semester dad teaches the seniors who are much more prudent of what to say and what to do. I guess that's the reason. They have their graduation evaluation and job assignments hanging over their heads."

Lishan shrugged her shoulders.

"Moderate as it is, I'm afraid the meager decency will soon be blown away. Look at his friend!" said Lishan. The black heart on Weihua father's white shirt flashed back.

"Then what's to be done?" Juhua's fidgeting returned.

Juhua opened the door. No one was home. The two girls entered Juhua's bedroom and cast away their blouses, pants and skirt. Too sultry and stuffy! They freed their limbs. How wonderful to be away from the madding crowds! How wonderful to be cocooned in your own corner! Campuses, auditoriums, sports fields, dining halls, classrooms, bedrooms, lawns, steps...all had turned rowdy and turbulent. Moreover, the two factions of the Red Guards, the Royalists and the Rebels, had recently escalated the clamor of their debates. Home seemed to be the only oasis.

They closed the door and lay down, locked in each other's embrace, caressing a bit and then their minds drifted into a deeper murkiness. In a minute their slumber grew profound.

A thud. Bang, bang! The door was flung wide open. Juhua and Lishan rubbed their eyes, groggily trying to make a connection between the opened door and the bed they were in. Why and how did they end up sleeping in this bed and what happened to the other beds buried beneath heaps of papers, pens and brushes?

A gang stormed in. The red and green was striking in these homey surroundings. Freshmen from father's department! Juhua was wide awake. She quickly grabbed anything at hand to cover herself. Lishan slipped out of Juhua's arms like a fish. The intruders were obviously impressed by what they saw in bed: two half-naked girls in each other's arms. The unexpected discovery was more interesting than ransacking a professor's house.

"Come here. We found something." Squinting, the boy called with a lewd smile. His comrades rushed to the scene from the study where they were dumping any books not by Chairman Mao into a big bag, and like him their jaws dropped. Their search for counterrevolutionary contraband immediately shifted to Juhua's room. They combed every corner and carpeted the floor.

Juhua dashed to her desk, blocking the top drawer with her back, "This is my desk. It has nothing to do with Professor Lu."

"Feudalism, capitalism, revisionism and their like, plus all sorts of ideological garbage are the targets of our revolution. We Red Guards have every right to confiscate them all!"

The boy thrust himself towards the desk and wrestled with Juhua who was still clutching the top drawer. Her fingers were prized open and the drawer jumped out of the desk, laying bare its contents on the naked floor: Lishan's Russian painting book, her own paintings and all three of Lishan's diaries since middle school.

A month ago, sensing the imminent danger at school, Lishan thought home might be a haven, a sanctuary for her art. Her relationship with dad however was only in a truce. Hoarding a load of suspicious stuff under her father's roof required additional intimacy and trust and that was beyond her frame of mind at the present. It would be even worse if these diaries were scanned by her father who had the habit of meddling in her affairs. She talked to Juhua about her problem and Juhua offered a sanctuary. That was how her treasures ended up here. At that time, ransacking was not yet in mode. Like paper hats and Yin Yang heads, ransacking was another revolutionary novelty which popped up unexpectedly, far surpassing Juhua and Lishan's predictions. The stationing of the diaries in Juhua's home now proved to be a fatal mistake.

Lishan snatched one of her diaries, "They are mine. I am also a Red Guard."

"Everything in Professor Lu's house is subject to examination." A tall girl strutted in. She spoke in a calm, professional manner. The girl collected the diary without further protest from its owner.

Lishan was lost in consternation.

The revolutionaries procured the diaries and left in triumph with their other trophies.

What will happen? What are they going to do with my diary? With me? With Professor Lu? Those diaries... the black heart on the white shirt flashed through her mind again. Lishan deeply regretted making an unscrupulous decision that ended up implicating Juhua's father and endangering her lover's whole family. She envisaged her reckless writings being broadcast and placed on the table for public dissection. She heard her name read aloud as a deep-rooted class enemy. *What will happen?*

Juhua's mom came back with more astounding news: the English professor suffered a sudden heart attack when the parade reached downtown. He was rushed to the hospital. His wife collapsed of sunstroke at her criticism meeting and died of a heart attack earlier in the day. The house was somber ...

"Where is dad?"

"He is in the hospital at his bedside. The doctor was not optimistic. There was really not much they could do. The heart simply failed."

Mom sank into a chair, silently sobbing into her handkerchief.

"His wife's death must have aggravated his heart condition," Lishan said.

"No. That's not the case. No one even had the chance to breathe a word to him about his wife's death. People were all busy making revolution."

"Maybe it is better for him to stay in the hospital; no one would drag a patient out," Lishan said.

"Yes, they would." Juhua's mom nodded, "I was there. The Red Guards called the hospital the hideout for the enemies."

"Let's hope for the best." Mom dabbed her tear-streaked face.

"What do you mean, 'The best'?" Juhua suddenly raved, "There has already been a death in that family!"

"Well, there could be two," Mom murmured.

Professor Lu came back at midnight, sullen faced. He headed straight to his room. Mom tailed him. Sobs burst out, from both.

"Good heavens! Husband and wife? The same day? Poor children!"

Juhua and Lishan looked at each other, dumbfounded. Tears trickled down. They held hands. From the dark ocean of their minds, rose the American Baby, his broad smile, happy-go-lucky manner, outstandingly ugly face, his eyes small and black like tadpoles. And beside him, sailed in the deft-fingered pianist whose breathtaking beauty contrasted with her brother's remarkable ugliness. *Will these siblings ever be able to smile again?* Juhua felt extremely lucky for her dad who so far remained intact. Their thoughts roamed randomly, from American Baby to Autumn Flute, then to the art salon which stopped its gatherings a year ago. *Will the salon be in trouble, too?* The salon was wreathed in black in their minds.

The four of them gathered in the living room. A moment of silence proceeded. Professor Lu took out a piece of crumpled paper from his pocket, "He squeezed this into my hand in the hospital. I almost forgot."

Lishan and Juhua looked. It was an English poem with a Chinese translation.

"What did it say?" Mom asked dazedly.

"Shakespeare's lines, from *Macbeth*. And a few words to the wife and children." Dad moved it to the reading lamp:

"A cynical reflection on life and death."

He pondered, "He must have prepared for this day for a long time."

"May I take a look?" Juhua asked.

Dad handed the paper over. Lishan read it as well. She went over the poem once, and then reread it a second time.

At ten, Lishan went back to school alone. The double death in her classmate's family had partially overtaken her concern for her confiscated diaries. Juhua remained at home trying to comfort her parents in the face of their present horror.

Chapter 4

Black List

Her legs dragged along the dimly lit street; they were heavy as if having run in a marathon. Her mind was a jumble of the day's events, scenes from a horror movie: paper hats, a black heart, tear-stained faces, "Yin Yang head"... and now her own betraying diaries. The question of Professor Lu's destiny kept nagging at her; his role in caching her counterrevolutionary writings and paintings might be his undoing. Now that she had classified herself and her works under the category of Anti-proletarian, Anti-Chairman Mao and Anti-Socialist, Lishan knew that she must calm herself and prepare to face the pending catastrophe.

Since June, her attitude towards the Great Proletarian Cultural Revolution had gone through three phases: resolve, doubt, renewed resolve. When the rebels adopted a stance antagonistic to the existing system, Lishan wasn't a complacent, aloof observer as she had been in 1957. No matter how despicable her dad appeared to her and how unmerciful she still was towards him and the corruption he represented, and despite the grievance she still nursed due to the arrest of her beloved Ms. Guan, the system that her father, Jianfei's father and thousands upon thousands of their comrades-in-arms had shed blood and laid their lives down for was something her instinct told her that she must rise in defense of. Defiantly her Da Zi Bao presented her defense of the authorities, her standpoint distinctively opposite that of the rebels. Her posters drew arrows from all directions. Juhua followed and talked to several students. Together they founded a team of their own, "The Winter Plum Blossoms." Lishan was its pen and very soon she became the school's most notorious "Royalist," one who stood in defense of the Party, but not of Chairman Mao.

However when news leaked from Beijing that Chairman Mao and his wife were actually Rebels themselves and the rumor was soon verified by Chairman Mao's first Da Zi Bao: "Bombard the Headquarters!" Lishan was totally confounded. *What did Chairman Mao want? To overthrow his own regime? How could he tolerate such inhuman atrocities?* Millions upon millions of loyal Communist Party members who had followed him south and north fighting to help establish his political and military power were being betrayed, ruthlessly, by him! Even the enemy during the war had failed to adopt the variety of tortures that the Rebels were now not only applying to the intellectuals but also using against thousands upon thousands of Party members and leaders of the government grass-root units. Within two to three months, Chairman Mao had accomplished what his enemy could not dream of accomplishing in decades.

Lishan knew her own family would not be in jeopardy since no one dared to topple the army. Chairman Mao could sacrifice anything but the gun barrel. Her mom was an insignificant clerk in a government department. *But what about Jianfei's family?* The thought unnerved her. Jianfei's father's promotion would put him square in the firing range. Though his research institute was directly under the Department of National Defense, it had no protection since the staff was all scientists wearing no uniforms. *Five thousand employees, five thousand bullets! And four fifths of these were factory workers, the mainstream of the current tide!* Jianfei's mom was a Department head of the municipal government, another tall tree drawing winds. Nowadays being any sort of a head put your own head in danger. *Back to the guillotine!* In a short period, China witnessed disorder and chaos and experienced tremendous sufferings from industrial and agricultural loss. Theft, lootings, fist beatings, verbal fights, not to mention the countless incidents of psychological, emotional, and at times even physical torture…once Pandora's box was opened, there was no return. New sufferings, largely unknown in recent years, continually cropped out to torment the whole of society. *Why, what, how* and *when,* unanswered questions kept popping into Lishan's head, not giving her a moment to try to formulate an answer. Nothing made sense any more.

Until yesterday, right and wrong were still ambiguous but the mushrooming episodes of torture and abuse she witnessed during the day had forced the conclusion clear and fast that no matter what *ism*'s lay behind this behavior, none could justify such barbarity. *No leader should be excused if he has issued permission to carry out such a plague and scourge, Chairman Mao included.* Lishan had reaffirmed her convictions and clarified her role in this anarchy. *No more poster writing for tomorrow, if there will be a tomorrow,* she ordered herself. *No more Red Guard meetings, nor hysterical debating. I will dig into Marx and Lenin and let the proletarian ancestors be the judge of Chairman Mao's Revolution. If I cannot stop this evil, I can at least withdraw from it.*

Unsurprisingly, there was no bus today. She took a shortcut through Juhua's father's campus again. The young radicals were all about despite the late night hour, showing no signs of wrapping up for the day. The Da Zi Bao's were ablaze in lights, as on a sunny day. The school's bulletin boards, constructed of large enforced bamboo mats and bolstered with solid pillars, were taken over by Da Zi Bao and other postings of the radicals. The boards stretched along the campus walkway for some hundred meters. The crowds were thick near this center of activity. Many people were found clustered along the whole length of the Da Zi Bao boards reading the latest accusations and praying that they themselves were not listed among the accused. The boards were well organized; each department had its own section. The newer ones led in the front; the older ones were gradually covered up and automatically moved to the back. The frequency of renewal was approximately half a day. Compared to those in the Art College, here the articles were longer, ten to twenty pages on average.

Readers began to pour in front of the history department section. Lishan joined the stream. The walls of posters that lined the walkway were lit by 100 watt bulbs. With caution, Lishan edged her way along the opposite side, staying in the rear of the crowd. Tides of readers in front made the posters inaccessible to her eyes. She was dependent on a loud voice from the front row that was trying to help to piece together the contents.

"Sweep the… den…with…iron broom…"

The reading went on but was faint. What fed Lishan's ears were actually fragments of conversation issuing from various listeners' mouths.

"So the English dean has turned his mansion into the headquarters of a handful of counterrevolutionaries..."

"And a homosexual club."

"Which professor? Is that the one with a black heart on his white shirt?"

"That's him."

"How did they find his diary?"

"No. You are confused. Not his, it belongs to an art student."

"What a mess!"

"Artists have such anti-social tendencies."

...

Though their references couldn't be clearer, Lishan still could not suppress the need to take a look with her own eyes. She steered herself around and found a small stool used to hang the higher posters. She stepped on it. A series of names crossed with red check marks greeted her eyes: "Juhua," "Autumn Flute," "Weihua," "Meihua." Her own name was scrawled on every section of the paper. *We have all been named*, she thought. *What is the source? Who provided the black list? A slap to her face: You! Yourself! Your diaries! Traitor!* The voice came deep from within her own vacant heart. The stool served as her pedestal. She could not afford such conspicuous terrain. She gingerly stepped down and stole into the shadows behind the poster boards. The bamboo mats shielded her and the darkness enveloped her. The sports ground lay behind with a wilderness of grass leading to an abandoned railway.

Crowds continued to mill around. Their anger went unabated.

"These homosexuals deserve life imprisonment."

"Exactly! So that their disease won't contaminate society. How disgusting!"

One finicky voice offered, "The Artists' club is a sewer, a trash can. Politically it is anti-people; artistically decadent."

A boy in the front started to address the audience, "The Artists' Association, too. They all should be abolished!"

People enjoyed their freedom of speech. If you went with the tide, free speech was yours for the taking.

Footsteps were heard rushing to her direction.

"I saw her just a minute ago on a stool."

A pair of feet stopped in front of Lishan who was now separated from her captor only by the width of a bamboo mat. She was on the shady side. The hunters in the light.

"Are you sure it was the same girl we ran into in the Lu's house? But isn't she in the art school?"

"Swear to Chairman Mao! Trust my eyes."

"Where could she be? She couldn't be far."

"Search!"

Lishan started to run.

"There she is, on the other side of the board!"

Footsteps were behind her. Gasping, Lishan ran towards the sports ground. In the dark, she tripped and lay buried in the grass, motionless. In a minute, her arms were locked from behind.

A voice said, "Run? Where to? Our revolutionary net spreads all over the world!"

Lishan was dragged to her feet. In the murky light, were the same faces she saw in Juhua's house.

Chapter 5

Silver Moon

At least it was cool in the basement. Mold oozed from freckled walls, a rickety table, stools and a double-decker bed. Melon rinds and fruit peels strewn on the cement floor competed in their stench. Hazy lamplight fell on fatigued faces and yawning mouths. The interrogation had been going on for twenty four hours. High up on the wall, through a small window, hasty feet could be seen passing by. The campus still clamored with midnight debate and spontaneous speeches.

The chairperson had a pair of drilling eyes which could turn any shady souls inside out. His eyebrows were two stumps, dark and bushy. His belt did not buckle his green uniform but was removed in the middle of his torso and hung in his hands. From time to time, his two palms grabbed each end, loosening and straightening in a spasmodic manner, cracking menacing sounds that lingered in the air.

"I believe your diaries have successfully portrayed your anti-populist, anti-Communist Party, anti-Socialist artistic tendencies. Your sympathy for the remnant of the KMT Youth League dates back to your middle school days. Your 'Sanctuary' already revealed a heart antagonistic towards our blazing revolution. Your counter-criticism of Autumn Flute a few days ago... all speak loudly of your true character…"

"I love our Party and..." Lishan retorted, but her defense sounded weak and waffling, holding no water even to her own ears.

"Shut your fat mouth!"

The belt roared, falling on her left side, then the right, avoiding a touch.

"You have no right to love. That word from your mouth is filth and blasphemy."

A chubby face cooperated with the leader.

"Since you have touched the topic, let's talk about your love."

The chairman lit a cigarette and squinted at her.

All at once the lethargy dissipated. Faces were lit with anticipation. Finally the lengthy flow of the boring river had entered the turbulent section as an interesting topic was introduced to the stage. All the attendants widened their eyes.

"What did you do in the English professor's house two years ago?" The inquiry was issued from a sharp voice and a pretty face.

"No. In the homosexual club," another sharper voice corrected her.

"We had a seminar on Qi Baishi's paintings, imagism. His art has opened a new chapter..."

"Bullshit!" a lanky fellow spat on the floor.

"She is picking up the trivial, avoiding the critical," a mellow voice reminded the chairman.

"Trying to pull the wool over our eyes!" heavy and angry.

"Down with the bourgeois artist Lishan!" chorused.

"What else did you do? Speak out!"

I will wear out your patience, Lishan said in her heart.

"Then we exchanged our annual works..."

"That's when you exhibited your vicious paintings. Right? Right? Every single piece was a bomb!"

"If you want my confession, you need to let me speak..." the sentence was chopped in half.

"Talk back?"

Lishan's left cheek burned and then the right. The slaps were crisp.

"How dare you talk back!"

Lishan's tit-for-tat strategy greatly agitated her investigators and brought herself more wallops from the belt on her back and shoulders.

"Then we listened to music..."

"Did you dance?"

"Yes."

"There you go! Stop there!"

The chairman moved his chair to Lishan and drilled into her eyes, "And the dancers were all paired accordingly! Right?"

A barbed smile followed the stressed "accordingly". The chairman started to pace. No one had ever vexed him like Lishan. She dared to talk back. The old-timers simply let the chairman and his flunkies knead the dough. They were much more malleable.

"Let's be frank. The dancers were pairs of homosexuals, weren't they?"

"No. We are good friends, who know each other through our art..." Lishan shrugged her shoulders, and that fueled the chairman's rage into a bonfire.

"She is smarmy!"

"She is smug and arrogant!!"

"She is indifferent!"

Pa, pa, pa! Belts rained on her. Welts swelled on her head.

"Shame on you!" they clenched their teeth.

"Rotten! Rotten to the core!" they clicked their tongues.

Lishan was firm, "No."

"No," she insisted.

"No."

Whack, whack, whack.

"Comrades," panting, the chairman paused and rested his wrists, trying to regain his equilibrium, "we all know that homosexuality is a disease. Its morbidity is beyond the comprehension of us healthy youths brought up under the red flag. It is the life style of the bourgeoisie."

"Disgusting!" people expressed their genuine sickness.

"Down with the bourgeois way of life!" a forest of arms thrust into the air.

The rising sun had dyed the east window from which footsteps were seen scurrying to the sports ground for the morning exercises. More mouths opened in yawns. It was the second sunrise they had witnessed during this interrogation session. The chairperson announced the dismissal but allowed the boys to "take care of" Lishan in their own dormitory where Lishan was shaved with razors and burnt with cigarettes on her scalp. She was then escorted to her own school for further investigation.

A silver disk hanging from the dark blue velvet, the moon had grown round again. In a month, the mid-autumn festival would be here, a time for reunion again, wax and wane, year in year out. Those moonlit tables piled with melons and cakes! Those full moons like tonight's! Those neglected, uneaten moon cakes! *How wonderful to bicker with one's brothers over the food portions and accuse dad of favoring the boys! How sweet to be tortured by dad's scathing tongue, to be taunted by her united brothers!* She missed the family's partisanship. *Dad, dad. I know you love me. May we shake hands now? Dad. Mom.* The moon was sailing, her pale face veiled in a wisp of cloud. The bitter sweetness numbed her heart and lulled her into drowsiness.

Huifang's white butterfly bow floated over the black sea of heads on the marble steps, attracting young cadets... Jianfei leaned on a birch tree, Tagore in hand... Juhua reclined on a red carpet posing for her "Reading"... Dad entered the school gate, hand in hand with the teeth-protruding principal... "Vienna Woods" breezed in the English tycoon's parlor... Dancers slouched on the sofa while others sidled by, tipping, sashaying, loping... A voice thundered, "Death is written on your face." Lightning cracked, illuminating a withered face and his beggar's kit...

Cold sweat stuck to her shirt. Lishan opened her eyes. Dream fragments brought on heart palpitations. Death! Was the old beggar a gifted psychic as well, hiding up his sleeve the card for her future? Death! It was a buzzard returning to spin in her head now. *What is there ahead that is worth dragging this pile of flesh on to? Why should I wait to be tossed over into the street with a denunciation plate hanging from my neck? Why should I wait for the spectators to stone me with their iron fists, or drown me in their revolutionary spit? Why should I submit my heart to a scalpel? Isn't this skinhead enough? And with the burning marks on my scalp like a newly recruited Buddhist nun?* The old man flashed again, somber like the sky above him.

Her hand touched her hairless head. *What will Jianfei think of me in this fashion? Jianfei!* She sighed. Sourly she pictured Jianfei with her blue sweater boy. She felt for Jianfei when Huifang revealed to her Jianfei's tears—maybe a failed love affair with Yang Bing? Jianfei had replied to Lishan's numerous letters only once since the salon, and her reply was cold and formal, expressing her viewpoint towards the Cultural Revolution and angrily criticizing Lishan regarding the proper course of revolution.

Jianfei's extremism was shocking and a little frightening to Lishan. Jianfei, the radical Communist and fervent follower of Chairman Mao, whose ultimate goal was to uproot all the grass-roots units of the Communist Party up to its Central Committee, advocated, "Our Party is standing on the brink of revisionism. We must save the International Communist Movement!"

Lishan could not entirely agree and she refused to accept her destructive activism. This political divide had somewhat diluted Lishan's worship of her childhood friend. Yet Jianfei remained the only constant shining spot in her life regardless of the rises and dips in their relationship. Lishan shook her head. *Jianfei! The romantic idealist!* For her, Lishan held no resentment. No grudge would ever be able to germinate in her heart for her first love.

There was no shred of sleep left in her head. The moon voyaged on. The pale-faced, cool-hearted lady looked on apathetically from her unfathomable navy blue ocean.

Suddenly, from a remote age, a melancholy child song returned to her heart:

> Silver moon, silver moon,
> The moon remembers,
> It shines on Sister Gold's face,
> It shines on Sister Silver's clothes,
> And on the child Autumn Fragrance.
>
> Sister Gold, you have a father;
> And Sister Silver, you have a mother.
> Where is your father?
> Where is your mother?
> Autumn Fragrance?
>
> They are on the beautiful mountain,
> Day in, day out,
> Herding the sheep, herding the sheep.
> Poor Autumn Fragrance!

Dad taught her this song when she was little. Dad told her that was where her name came from, "Beautiful Mountain," Lishan. Tonight as she surveyed her short life, this long-forgotten melody rocked back to her, together with her childhood, like a cuckoo echoing from a remote mountain. The pathos lingered.

How long she lay there unleashing her thoughts, she did not remember. All she knew was that the nightmare had to stop and her tragedy must end. In several hours, she would be a fly returned to wanton schoolboys again.

She turned over, coughing slightly. No response. The air was vibrant with the girls' faint snoring. With feline agility, Lishan tiptoed out.

The moon splashed on the Beautiful Mountain.

Chapter 6

Red Sun

Two days after her home's invasion Juhua returned to school where the revolution witnessed a new phase. The politically less sensitive Art College was always one step behind, and the earnest artists endeavored to keep abreast with the prestigious university next door. The Art Association's latest visit proved efficient in promoting revolution. Here dozens of criticism meetings were generated to repudiate the professors' fallacies and culminated in triumph. Splashing black hearts on their white T shirts and carving Yin-Yang heads were successfully imitated. One death was procured so far; the artists needed to catch up in this arena. The revolutionary act of ransacking professors' homes was also introduced and swiftly carried out. Visiting their prestigious neighbor on a daily basis to refill their inspiration turned out to be a must.

On the walls and bulletin boards, fresh big-character posters replaced the old ones without even waiting for their ink to dry, leaving a bunch of slow readers to lament over their missed lessons. Some posters were marked with shrieking warnings, "Keep posted for two days, don't cover!" But impatient brushes swept glue over them anyway. Get out of my way! Everyone needs to make revolution!

Entering the dorm, she was perplexed to find that all her roommates, the Royalists and the Rebels, were working shoulder to shoulder over the desk, including the members of her own team, "The Winter Plum Blossom". Six heads clustered over one piece on the desk, on the floor their feet were surrounded with finished pages, ten or more. Lishan's name like nettles clung to the sheets, stinging Juhua's eyes.

…"Sanctuary" is an out-an-out anti-Socialist, anti-Party and anti-Chairman Mao poisonous weed. What Lishan strives for is a shady corner away from revolutionary sunny sky which is represented as the unbearable heat under the bright sun. We all know who the sun is … The painting smolders with the emission of her long harbored hatred. We may as well ask: What is your sanctuary? The answer is apparent: bourgeois life and capitalism!"

One of the roommates was reading the draft; another brandishing the brush; a third one marking the page numbers: 10, 11, …

"…A despicable soul that dares not assert herself in broad daylight…"

The dictating mouth did not pause due to the entrance of Lishan's friend,

"… 'Reading' reeks of a moldering carcass. It is an art style abandoned by our healthy Socialist cause a decade ago. It is morbid, perverse, freakish and toxic. Lishan's so-called body art is nothing but the reproduction of a cheap whorehouse painting. This kind of art is like colorful mushrooms attracting our eyes but poisoning our hearts. It is spiritual opium as Chairman Mao defines …"

Eyes turned to her as if Juhua were Lishan. Juhua had no time for her roommates' contemptuous and jeering looks. She must find Lishan. She went downstairs and darted out of the building. *Lishan, Lishan!* The consequence of leaving her alone at this juncture loomed up in her mind.

As she browsed among the big-character posters, she noticed that Lishan's names dotted the posters like nails in a construction site. She was now a target of the whole school.

"Probe Lishan's soul!"

"Dig out the deep-rooted enemy, Lishan!"

One poster entitled "Counterrevolutionary student—Lishan" enumerated her misdeeds in a fairly lucid, level-headed manner:

   ...

Sympathy for her rightist teacher at an early age;
Homosexual fantasies in high school;
Assertive in the artists' club; (we all know what it is now);
Making love to her girlfriend Juhua;

   ...

For the first time Juhua saw her own name crossed out in red which announced a death sentence, banned her from any political activities, blocked all her paths and dimmed her artist career.

Juhua forced her eyes to go on:

"...the latest towering crime Lishan committed is to slander the great Cultural Revolution. By now we have portrayed a full-fledged counterrevolutionary student whose soul has been corroded by a nihilistic acid and contaminated by exposure to a bourgeois way of life. Her diary also serves as an eye opener and will help us to fathom deeper the answer to the questions why and how? Her total corruption is a mystery because she is from a red family, with perfect revolutionary parents. The so-called salon, which we will dissect in a separate chapter, gathers a handful of reactionary artists. It is not exaggeration to refer to it as 'an anti-Party clique'..."

Membership in a "clique" scaled very high in the spectrum of serious political crimes which the enemy might commit because it symbolized a united force. She had seen "clique" members handcuffed on the eve of their graduation and never heard from again.

Juhua collapsed on a wooden bench.

Lishan, Lishan! It was an urgent call now because she knew her friend only too well.

The prestigious university's singing and dancing troupe, now *The Mao Tsetung Thought Propaganda Team*, was rehearsing behind an abandoned building. Their performances were scheduled every day from afternoon till midnight. They went to all the squares in the city where citizens gathered in droves to read the increasingly critical posters that speared the municipal government, and to the river embankment where construction workers labored night and day trying to piece together the Yangtze River Bridge abandoned by the Soviet experts; they would also take the ferry across the river into the countryside where peasants watched them perform as they used to watch the monkey shows in the old days.

"Our beloved Chairman Mao, you are the red sun in our hearts…"

The girls stood on their tiptoes and raised one arm to the sky, pressing the other arm on their left chests.

A boy in the abandoned building was watching them.

The boys were supposed to step in but they were absent-minded.

"Stop!" the team leader ordered. "Boys, it's your turn! One, two!" The accordion played a lively interlude.

"Our beloved Chairman Mao, you are the red sun in our hearts…"

The boys jumped in, arms crossing shoulders, legs kicking gingerly, each making a synchronized pair with the girl in front of him.

The boy in the abandoned building was watching them.

Nowadays the most fashionable dance movements to be seen in the propaganda troupes based on the frequency of their occurrence onstage were: hands spreading over hearts; arms stretching to the sun; heads uplifting; bodies leaning forward to meet an imaginary hostile object; one bent leg, one flattened arm, dashing into a storm.

The boy in the abandoned building was watching them.

The rehearsal had never been so efficient as today. The team leader smiled. There was only a single audience member today. There used to be too much distraction from the surrounding spectators who often harbored the intention to date one of the beautiful dancing girls or cast amorous eyes on the imposing male figures. Friends, roommates and secret lovers made things even worse. Joking, flirting, endless laughing, messy steps… The derelict building projected no warmth and no one bothered to visit during the daytime. This evacuated building was nestled in a corner by the back gate that led to an abandoned railway. Only months ago, this building bustled with the noise and enthusiasm of zealous international youths from Vietnam, Korea, Albania, Yugoslavia and Romania who looked upon China as a beacon in their voyage towards Communism. Then the red storm swept away their illusions one by one until finally these foreign students were pulled out by their governments and called home. In brief, this was how the once sparkling building had become a relic. Although the entrances were officially sealed, the downstairs windows had been vandalized and offered easy access for lovers who dwelled in the dark paradise of sex.

The boy in the abandoned building was still watching them. The transom window slanted outwards and was half-open, leaving a gap which allowed him to insert his placid, motionless head. The committed audience had maintained the same posture the whole morning. The pale face from the transom was a consistent presence but the busy dancers never bothered to cast a serious look. A curious audience was never a stranger to them. A loyal boy like this one always served as an incentive for a better performance. Girls' limbs swayed with more agility and their bodies grew suppler. From time to time, they cast a coquettish smile towards his direction.

The team leader announced dismissal. His members began to gather their bags and cups, ready for lunch.

"Back at two! Don't forget your props!" the leader said.

"It is strange that the boy did not budge an inch the whole morning. There is something odd about him," one of the girls commented.

Then she turned to the pallid face that stared at her through the gap between the slanting window and the frame. Her eyes encountered a pair of glassy eyes that seemed to have fastened ahead yet meanwhile scattered into a spacious eternity, whose opacity reached its conclusion never to let any light seep through them again like drawn shades, a pair of lenses that could no longer focus, a telescope blocked by mud. This pair of eyes failed to emit any grain of comprehension when the dancer's hand waved a greeting. The lonely onlooker had purple lips that slightly parted, on which seemed to hang an unanswered question. They, too, showed no ability to respond. The grey scalp seemed to gradually reveal its original gender, together with a pair of gentle arches in the front. Ghoulish. The dancer yielded.

"…He…he…she…she…" and stopped, eyes dilated, agape, face ashen.

It began to dawn on her that the eyes she had just looked into were sightless and the face lifeless. Her friends followed her sightline and looked in the same direction; they shrieked and started to run. Some feet were frozen to the ground. The team leader was called.

A girl pointed at the sole audience and trembled, "There, there!"

All the boys darted into the abandoned building.

When Lishan was unleashed from the shower rod, her body was hard and stiff.

"She is not our student," a boy identified the corpse. "She is from the neighboring art school."

The leader frowned, "Why the hell did she choose to hang herself in our school? As if the lots were all sold out in her own school."

"She was arrested by our history department."

Several others also recognized Lishan through her bluish complexion.

The shower room, once the bathing place for the world revolutionary youths was now renowned for the ghostly scene that frightened dozens of Mao propagandists.

On the wall, pasted squarely was a small piece of Shakespeare taken from the Chinese version.

> Out, out, brief candle! Life's but a walking shadow, a poor player that struts and frets his hour upon the stage and then is heard no more. It is a tale told by an idiot, full of sound and fury, signifying nothing.

Then at the bottom:

> Forgive me, Juhua. I am sorry.

Chapter 7

Red Love

"Telegram!"

A loud voice woke up Jianfei, who, groggy with sleep, met the day with a big yawn. The words immediately threw her up from her covers. She sat up, rubbed her eyes repeatedly, trying to clear her mind from a broken sleep.

"Lishan passed away. Come back."

It was from Huifang. The words "passed away" took a detour to reach her head. She simply couldn't juxtapose Lishan and Death. No, Lishan was too cynical to give up life. And there never was any symptom of world-weariness. Jianfei argued with the piece of paper in hand. Slowly, rejection gave way to acceptance. Immense grief and profound perplexity penetrated and enveloped her. The photo Huifang sent her two years ago stood on her bookshelf, the three of them, smiling from ear to ear, waving at Jianfei. Gazing at Lishan, her eyes brimmed. Lishan was gone and gone forever. Her melancholy figure carried by a somewhat sluggish gait walked over. With her almond-shaped eyes, a pair of dimples that floated over her warped lips, her ballooning uniform pants, her hard-working mouth that dripped acid, her faked indifference, her throaty voice, grumpy temper, waspish tongue, penetrating insight, logical didacticism, Lishan emerged conclusively in her full regalia.

The heat did not abate in her hometown. Red flags sagged on top of buildings.

"Ice-lollies! Horsehead brand ice-lollies!" a peddler's lethargic voice added monotony to the railway station.

Jianfei arrived at noon. Huifang was waiting. The black arm band stung Jianfei's eyes.

"How did it happen?" Jianfei's voice was hoarse.

"Hung herself," Huifang's voice was the same.

"Where is she now?"

"Buried in the south suburbs."

"How is Juhua?"

"Confined somewhere, I was told by her roommates."

Huifang took out an envelope, "Lishan sent me a letter, enclosed was this for you."

Rubbing her eyes, Jianfei walked away to a quiet corner.

Dear Jianfei:

By the time you read this letter, we will be in different worlds. It is a pity that we will no longer be able to laugh and argue together. When was the last time we saw each other? In the temple? No, at the salon.

I love you. I love you because I believe human hearts should all be like yours. I hope you understand me. Now I am kissing your name. Don't be mad at me.

Don't cry for me. I will be happy. I am leaving just to roam among the colorful clouds. I will visit you in your dreams and join you in your laughter.

Your childhood friend,

Lishan

Jianfei cried her heart out. Tears soaked the letter. At her last breath, Lishan still tried to pose as the western figure, Gadfly.

They bought a paper-flower wreath. The wreath leaned against Lishan's grave. The small yellow mound squatted like a shriveled old woman, separated from its neighbors. Away from hundreds of workers, poor and lower-middle class peasants whose tombs covered a larger stretch of land on the sunny side, her lonely grave rested on the shady side of the hill. A starved elm tree canopied her, its leaves meager and sparse. "Lin Lishan, 1945-1966" was engraved on dark gray slate. Obscure and humble, it yielded to hundreds who had earned glorious deaths because of their class ranks. Lishan, a prodigy, a muse, whose name meant beautiful mountain, now finally owned a piece of that mountain. Jianfei suddenly felt mentally drained. She slumped down on a large rock, gazing downhill at the Yangtze. The river meandered in broad haziness, merging with the dreamy horizon. Above, wisps of clouds drifted leisurely, gilded by the setting sun. A brush of orange dazzled in the far distance. *Lishan, are you there? In the clouds, as you wrote, roaming freely? Will you show up in my dreams, in my laughter, with your dimples?* Jianfei stared at the dyed clouds, her eyes brimming again.

Huifang dug a hole and buried a handful of colorful pebbles. She whispered in a sob, "Dear friend, may you sleep in peace and beauty."

Their hands rested on the tombstone. Jianfei gathered two pine branches; Huifang tied them to the gray slate with her tear-stained handkerchief. The two friends hung their heads, paid their last tribute and went down the hill. The mountain was beautiful in the pink sun.

"When did you come back to town?" Jianfei asked Huifang as they sat on the bus, bumping along the country road.

"I have been home for two weeks...on vacation." Huifang answered, eyes turning outside.

"How is everything?" Jianfei caught Huifang's evasive looks. She wondered whether there was something worth digging deeper for.

After a short silence, Huifang said, "I am here for a pregnancy check-up."

What went wrong with the world? One death, one birth. Jianfei looked straight into Huifang's eyes, "Pregnancy? You are not even married. Are you?" Bewilderment angered her.

"No. But I am going to be...on National Day. My fiancé is a Communist Party member working in the commune. A young man with power."

"The bastard! How dare he blow up your belly without giving you a decent wedding?" Jianfei had never talked in this manner, she felt somewhat relieved.

Huifang bit her lips and looked away again. The bus was galloping amidst yellow horses of rampant dust; the engine deafened them and muffled their voices. One death, one birth. Jianfei's mind raced with the yellow horses that carried them back to where they came from, not knowing what to think. They remained silent until they got off the bus and walked under dim street lamps.

Huifang pulled Jianfei's sleeve and breathed into her ears, "I have something to tell you."

They strolled to the street corner and settled on a cement bench. The grass blades had cooled down and stood erect in the evening breeze. Jianfei hoped this time something good would come out of Huifang's mouth.

"Sometime in late spring my brigade leader broke into my room at midnight and raped me. I hated him at first sight when he came to visit dad," Huifang sounded calm.

"My goodness! You should bring him to court," Jianfei was ignited again.

"Court?" Huifang sneered, cold flinty looks worn on her face.

For a moment, Jianfei saw Lishan's smile hanging on Huifang's lips. Jianfei sank into a deeper sadness.

"It happens everywhere. Fighting against the local despot means burning your own bridge back to the city," Huifang said in a matter-of-fact tone.

"Does the young man know?" Jianfei asked.

"I think so."

"Do you love him?"

"Love?" A glint flickered in Huifang's eye. Huifang curved up her lips, "What is love? I don't know."

Jianfei never mentioned Tang Wei though he was in her mind and on the tip of her tongue during the whole conversation.

Leaves rustled lightly like a baby's whimper. Darkness thickened.

Epilogue

Jianfei opened her mailbox. Fliers of all sorts tumbled out. She dumped all the stuff on the kitchen counter: Star Market, Ann & Hope, frequent flyer's mileage... lobster $4.99/lb, cherry $2.99/lb, buy one get one free, 20% discount... As she shook the pile, a handwritten envelope stuck in a folded brochure slipped out. Beijing, China, Yang Bing. The handwriting opened an old wound. Jianfei reclined on the couch and read. A thirty-year-old story unfolded, starting from the click of the telephone.

The breakup was simply beyond what he could bear. The trauma brought him to the hospital.

"When the phone clicked, I felt my life line was unplugged," he wrote.

For eight years he marked the day on the calendar when the fatal phone conversation occurred. For him, it was a black memorial day. For her, Yang Bing had never faded even after her marriage. For many years, she tried to locate him but failed. He dug her out by mere coincidence. He and Xiaoshi had a chance meeting at a conference.

She continued with the letter, "Of course, we can blame our fathers, blame that ridiculous policy, and blame the old time and its system. But I have to say we were the victims of ourselves. Like our fathers, we were idealists. Every minute of our lives had to be subjected to the noble cause. Soldiers make physical sacrifices. Ours were emotional."

What could Jianfei say? For decades, she could not escape from her self-reproach. Too naive and gullible, they both were impeccable products manufactured in the Communist factory during that specific historical period.

It was a four page letter. Jianfei put down the letter and went to the kitchen. Yet she was in no mood to prepare anything for dinner. The old passion was still simmering, but a new fire had already been set. His last few lines were, "I am not coming to say hi or chat about Boston. I am coming to claim what belonged to me in our youth. If I lose you the second time, I'd rather stay in Beijing. I am coming with a government group and the tickets were already booked. Please don't disappoint me this time."

She went to the backyard. In the one week since he called her from Beijing, the forsythia had bloomed into a daring gold. Scanty furry grass blades cautiously spread a thin, tentative green sheet over the black earth. Halfheartedly, she started to rake the remainder of last year's leaves, preparing the flower bed for the pansies. Yet her mind kept sliding back to the letter that was claiming its old debt. She had three choices: *Bring Jeff with me; let Yang Bing stay in Beijing; or, meet him in his hotel, alone.*

Am I going to act in the old way again? Slowly she came to her conclusion.

"Legal Seafood." As Jianfei and Jeff waited at the entrance, a Chinese man approached. Unlike his handwriting that still carried the strokes of the young hand, Yang Bing showed up with little resemblance to the old days. What caught Jianfei's eyes was his nearly bald head. *Where has his thick, sleek hair gone?* She stretched out her hand. He smiled. Jianfei narrowed her eyes. Gradually the young old friend of hers came into being. *Yes, the same eyes, the same smile.* Behind the glasses, with sparse hair, was a dynamic engineer. The reserved and timid boy kept dragging Jianfei back to the sports ground. His glasses (those glasses!) were gold-framed. His suit was subtly expensive; his tie was pure silk. Yet the blue sweater popped up in competition.

The letter and the telephone conversation were never brought to the table; instead, lobster and The Freedom Trail were their topics. They asked the waiter to take a picture: Three smiling faces; three bright red lobsters in hands, their claws spread as if flying; three bibs clinging to their chests under doubled chins. Were they happy? Yes, they both had a happy marriage. As they cracked the shells, scooping out the roe, sipping the red wine, scrutinizing each other's crow's-feet that had taken over the corners of their eyes, and the thin frost that had vaguely dyed their temples, the laughing, the whipping of the rope, the old songs, the posters and slogans echoed from their youths. The meeting was not what Yang Bing had expected but happy enough to put an end to his life-long chagrin.

"How is your dad?" he asked.

"Passed away after the Cultural Revolution. And your dad? Is he still alive?"

"Retired. Living in Shanghai." He looked into his dark cabernet, and said with some hesitation, "He didn't say a word when I told him I was coming to see you."

That evening, that was the only touch of their past.

— Finis —

Printed in the United States
By Bookmasters